The Jalak

BY JAMIE EDMUNDSON

THE WEAPON TAKERS SAGA
TORIC'S DAGGER
BOLIVAR'S SWORD
THE JALAKH BOW
THE GIANTS' SPEAR

BOOK THREE OF
THE WEAPON TAKERS SAGA

THE

JALAKH

BOW

JAMIE

EDMUNDSON

Rarn
Publishing

The Jalakh Bow
Book Three of The Weapon Takers Saga
Copyright © 2019 by Jamie Edmundson. All rights reserved.
First Edition: 2019

ISBN 978-1-912221-04-2

Author newsletter
http://subscribe.jamieedmundson.com

Cover: Streetlight Graphics

For Dad

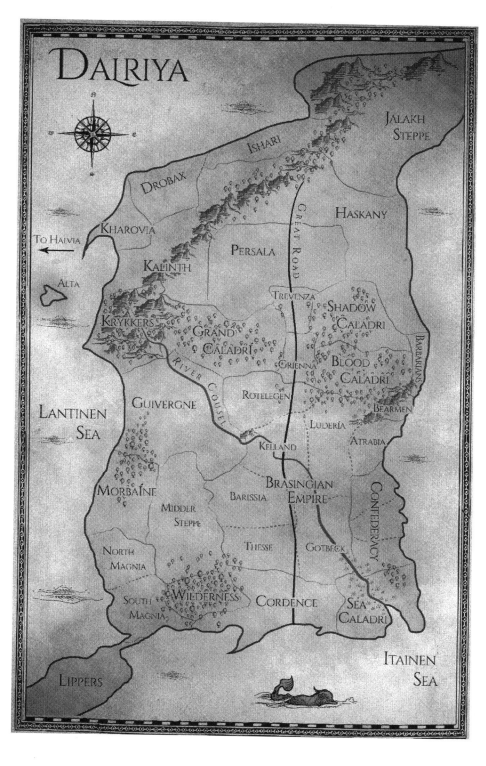

Dramatis Personae

South Magnians

Soren, a wizard

Belwynn, Soren's sister

Herin, a mercenary

Clarin, Herin's brother

Farred, a nobleman of Middian descent

Gyrmund, Farred's friend, an explorer

Edgar, Prince of South Magnia

Brictwin, Edgar's bodyguard

Morlin, Edgar's bodyguard

Wilchard, Edgar's chief steward

Wulfgar, high-priest of Toric

Otha of Rystham, magnate, Wulfgar's brother

Aescmar, a magnate

Ulf, a smith

North Magnians

Elana, a priestess of Madria

Cerdda, Prince of North Magnia

Mette, Cerdda's mother

Elfled, Cerdda's sister

Irmgard, Cerdda's wife

Middians

Brock, a tribal chief

Frayne, a tribal chief

Kellish

Moneva, a mercenary

Baldwin, Duke of Kelland, Emperor of Brasingia
Hannelore, Empress of Brasingia
Walter, Baldwin's younger brother, Marshal of the Empire
Rainer, Baldwin's chamberlain
Decker, Archbishop of Kelland
Ancel, Bishop of Coldeberg
Gustav the Hawk, Archmage of the Empire
Inge, Gustav's apprentice

Rotelegen

Jeremias, Duke of Rotelegen
Adalheid, Duchess of Rotelegen, his mother
Rudy, an escaped prisoner from Samir Durg
Jurgen, his cousin

Other Brasingians

Arne, Duke of Luderia
Tobias, his son
Godfrey, Archbishop of Gotbeck
Coen, Duke of Thesse
Werner, a steward in Coldeberg
Heike, a servant in Coldeberg
Gervase Salvinus, a mercenary leader

Guivergnais

Nicolas, King of Guivergne
Bastien, Duke of Morbaine
Russell, Bastien's man

Kalinthians

Theron, Count of Erisina, Knight of Kalinth
Evander, Theron's squire
Sebastian, Count of Melion, Grand Master of the Knights of Kalinth
Alpin, Sebastian's squire
Galenos, former Grand Master of the Knights of Kalinth
Tycho, Knight of Kalinth, Theron's friend
Remigius, Knight of Kalinth, Sebastian's friend
Euthymius, Knight of Kalinth
Philon, Knight of Kalinth
Leontios, Knight of Kalinth
Coronos, Knight of Kalinth
Proteus, Knight of Kalinth
Jonas, King of Kalinth
Irina, Queen of Kalinth
Straton, eldest son of Jonas
Dorian, second son of Jonas
Diodorus, Count of Korenandi
Bemus, a disciple of Elana
Lyssa, a girl from Korkis

Jalakhs

Bolormaa, a Jalakh woman, elder of the Oligud tribe
Gansukh, warrior, Bolormaa's son
Qadan, warrior

Haskans

Shira, Queen of Haskany, member of the Council of Seven
Koren, Shira's uncle
Rimmon, a mage

Persaleians

Pentas, a wizard
Cyprian, an escaped prisoner from Samir Durg
Zared, an escaped prisoner from Samir Durg
Mark, deposed King of Persala
Duilio, soldier
Aulus, flamen of Ludovis
Ennius, flamen of Ludovis

Krykkers

Kaved, a mercenary
Rabigar, an exile

Maragin, chieftain of the Grendal clan
Guremar, chieftain of the Plengas clan
Hakonin, chieftain of the Swarten
Jodivig, chieftain of the Dramsen
Stenk, a young warrior

Crombec, chieftain of the Pecineg clan
Wracken, chieftain of the Binideq

Caladri

Dorjan, King of the Shadow Caladri

Lorant, King of the Blood Caladri
Hajna, Queen of the Blood Caladri
Szabolcs, a wise man
Gyuri, a carriage driver
Marika, a carriage attendant
Dora, a carriage attendant
Vida, a carriage attendant
Joska, a carriage attendant

Kelemen, a leader of the Grand Caladri
Ignac, a wizard

Sebo, a Sea Caladri captain
Darda, a Sea Caladri soldier

Isharites

Arioc, King of Haskany, member of the Council of Seven
Siavash, High Priest of Ishari, member of the Council of Seven
Ardashir, a wizard, member of the Council of Seven
Rostam, lieutenant of Arioc, member of the Council of Seven
Harith, servant of Diis
Peroz, servant of Diis

Other

Tamir, a Barbarian chieftain
Sevald, a Vismarian leader
Gunnhild, a Vismarian
Kull, a Drobax

Recap: Toric's Dagger, Book 1

Toric's Dagger, a holy relic, is apparently stolen by Gervase Salvinus and his group of mercenaries from its resting place in Magnia. Prince Edgar asks his cousins, Soren and Belwynn, to lead a team tasked with its retrieval. The twins are joined by their friends, warriors Herin and Clarin; Krykker bladesmith Rabigar; mercenaries Moneva and Kaved; priests Elana and Dirk; and the ranger, Gyrmund. They follow the trail into the Wilderness, where they are attacked by the vossi. Surrounded and close to defeat, Soren casts an illusion that makes the vossi's god appear. They turn and run, but Soren has overextended himself and lost his ability to use magic.

They continue to follow Salvinus to Coldeberg, in the Brasingian Empire. On the road to Coldeberg they are attacked by a powerful Isharite wizard, Nexodore, and saved from him by Pentas, a red-eyed wizard. In Coldeberg, they learn that Emeric, the Duke of Barissia, has declared himself king. Many of the group are captured by Salvinus, and taken to Emeric's castle. Belwynn, Soren, Clarin and Dirk must rescue the others from the castle prison. Dirk reveals that he stole Toric's Dagger from the temple and has had the relic all along. In the castle dungeon, Rabigar is tortured and loses his eye. He is rescued by Moneva. In the duke's private rooms, it is revealed that Kaved betrayed them to Emeric. They escape the castle, chased by Salvinus. Walter, Marshal of the Empire, saves them from Salvinus and takes them to the capital of the Empire, Essenberg.

After a meeting with Emperor Baldwin and his Archmage, Gustav, Soren decides to take Toric's Dagger to the lands of the Blood Caladri, and his friends are persuaded to go with him. Here, they learn that Toric's Dagger is one of seven weapons made by Elana's goddess, Madria, that can be used to defend Dalriya from the Isharites. Elana is attacked by Nexodore, who is killed by Dirk, wielding Toric's Dagger.

Farred leads an army of Magnians north, to help the Brasingian Empire against the imminent Isharite invasion.

Looking for more information about the weapons, as well as a way to restore his powers, Soren leads the group to the lands of the Grand Caladri. When they reach the capital, Edeleny, they find it under attack by the Isharites. Amidst a magical battle, Soren finds a way to restore his lost powers. Belwynn, Elana, Dirk and Rabigar retrieve a second weapon, Onella's Staff. They are then transported to safety by Pentas. The rest of their friends are captured in the invasion by Arioc, King of Haskany.

Belwynn and her friends find themselves in Kalinth. Rescued by a Knight of Kalinth, Theron, and taken in by his uncle, Sebastian, they find themselves involved in a conflict between the Knights and the crown. Taking on the mantle of Grand Master, Sebastian takes the capital of Kalinth, Heractus, and seizes control of the government.

Brasingia is invaded by a huge Isharite army led by Queen Shira of Haskany, containing hundreds of thousands of Drobax. Farred works with Prince Ashere of North Magnia to frustrate the invasion. Ashere is mortally wounded and Farred's Magnians take refuge with the army of Emperor Baldwin in his mighty fortress, Burkhard Castle.

Moneva and the rest of her captured friends ae taken to Samir Durg, capital of Ishari. Moneva is taken to the rooms of King Arioc. Herin, Clarin and Gyrmund are sent to work in the mines and Soren is delivered to the Order of Diis. Submitting to Arioc, Moneva is given some freedom by him, and meets with Pentas, who tells her where her friends are being held.

Rabigar leaves Kalinth to return to the lands from which he is exiled. Despite his past crimes, he persuades the Krykkers to make a stand against the Isharites. The Krykkers lead an army to Kalinth, bringing with them the third of Madria's weapons, Bolivar's Sword. The combined Krykker-Kalinthian army invades Haskany, causing panic in Samir Durg.

Prince Edgar personally leads a Magnian army the Empire. Allying with Duke Coen of Thesse, he defeats the army of Duke Emeric. After a failed attempt to assassinate Edgar, Emeric is besieged inside Coldeberg. Gervase Salvinus betrays his master and brings Coen the head of Emeric, ending the siege and the Barissian rebellion.

Moneva successfully frees Herin, Clarin and Gyrmund from the mines. With a small force of escaped prisoners, Herin and Clarin cause havoc in the fortress of Samir Durg. Moneva and Gyrmund locate Soren and free him. Soren insists that he is taken to the throne room of Samir Durg. Here they find that Pentas has taken Belwynn to the throne room, too. Their attempt to kill Erkindrix, the Lord of Ishari, looks like it will fail, until King Arioc betrays his master. Moneva kills Erkindrix with Toric's Dagger.

The death of Erkindrix sees the recall of the great Isharite army, saving Burkhard Castle and Brasingia. It also saves Clarin and his force of escaped prisoners. Herin, however, is missing.

Prologue

ERKINDRIX IS DEAD,' Shira said, keeping her voice steady. 'Arioc and the other members of the Council are at each other's throats. Now is the perfect time.'

The men in the hall didn't look convinced. Many of the most powerful noblemen in Haskany had made the journey to Shira's estate. She had fed them all and plied them with arak to drink. But evidently, none of that meant that they were going to commit to her cause.

These were hard looking men. Wrapped in furs that made them look twice as big as they were, they had agreed to come despite a cold snap that signalled late autumn was turning to winter.

They had served Arioc since he had become king. They would continue to serve him if necessary. But Shira knew, at the same time, that their country's servitude to Ishari chafed at each and every one of them. They were proud Haskans, who would see their country become independent. But they were careful. A failed rebellion could see them and their families destroyed.

'Together we could raise a reasonably strong and well provisioned army,' suggested Etan, a widely respected figure. 'I have no doubts over your leadership of it, or that of your uncle,' he said, nodding at Koren, who was standing to one side of Shira, arms folded. 'But Ishari have magi. They have the Drobax. While that remains the case, we are not in a position to act against them.'

'They are not in a position to act against us,' she retorted, not willing to give in. 'Arioc, Ardashir and Siavash all fight each other to succeed Erkindrix. Not one of them has the resources to take on a united Haskany, and who knows how long their conflict may take? Even if one of them should emerge victorious, how likely is it that they will have the same power and reach as Erkindrix did? Would you cower in your halls, year after year, waiting until the Isharites return to claim our throne?'

There was anger at that—murmurs and whispers filled the hall. Maybe she had pushed them too far. But she knew that she needed to win these men over now. Should they drift aimlessly into the spring and summer months, divided and purposeless, a year would go by and they would have done nothing.

She looked at the faces in front of her. As many were against her as with her. And most weren't in either camp, unpersuaded and reluctant to commit to any path.

A knock at the door to the hall. Koren walked over to investigate. A whispered conversation followed. The attention of Shira's guests shifted in that direction. Uncertain, Shira turned to look.

Koren pulled the door wide open.

'Lord Pentas,' he announced in a strong voice, that gripped the attention of those in the hall.

Pentas sauntered in. It was the first time that Shira had ever been pleased to see him. He surveyed the hall, his red eyes fixing on the key figures in the room, making eye contact, a half-smile playing on his lips.

The atmosphere in the hall switched instantly. Pentas possessed powers that none of these men could understand or measure. Shira was their Queen, a member of the Council of Seven, yet Pentas exuded an authority she could never possess. It galled her, and yet she knew it might make the difference between success and failure.

'So,' Pentas said, drawing out the syllable, and raising his arms to encompass everyone who had gathered in the hall. 'Here are the new rulers of Haskany.'

And that, Shira said to herself, as she observed her countrymen, *is that.*

I

COLD COMFORT

WINTER HAD SMOTHERED the north of Dalriya.

Belwynn, raised in the temperate south, had never seen anything like it.

She thought that the city of Heractus, capital of Kalinth, was made for winter. Here the snow that fell in the streets turned to a dirty slush, complementing the grey walls of the city and its castle. The citizens of Heractus stoically endured the freezing conditions.

These people love being miserable, Belwynn told her brother. *Cold days and winter rations make them happy as pigs in shit.*

It was a slow time of the year. The Kalinthians had worked hard from spring to autumn, brought in their harvest, and most people had full enough larders to see them through comfortably enough. They flocked to the inns of the city, drank strong beer, told tall stories and sang old songs. For all she tried to resist it, Belwynn found herself liking the people here a little bit more each day.

Travel seemed to be virtually non-existent. On the occasions she ventured out beyond the city limits, accompanied by Theron, or sometimes Gyrmund, she never tired of the spectacle of a land blanketed in white. Thick snow crunched underfoot. Streams and lakes were frozen, some hard enough to walk across, others dangerous, with quick flowing, icy water beneath a thin top layer.

Otherwise, she spent her time in Heractus. She helped Elana with her work. She slept; she ate; she drank. She talked with her brother and her friends. It was a slow time of the year, and that was exactly what they all needed.

Belwynn and Gyrmund stood before Dirk's grave.

It was easy to find, since it was the only plot in a brand-new cemetery in Heractus. It was connected to the new Church of Madria, where Elana performed her healing. The land had been paid for by Elana's many supporters. The rich and powerful men of Heractus had contributed: Theron and Sebastian, and many other Knights of Kalinth—even Prince Dorian, second son of King Jonas, had supported the project. But so too had the ordinary men and women of the city. Elana's reputation had followed her from the High Tower, the seat of the Knights of Kalinth, where her earliest miracles had been witnessed. She had accompanied the Kalinthian army into Haskany, and there, word of her powers grew further.

Now everyone knew about her. She was visited daily, with ailments from the most serious to the most petty, to the purely imaginary. The Church of Madria had become the most visited in the city, and a source of envy from the other temples who had seen their congregations diminish. But with powerful protectors like Sebastian, the new Grand Master of the Knights, whose army still occupied Heractus, there was little they could do.

'I am sorry I wasn't able to speak with him before he died,' Gyrmund murmured, staring down at the tombstone. 'He helped to rescue me from Coldeberg prison. I never thanked him properly for that.'

'He died at peace, Gyrmund,' Belwynn said. 'With no regrets. You should have none too.'

Gyrmund nodded, looking up at her. 'And how are you and Soren?'

Both twins had been in a bad way for a while, not that Belwynn herself had known much about it. The wizard, Pentas, had spirited them out of Samir Durg, all the way to the Kalinthian army and Elana. Belwynn had been knocked unconscious by Rostam in the Throne Room of Samir Durg, shortly before the assassination of Erkindrix and their miraculous escape. She had remained in and out of consciousness for some time.

'I'm fully recovered,' she assured him. 'Soren isn't, though.'

Her brother had been tortured in Samir Durg, in ways she did not fully understand. Moreover, the Isharites had kept him in a box, never letting him out until Gyrmund and Moneva had found him. Never physically strong, his body seemed irreparably damaged from the ordeal.

'His back still troubles him, and he tires easily from physical exertion. His eyesight hasn't recovered, either. Elana thinks it never will. He clutches that staff all the time now, it's the only way he can see properly—he's virtually blind without it.'

'I'm sorry.'

'Well, don't be too sorry. I thought I would never see him again. And you and Moneva rescued him. So, for the thousandth time, thank you. And I remind myself of how desperate I was to see him again, every time he moans at me, which is at least half a dozen times a day.'

Gyrmund smiled at that, something he rarely did these days.

'How is Moneva?' she asked, already knowing the answer, but knowing that it was a subject that Gyrmund needed to talk about. Moneva had been remote and uncommunicative ever since their return from Samir Durg, and it was Gyrmund who suffered the most from it.

'No change,' he said. 'She won't speak to me properly. I know that she suffers, but she won't share it with me. I was wondering if you could try talking with her?'

Yet again? thought Belwynn. She and Moneva had built a friendship during their weeks together. But since Moneva, Soren and the others had been captured in Edeleny, and taken to Samir Durg, while Belwynn had escaped to Kalinth, their paths had been very different. There didn't seem to be much of that friendship left.

'Yes. I'll try,' Belwynn found herself saying. She knew that she should.

'I've been thinking,' Gyrmund said, 'of what I should do once this snow melts. I've been treated well here, and I get on with Theron. He has asked me to stay for a while, help to train new soldiers, that kind of thing. But I don't think that's me. I can't stop thinking of Herin and Clarin. I bear a huge guilt that I left them to their fate. I feel like I should go back.'

Belwynn nodded. She had spoken with Gyrmund a number of times about the two brothers. Once they had broken out of the slave pits in Samir Durg, Gyrmund and Moneva had gone to find Soren, while Herin and Clarin had remained behind, occupying a tower of the fortress along with a ragtag band of escaped prisoners. Anything could have happened. Clearly, the most likely outcome was that they had all been slaughtered. But the chaos engendered by Erkindrix's assassination may have given them a chance of escape. She knew that the two of them weren't easy to kill and there was a chance, however slim, that they lived.

'I will talk with Soren about Herin and Clarin. Though I'm not sure what we can achieve without Pentas. And I will talk with Moneva, too.'

'Thank you,' said Gyrmund, and he smiled ruefully. 'I'm sorry I've passed on all my problems to you.'

Eudora's Tavern was a small place, centrally located in Heractus; not too rough and not too expensive, either. It was where Moneva had chosen to spend her time.

The brief hours of daylight were already disappearing, and the inside of the establishment was dim, meaning Belwynn had to search before she saw her, sitting at a table by herself. A plate of food sat in the middle of the table, seemingly untouched, while Moneva had clearly begun drinking. As Belwynn sat down next to her, Moneva gripped both handles of her cup and tipped it back, guzzling it down.

'Hello, Belwynn,' she said when she was done, her breath strong with alcohol.

'Hello. How are you?'

Belwynn refused to play the role of mother, asking Moneva how much she had drunk, or similar interrogation. That was her business.

'Fairly bored. But there will be music later.'

Moneva gestured over a serving girl.

'Same again for both of us,' she said, indicating herself and Belwynn. Turning to her side, she said, 'I'm still sober if it's something important you've come to discuss. It's taking me longer to get drunk now I'm doing it regularly.'

'Why are you doing it so regularly?'

Moneva shrugged. 'It's fun. And what else is there to do around here?'

Belwynn studied her friend, the woman who had killed the dread Lord Erkindrix. She knew if it had been someone like Theron he would have become a legend by now. It would have been all too easy for him to capitalise on it, turn himself into a hero. And to be fair, everyone had been perfectly ready to treat Moneva in the same way at first. The Knights; the citizens of Heractus; even the royal family had acclaimed her in their own ways. When they first got back from Haskany, Moneva couldn't walk the streets without people buying her drinks, asking her about the events in Samir Durg. But she wasn't interested in that. She was tight-lipped, suspicious—almost contemptuous of the accolades. And so, people had backed off. Moneva had built a wall around herself that no-one, not even Gyrmund, was allowed to get through.

The serving girl brought them their drinks. Belwynn took a sip. The wine was watered down. Someone had put some food on Moneva's table. Maybe people hadn't completely backed off after all.

'Gyrmund asked me to talk to you,' Belwynn said tentatively.

Moneva sighed. 'Can't he just leave me alone?'

'No. He cares about you too much to do that.'

Moneva sneered at that, taking a swig of drink, before looking Belwynn in the eye.

'Do you know what happened to me in Samir Durg, Belwynn?'

Belwynn didn't know, not for sure. But she could guess.

'What happened?'

'He raped me. Not just once. Over and over again.'

Belwynn knew that *he* was Arioc, King of Haskany—the man who had captured Moneva and Soren, in Edeleny. Their escape from Samir Durg felt miraculous and had depended on the intervention of the wizard, Pentas. What would have become of them if they hadn't been rescued, she wondered? As it was, Soren and Moneva were still suffering.

'I'm sorry,' she said. 'Have you told anyone else?'

'No. And I don't want you to tell anyone. Especially not Gyrmund.'

'Whatever you say. Though I would suggest that you speak with Elana about it.'

'Why? What's *she* going to do?'

'I don't know, but you won't know either until you talk to her.'

Moneva shrugged. She turned her attention back to her drink, knocking it back, her need for it all too clear.

Belwynn knew about that well enough. She had watched her father descend into the same kind of addiction after the death of her mother. The alcohol had taken the edge off the raw emotions. But it had made him less of a man in the end. She didn't want to see Moneva do the same thing to herself.

'You know we're all here for you,' she persevered. 'We all care for you. Gyrmund most of all.'

Moneva curled her lips into a cruel smile.

'He cares about getting into my pants.'

'That's not fair.'

Moneva turned to her, face red, eyes red. 'I know, Belwynn,' she said, her voice raised, struggling to keep her emotions in check. 'I know I'm not being fair. That's why I don't want to see him.'

Belwynn nodded. She actually felt pleased. She had got more out of Moneva than their previous conversations.

'I have something for you,' she said, producing an intricately made leather scabbard and belt, the cross-guard and hilt of a dagger exposed.

Moneva took the weapon, pulling it free from the scabbard.

'Toric's Dagger?'

'When Dirk died he entrusted it to me. I think you should have it.'

'I thought we were supposed to return it to Magnia?'

'I think things have changed since then. Theron had the scabbard and belt made for you.'

Moneva twisted the weapon around in her hand, staring into the blade, seemingly lost in thought.

'Thank you,' she said at last, as if awakening from a stupor. She reached for her drink, hesitated, then pushed it away, before grabbing her plate of food.

Belwynn left the tavern and took the street that led up to Heractus Castle. Evening had arrived. The sun had departed the scene and the temperature had dropped, Belwynn's breath hanging mistily in the air. Most people out and about were heading in the opposite direction to her, small groups going down to the taverns and inns in the city centre, where there would be a welcoming fire, plenty of ale and wine, and the stories and songs would continue deep into the night.

For a city that seemed so peaceful and happy, there were still plenty of soldiers on duty at the gatehouse and on the walls. That was Theron's doing, since he always insisted on strict routines and discipline. But Belwynn also knew that beneath the surface all was not so calm in Heractus. Sebastian and Theron had occupied the capital with their army in the summer, drawn from those Knights of Kalinth who had switched their loyalty to Sebastian as the new Grand Master of the Order. But King Jonas of Kalinth also resided here, not imprisoned by Sebastian, but kept under close watch. His wife, the Queen Irina, and his sons Straton and Dorian, were here also. All of them, except perhaps Dorian, wanted the Knights gone and their freedom to rule restored. In the city and out in the wider kingdom, their supporters would be plotting just such a restoration. This winter, with its harmony and its merriment, would not last forever.

Not that Belwynn had any trouble with gaining access to the castle.

The Lady of the Knights they called her. Since her performance at the High Tower, she had become a figurehead of sorts for the movement, much to her own embarrassment. All of them now believed that she brought luck, confirmed by their victory in the Battle of Masada, the culmination of the Kalinthian invasion of Haskany. Outnumbered by the Drobax, Haskans and other forces of Ishari, she had blessed the swords of each knight before the battle. And, with no small help from their Krykker allies, they had won a seemingly miraculous victory. If any had doubts before, they had now evaporated. And so it was that if Moneva had become the mysterious, enigmatic killer of Erkindrix, Belwynn had become the angelic saviour of the Knights of Kalinth. It was bullshit, but nonetheless, it was a role that now felt impossible to escape.

The guards waved Belwynn through into the castle, and she took the winding steps up to her tower room, that she now shared with Soren. Inside, she found her brother lying face down on the floor, with Elana knelt by his side. She had her hands on his back, doing her best to heal his twisted spine and torn muscles.

'How is it going?' she asked them.

'His muscles are getting more relaxed,' commented Elana, a look of concentration on her face. Belwynn had some small experience of receiving Elana's healing powers, the warm sensation that repaired damaged tissue. It didn't always completely heal an injury, but she had already noticed Soren's movement improving.

'They tense up again by morning,' Soren complained, his voice muffled by the floor.

'You need rest,' reprimanded Elana, in the authoritarian voice she had developed to use with her patients. 'You can't expect an immediate recovery, even with my powers. And you must continue to exercise during the day.'

'I can't be bothered with all that,' he grumbled.

You really should listen to her, said Belwynn to her brother, using the telepathic link they shared.

'He just sits around and reads,' she added out loud, keen to tell tales on her brother.

'Too much sitting will tighten your back,' said Elana strictly. 'You should be stretching out on the hard floor and going for short walks.'

An indecipherable noise emerged from the floor where Soren lay, while Elana got to her feet.

'I should go,' she said to Belwynn, 'it grows dark. How are you?'

'Good. I had a productive talk with Moneva just now. I suggested she speak with you about something.'

'Of course. Well, I shall see you tomorrow.'

Elana left them to it.

'Well? Are you going to take her advice, or end up a cripple?' Belwynn demanded of her brother.

'I know. Still, I'm getting better. If I don't move from this position it doesn't really hurt that much.'

'Well, at least Elana's treatment is working. She has truly been blessed by Madria.'

'Please,' said Soren. 'Don't start with that nonsense.'

The words were so rude, Belwynn was taken aback, even if the fact that they came from someone lying prone on the floor lessened their impact somewhat.

'What do you mean?' she said at last. 'Have some respect for my choices.'

'I can't respect it,' countered Soren. 'You were vulnerable when I was in Samir Durg. That's how they take advantage of you. There's no doubting Elana's powers, but all this religious hogwash that she's sucked you into is ridiculous.'

Soren's arrogance galled her, and it was getting worse. It wasn't just that he had to be right and therefore she was wrong. It wasn't simply that her decision to follow Madria was, in his estimation, all about his absence from her side. It was also the disrespect he showed to Elana, who had just gone out of her way to come here and treat him. Yes, she knew that Soren was in pain, and was short tempered as a result. But her patience with him was wearing thin.

She was just formulating an appropriate response when there was a knock on their door.

'Can I come in?'

It was Theron.

'Yes,' she said automatically, before thinking Soren might prefer to be on his feet before Theron entered the room.

'Hi Soren,' Theron said, cheerfully enough. 'Everything alright?'

'Yes,' replied Soren gruffly. 'Are you two going to help me up?'

Theron grabbed Soren around the chest and Belwynn took his hands, and the three of them somehow got him to his feet, Soren grimacing the whole time and letting out a cry of pain as he straightened up. Belwynn passed him

Onella's Staff and he instantly looked better: his eyes focused on them, the grimace and frown disappeared.

'We've got a visitor,' Theron said, 'and he's asking after you both, you especially Soren. A mage, by the name of Gustav.'

Theron led them to Sebastian's private room in the castle. It wasn't any bigger than the room she shared with Soren, which was typical of Sebastian. He had attained the highest position in the Order of the Knights of Kalinth, was now de facto ruler of the kingdom, but would always be frugal in his tastes.

It was clearly meant to be a small, private gathering, since only Sebastian and Gustav the Hawk were there. As she took a seat offered to her by Theron, she looked at their visitor. He was pale and tired looking. He had been given a woollen blanket, which he clutched around him, but she could see that he still shivered from time to time. Next to him on a table was a cup of spiced milk, still steaming, which he would occasionally blow on before taking a sip.

'Well,' Sebastian began, 'thank you for coming. You have both met Gustav before, at the Brasingian Court. We both felt it only right that you should be included in this conversation. His visit here should remain a secret, so please think carefully about to whom you repeat what you hear here.'

'Of course,' said Soren. 'It is good to see you again, Gustav.'

'Likewise,' said the Archmage of the Empire, his voice deep and confident, but Belwynn could hear the exhaustion in it too. 'We parted as you and your friends undertook what seemed like an important quest, to the lands of the Blood Caladri. I have heard nothing substantial of you since, so it is good to see you both alive. I have heard rumours of significant events in the north, however, and based on these my master, Emperor Baldwin, has had me travel here to find out the truth of them.'

Soren smiled. 'It has been so eventful that it is hard to know where to start. Our visit to the Blood Caladri was brief and led us to journey into the lands of the Grand Caladri. There I was lucky enough to resolve the——,' he paused, 'personal issue that we discussed.'

This, Belwynn knew, was the loss of magic that Soren had suffered, only restored when he had formed a connection with the broken Caladri wizard, Agoston.

'Our time in the lands of the Caladri confirmed the importance of Toric's Dagger to us, and revealed that it is one of seven weapons that can be used to protect us from the Isharites. In Edeleny, we found a second such weapon, the Staff of Onella which I now hold.'

'Truly?' asked Gustav, leaning forward in his seat and reaching out a hand for the staff.

Soren hesitated. No doubt, Belwynn supposed, Onella's Staff would be a great boon to Gustav's considerable powers. If her brother handed it over, would he get it back?

Soren decided to give up the staff, and as soon as he did so, he slumped back in his chair, weakened.

Gustav, meanwhile, intently studied it, looking along its length from all angles, touching it in various ways and whispering under his breath. Eventually, and with a similar look of reluctance to Soren's, the Archmage returned it.

'That was where our luck ended,' said Soren, restored. 'Half of our number, including myself, were then captured, when Arioc's forces invaded the lands of the Grand Caladri.'

'I heard of this event,' said Gustav, 'Such an utter calamity. It is hard to put into words the loss to the world of magic that Ishari inflicted in that one episode. The Empire has carried out various reconnaissance missions in the region recently. So far they all suggest that Ishari has abandoned the area.'

Soren nodded. 'My sister escaped with both the dagger and the staff,' indicating that Belwynn could take up the story.

'How?' asked Gustav.

'Through the intervention of the wizard, Pentas,' she replied.

Gustav raised his eyebrows in recognition of the name but chose to say nothing.

'He sent us here, to Kalinth, where we were lucky enough to be taken in by Sebastian.'

'And Kalinth has seen its own share of excitement?' Gustav asked, looking from Theron to Sebastian.

'Indeed,' Sebastian replied, 'much of it necessary but regrettable. Our former Grand Master, Galenos, has been deposed, and I have taken over the position. Acting in what I believe to be the interests of the kingdom, Theron and I have secured control over the government here in Heractus. Acting in alliance with the Krykkers, we led an army into Haskany last summer.'

'Incredible,' said Gustav, impressed. 'Kalinth has been asleep for a long time. Thank you for waking your nation, just in time.'

'That's not the half of it,' said Theron. 'While we scored a victory over Ishari, the wizard, Pentas, and Belwynn here, broke into Samir Durg itself, rescuing Soren—and one of their friends, Moneva, killed Erkindrix himself.'

As Theron told the climax of their story, he looked at Belwynn, and his words were said with such pride that she found tears in her eyes and a lump in her throat, which she swallowed away.

'Then the rumours I had heard are true? I hadn't dared to believe them. Erkindrix dead? Then, let me tell you all of the news from the Empire. A great army of Drobax and Haskans was sent to the Empire. They first struck in Rotelegen, killing its duke, Ellard, and taking over the whole duchy. We were forced to evacuate the entire area.'

Gustav paused, noting the reactions of Belwynn and Soren, who had shared shocked looks.

'Of course, I forget, you left Essenberg with Ellard. I am sorry to bring you these tidings. Emperor Baldwin then decided to defend our greatest fortress, Burkhard Castle. It became a scene of great slaughter, but we were able to hold out until this great army departed. We didn't understand why they left at the time, but I presume that the death of Erkindrix left Ishari without clear leadership and the army was recalled. I should add that we were aided by a force of Magnians, led by Prince Ashere of the North, who was killed by the enemy, and a man from the South by the name of Farred.'

'Did Farred survive?' Belwynn asked quickly.

'He did.'

'His friend is here in Heractus. He will be pleased to know.'

'There is more regarding your home kingdom. I won't need to remind you of the treachery of Duke Emeric of Barissia.'

The name struck Belwynn cold. She was immediately transported back in time to Coldeberg, where she had given a private performance in front of the duke, distracting him while they attempted a rescue of their friends. She remembered Kaved, who had betrayed them to Emeric's forces, wandering in while she played, and the desperate struggle and escape that ensued. Most of all, she remembered Rabigar, blinded in one eye by the savage jailers of the castle.

Soren glanced her way, checking on her reaction.

'Go on,' he said.

While we were besieged in Burkhard, Emeric was attacked by Duke Coen of Thesse, fighting alongside a Southern force led by your own ruler, Prince Edgar.

'Our cousin,' said Belwynn, wonderingly. 'Really? Edgar fighting in the Empire? It doesn't seem real.'

'It happened,' said Gustav, 'and by all accounts Edgar and the South Magnians played a crucial role in the Battle of Witmar. Emeric escaped, but was killed by his own men.'

Belwynn laughed, covering her mouth as she did. It felt inappropriate, but the thought of Emeric defeated, by Edgar no less, had made her feel incredibly happy. It had been such a dark year. That it had all ended like this was truly the work of Madria.

'And so, to the final purpose of my visit,' said Gustav. 'Baldwin has appointed his brother, Walter, as the new Duke of Barissia. There will be a formal ceremony and celebration in the spring. Baldwin would like to extend an invitation, both to Kalinth, and to the heroes of Samir Durg. He wants to meet with you and discuss the future of Dalriya. When the snows have gone, you are all cordially invited to Coldeberg.'

II

THE HANDMAID, THE DUCHESS AND THE QUEEN

MY PLACE IS HERE,' said Elana, her gesture taking in the newly built Church of Madria. Her patience, Belwynn could tell, was starting to wear thin.

Belwynn had tried a number of times to persuade the priestess to accompany them on the journey to the Empire. Elana had stood firm, however, insisting that her role was to serve her new flock in Heractus. She had even, in preparation for Belwynn's absence, already appointed a new disciple from among those who regularly attended on her. Belwynn couldn't help but feel like she was being replaced.

'That's settled then,' said Moneva with finality. Moneva, in turn, had declared that if Elana were to stay, she would too, since the priestess would need someone to look out for her. 'Success breeds enemies,' she said darkly, and Belwynn wondered what kind of conversations Moneva had overheard whilst deep in her cups in the city's taverns.

'Then I will need the Dagger,' responded Belwynn. 'Edgar and the others deserve to see it,' she added, when Moneva looked like she was about to argue.

'You've only just given it to me and now you're taking it away,' complained Moneva, who nonetheless unbuckled her belt before slapping the weapon into Belwynn's palm and stalking off.

It was, no doubt, a self-indulgent emotion, but Belwynn felt a loss at their decisions. She had always tried hard to keep their group together. Now it was to become more divided than ever. Rabigar had returned to his homeland, his exile seemingly at an end. Herin and Clarin were lost, left behind in Samir Durg. Now Elana and Moneva were staying behind, while she would travel with Soren and Gyrmund to Coldeberg.

So be it. She wouldn't beg them to come. She said her farewells and returned to her room in the castle to get her pack. Soren and Gyrmund were there, waiting for her, and she soon found herself in the courtyard of Heractus Castle, mounted on a beautiful mare and ready to go.

Also staying behind was Sebastian, the position in Kalinth too precarious for him to take an extended absence. Theron would represent Kalinth in the Empire. His absence was enough of a loss, since while Sebastian was the leader of the new regime—respected and diplomatic—Theron had provided much of the energy and organisation.

Sebastian had come to see them off. He shared some last private words with Theron, before wishing them all good luck. Accompanying him was Prince Dorian, younger son of the king, who had formed a friendship with Belwynn despite her role in his family's diminution.

'Don't worry about your friends,' he said, coming over to give her horse a pat. 'I'll keep an eye on them.'

There was little talk as the four horses clip-clopped their way along the city streets, making for the East Gate. Gyrmund was subdued, upset at leaving Moneva behind, their relationship still not fully repaired. Soren was focused on the physical requirements of riding while clutching his staff in one hand. His condition had continued to improve, but he would now be without Elana's help. Belwynn rode next to Theron, who seemed to have a contented expression on his face.

'Looking forward to the trip?' she asked him.

'To be honest, yes. I've felt the responsibility of the last eight months. It's unrelenting. It will be a pleasure not to worry about everyone else for a while. And to spend so much time with you,' he added.

Soren snorted behind them, but they both chose to ignore it.

Evander was waiting for them at the gate, already opened, and as they nudged their horses through he fell in on the other side of Theron.

'Have you spoken with Tycho?' Theron asked his squire.

'Yes my lord, his force is ready, they are waiting on the road up ahead.'

'Very good, it's not like him to be so organised,' commented Theron. 'When we were young knights I used to have to wake him up every morning, or he would sleep in 'til noon. I suppose we've all grown up since those days,' he said wistfully.

They soon joined with Tycho's force of fifty knights. They were too disciplined to shout out, but to a man they all smiled and grinned as soon as they saw her. It was the strangest thing, but in truth, she was getting used to it. She knew all their faces now, and could name all but a handful. She recognised the handsome face of Leontios, big brown eyes framed by shoulder length brown hair. He always beamed when he saw her, puffing up in importance, since he was the first knight whose sword she had blessed, on the road from the High Tower to Heractus, and he was ever keen to remind his peers of that fact.

Tycho trotted over to greet them, shaking hands, kissing Belwynn's, and giving Evander a big slap on the back. It used to be that a slap on the back from Tycho would send a shudder through the boy, but not so now. Not only had Evander grown as tall as Belwynn, he had filled out as well, after spending the autumn and winter months on the exercise yard, training to become a knight.

'How far will you be travelling with us, Lord Tycho?' asked Soren.

'As far as Korkis,' Tycho replied. 'I have my orders,' he added, with a sly grin at Theron, 'to ensure the town is fully—what word did you use, Theron?'

'Integrated.'

'Yes. Fully integrated into the kingdom.'

Quite right too, Belwynn said to Soren.

Of all the dangers they had faced, the flight from Korkis somehow felt the most terrifying. It was perhaps because as a group they had been so vulnerable. Dirk had been ill, Elana and Belwynn helping him along, Rabigar was the only fighter with them, and he had recently lost an eye. If Theron hadn't intervened, at the last minute, they would likely all be dead.

That moment would forever be emblazoned on her memory, Belwynn thought. Theron, a lone knight, charging down the hill at the men who had been chasing them. She knew that regaining control over Korkis was politics. But she thought that a part of it might be to punish them for what they did.

They made surprisingly good progress. Belwynn wasn't at all convinced that spring had come yet. It was cold, and snow still lay on the hills of Kalinth. But Theron had argued that of all those invited, they would have the longest journey to Coldeberg, and would need to set off earlier than Baldwin's other guests. Although the ground was wet, they were amongst the first to journey on the roads since the snow had melted, and they weren't as torn up as they were likely to get in a few weeks. Their horses, kept indoors and fed on hay for the winter, also seemed enthusiastic to stretch their legs. The stark but beautiful Kalinthian countryside rolled by and as the evening of the second day drew in they had reached Sebastian's house, Sernea, where Soren and Belwynn were allocated a room for the night.

The next morning, they began the short journey to Korkis. As they neared the town, Belwynn recognised the countryside they passed through. Rolling hills with grazing animals, which today on horseback seemed gentle and innocuous, but last time she was here, escaping from their pursuers on foot, seemed impossibly steep and forbidding. To her right was the woodland where they had spent the night, and where the horseman from Korkis had followed them, taunting them, as his companions and their hunting dogs closed the gap to their prey.

The wooden palisade of the town came into view, Belwynn recalling how Rabigar had known about an exit in the north of the wall, a section swinging open that allowed passage in and out for those who didn't want to be seen. She thought about mentioning it to Theron or Tycho, but decided she liked the thought of it remaining there.

Anyway, the Knights had arrived with a far superior force to anything the town could muster. They were content to wait patiently outside until the authorities inside reacted.

More and more heads bobbed into view along the wall, staring out at the force that had arrived unannounced outside their town, until the gates opened, and half a dozen men walked out to greet them. Belwynn stared at their faces but didn't recognise any of them.

'I am Peros, Mayor of Korkis,' said one of them, trying to sound confident but in truth looking more than a little intimidated.

'Unfortunately for you,' said Tycho, pitching his voice so all could hear, 'you are mayor no longer.'

He produced a roll of parchment from his saddle bag. 'By order of the king, I have been appointed the new mayor of Korkis.'

He moved his horse slowly towards Peros before holding out the document. Peros took it and began reading.

I wonder how they persuaded Jonas to sign that, Belwynn said to Soren.

Assuming they didn't forge his signature, said Soren.

'Under our constitution,' said Peros, looking up from the parchment, eyes wide and anxious, 'the townspeople choose their own mayor.'

'This is an emergency royal writ agreed by the council,' said Theron.

'Have I done something wrong?' asked Peros.

'I don't know,' said Tycho. 'But if you have, you can be sure I'll find out about it. Now, let's get moving, I need to garrison my knights.'

Belwynn knew Tycho as a light-hearted, friendly man. But he could clearly be intimidating when needed, and Peros and the rest of the men turned around and began leading them into town.

'Come,' said Theron to the others. 'We will be leaving soon but we might as well get an early lunch here to send us on our way.'

Tycho had the knights' horses stabled and food brought out, while the people of Korkis started to organise how they were going to quarter fifty knights. He had already gone a long way towards asserting his authority over the place and Belwynn felt sure he would soon identify the corrupt members of the town guard and remove them.

Belwynn, Theron, Evander, Gyrmund and Soren had found a place to sit and eat in the central plaza, giving their horses a chance to rest before it was time to move out.

'Are you not itching to get involved yourself?' asked Belwynn with a smile, knowing that Theron usually couldn't help man-managing.

'No. I trust Tycho. My problem is there aren't many others I trust. With Tycho here, I hope that Sebastian has enough help in Heractus.'

'Belwynn,' said Gyrmund quietly, nodding to a location over her shoulder. 'Looks like you have a visitor.'

Belwynn turned around, wondering what he meant. A young girl was standing awkwardly nearby, and she startled somewhat when Belwynn looked at her. She looked familiar. Belwynn suddenly let out a gasp when she recognised who it was. She had tried to defend this girl when she was accused of stealing bread. It was that intervention that had prompted the Korkis soldiers to try to arrest them. The girl had obviously survived the winter, but she looked pale and malnourished.

'Come here,' said Belwynn, holding up a hand.

The girl looked warily at the men sitting with Belwynn, weapons lying by their sides. Belwynn kept her hand up, smiled, and waited patiently. Hesitantly, the girl came over, then flopped down next to Belwynn.

'I'm so pleased to see you,' said Belwynn, handing her some bread and cheese. Theron passed over a drink and the others donated some food, until the girl had a mini-feast in front of her, which she tucked into with vigour.

'This is the girl I tried to help last time I was here,' she explained to the others, all of whom had heard the story, but hadn't been with Belwynn at the time.

The girl nodded seriously in confirmation, her mouth full of food.

'What is your name, child?' Belwynn asked.

'Alyssa.'

'And where are your parents?'

'My mam died when I was seven,' said the girl matter-of-factly.

Belwynn guessed that was about two years ago.

'So who looks after you now?'

'No-one.'

That explained why the poor thing was taking the bread. She would ask Tycho to make sure she was looked after.

Alyssa looked at her. 'You can look after me if you want.'

Belwynn's heart broke. She found herself thinking of how to explain why she couldn't look after her. But *why* couldn't she? No-one else in this town had done so in two years. And the truth was, Belwynn was in a far better position to care for this child than most people were.

'She could come with us,' she found herself saying.

Don't be ridiculous, said Soren, but she ignored him.

She looked at Theron. 'You have a squire attending you on this journey,' she said to him. 'Why shouldn't I have a handmaid?'

Gyrmund chuckled, Soren scowled, and Evander looked expectantly at Theron.

'Should I fetch a horse for her, my lord?' asked the squire.

Theron looked at them all, keeping a neutral expression, before his eyes settled on the girl.

'Go on then, Vander,' he conceded.

Evander grinned, leapt to his feet, and ran off to find Tycho.

The route from Korkis to the Brasingian Empire wasn't straightforward. The fastest way was to head due east into Persala, and then south down the Great Road. But that involved heading into territory that was, they suspected, still controlled by Ishari. While Gustav had suggested that Ishari had withdrawn from their more southerly conquests, no-one was really sure what the situation was, and so it was deemed safer to avoid that option. The alternative was to head south-east, to the border with the Grand Caladri, and follow it east all the way to Trevenza, avoiding population centres. It was a more difficult route to navigate, but Gyrmund was confident of leading them, and they were in no rush. Borderlands could be dangerous places, but Soren's powers seemed enhanced, especially with Onella's Staff, and Belwynn had few concerns that they would face a threat that this company couldn't handle.

More of a problem was Alyssa. Belwynn's spur of the moment decision to bring the girl immediately looked foolish when they discovered she had never ridden a horse before. She therefore had to ride with Belwynn, gripping her tightly around the waist and screaming with alarm when they went too fast. As soon as she got used to the sensation of riding, she developed saddle sores, and spent two days crying, both on and off the horse, until she toughened up.

After a miserable few days with her, they had a go at teaching her to ride, short stints at first. Theron spent a lot of time with her, since Gyrmund was often way ahead of them, scouting the route. But she liked Evander best, would listen intently to everything the squire said and never moaned, which she did with the adults. Like most children, she was a fast learner. The short rides gradually got longer, until Belwynn found herself riding alone again, and much to everyone's relief, the crying and whining stopped.

Perhaps because of Alyssa's presence among them, everyone made an effort to entertain when it came time to sit around the fire. Soren would tell stories of the past, Gyrmund would tell stories of his travels to strange places, and Belwynn would sing for them. If there was enough light, Theron and Gyrmund would give Evander weapon training. At such times it was up to Belwynn to keep Alyssa occupied, especially after Soren's attempt to teach her how to read ended badly. The girl liked having her hair plaited, and so one night Belwynn let her practice on her hair, Alyssa sitting behind her by the fire, quietly working away. It was a peaceful, contented moment.

'How is it going, Alyssa?' asked Belwynn, not able to turn to face her because the girl had her hair in both hands.

There was a pause before the girl replied.

'My mam used to call me Lyssa. You can call me that if you want.'

Belwynn swallowed, and decided it best not to turn around.

'Thank you, Lyssa. I will.'

She shared a look with Soren across the fire, his expression unreadable, before he returned to his book.

In this way they spent their days and nights, until Gyrmund announced they had left the borderlands and had entered the province of Trevenza. Along with Grienna, Trevenza had declared independence from Persala so that they could join the Brasingian Empire, only to find themselves conquered by an army of Haskans and Drobax. They were likely to find a ravaged country, and Gyrmund felt more comfortable riding straight for the Great Road. They had sufficient provisions and the horses remained in good condition, so there was no need to stop.

As soon as they set foot on the road Belwynn felt more relaxed, since all they now had to do was follow it due south to Grienna and then to Rotelegen, the most northerly of the seven duchies of Brasingia. The temperature was milder than when they had set off, and it was easy travelling compared to the first part of the journey. Their horses ate up the miles. Despite the warmer weather there was very little traffic on the road. The people they did meet were groups of travellers heading south like them, but at a slower pace, with wagons full of possessions and sometimes livestock accompanying them. When Gyrmund asked, they explained they were heading to Rotelegen to start a new life in a safer part of the world. Belwynn wondered whether they would be welcomed in the Empire, but they all seemed convinced they would be.

In Grienna Belwynn was reminded of their journey from the lands of the Blood Caladri to those of the Grand Caladri. When crossing the Great Road, they had encountered the corpses of the Drobax who had died on their march south to invade the Empire. Presumably, similar casualties were suffered on their retreat north. But there was no sign of either now, and Belwynn speculated that the birds and other creatures of the forest, that ran either side of the Road, had feasted on the remains.

There had once been a sizeable settlement on the Brasingian side of the border with Grienna, giving the dukes of Rotelegen the opportunity to inspect and monitor the people and goods leaving and arriving in their duchy. But there was little left of the buildings and it was empty of people. Gyrmund had planned to spend the night there, and so that was what they did, making a small camp amongst the unclaimed debris. Their mood was sombre, as if they were sharing the land with the ghosts of the settlement.

Next morning, they were quick to pack up and leave, heading for Guslar, the capital of Rotelegen. After the devastation at the border, Belwynn was unsure what to expect from the city, but as they approached she could see that the defences were intact. Soldiers manned the walls and waved them through an open gate. It looked like a city open for business.

The straight roads of Guslar took them to the central plaza. Belwynn enjoyed sharing Theron's interest in the city, the layout and building designs all a novelty to him. Lyssa showed little interest, wondering instead when they would stop for lunch.

It was agreed that Belwynn would accompany Theron as envoys of Kalinth and present themselves at the castle, while the others sourced supplies for the journey south. A brief meeting was organised with Adalheid, mother of the young Duke of Rotelegen, and with little ceremony they found themselves waiting in what looked like one of her private rooms. After a couple of minutes, the door swung open and Adalheid entered, accompanied by only one minister and a bodyguard, who stood by the door and looked straight ahead, avoiding eye contact with those in the room.

'Lady Adalheid,' said the minister, making the introductions, 'Count Theron and Lady Belwynn.'

'You're on your way to the festivities in Coldeberg,' said Adalheid with a note of sarcasm.

'Yes indeed,' replied Theron. 'Will you or the Duke be attending?'

Adalheid snorted. 'We don't have time for that. The rebuilding task here is enormous; never ending. Jeremias needs to be seen to be leading it, not trying to curry favour with the Emperor who will never lift a finger to help us here. He'd rather spend the Empire's money on a party in Coldeberg.' She shook her head in distaste. 'Giving Barissia to his own brother...'

At least, thought Belwynn, Theron and I are used to the awkwardness of the royal court in Heractus. It's been good preparation for this.

'The people of Kalinth offer their support to Rotelegen. If there's anything we can do to help, please ask,' said Theron.

Adalheid studied him. 'You in Kalinth know what it is to share a border with Haskany and the Drobax. When the time comes, fight them. You may buy us some time here. Should they come for us first, we will do the same for you. I think that is all we can do for each other.'

'We noticed immigrants heading here from Trevenza and Grienna,' said Belwynn.

Adalheid turned to her. She looked prematurely aged to Belwynn, who thought she could just make out the features of a younger, carefree Adalheid. If she had really existed, that Adalheid must have disappeared on hearing the news of her husband and sons.

'Yes. We're depopulated. Many died in the fighting. Others, who were evacuated, have decided to stay where they are rather than return here to their homeland. So there are opportunities in Rotelegen for those from the north, and for those from across the Empire. Where else could you be given your own plot of land to farm for free? Unfortunately, it means that we have become a magnet for the indolent and the criminal. But that is what the Gods have given us to work with. We must do our best. Anyway, it was a delight to have met you both.'

With that, Adalheid was on her feet, and as soon as Theron and Belwynn muttered their pleasantries she was gone.

'I feel sorry for her son,' commented Theron once they were out of the castle, 'such a dragon for a mother.'

'I disagree,' said Belwynn. 'Surely it's better to have a dragon on his side than to have been left alone.'

Theron nodded. 'Alright, you win.'

We've finished early, Belwynn said to Soren. *Where are you?*

I'll give you directions, Soren replied instantly. *I think you'll be surprised who we've bumped into.*

Intrigued, Belwynn led Theron a few streets away towards the market area of the city. Evander saw them and waved. He was standing with Soren and Lyssa, next to a carriage which had been parked up on the other side of the street. Attached to the carriage were four gaurs.

'It can't be,' said Belwynn out loud, a stupid grin appearing on her face.

Theron frowned at the spectacle, but followed on as Belwynn practically skipped over to the carriage. As she neared, Gyrmund came into view from behind the carriage, talking animatedly with two Caladri women. She recognised them immediately as Marika and Dora, the carriage attendants they had met when they had entered the lands of the Blood Caladri the previous summer. When they saw her they both let out a little scream and rushed over to give her a hug.

Belwynn introduced them to Theron, and in their excitement they hugged him as well, making her giggle.

She peered into the carriage, but it was empty.

'They can't be here on their own?' she asked Gyrmund.

'From what I can understand, the men are out buying provisions and left them here for a short while.'

Sure enough, it wasn't long before the Caladri returned. Amongst them was Hajna, Princess of the Blood Caladri. She walked over, poised and elegant, all the more noticeable when her attendants were so excitable and over-familiar.

'How nice to see you all again,' said Hajna once the various introductions were made. With her were Gyuri, the same carriage driver who had driven them before, and two of the male Caladri attendants, Vida and Joska. The three of them were carrying sacks of items they must have purchased at the market. In addition, Szabolcs, the wise man they had met during their visit, was with them. Soren immediately gravitated towards Szabolcs and drew him away for a private conversation.

'I presume you are also on your way to Coldeberg?' Belwynn asked.

'You are correct. We were invited to attend by Gustav the Hawk. It is very important that Szabolcs and I meet with the leaders of Dalriya.'

'Prince Lorant is not with you? Is he well?'

A look of grief passed over Hajna's face. 'Lorant is well. We faced very serious fighting soon after you left, the worst I have ever known. My husband's father, King Tibor, was killed in the fighting. So Lorant is not a prince anymore, but a king.'

'And you are a queen?'

'You are correct. We agreed to a truce with the Shadow Caladri not long after our king's death, and it has held over the autumn and winter seasons. But Lorant dare not leave our lands and so I have come without him.'

'Are you about to leave now?' Belwynn asked.

'Yes. We thought it wise to replenish our supplies here first.'

'Can we accompany them?' Belwynn asked, looking at her companions.

'Of course we will,' said Soren.

'That is so kind of you,' said Hajna.

Gyuri climbed up to his seat, while Hajna and her four attendants took their places inside the carriage. Giving a shout and a pull on the reins, Gyuri got his gaur moving.

Belwynn and the others looked at each other with a mixture of expressions.

'So we just bumped into the Queen of the Caladri?' asked Theron, disbelievingly.

'I liked the cows,' said Lyssa.

III

COLDEBERG

SPRING RAINFALL HIT THEM on the road from Guslar to Essenberg. It was incessant, and Belwynn soon gave up on trying to keep dry, reconciling herself to travelling while soaked through. Her inner things got sore from the constant rubbing of riding. The Caladri were able to keep out of the rain inside the carriage, the men taking turns driving the gaur. But their slow pace became a source of frustration. In the end, Belwynn bundled Lyssa into the carriage with Hajna and the rest of them rode on ahead: the sooner they reached Essenberg, the sooner they could get warm.

The Great Road took them to the northern Castle Quarter of Essenberg and they went straight to the royal castle. Baldwin and his court were probably already in Coldeberg, but someone would have been left in charge of things, and both the Kalinthians and the Caladri were invited guests of the Emperor. After explaining who they were, Belwynn and the others were admitted to the castle but had to wait a while before someone arrived to greet them. That someone was a priest.

'His Grace is on his way to meet you. I can take you to your rooms first.'

Belwynn shared a little smirk with Gyrmund as they both recalled the pace at which the Archbishop moved.

'Is Decker in charge in the absence of Baldwin?' asked Soren.

'That's right.'

'Well, you might want to mention to him that the Queen of the Caladri is on her way here too.'

The priest's eyes widened at the news, but he otherwise kept his composure. 'I will certainly tell him. Please, follow me.'

It was a few hours until the Caladri were settled into the castle and ready to meet with the Archbishop. Outside, the sun was setting, and a chill descended, much to Belwynn's disappointment, since she had only just got herself warm again. Hajna and Szabolcs attended, leaving the rest of the Caladri in their rooms. Theron left Evander to look after Lyssa, adding babysitting to the list of duties expected of a squire. Decker was alone. He had found them a cosy room to meet in, with a roaring fire, and while the Archbishop was best positioned to take full advantage of it, the heat spread nicely through the room. Belwynn wasn't the only one whose eyes looked droopy, as the heat, a generous helping of Cordentine red wine, and a long day of travelling combined to make everyone feel sleepy.

Decker was naturally eager to hear their news and mostly listened at first. But after a while Belwynn had a few questions for the Archbishop.

'You did not want to go to Coldeberg, Your Grace?'

'Well, I might have enjoyed it when I got there, but I don't enjoy travelling so much these days. And a city this size needs to know that someone is in charge. Otherwise people get to thinking they might be the ones in charge.'

'Wouldn't you have been involved in the coronation?'

'Dukes do not get crowned,' explained Decker. 'That's what went wrong with the last one,' he added mischievously.

'Oh,' said Belwynn, slightly confused with the politics. 'They are just appointed by the Emperor?'

'No, not that either. The duchies choose their own rulers, usually in line with the laws of inheritance. Emeric had no direct heir. In the situation they are in, the wise people of Barissia would want their ruler to be both able and, most of all, be loyal to the Emperor beyond a shadow of a doubt. I think you will agree that Walter is the perfect candidate.'

'Of course,' said Belwynn, not wishing to appear that she was suggesting otherwise.

'And the not so wise people of Barissia?' asked Soren.

'Well, they are the ones who brought the duchy to its knees. Baldwin has been merciful with Barissia, placing all the blame for their treachery on Emeric's shoulders. But neither he nor Walter will tolerate any further opposition. The Barissian rebellion nearly led to the fall of the Empire, let's not forget. Emeric was in alliance with Erkindrix himself. And how would Emeric and his minions have treated us if Burkhard Castle had fallen and the Emperor had been slain?'

'That would have been a disaster,' suggested Hajna softly.

'I agree, Your Highness,' said Decker. 'None of us have forgotten what Barissia did. This meeting of the rulers of Dalriya has many purposes, of course. But one of them is to affirm, for all to see, who is in charge of the duchy now.'

Everyone was up early for the final leg of their journey. The sky was overcast, but the rain was holding off for now.

Theron had a brief opportunity to see the sights of Essenberg, all of which held memories for Belwynn of their time in the city last year. On their left, Decker's cathedral dominated the skyline. Ahead of them lay the River Cousel, swelled by the recent rain. They used Albert's Bridge to cross the river. Downstream of them was the First Bridge, that used Margaret Island to cross the river. Belwynn pointed it out to Theron and Evander, explaining that they had spent a night on that island, hiding from their enemies.

Far to their left, out of sight, was the Imps, the headquarters of the Imperial Army. It had been Walter's to command, perhaps would be still, though surely he would be spending less time in Essenberg now that he had become a duke. It was to Walter's duchy that they now headed, riding straight on through the Coldeberg Gate, from where a road took them directly to the capital of Barissia.

The rain that had threatened them never came, and so they were content to ride along at the same pace as the Caladri carriage. Just as the light was fading Coldeberg came into view. They saw its distinctive slope, descending from the high point where the castle adjoined the city walls, down to the southern end at the bottom of the hill. The sight made Belwynn's insides twist. Her memories told her that Coldeberg was a place of evil, but she knew it didn't have to be, now that Emeric's regime was gone.

The gate into Coldeberg was closed for the night, so they had to request entry from the night watch. That would involve the soldiers finding someone with enough authority to give permission, so Belwynn expected a long wait.

She was surprised when the gates opened after a few minutes. Waving them into the city was Rainer, Baldwin's chamberlain, who had assembled a team of officials to expedite their arrival. As she entered the city a stable-boy ran up to grab the reins of her mare and take her away. Another boy jumped up beside Gyuri and guided him away to a suitable place to leave the carriage.

'Lord Rainer,' Belwynn greeted him.

'Lady Belwynn,' the chamberlain replied.

She was impressed that he remembered her, but he had always seemed a man in control of the details.

'May I present our travelling guests? Queen Hajna of the Blood Caladri and Count Theron of Erisina, representing King Jonas of Kalinth.'

Rainer took their hands.

'On behalf of Emperor Baldwin and Duke Walter may I extend you all a warm welcome. You are expected, and I have already organised your accommodation. Queen Hajna, Gustav insisted on taking charge of your rooms, so I will personally take you and your attendants to see him right away. As for the rest of you, I have a town house picked out for you by Duke Walter. I hoped you would be able to share it with Prince Edgar and his entourage?'

Belwynn briefly checked with Theron, who nodded his approval. 'Is Edgar here already?' she asked.

'Yes, you are the last of our guests to arrive, everyone else who accepted our invitation is here.'

'We are very grateful,' said Theron. 'I can only imagine the amount of work such an operation has given you.'

'Yes indeed, but once I accepted the inevitability of the odd mistake here and there, I have been able to embrace the challenge. Werner!' Rainer said, calling over a member of his staff. 'Please take our guests to their house.'

They said their farewells to Rainer and to the Caladri, before the six of them followed Werner on foot through the dark streets of Coldeberg. Belwynn had never felt safe in this city, and made Lyssa hold her hand as she peered down dark alleys suspiciously. In truth, however, Werner was leading them to the wealthy part of the city, where the houses were sheltered by the looming presence of the Duke's castle. Whereas before the castle had been crawling with Emeric's mercenaries, she knew that now it was Walter's soldiers who kept an eye on things, and her fears subsided.

When Werner approached the door of the building and gave a knock she almost gasped in surprise, for he had led them to one of the most expensive looking buildings she had seen. It was brick built and no expense seemed to have been spared in the choice of materials, with glass windows and clay tiles on the roof.

The door was opened by a young woman who Werner introduced as Heike, before explaining to Heike who they were.

'You will have a staff to attend to you here during your stay,' Werner explained. 'Any concerns please ask for me—I am more likely to be available than Lord Rainer himself,' he said with a smile.

With that said, Werner hurried off down the street and Heike took them all in to the hall of the house.

As they gathered there, looking about them, the far door opened, and Edgar suddenly appeared in the room, flanked by Gyrmund's friend, Farred. Farred and Gyrmund embraced; Edgar shook hands with Soren, then found Belwynn for a hug; Belwynn introduced him to Theron; and soon the hall was filled with so much talk that Belwynn couldn't really follow any of it.

In the end the travellers discarded their cloaks and were taken into the kitchen, where they were seated at a table. Heike began to pile the table with a cold supper and Belwynn, realising that she was famished, didn't hesitate to begin tucking in. Soren and the others, even little Lyssa, all did the same, and so it fell to Edgar and Farred to relate their news first.

And what tales they had to tell.

Edgar went first. He began with the worst of it, recounting how Gervase Salvinus, Emeric's Isharite wizard, Tirano, and their former friend turned traitor, Kaved, had broken into his camp, killing Soren's mentor, Ealdnoth, before attempting to kill Edgar himself. His bodyguard, Leofwin, had died in the desperate fight, but not before killing Tirano. Belwynn took a look at Soren on hearing the news, who had bowed his head in grief. The others looked to her and she shook her head, indicating that Edgar should carry on with his account and let her brother be. Edgar then filled in the bare bones of the campaign in Barissia, which had ended with the surrender of the very city they were now in, and Salvinus emerging free from Coldeberg in return for the head of his former master.

'This was Salvinus's house,' added Edgar, with a wry smile. 'Walter thought it apt that we should be the ones to enjoy it.'

Next it was Farred's turn, whose story was no less dramatic. He had taken a force of South Magnians to the Brasingian Empire where, led by Ashere of North Magnia, they had engaged with the invading Isharite army. The idea of this small force taking on an impossibly large army sounded like it should be made into a song. Farred's story had its own share of tragedy, when Prince Ashere died of the wounds inflicted on him. Farred then found himself, along with Emperor Baldwin and the imperial army, under siege in Burkhard Castle.

They had been surrounded by the huge Drobax army that had descended the Great Road, having to defend their position from daily onslaughts. When Farred explained that the Isharites had suddenly and unexpectedly retreated north, he and Edgar looked at them quizzically, and it was time to tell their story.

Before that, Belwynn insisted on putting Lyssa to bed, whose eyes had glazed over, despite her best attempts to stay awake. Gyrmund ended up carrying her to her bed, where she was too tired to resist and went straight to sleep. When they returned to the kitchen, they had a glass of wine waiting for them. Heike had cleared the table.

'Please, Heike, there's no need to stay up,' said Belwynn. 'We can sort ourselves out.'

'If you don't mind,' replied the young woman, 'I asked if I could stay and hear your story.'

Soren and the others gave a smile, and so Belwynn took a seat and helped her brother and the others relate their adventures since leaving Edgar's court at Bidcote in Magnia. It was less than a year ago, but seemed so much longer, and at times during the telling it felt like the events had happened to someone else and not to her at all. The chase through the Wilderness; Kaved's betrayal in Coldeberg; Arioc's invasion of the Grand Caladri; Belwynn's escape to Kalinth; Soren and Gyrmund's imprisonment in Samir Durg. When Gyrmund finally told how Erkindrix had died, betrayed by Arioc in his own throne room, the hour had grown late, the wine had been finished, and everyone looked eager for sleep.

At the end, Belwynn produced Toric's Dagger and handed it to her cousin, who drew it from its new scabbard and studied it carefully.

'So this blade killed Erkindrix?' he asked wonderingly.

'We brought it back,' said Belwynn. 'It just took a little longer than expected.'

'I had total faith,' said Edgar, grinning. 'But what to do with it now? From what you say, returning it to Toric's Temple isn't the wisest move.'

'I hope we will gain some answers tomorrow,' said Soren. 'Szabolcs has been researching the history of the weapons. He tells me he has more substantial information than he did in the summer.'

Edgar nodded, returning the weapon into Belwynn's keeping.

'Then I for one am looking forward to what tomorrow brings, a day that was already threatening to be very busy. But now my bed is calling me.'

The early morning event of the day was a service celebrating Walter's elevation to the duchy. After a quick breakfast, they left the house to walk the short distance to the cathedral, leaving Evander and Lyssa behind.

Mingling outside Coldeberg Cathedral was a veritable who's who of the Brasingian aristocracy, not to mention representatives of states beyond the Empire's borders. Between Edgar and Farred, there were few individuals their group were not familiar with, and they found themselves greeted by a bewildering array of powerful figures, Theron struggling to keep up with so many new faces.

Baldwin himself was there, accompanied by his queen, Hannelore. It was the first time Belwynn had ever seen Hannelore. She was tall and full-figured, her brunette hair elaborately piled on top of her head, making her appear even taller. Their children accompanied them: two daughters about to enter adolescence and a younger boy. The children seemed somewhat shy and stood to one side of the gathering, until someone familiar approached them and engaged them in conversation.

Hannelore's father was Arne, Duke of Luderia, and his son and heir was Tobias. The whole family had the same, large framed look to them, but whereas the men, Belwynn felt, ended up looking corpulent, Hannelore looked shapely, turning the heads of those present. Arne had been a defender at Burkhard Castle, and came over to talk with Farred and to introduce himself and his son to everyone else. He was friendly, down to earth, and proud of his family.

Most of the other great men of the Empire were also here with their entourages. Duke Coen of Thesse, energetic and bald headed, spoke at length with Edgar. Archbishop Godfrey, ruler of Gotbeck, had the kind of voice that could be heard wherever he happened to be standing. And, of course, Walter himself came over to see them, enquiring about the house he had chosen for them. There was a touch of humour in his eyes as he asked, all of them recalling the first time when they had met, on the road from Coldeberg to Essenberg, when he and his soldiers had intervened at the last minute and saved them from Gervase Salvinus.

'Any news of him?' asked Edgar, a hungry look in his eyes, as if he could not wait to hear that the man was dead.

'Possibly in Cordence, last I heard,' said Walter. His humour had disappeared. 'Unfortunately, men like him can always find new work.'

From beyond the Empire had come a collection of chieftains from the Midder Steppe. They strolled around in their flowing kaftans, with their distinctive long hair tied behind them. There was a delegation from Guivergnais, and one from Cordence. Queen Hajna was there, along with Szabolcs, talking quietly with Gustav, the Archmage of the Empire. They, of course, attracted the most stares. For the vast majority of guests, this was the first time they had lain eyes on a Caladri, and their clawed feet, bird-like head swivels, and delicate frames marked them out as something alien and other.

The last group of guests to emerge onto the cathedral precincts, guided by Rainer the chamberlain, were three Krykkers. Once Belwynn's group had been seen they came striding over in their direction, swords strapped to their belts, as if they were marching to war rather than attending a church service.

Belwynn smiled, for the Krykker in the middle wore an eye patch: Rabigar. He smiled too, giving her a rough hug when he reached them. Flanking him were Maragin, chief of Rabigar's clan, the Grendals, and Guremar, the stern faced chief of clan Plengas. They made a bee line for Theron, each clasping his arm in greeting, a mark of their respect for him as a warrior who had fought by their side. Belwynn could tell that he was pleased: finally, Theron was the one with connections. Meanwhile, many of the other guests were staring at the Krykkers as a curiosity. With the armour-like skin covering their torsos; Rabigar's eye patch; the fact that Maragin was carrying a sword as large as the men's; and the confident, bordering on superior way in which the Krykkers stared back at the humans, there was something slightly menacing about them.

Now that everyone had assembled in one place, Rainer was keen to press on with the programme, and began politely coercing people into the cathedral. Belwynn's group filed through two sets of doors into the nave, which stretched before them, a huge space both length-ways and in height. The vaulted ceiling of the cathedral must have been thirty metres high, and the myriad conversations taking place echoed around the vast space.

Wooden pews filled out the space, with a clear path down the centre. Ushers were on hand to take the guests to their seats. The Magnians were allocated to one of the pews in the middle of the nave. Belwynn looked about, watching as the seats quickly filled. She didn't envy Rainer the headache of organising such an event. Not only did he have to decide who made the guest list in the first place, but then where they should sit. Not everyone would end up where they felt they deserved to be. Did a count from Kalinth outrank a chief from the Midder Steppe, for example? There was surely no definitive answer, but somehow everyone was seated without incident and the ceremony could begin.

The bishop of Coldeberg ascended his podium and began to welcome his unusual congregation. There was something familiar about him, but she couldn't quite place her finger on it.

Do we know him? she asked Soren.

Soren already had the bored expression he used in churches, but perked up when he heard the question. He placed one hand onto the staff that had become his sight aid and focused on the man who, though young looking, was talking in a rich, smooth voice.

Ancel, he said definitively. *The priest who found us in Essenberg and took us to see Decker.*

He was right. They had been caught in two minds about where to go, fearing that Emeric's agents in the city were waiting for them. Ancel had led them to a side door in Essenberg Cathedral, and Decker had then taken them underground, via the Crypt of the Dukes of Kelland, to Baldwin's Castle.

You're right, she agreed. *But how is it that he is now the Bishop of Coldeberg?*

I don't fully know the politics of it, Soren said. *But presumably, the previous Bishop of Coldeberg was the one who crowned Emeric as a king. Baldwin will have wasted no time in ejecting him and needed a replacement. No doubt Decker recommended Ancel, who I suppose is someone they can trust.*

Yes, said Belwynn. *But that means they have replaced both duke and bishop with Kellishmen. That surely can't be popular.*

Well, they defeated the Barissian rebels in battle. I think Baldwin is more concerned with asserting his authority than being popular.

That said, and with Ancel moving from his introduction to his sermon, Soren placed his staff on the floor in front of him, adjusted his position to get more comfortable, and closed his eyes.

Since the Brasingian Church worshipped many gods, Ancel's sermon was theologically vague and, Belwynn believed, had nothing in it to offend the ears of most of the guests, be they Middians, Cordentines, or even Caladri.

Compared to Elana's ideas it lacked a singleness of purpose. Belwynn was interested in the references to Lady Alexia, however, who provided protection to the people. She remembered something Hajna had said once, that she had taken little notice of at the time. Hajna had equated her goddess, Onella, with Elana's Madria, and also with Alexia. Were they one and the same, worshipped by different peoples under different names?

After expounding on the duties that Walter owed to the Barissian people, and on the obligations they had to him in return, Ancel and his audience seemed satisfied with the ceremony and stood up, before filing out of the building.

Their next destination was Coldeberg Castle, as the guests of Walter and Baldwin. It was a short walk to the castle, where Walter's hall was already set up with tables of food and drink. The Magnians sat around a table with the three Krykkers. Belwynn took something but it was so soon after breakfast that she wasn't hungry, and anyway, she hadn't come all this way to eat, drink and be merry. She wasn't the only one who felt this way and within a few minutes the tension in the hall grew, conversations became muted or stopped altogether, and the gathering waited for someone to speak.

Into the void came a bang from the top table, and everyone turned to face Walter, who had read the mood.

'Thank you all for being here. I am not a man for ceremony, so I would like to turn our collective attention away from myself and my new responsibilities, and to the real reason why most of you have been invited here. Everyone attending today, in different ways, to a larger or smaller degree, has experienced the threat posed by Ishari. Only recently have we started to unite together to face it. Late, but I hope not too late. There is much we can do here. There are individual alliances to be made. If I know my brother at all, I know the Emperor is itching to speak with the leaders, or their representatives, of the other nations who have graciously agreed to his invitation.'

Heads turned to Baldwin, seated next to the new duke. He looked older than Belwynn remembered, more grey in his hair now, but he was still a formidable presence in the room. He held his hands in the air, 'he knows me,' he conceded grudgingly, with a smile, before gesturing to his brother to continue.

'But,' continued Walter, 'we have agreed that first, we must address the most difficult issue, or at least the issue that the Emperor and I find the most difficult. Magic. Whatever anyone's personal feelings on this issue, it cannot be ignored. Last year Ishari used magic to destroy the Grand Caladri, they used magic to aid their invasion of the Empire, and it has been used in many other ways. In turn, magic had a role to play in the death of Erkindrix, the event that arguably spared many of us from further disaster. Anyone who is not comfortable with the topic is not required to stay and hear this. But the truth is, magic will play a role in the future, too, and if we pretend otherwise, we are giving the enemy an advantage.'

There was a pause, then, between Walter taking his seat and Gustav getting to his feet. It allowed some to leave the room. Queen Hannelore quietly vacated her seat, along with her children. Archbishop Godfrey left much more loudly, not able to resist uttering dire warnings about the use of magic. But most people stayed.

'Amid the battles, sieges and other acts of war,' Gustav started, calmly and clearly, 'a second conflict raged last summer. It revolved around weapons, and this conflict was started by none other than Duke Emeric, in alliance with Erkindrix. Emeric's servants attempted to steal a holy weapon, Toric's Dagger, from Magnia. Not only was this attempt foiled by the Magnians, but a small group of them went further, to Edeleny itself, where they took a second weapon, Onella's Staff, before Arioc could get his hands on it. The Krykkers, sensing the threat, raised an army and took their own weapon, Bolivar's Sword, deep into Haskany, where together with the Kalinthians they inflicted a defeat on the Isharites. Finally, this group of Magnians went one step further, getting into Samir Durg itself, where the staff and dagger were used to kill Erkindrix himself.'

Gustav then gestured at their table. Not everyone in the room knew of these events, and many turned to look at Belwynn and the others with curiosity. Rabigar did not hesitate, getting to his feet and drawing Bolivar's Sword from its scabbard, before holding it in the air for all to see. Somewhat more self-consciously, Belwynn and Soren also rose, revealing the weapons they carried.

'So,' continued Gustav, 'events would have turned out rather worse without these weapons. It turns out, however, that there may be seven of them altogether. As I have said, the Isharites were keen to get their hands on these weapons for themselves, or at least to prevent us from using them. It would be logical to presume, therefore, that it would be in our interests to find the remaining four. To do so, we need to know two things. What they are, and where they are. Master Szabolcs of the Blood Caladri has spent the winter consulting the ancient texts of his people, and has found that these histories will help us in this respect. So, I invite him now to address us.'

The aged Szabolcs stood up and turned to address the room.

'I have been instructed by my Queen to keep this simple,' he said with a self-deprecating smile. 'She believes there may be little general interest in the sources I have used to ascertain my information. So here it is. Many years ago, when the Isharites first invaded Dalriya, they were resisted by the peoples of our world, who fought together. Lady Onella, known in the Empire as Lady Alexia, provided us with the seven weapons that Gustav has mentioned. These weapons were used to fight a war with the Isharites, a war that ended with an event known as the Cracking of the World. The texts say that this is when the continents of Dalriya and Halvia split apart.'

Murmurs greeted this assertion, but Szabolcs continued.

'Each of the seven weapons was then taken home by a champion, to be kept safe should it be needed again. Time has passed and much of this story has since been forgotten, or corrupted into stories and songs.'

'Not by us,' Belwynn heard Guremar say under his breath.

'And so, to the weapons themselves. The Caladri took away the staff. The Krykkers, the sword. The Lippers had the dagger, later taken from them by the Magnians.'

Belwynn knew all this. Now, it was going to get very interesting.

'The humans took back a shield. It was not easy to find where they took it. Our texts gave them a different name them, but I am now sure that they were referring to the Persaleians.'

Mutterings of dissension could be heard in the room, at the idea that the great enemy and conqueror of Brasingia, the Persaleians, were the heroes of this story.

The Empire grows arrogant, said Soren darkly as he observed the response from the Brasingian nobility.

'To the north,' Szabolcs continued, 'the Jalakh people took a bow. To the west, in Halvia, a people known to the Caladri as the Orias, but commonly known as the Giants, took a spear.'

Now the mutterings in the hall got louder, and there was laughter at the idea of Giants.

Giants? Belwynn asked Soren.

I have read of their existence, her brother replied. *But they must have died out years ago.*

Szabolcs persevered, though his voice now struggled to be heard. 'Finally, a people referred to as the Asrai. They are the most obscure by far. The weapon is referred to as a cloak, or coat. The location given appears to be somewhere in the Lantinen Sea. I could speculate that their lands were submerged when the Cracking caused a great flood, but—I can't be sure.'

Belwynn could see that this had not gone well. There were those—the Caladri, the Krykkers—who believed everything Szabolcs had said. There were others—the Cordentines, Guivergnais, the majority of the Brasingians—who now thought the entire subject ridiculous.

Baldwin stood. Walter angrily banged a cup on the table for silence.

'At this point I will pass this matter on to my Archmage, who will discuss it further with those who wish to make a contribution.'

He's washing his hands of it, said Belwynn.

Don't be surprised, Soren replied. *His head is full of supply requests, military affairs. He has no understanding of this. We should feel lucky he agreed to raise it in the first place.*

'As my brother said, I am now holding talks with the other leaders of Dalriya or their representatives. I will not bring advisers—no Dukes of Brasingia, not even my brother. I hope the other leaders can do the same, to keep the numbers small and the meeting efficient. Please, step this way to my apartments.'

The Krykkers looked at one another.

'He's not coming,' said Guremar, jabbing a thumb at Rabigar.

Rabigar held his hands in the air to signify his acceptance, and Maragin nodded. The two Krykker chieftains stood and made their way to the exit from the hall, followed by Edgar.

'I'll see you later,' said Theron, before following them.

Once Baldwin and the other rulers had left, most of the assembled guests began to drift out of the hall, their participation in the day's events over. Those who remained in the hall were those with an interest in the subject matter raised by Szabolcs. Belwynn was a little surprised to see that Walter had remained. He called everyone over to the top table and Belwynn and the other Magnians joined him there, along with Gustav, Szabolcs and Rabigar.

'So, we have an idea what we are looking for,' said Soren. 'Can we come up with a plan?'

'Szabolcs mentioned the Orias, in Halvia,' began Rabigar tentatively. 'It might be possible to contact our Krykker cousins in Halvia, and ask them what they know of this people, where they lived. The problem we have had is the crossing of the Lantinen Sea. The Kharovians control the waters now, they sink any ship that is not theirs.'

'The Jalakhs had a bow?' Soren asked Szabolcs, who nodded in confirmation. 'That is perhaps the most precisely identified location. It makes sense for those of us who are based in Kalinth to travel to the Jalakh Steppe. But it won't be easy, we would have to travel through Haskany. Gyrmund?'

'There is no easy route. It would be impossible to sail past Kharovia. Overland, it may be possible for a small group to travel unnoticed, through the Dardelles mountain range, where few people live. But it would be time consuming and dangerous.'

'If myself and a group of companions were to go for the bow,' said Soren, 'the Empire can focus on the shield, in Persala. This is the perfect time to send a force there, while the Isharites remain leaderless. The Blood Caladri are also positioned well to help with that.'

Walter and Gustav looked at each other. 'Don't count on my brother sending a force north of Rotelegen.'

'Why not?' demanded Soren. 'Now is the perfect time for Brasingia to assert itself to the north—you are unchallenged. The Drobax are gone, the Haskans have thrown off Ishari's dominion, Arioc is fighting his rivals. Why not?' he repeated.

'I will be asking him for resources here in Barissia. Adalheid will do the same, more shrilly, for Rotelegen. Our soldiers, who sacrificed so much at Burkhard Castle, have still not been fully paid. Farred knows what it was like there, what they went through. It is too much to expect him to invade Persala.'

'If he doesn't strike at Ishari now,' countered Soren, 'he is merely waiting for them to regain their strength. And when they do so, they will return to Burkhard Castle. If he liberates Persala, he can create a buffer state between them. Maybe then form an alliance with Haskany against Ishari. Surely, you both see that?' Soren asked them, looking from Gustav to Walter.

'If Baldwin and I tried to raise an army to invade Persala, no-one would go. Our people have had enough of war, and your arguments won't work.' Walter looked at them all and sighed. 'Look, Baldwin's meeting with the other leaders will decide the extent of his participation. But I am warning you. Don't expect too much from him.'

'Theron will persuade him of the need for more,' said Belwynn.

'What about you?' Soren asked Gustav.

Gustav spread his hands open. 'I serve Baldwin. But I will do what I can.'

'And the Caladri?' Soren persisted, turning to Szabolcs.

'We do not have the power to invade Persala, with our enemies pinning us down. Further, we cannot easily enter the country unnoticed. But my queen will decide what our contribution is to be.'

Leave it for now, Belwynn warned her brother. She knew he was angry, but if he kept pushing for more it could do more harm than good.

'Then there is the cloak,' Farred reminded them all.

'Yes,' said Szabolcs. 'Owned by the Asrai people. I am afraid I don't know who they are.'

'What is said of them?' Soren asked.

'Virtually nothing. They are mentioned by name by two different writers, neither of whom take the time to explain who they are. By all means, Soren, I can show you my texts. But what I have told you is all that they reveal, and I have exhausted all my sources. It is possible the Grand Caladri had other books, but those are now gone.'

So that was it. Soren had volunteered to lead a perilous mission to the Jalakh Steppe. Beyond that, nothing much, except to hope that more would come from the Emperor's negotiations than his brother expected.

IV

IT TAKES AN ASSASSIN

MONEVA LET THE SHARP TIP of the knife slide along her neck. She had come close to shoving it in since her time in Samir Durg. She should have been happy to have escaped, that was the part of it she didn't get. Why was she feeling so low all the time, so tired of it all?

Maybe it was just as well that she'd found an enemy in Heractus. It had given herself something to focus on.

She had noticed the same faces on three separate occasions, watching Elana. Moneva had been trained to kill people and she knew exactly what to look for. *But even when I was thirteen I wasn't as inept as these fools.*

She shifted her position on the warehouse roof, stretching her legs and then giving them a good rub to make sure they didn't go to sleep. She then turned back to the alleyway that Elana took when she walked from her house to the church.

She heard them first, talking to each other, then saw them. It was Elana with one of her new disciples: the big, dopey man called Bemus. He was the size of a warrior, but instead spent all his time praying. They might try it now, even with him there.

Yes, behind them, at the top of the alleyway, Moneva made out a third figure, trailing them. Elana and Bemus were too busy talking to each other to have noticed, exiting the alleyway into the courtyard. Then, to her left, Moneva saw two more figures emerge from the direction of the Church of Madria, walking towards Elana. It was a simple trap, but it had worked, and Moneva knew she had to act fast.

Jumping to her feet, she leapt off the warehouse roof, over a wall, and landed on all fours in the courtyard. Grabbing the knife from her boot, she stood and looked around. The two figures, a man and a woman, had drawn wicked looking long knives of their own, and were staring at her. Bemus had put himself between them and Elana. The third assailant had remained in the alleyway, ready to cut off their escape.

'Moneva?' said Elana.

The man lurched towards Moneva.

'Kill them!' he shouted to his partner.

Moneva made a feint towards him, making him thrust forward with his weapon, before, in one fluid motion, jumping sideways and throwing her knife at the woman. It hit her in the chest and she fell over from the force of it, dropping her knife. Moneva then drew her short sword from her hip and spun around to face the man. She sensed behind her the third assailant coming at her from the alley and knew she had to act quickly. The man was wary of her now, backing away, and she used that to her advantage. She ran at him and instead of thrusting his knife at her he tried to sidestep out of her way. But his footwork was clumsy, and she hacked the length of her sword into his neck with considerable force, knocking him to the ground in the process.

She whirled around to see the third assailant stop in his tracks, turn around, and run for the alleyway.

'Pick up her knife!' she shouted at Bemus, indicating the dropped weapon. But where he was slow to respond, Elana was fast, darting forwards to grab it.

Moneva saw no more as she gave chase. She approached the alleyway with some care, in case he tried something, but when she looked around he was already at the far end, running at top speed. She sprinted down the alleyway, looked in both directions, and saw that he had turned right and was running down one of the main city streets.

'Stop him!' she shouted, before saving the rest of her energy for the chase. The bystanders in the street backed away from them, avoiding the blades they both carried.

A few months ago, she might have lost him—spending her time sitting and drinking in the taverns of Heractus had left her slow and weak. But she had stopped all that nonsense now, had made herself stick to a rigorous training schedule, easy enough to follow when she had nothing else to do. So it was that she began to run him down, sticking to an even pace that she could keep up for half an hour if necessary. The man she was following, however, had been very fast at first but was now slowing, looking more and more ragged.

She was gaining on him, and he must have known he couldn't outrun her, because he turned around, red in the face, holding out a long knife of the same type his accomplices had. Moneva wasn't sure, but she may have killed both of the other assailants, and so she wanted this one taken alive. She didn't make a rash move, but stood opposite him, controlling her breathing, taking her time.

'I would advise you to drop that,' she told him.

He said nothing, his breathing still heavy from his exertion.

Footsteps came from the left. Two men were running over. Young knights, she was fairly sure she recognised their faces from somewhere or other, but had made a conscious decision not to bother learning any of their names. There were so many of them, and they all acted the same.

'Moneva?' said one of them, obviously perfectly aware of who she was. 'What's happening here?'

'This man tried to kill Elana,' she said.

The eyes of the knights grew wide and they both drew swords, turning to the accused.

Now facing three opponents, he knew he had no chance, and threw his knife to the ground.

As it happened, Moneva had only killed one of them. As well as the man she had chased, the woman was alive, and they were both now in the process of being interrogated. Two adjoining cells had been found for them in the castle dungeon, so that when one screamed, the other could hear.

Moneva had to admit that this Sebastian, Grand Master of the Order of Who Cares, had a much more robust approach than she had imagined he would take. She had been worried that it might all be polite requests, but he was quite willing to use threats and violence, attested to by the row of sharp instruments he had deployed. Yes, much of it was for show; they had barely used them. No, it wasn't anything close to the savagery inflicted on Rabigar by the jailers at Coldeberg. But it was getting quick results, and that was what Moneva was concerned with. The people who wanted Elana dead were still out there, after all.

They had ascertained from the woman, the more talkative of the pair, that they had been hired by a representative of the temples of Heractus. When they had put this to her colleague he had confirmed it. These were the people whose flock, and funding, had largely been taken from them by the success of the Church of Madria, and their motive was clear. Neither was Moneva surprised; she had picked up on this source of animosity herself. But neither she nor

Sebastian were convinced that this was the full story, and so the questions continued.

'You know that I will happily use this,' Moneva said to the woman, holding a scalpel just close enough to her face to be uncomfortable. Arms and legs bound, and strapped to her chair, there was little the woman could do to avoid it. 'These knights wouldn't do it to a woman, but you know I would. As a fair punishment for trying to kill my friend. It would require a lot of work, however. You're so ugly in the first place I'd have to make quite a few changes so that people would really notice. Cut the ears off for a start,' she said, walking slowly around to the side and then behind the woman, so that she couldn't see her any more. 'Give you a big sad smile,' she continued, walking back around to the front and miming cutting either side of the woman's mouth.

'Gods, what do you want?' said the woman.

'Your accomplice has told us who else was involved,' came in Sebastian, voice hard. 'Confirm it and we're done.'

'He wasn't involved with us, with our orders. But I saw him speaking with my elders.'

'Him? Who?'

'Straton.'

Even Moneva knew who Straton was, the king's oldest son. Sebastian's expression went cold. He jerked open the door of the cell. Moneva saw him speak with one of the young knights who had helped her to apprehend the man. When he was done, the young man turned and ran off down the corridor.

Sebastian gestured to her. She left the woman in the cell and shut the door.

'Let's check with him,' said Sebastian quietly.

He opened the door to the second cell and they entered, staring at the man. He had said little, even when under torture, but it had been enough.

Moneva smiled at him.

'We know,' she crowed. 'Straton.'

'What about him?'

'We know he's a part of this.'

'He wasn't involved.'

'But?' asked Sebastian, his voice loud, full of authority.

'I don't know. I don't know what his role is. But he wasn't involved with us. I never spoke with him.'

But you're not denying he was there, in the background, Moneva said to herself.

'We'll find out if you're holding something back,' she said.

'That's it. They don't tell me anything.'

Sebastian nodded, and they left the cell, waiting in the corridor.

It wasn't long before the young knight returned, his face flushed.

'Well, Philon?'

'Straton's not in his chambers, he's not been seen by anyone since yesterday evening. He may have left the castle last night.'

Sebastian banged his hand into the wall.

'Damn it. If he's out there recruiting an army we could be in serious trouble.'

***

FARRED CLASPED hands with Edgar.

'I hope to see you before too long,' said the Prince.

Farred smiled, a little nervous about his new mission.

'I hope so.'

Edgar said his farewells to the others, giving his cousin Belwynn a hug, before climbing onto his horse. Brictwin was waiting for him, and without further ado they trotted away to meet up with the Middians. They would travel with them through the Steppe before returning to Magnia.

They left behind a sombre looking group. The decisions taken at Baldwin's meeting had not been to the liking of Gyrmund and his new friends.

'What now for you?' Gyrmund asked him.

'Rainer says he will bring the Queen here, then we will set off.'

Gyrmund nodded, unhappy about it. He had hoped that Farred would accompany him back north, but that wasn't to be.

'Visiting with the Sea Caladri may be very helpful,' said Soren, the wizard, a tone of complaint in his voice. 'But we're leaving with too many things unresolved. Most of all, no-one is taking responsibility for the shield, in Persala. I'm in two minds about what we should do.'

'Well, Edgar is doing his part, don't blame him,' Belwynn reprimanded her brother.

'I don't enjoy saying so about your cousin, but he was on Baldwin's side in everything,' said Theron, the Kalinthian knight, nodding in the direction Edgar had departed to. 'All he could say was how much sacrifice his people had already made.'

Farred bridled at the arrogance of the knight, who had won a single victory with the help of the Krykkers and thought himself superior to everyone else. Magnians had spilt blood fighting the Isharites and the Barissians—fighting other people's wars.

'And what would you have Edgar do?' he demanded. 'Send an army across the Lantinen to go looking for giants?'

'It's the Brasingians,' said Theron. 'They have the resources of an Empire at their disposal, the largest army of all of us, and what was decided yesterday? That they would do nothing. My people are surrounded by enemies and all we have received from anyone is good luck wishes. Why call this meeting in the first place? It has been a waste of time.'

'The last time they sent an army north,' countered Farred, 'it was destroyed to a man, leaving the whole of Rotelegen defenceless. The only reason the Empire still stands is because they threw everything into defending Burkhard Castle. It's unreasonable to expect them to change that strategy.'

'Unreasonable?' repeated Theron.

'Stop it!' said Belwynn. 'This isn't helping. Look, the Caladri are here.'

Farred turned to look. The Caladri carriage, pulled by the strange horned creatures, was ambling down one side of the street. On the other, Queen Hajna and two of her companions were riding horses, accompanied by Rainer. They seemed ready to go. It was time to leave. Gyrmund was already offering his hand.

'I wish we could have had longer,' said Farred.

'The times won't allow it, it seems. I wish you all the luck in your mission.'

'Thank you. I wish the same for you, whatever you decide to do.'

The squire, Evander, was already leading his mount over. They had these boys well trained, the Kalinthians.

'Thank you, young man,' he said as he climbed into the saddle.

'I appreciate your offer to ride with the carriage,' Hajna said.

'You're welcome,' Belwynn replied for her party.

'Take care of Onella's Staff,' she said to Soren. 'My husband, Lorant, asked me to bring it home with me. It does, after all, belong to the Caladri. But you will be putting yourselves in danger if you are heading for the Jalakh Steppe. I will explain to him that you need to keep it a while longer.'

'You should perhaps explain to him,' Soren replied, 'that I will be keeping it permanently. I have suffered for this weapon, and it is now mine, whatever its history.'

It was an unnecessarily rude response and, to Farred, seemed typical of Gyrmund's new acquaintances. But in the end, that was his friend's lookout, not his.

'I will pass on your words,' said Hajna. 'I do not keep anything from him.'

She nodded at the rest of them and turned her horse around. Rainer followed her lead and led them off, heading for the eastern gate.

Farred followed on before turning around and took one last look at Gyrmund, wondering as he always did whether he would ever see him again, and then turned back to his present task. He had a job to do, and it was important. Control of the Lantinen Sea had been lost to the Kharovians. The Sea Caladri were apparently the only people with a strong enough fleet to take them on. If Hajna could persuade them to act, the harbours of South Magnia would be the ideal location for them to base their fleet, and that was the reason Farred was getting involved with the mission.

Rainer, as organised as ever, led them to the east gate where Archbishop Godfrey's small entourage was waiting for them. Baldwin had asked Godfrey to ensure they had safe passage through his duchy of Gotbeck. The Archbishop approached them. His horse was lively, and he had to give it a good slap on the neck to calm the beast down. Farred couldn't help thinking that the forthright churchman and the enigmatic queen had very little in common, but the Archbishop was meticulously polite.

'Your Highness,' he greeted her. 'The weather looks set fair for our journey.'

'Good. I am most grateful to you for offering to escort me.'

'Not at all. We certainly can't have you navigating the swamps of South Gotbeck by yourselves. It's not just the risk of getting lost. Lizardmen still inhabit the marshland. I have done much to cull their numbers in recent years, especially since the death of the evil witch who protected them. But it's nigh on impossible to completely eradicate them, especially since the Caladri won't lift a finger to help.'

Extraordinary, Farred thought to himself. *In one little speech he has insulted magic users, the Caladri, and expressed his regret at not being able to commit genocide.*

'Well, I will leave you to it,' said Rainer. 'I wish you all the best of luck.'

The chamberlain gave Farred a brief look, suggesting that he might need a good share of luck, before leaving them for the castle.

'Lord Farred,' said Godfrey, acknowledging him. They had got to know each other pretty well, having spent the summer stuck in Burkhard Castle together.

'Your Grace.'

'I think we may have an interesting few days ahead of us,' muttered the Archbishop.

'I couldn't have put it better myself, Your Grace.'

V

THE BATTLE OF SIMALEK

S HIRA STUDIED THE ARMY arrayed before them.

Pentas had been right. The forces facing them were deadly, yes. Isharites with their crystal swords, no doubt laced in poison, that left you paralysed when it entered the bloodstream. She heard the barks of the Dogmen rather than saw them: kept in reserve, perhaps, as a weapon to shatter her own lines. But no Drobax. And as for numbers, Arioc had raised no more than they had. Maybe less. Arioc hadn't won complete control in Ishari, then. He was taking a risk bringing this army into Haskany. That gave her Haskans a chance. And that was all she had asked for.

The plain on which the two armies met was flat, with a tree-line to the rear of Arioc's position, from which his force had arrived, hoping to surprise them. But Pentas had given them good warning of the enemy's approach. The flat terrain meant that the cavalry contest would be decisive, and so Shira had chosen to lead the Haskan cavalry herself. The infantry divisions were under the command of her uncle, Koren. As she thought of him, she heard the Haskan trumpets blaring, and ahead of her cavalry position the infantry started to march. This was a battle she wanted, and so she couldn't wait for the Isharites to attack. If she did, Arioc might choose to stay where he was and slink away in the night to fight some other time.

Behind her lines lay the watchtower of Simalek. That was where Pentas would observe the battle and help when needed. He had the task of neutralising Arioc and any other magi her husband had brought with him. Could he hold them off long enough for her to win a victory? She knew nothing of magic, and so had to put her faith in the red-eyed magus. He had his role and she had hers.

The waiting before a battle was the worst part. The battle itself was horrible, but at least then time rushed by, as the mind and body were fully occupied. But as Shira's infantry slowly marched forwards, she experienced the gut-wrenching anticipation with none of the physical release.

The Haskan infantry marched farther and farther away, individuals disappearing into units, units disappearing into a line on the horizon. The Isharites didn't move, waiting for the Haskans to come to their position. But Shira and her generals had expected as much.

Eventually, the sound of trumpets blared; the clash of wood on wood and steel on steel; the shouts and the screams of men killing and men dying; all the noises of war came to them on the air. Moneva's cavalry waited. They were too far away to see which side had the advantage, except that there was little movement, and the fact that the sounds continued unabated indicated that the fighting was fierce.

Shira's stallion raised its head and she patted his neck as gently as she could with steel gauntlets.

'Easy, Shadow,' she whispered in his ear, 'not our turn yet.'

He relaxed, putting his head back down. She loved this one. He was black as night, muscled, and savage in combat.

And then, the infantry sent them the signal. First one, then two riders could be seen, detaching themselves from the infantry units, riding hard in their direction, and waving red flags as they did.

Her force readied themselves to go. Shira stood up in her stirrups and twisted around, to look at her main cavalry force, and the smaller reserve force who would stay put for now. She pulled her visor down, limiting her vision to a narrow strip. She raised one arm.

'For Haskany!' she shouted, and her soldiers repeated the war cry.

Shira turned back, picking up the lance she had skewered into the ground. She leaned forward, saying 'Now, my friend.' He didn't need much encouragement, springing ahead, leading the other horses who followed him, as she led her subjects.

'You can be my new king,' she told him, exulting in her freedom, in the moment. 'We don't need the old one anymore.'

The signallers waved their flags to the right, and so they swung around in that direction. When they straightened out, on the flank of the infantry battle, they could see the Isharites up ahead. The enemy didn't carry lances, instead they already had their swords drawn. The Haskans would have the initial advantage on impact, but would then have to be wary of the Isharite weapons. Shira and Koren, knowing full well the threat of poison, had insisted on covering all their soldiers head to toe in metal armour, to give them the best protection possible.

As they gained speed, the distance between the two forces rapidly diminished. Shira could now see the individual riders who were coming at her, identifying one with a bluish coloured sword as her target. The clash of cavalry could be terrifying, but she knew that neither she nor her mount would pull up.

She levelled her lance at her target, and then the two lines crashed together. As the Isharites tried to avoid the lances aimed at them, they crashed into one another. Shira's target was buffeted to the side at the last second and her lance missed, but connected with someone else; she couldn't see who. Her mount was kicking and biting, turning around in a circle, and it was hard for Shira to get her bearings. She drew her sword and pulled on the reins, wresting control back over the beast.

She looked around her, trying to focus as the noise of battle engulfed her—men's shouts combined with the screams of horses, some of which were writhing and kicking on the ground; others were riderless, their riders now fighting on foot if they had survived the fall. She could see her soldiers slashing a path towards her. She waited for them to arrive before striking out with them, working as a unit to gain the advantage over the Isharites. One of her men lost the point of his sword, shattered by the hard crystal of an Isharite blade.

Nonetheless, they were forcing the enemy back. Until they came upon a line of Isharite cavalrymen. They had the biggest horses, the most expensive armour. And in the middle of the line sat Rostam, newly appointed member of the Council of Seven, and Arioc's chief henchman. Until recently they had been on the same side, both working to further Arioc's ambitions. Now Shira had chosen her own side, but Rostam had remained loyal.

She raised her visor, making sure that he had seen her. He held his sword vertically in front of him, in a kind of salute. Instinctively, the soldiers around them left a space. Shira would fight with Rostam, and the outcome, she knew, was likely to swing the course of the battle.

She pushed her visor down, kneeing her horse so that it circled to the left. Rostam copied her movement.

There are many ways to win a fight, Shira knew, and one of them is to know your enemy. Predict what they will do. She knew Rostam well enough, knew that he would consider himself superior to her in every way: strength, skill, stamina. He believed he could win any number of ways: beat her down with strength, or kill her with a thousand cuts, especially if he had applied poison to his blade. Shira knew that her enemy might have one weakness: over-confidence in himself, and an underestimation of her.

Shira suddenly kneed her horse forwards into a charge. She pulled her sword back and put everything into a massive strike. If Rostam had evaded her, she may have toppled off her horse. But he chose to block. He blocked, thinking he could parry and counter-attack; demonstrate his superiority. He hadn't realised quite how strong she was. He hadn't anticipated she would take such a huge risk. Rostam's block was too weak—Shira's strike forced through it, her hips, core and arms working together to push him back. The power of her blow pushed his blade back against his body, pushed his body back in his seat so that he lost his balance. Shadow bit at the face of Rostam's mount, causing it to skitter away.

For a moment, that seemed to linger longer than it really lasted, Rostam tottered back in his seat, arms windmilling to regain his balance. Shira brought back her sword over her left shoulder, then struck down. Her strike was true, connecting with Rostam's neck and virtually severing his head from his shoulders. His body sprawled to one side, feet still caught in the stirrups.

There was a moment of shock on both sides, at the speed of the outcome as much as anything else. Then the fight resumed.

That one incident changed the course of the contest. Rostam was just one man, but his death boosted the confidence of the Haskans, just as it put doubt in the minds of the Isharites. Slowly at first, then faster, Shira's soldiers gained the upper hand, pushing the enemy back, until one turned around and fled, then others, then all of them. The Isharite cavalry escaped back the way they had come and the Haskans gave chase, hoping to run them back to their camp and into the woods, making sure that they didn't regroup.

Shira was with them, a grim smile on her face. Then something, an intuition maybe, made her slow down and stop. Some of her soldiers saw and stopped the chase too, started calling to those ahead. Shira raised a hand for silence.

To her left, she could see that the infantry had stopped fighting. The two sides stood a few feet apart, and an eerie silence had descended over them. And they weren't looking in her direction. They weren't reacting to her victory. They were looking in the opposite direction. To the south.

***

PENTAS STOOD on the roof of the watchtower of Simalek, which rose almost one hundred feet into the air, a marvel of Persaleian engineering. Here the wind battered him, but the position allowed him a unique view of the plain around the tower. He observed the clash of cavalry on the battlefield. He had found two Haskan magi, an older man and his younger and more gifted protege. The younger of the two, Rimmon, could also ride a horse, and so Pentas had sent him with Shira.

Rimmon helped him to see Shira and Rostam circling each other, and when Shira attacked, Pentas and Rimmon were able to suppress the use of magic. He could see Shira strike Rostam down, see the battle turn in the favour of the Haskans.

But he didn't see the black kite gliding towards the tower, until it was too late. The bird landed on the parapet and only then did Pentas give it his full attention. The bird transformed before him, taking the form of Arioc.

They looked at one another for a short while. Pentas felt a brief feeling of despair. He hadn't wanted to die, and now that the time had come, he regretted it. And yet, he told himself, this was always going to be the likely outcome.

'What's happening?' Arioc asked him, gesturing at the battle down below.

'Rostam has fallen.'

'That's a shame.'

'He was your son, was he not?'

'I believe so. But I can always raise another army. It is you I have come for.'

'I feel honoured that this is all for me,' Pentas waved his hand at the spectacle before them ironically.

'Don't be surprised, Pentas. I have killed Ardashir. Now I will kill you. That only leaves me Siavash, and all my rivals will be gone. Then Diis will join with me.'

'He has not done so already?' Pentas asked.

He genuinely wanted to know. He had wanted this Haskan rebellion to be an inconvenience for the Isharites. But their failure to crush it in its early stages had surprised him. If Diis had not intervened, leaving the Isharite leaders to their own devices, that would explain their weakness.

A look of annoyance, maybe even insecurity, flickered across Arioc's face.

'He will not join with me until I have proven myself. I would expect nothing less. But the time draws near. And so it is your time, Pentas. I have wasted some of my own time wondering why you engaged in this foolishness. Surely you knew it couldn't last long.'

'I am Madria's servant, Arioc. I always have been.'

A look of surprise now crossed Arioc's face. He smiled then, and looked at Pentas with a new expression, almost one of respect.

'Well, I admit at times it had occurred to me. It certainly explains your regular incompetence. Your failures regarding her weapons, of course. You were in Edeleny, then?'

'Yes. That was me.'

'And you were behind the attack on Erkindrix?'

'I helped them,' said Pentas. 'But then so did you.'

'Indeed. We just had very different motives. Well, you have played a good game Pentas, I will give you that.'

Pentas looked past Arioc.

'You may think this one last game,' he said, 'but perhaps you should look behind you.'

'Really. Now you disappoint me. This is more like the Pentas I thought I knew.'

'This is no joke, Arioc.'

Arioc turned, and saw what Pentas could see. Seven crows, flying in a V-shape towards them.

'Not your magi?' Pentas asked him, already knowing the answer.

'No.'

Arioc seemed to tear his attention from the birds to the battle below them.

'See there,' he said.

Pentas looked where Arioc pointed, to the south of the fighting, and saw nothing. Then he realised what he was seeing. The Isharite fog, creeping towards the two groups of infantry. A third force had arrived, concealing its presence, and was now not far from the two armies. He could see on the battlefield, but he had no way of communicating over such a distance. The twins, Soren and Belwynn, were surely the only ones with that power. But maybe he could send a kind of warning; encourage Shira to notice the trap. He tried but would not know whether he had succeeded.

'Siavash,' he said to Arioc. 'And I think now we know who Diis has chosen. And perhaps has chosen for some time.'

'I have been fooling myself,' Arioc admitted. 'Diis has not forgiven my role in Erkindrix's death.'

'Maybe you are altogether too human for him, Arioc.'

'Enough of your silver tongue, Pentas. What do we do?'

'It's 'we' now, is it?'

'Of course it is. That's the only chance we have of survival.' Arioc looked him in the eyes. 'My assumption is we can't beat them, even working together.'

'I would agree,' Pentas replied cautiously.

'Then we flee,' determined Arioc. 'Then they must decide whether they chase one or both of us. It may give one of us a chance to escape.'

'Agreed,' said Pentas. He paused, not quite believing he was saying it. 'Good luck.'

But Arioc had already transformed into his kite. The bird took one last look at him then flew away, heading north.

Pentas looked at the approaching crows, no doubt seven masters of magic. Maybe even Siavash himself was amongst them. The truth was, Pentas had never learned to transform into animal form. It was a highly complex piece of magic, generally only mastered by the Isharites.

But he had mastered an alternative means of travel: the teleport. It was equally difficult, and perhaps more dangerous, requiring him to focus on a precise location to send his body. If he got it wrong, he could send himself to his death. He concentrated, focusing on a location he had identified before the battle. It was, after all, always prudent to be prepared. As he felt himself begin to move, as the sensations of blurred vision and stomach churning began to take hold, he was able to spare a brief thought for Arioc.

Good luck escaping from all seven of them, you bastard. You're going to need it.

***

SHIRA TROTTED her horse back the way they had come, then stopped again, listening.

This time, she knew she heard it. It was a sound she was all too familiar with. Drobax. Thousands upon thousands of Drobax, marching in their direction. She could hear them and, she now thought, even smell them. But she couldn't see them.

It was magic. Arioc had brought the Drobax with him, somehow circled around their position without them noticing. He had concealed them with magic, the same trick her magi had used in Rotelegen.

Pentas had missed it. Had failed.

But if it was Arioc, she asked herself, why had his soldiers stopped fighting too? She smiled, a mirthless smile, when she understood what was happening. Siavash. He had outwitted the pair of them.

One of Pentas's pet magi, the one with the red hair, rode up to her.

'We must flee,' he said urgently.

But Shira knew deep in her bones that she wasn't fleeing from this.

'You go,' she told him. 'And rescue my uncle if you can.'

She raised a hand and the Haskan cavalry rallied to her. She took them south, in the direction of the enemy, and the Haskan reserves joined them. They peered ahead, listening to the noise of the Drobax getting closer. She remembered the fears of the Haskans when she had called for this rebellion. They had warned her of the Ishari magi; of the Drobax. And she had not listened, and Pentas had sweet talked them into doing his bidding.

Shira never hid from the truth. She knew this was her doing. But she would ride against the enemy and show them what free Haskans could do. And maybe the rest of her soldiers could make their escape, return to their homes, and live to fight another day, when the odds weren't so stacked against her country.

The fog was slowly dissipating. The work of Siavash's magi was done, and now his Drobax could be seen, emerging through the tendrils of smoke like the monsters they were. And not just Drobax, but other creatures too. Shira could see a unit of Isharite infantry, men who had chosen Siavash over Arioc. And small groups of spindly legged creatures had been positioned in between the Drobax, creatures Shira did not recognise at first until she realised she had met one of them before. Dorjan, King of the Shadow Caladri. He had led his people here too. Well done, she silently acknowledged. You chose well. You chose the winner.

Shira raised her arm one last time. Her cavalry gave a shout. Those who still held lances held them to the sky. Most, like her, now had to make do with swords. She pointed hers at the enemy.

'For Haskany!'

They rode hard, gaining speed, the lancers moving to the front, Shira and the rest positioned behind.

The Drobax came, relentless and unthinking. The Shadow Caladri raised bows. No, Shira thought, but it was too late now.

A hail of missiles rose high into the air, before dropping from the sky towards them, as if they were sentient creatures that could target their victims. They rained down onto the Haskans. Shira had insisted that her cavalry were equipped with the strongest metal armour, many of them covered head to toe in plate, their horses protected with scales. The casualties weren't therefore as bad as they might have been, but they were bad enough. Horses went down in front of her, to the sides. The riders following behind crashed into them, causing more devastation. The Haskan line was now uneven. But it hardly mattered.

Twenty yards out. Ten. And now they were into the enemy and Shira could swing her sword, Shadow could kick, and the Drobax fell under her fury. Her arm tired from swinging her sword and still she swung it, in a fierce desperation to kill as many of the creatures who had invaded her land as she could.

She mistook it at first for another Drobax. She swung down to her right dismissively, but it blocked her stroke with a shield, then casually stepped inside and shoved a short sword into Shadow's throat, finding a gap in his armour. The sword came out with a gush of blood and Shira barely had time to get her feet out from the stirrups before her mount collapsed.

She landed on the ground heavily, her armour making it difficult to move well, but she had kept her grip on her sword. A blow landed on her back, nearly knocking her over, but it felt like it skidded off her armour rather than penetrating through.

She struggled to her feet and turned to find a Drobax coming in for a second attempt. She backed off just in time to avoid the thrust, then lunged forward and thrust her own sword into the creature with both hands, skewering through flesh and bone, before tugging the blade out again.

It collapsed, dead.

Shira walked around Shadow, assessing her situation. Fighting raged all about, and she could see more and more Haskans being pulled from horses as her force became overwhelmed. She reached his head, where the soil was drenched in his blood, and there it was, waiting for her.

It was fighting bare-chested, but appeared to have a naturally armoured torso. Then she knew it as a Krykker, but what it was doing here, in this fight, she had no idea.

A couple of Drobax approached her, but the Krykker shouted at them, waving his sword, and they retreated to find some other victim.

The Krykker discarded his shield and took a hand-axe, readying himself to fight with a weapon in each hand. He gave her a smile before walking towards her.

She let him approach, before launching a two-handed strike. But, not weighed down by as much armour as she was, he seemed to move so much faster than she did. He blocked her sword with his own, before going down on one knee and bringing in his axe in a long horizontal slash. The axe blade connected with her knee and her leg was taken from under her, causing her to collapse to the ground.

Excruciating pain erupted from where the blow had landed. She tried to stand back up but she screamed out loud in agony when she tried to put her weight on the injured leg, and had to give up. Instead she knelt, putting her good foot on the ground in front of her.

The Krykker approached, in no rush. She fished her sword in front of her and quick sharp he flicked his sword at her wrist, trying to disarm her. She pulled back just in time, then swung for his legs, trying to repay him in kind, but he managed to skip away just in time.

She knew his game now. He knew who she was, and he would get a nice reward for capturing her alive. She held her sword out in front of her in one hand, before grabbing a dagger from her belt in the other. She smiled at him now, and he smiled back, pleasantly enough.

She flung her sword at him.

His natural reaction was to move out of the way.

Shira went down on both knees now. She grabbed her dagger in both hands and put the sharp point of the blade to her throat.

'No!' he shouted.

Shira held the dagger in place, elbows spread out wide, and let herself fall to the ground.

VI

BROKEN VOWS

THEY RETRACED THEIR JOURNEY back to Heractus.

Once they were through the Empire, Szabolcs and the other Caladri said their farewells and returned to their home. Belwynn and the others continued on, through the disputed lands of Grienna and Trevenza, then west, skirting the southern border of Persala.

Slowly, their spirits rose. Most of them had things to look forward to in Kalinth. Belwynn could resume her work with Elana. Gyrmund would see Moneva again. Theron, she could tell, was keen to get back to work. His mind had moved on from the disappointments of diplomacy in Coldeberg. He started talking to her about the Kalinthian army, mainly on the subject of the need to develop an infantry force to complement the Knights. She understood the basic problem he had. It had been the Krykker infantry and the Kalinthian cavalry that together had defeated the Isharites. Neither could have done it alone.

Soren, while not exactly a force of optimism, had also come to terms with the meeting in Coldeberg. He still smouldered with anger at what he saw as a lack of action from others. But he had learned from Szabolcs the locations of the remaining weapons. That had helped him to focus on what he needed to do.

'Yes,' he said to her out loud, as their horses clipped along, the deep forest of the Grand Caladri on their left, the ancient kingdom of Persala to their right. 'The shield is on our doorstep, somewhere there,' he continued, indicating Persala. 'But who else is going to travel to the Jalakh Steppe but us?'

That was a question that did not require an answer. And though Belwynn took issue with the word 'us', she kept that to herself for now.

When they entered Korkis they found a town in some turmoil. The central plaza was a mess of wagons, horses and soldiers. In amidst it stood Tycho, normally so relaxed, red-faced and barking out orders.

'Thank Madria you are back,' he declared when he saw Theron, with little humour.

'What is going on?' Theron asked.

'Straton is raising an army,' Tycho replied. 'Sebastian has ordered me to bring a force back to Heractus.' He looked at Belwynn. 'Elana was attacked— she's fine, don't worry,' he assured her. 'But Straton seems to be making alliances with our enemies.'

'What are Sebastian's orders?' Theron asked him.

'Bring back most of the knights and recruit infantry. I have enlisted fifty townsfolk. It means leaving a skeleton force here. I've put Leontios in charge.'

Theron nodded his approval.

'It's not as simple as you might think, Theron. I've had reports of armies marching up and down Persala, of war in Haskany. The Isharites are on the move again. If they strike at our eastern border now, there's nothing to stop them.'

'Then we need to deal with Straton as soon as possible.'

They rode to Heractus with all speed, leaving behind the soldiers who had to travel on foot. As they approached the capital, they saw that a tented camp had been established on the fields to the south of the city. They could see some soldiers there, being drilled on spear work. But there were not many.

When they were admitted past the city walls, the others went straight to find Sebastian, but Belwynn had a job to do first. Little Lyssa, tired out from the ride, needed a place to stay. Belwynn took her to the room in the castle that she shared with Soren.

'This is where you will stay now,' Belwynn explained to her. 'That is Soren's bed and this is mine.'

'I don't have a bed,' observed Lyssa.

'You can sleep with me for now,' said Belwynn. 'And soon Soren will be leaving. Then you can have his bed.'

Lyssa nodded sleepily.

'I will fetch you something to eat and drink. Then I need to speak with Soren and the others. But I will come back here when I am done.'

When Belwynn found them, in Sebastian's office, they had already talked much of it out. Who the enemy was, where they were, what they should do. Belwynn found that she wasn't as desperate to know all the details as she once would have been.

Sebastian, Theron and Tycho had a map before them and a pile of letters, no doubt reports from their supporters on the situation in the different parts of the country. Gyrmund and Moneva were sitting, not far apart, both of them looking more contented than she had seen them in a long while. Soren sat with his arms folded, one hand resting on his staff. Finally, Elana was there too. She looked perfectly well despite her scare. Belwynn slipped in while Sebastian was talking and sat next to the priestess, placing a hand on her shoulder.

'You are well?' she whispered.

'Of course,' Elana whispered back. 'Soren tells me you know the whereabouts of the rest of the weapons?'

Belwynn nodded. Elana smiled and returned her attention to the conversation.

'So,' said Soren, 'you are suggesting that it won't be a week until your army can leave Heractus?'

'I would say so,' replied Sebastian. The Grand Master looked disappointed in the delay. In fact, Belwynn thought, he looked older, more careworn.

'And you are sure you won't need my help?'

The Knights all looked at each other.

'We need to match their infantry force,' Theron said eventually. 'Once we do that, I am convinced of our superiority. So, thank you Soren, but I don't think that will be necessary.'

'Then it is decided,' said Soren. 'I don't think we should waste any time. Gyrmund, Moneva, Belwynn and I will make plans to head to the Jalakh Steppe. If tomorrow is too early, then the day after.'

I'm not going, Belwynn told him.

Soren turned to her, looking unsettled, and she felt a rush of guilt for not discussing this before. He opened his mouth to say something else to the group, then closed it again. 'Belwynn,' he said. 'Can I talk to you?'

While the rest of them looked on, Belwynn got up from her chair and followed her brother out of the room.

Soren walked on a bit farther and then turned to face her in the corridor.

'I'm sorry,' she said. 'I should have said something to you. But you did kind of assume I was going without asking me.'

'Why?' he asked, looking genuinely baffled. He was hurt too, he couldn't hide it from her.

'I have people here who need me, Soren. I have left Elana for too long. You know that Theron—' she paused, embarrassed. 'However foolish it might be, the Knights find strength when I am there.'

'Yes, but I need you too, Belwynn. I'm your brother. No-one else is doing anything to find these weapons. I need your support. I always have. You know that.'

'Soren,' she chided. 'Gyrmund and Moneva will be with you. Besides, what real use am I going to be to you? I'm more use here. And, although I don't like us being apart, our abilities may be useful this way. We can keep in touch with each other.'

Belwynn thought better of mentioning one other factor. Lyssa. She really didn't like the idea of leaving her, even though she knew that Elana would look after her.

'Belwynn,' he said. 'I'm asking you to come with me.'

She smiled. He knew he always got her to do what he wanted. That had been at the heart of their relationship for years.

She took his hands. 'And I'm telling you no.'

It was time for that to change.

They stood for a while, his hands still in hers, looking into each other's eyes. Something important and unspoken passed between them.

I understand, said Soren.

When they returned, everyone was standing, ready to go. The hour was getting late and everyone looked tired.

Belwynn undid the belt that held Toric's Dagger and held the weapon out to Moneva.

Moneva took it and then embraced Belwynn.

'Thank you,' she said quietly in Belwynn's ear. 'Not just for the Dagger.'

Belwynn smiled as Moneva released her. 'Thank you for looking after Elana for me. I heard you did a pretty good job.'

'I'm walking Elana back to her house,' said Moneva. 'Everyone has agreed that someone will be with her at all times. Haven't they, dear?' she asked the priestess.

Elana rolled her eyes. 'I'm sure I'll be perfectly fine now.'

'I'll come with you,' said Belwynn.

'What was that about?' Moneva asked her as the three women were ushered through the gates of the royal castle and began to walk down to the town. 'With your brother?'

'I told Soren I'm not going with you.'

'Thought so.'

'It's not because of me, I hope,' said Elana. 'I am perfectly happy to carry on by myself, Belwynn. I feel that my current duty is to build this community. But getting the weapons is of the utmost importance, of course.'

'It's not just because of you, Elana,' said Moneva. 'She needs to stay with Theron, too, don't you Belwynn?' she asked with a knowing look.

'Of course, how silly of me,' said Elana, unable to suppress a little smile from hovering about her face.

'Yes, the Knights need me,' said Belwynn archly. She was damned if she was going to let these two embarrass her over Theron.

Moneva made a face and puffed air out of her cheeks in mock outrage at this remark, but let the topic slide.

'So, who is raising an army against us?' asked Belwynn.

'The head priests of the temples, who want Elana dead,' said Moneva. 'They're formed an alliance with Straton, who wants rid of the Knights. His friend, the Count of Ampelios, escaped with Straton last week. Straton has authority as heir to the throne, Ampelios apparently has money, making them a dangerous pair.'

'Sebastian's enemies within the Order are also rumoured to be involved,' added Elana. 'Do you remember a knight called Euthymius, Belwynn?'

'A little.'

She remembered him from The High Tower, as the most vocal supporter of Galenos, the former Grand Master of the Knights whom Sebastian had displaced.

'He is supposed to be gathering knights who are loyal to Galenos, even though Galenos himself is still imprisoned in the Tower. Sebastian is worried about it. He fears not only the force that Euthymius might raise, but also the affect it could have on the rest of the Order. Many knights may choose not to get involved on either side, for fear of having to fight their own brethren. And that could give an advantage to Straton.'

They had reached Elana's house. They had told Belwynn enough to make her realise that the threat was serious. But while she acknowledged it, she felt too tired to worry about it until tomorrow.

They said brief farewells to Elana, before Belwynn and Moneva retraced their steps back to the castle, where the guards saw them coming and had the gates open for them.

Saying goodnight to Moneva, Belwynn made her way to the tower where her room was. She quietly opened the door and peered in. Soren lay asleep in one bed, and Lyssa in the other. The thought of an uncomfortable night squeezed in next to Lyssa didn't appeal. She let the door shut, then padded back down the tower stairs.

Without really thinking about it, Belwynn found herself outside Theron's room. She raised her hand to knock on the door. Maybe she *should* think about this. She knew if she did, she would leave, so she knocked on the door before she could talk herself out of it.

The door opened slightly, and Theron peered out. He opened it fully when he realised who it was.

She had got him out of bed. He was half dressed.

'Belwynn, is everything alright?' he asked.

'Everything's fine,' she reassured him. 'I've just lost my bed, that's all. So I came here.'

'Come in,' he said.

She entered his room and he shut the door behind her. Her stomach was swimming with butterflies. What did she think she was doing here?

She turned to face him. He was looking at her and she looked back at him, feeling her heartbeat race, her breathing getting shallow.

We both want this so much, she told herself.

'Can I sleep with you tonight?' she made herself ask him.

'What are you saying—' he began.

'You know what I'm asking,' she told him.

He moved in close. 'Belwynn,' he murmured, his voice sounding husky. 'You know I have my vows.'

'I don't care about them,' she said.

He put his arms around her, pulled her into him. She looked up at him, parting her lips, putting one hand around his neck, and then his lips were on hers, his hands on her body, and she knew that his vows were broken.

65

***

NINETEEN OF them had made it through the winter. Nineteen had come down from their camp in the Dardelles mountains, and the irony was, that was when they had come closest to death. Hordes of Drobax were crossing the mountain range into Haskany, and they had nearly got trapped. They had hidden in a cave and had to wait out an entire day before it was safe to move.

The original plan to cross into Persala was dead. Each time they made an attempt they had encountered armies, or scouting parties: if not Drobax, then Haskans or Isharites. So they had hugged the mountains, gradually heading south-west, getting hungrier and weaker every day.

Nineteen emerged onto the Plains of Kalinth. Eight Barbarians; six Persaleians; two men of Rotelegen; two Dog-men; and a Magnian.

Clarin, worn down by the burdens of leadership, prayed to Toric, Madria, and every other god he had ever heard of. If the Drobax hadn't crossed into Kalinth, they had a chance.

They had left the mountains behind them but Kalinth remained a rugged landscape, and their progress was painfully slow. They walked at the pace of the slowest, which was the pace of Jurgen, the Rotelegen. He had a permanent limp, the result of a spear wound he sustained in the fighting at Samir Durg. He used a stick to help him balance. The Dog-men carried his possessions. His cousin, Rudy, was always by his side, usually by the end of the day with Jurgen's arm around his shoulder, taking his weight, encouraging him. But still, Jurgen was the slowest.

At the worst times, when he was tired and fed up, Clarin had thought about killing him. Just thoughts, crossing his mind, when there was nothing else to think about except putting one foot in front of the other. He'd sometimes see the same thoughts in other people's faces, but no-one had talked of it, Clarin hadn't seriously considered doing it. If they killed Jurgen, would they then turn on the second slowest? What if Clarin himself got injured? Would they finish him off? No, they had survived this far by sticking together. As unlikely a group as you would find in the whole of Dalriya, but they all shared the experience of slavery in the mines, had fought their way out of Samir Durg together, and they weren't going to turn on each other now.

Kalinth was a sparsely populated land. There were few villages like they had in Magnia. Mainly isolated farms and hamlets, with more sheep than humans. They avoided contact. Clarin was certain that the local population, tough border people, would see them as a threat, and he didn't fancy getting stuck with an arrow by an anxious farmer. They didn't—couldn't—avoid the sheep, however. On an evening they got a fire going and ate roasted lamb; Clarin genuinely believed he had never tasted anything so good.

It was only a matter of time before they were challenged. When the Kalinthians arrived, there were only ten of them. They looked good, though. Fine horses, fine clothes, tall lances, armour polished and shining in the mid-morning sun. Clarin had heard all about the Knights of Kalinth, supposedly the best heavy cavalry in Dalriya. He was sure he was looking at them now.

'They're keeping their distance,' observed Cyprian, the Persaleian, as the riders drew up a hundred yards away.

'They're outnumbered two-to-one,' said Clarin. 'And we must look like mean sons of bitches by now. And not just them,' he added, indicating the Dog-men, which got some laughs, easing the tension a little. 'I'll go and talk to them.'

'I'll come with you,' said Zared. Zared was a young man, only in his early twenties, yet he was clearly the leader of the Persaleians.

The two approached while the Knights sat astride their horses, waiting for them. They were an intimidating sight, and Clarin couldn't help feeling nervous as he approached.

'Well met,' he began. 'I should explain our presence in your lands. We are men from all over Dalriya—from Persala, the Empire and elsewhere.'

'What are you doing here?' asked one of the knights, interrupting. He was a young man, perhaps Zared's age. But he presented himself as the leader and so that was who Clarin addressed.

'We have escaped from the prisons at Samir Durg. We have been on the run since last summer. We tried to head through Persala, but it's impossible.'

'Samir Durg?' repeated one of the other knights. 'Leontios,' he continued, talking to the leader, 'isn't that where Lady Belwynn went to rescue her brother?'

'Wait,' said Clarin, looking from one knight to the other, not quite believing what he had just heard. 'You know Belwynn?'

Leontios, to his credit, loaded them up with precious supplies before sending them on their way to Heractus. Perhaps that was his way of ensuring they weren't tempted to butcher any more sheep. He couldn't spare horses though. Indeed, it turned out that those ten knights were all that remained of the garrison of a town called Korkis. Furthermore, from what Clarin could tell, that garrison was the only one anywhere near the Persaleian border. If—more like when—the Isharites turned their attention here, Kalinth would be in terrible trouble.

The reason, Leontios had explained to him, was a civil war brewing in the country. Even the Knights themselves were divided in their allegiances. It was a strange and confusing situation for Clarin's group to find themselves in. The idea of fighting a civil war, when the Isharites and Drobax were on the march, seemed to Clarin the height of lunacy.

Be that as it may, his group found themselves walking again, albeit with the permanent, exhausting fear of the previous weeks now gone, and enough food in their packs to get them to their destination. It wasn't such a long way in the end, and two and a half days after leaving Korkis, the city of Heractus appeared before them. It was a sizeable settlement, with grey stone walls surrounding the main city and a camp to the south. Once they got closer, Clarin could see that it was an army camp, well-made tents set out in organised rows. More evidence of the threat of war, though the camp looked new and the soldiers cared for.

Another good sign was that they were challenged promptly upon approaching. Clarin handed the wary looking soldiers a letter written by Leontios, which Zared had assured him vouched for who they were and asked that they be taken to one of two men, either a Theron or a Sebastian. Once the soldiers had found someone to read it, they agreed to let them enter the city, on condition that they handed in their weapons.

Clarin's group balked at this demand. These were men who had sworn never to let themselves be taken captive again, and so persuading them to disarm was nigh on impossible. In the end, it was agreed that the group would be found spare tents in the camp and Clarin would go into the city alone.

Heractus had a solid, if unspectacular looking castle, made with the same grey blocks of stone as the city walls and many of the houses. It was to the castle he was taken, and at the gates the letter did the trick once more, a castle guard leading him into the main hall where he was offered a place at the fire and told to wait until someone fetched him.

He took a seat on the floor by the fire, and let the flames warm his tired body. In the mountains, during what seemed to be an unending northern winter, he had thought he would never feel warm again. Now he sat so close that the fire burned him. His face felt red, a trickle of sweat ran down his side, and yet he was loathe to move farther away. He felt like he could sleep for a week, and had to stop himself from lying down there and then. The trouble was, with all the military activity going on, these two knights whom Leontios had mentioned in his letter probably had a dozen better things to do than meet with him.

'Clarin!' came a voice from the other end of the hall, and he turned to see someone he had thought he would never see again.

Belwynn, smiling, came running over, closely followed by Elana. He got to his feet and opened his arms to grab her. She pushed away too soon, and then he was hugging Elana, though in truth he only had eyes for Belwynn. He had promised himself many things since his capture in Edeleny, and one of them was that if he ever found this girl again, he would never leave her. She looked more beautiful than ever and she looked happy; happier than he remembered her.

'You're a lot thinner,' said Belwynn.

'Yes well, being starved for eight months will do that. I swear, I never understood what hunger meant.' He looked around. He had hoped there would have been more. 'Soren? Gyrmund? Did they not make it?'

'You've just missed them, by two days,' Belwynn replied. 'They're heading north, to the Jalakh Steppe. I'll explain why later. Moneva is with them, too.' She looked at him. 'I forget, there's so much you don't know. I am so sorry we left you. Herin?'

We left you? Had Belwynn been in Samir Durg? It sounded like there was much he didn't know.

'Herin,' he began, answering her question. 'We held out in one of the towers of Samir Durg. He went missing. I looked for him as best I could, vowed to myself that I would never leave without him. The others helped me, but there was not a single sign. If he was dead, I am sure we would have found a body. But nothing. And there was little time. If we didn't leave when we had the chance, we wouldn't have left at all.'

'Who's we?' Belwynn asked. 'The other prisoners? Gyrmund told us about them. What did he say?' she asked, turning to Elana.

'There were humans,' said the priestess. 'Dog-men. A Bear-man?'

'Yes,' said Clarin, smiling, and told them about his new companions, those who had survived. Then they in turn told him of what had happened in Kalinth, of Dirk's death, of their invasion of Haskany, and finally of Belwynn's time in Samir Durg, teleported in by Pentas the wizard. How Gyrmund and Moneva had somehow rescued Soren, how they had all ended up in the throne room, and how Moneva had used Toric's Dagger to kill Erkindrix.

'That makes sense,' said Clarin. 'The Isharites had all but defeated us, we were ready to make our last stand on the roof of the tower. And then they all left. That must have been when Erkindrix was slain.'

'I am sorry we left you,' said Belwynn. 'I don't know whether it was the right thing to do. I was unconscious—'

'Nonsense,' said Clarin. 'You saved us, when you all helped to kill Erkindrix. They had to take you to safety at that point. Anyway, what now?'

'Oh, I completely forgot,' said Belwynn. 'Theron told me to take you to see him.'

Belwynn and Elana led Clarin to a room where the knight, Theron, was sat at a desk, bits of parchment spread about it. He stood up and welcomed them in. He was young, confident, but looked careworn. Clarin understood. Many were counting on him to win this war the Kalinthians were involved in.

'It's an honour to meet you, Clarin,' said Theron once they were all seated. 'Belwynn and the others have told me so much about you. To have a warrior of your prowess here is a boon, I can tell you. The letter Leontios wrote,' he said, trying to find it amongst the various bits of parchment on the table before giving up, 'mentioned a number of other escaped prisoners?'

'That's right, there are nineteen of us in all. Two of them are Dog-men. I know that may sound strange, but they have been loyal to me and we wouldn't have survived without them.'

'I understand. I'm in no position to discriminate against them, even if I was so inclined. Look Clarin, I will be frank with you. You will have picked up that we are in a dangerous situation right now. I can offer you and all your friends accommodation, food, and even wages. On one condition. You all join the Kalinthian army.' Theron looked at Clarin's expression. 'I'm sorry to have to do it, but I have no choice. We're desperate.'

Clarin looked from Theron to Belwynn and Elana, then back to the knight, but none of them cracked a smile.

They all looked at him, with deadly serious expressions. But they had to be joking. They *had* to be fucking joking.

VII

RED SERPENT

THEY USED THE GREAT ROAD to travel south, before leaving it to travel south-east through Gotbeck. This part of Godfrey's duchy was well-organised and flourishing farming country, and he admitted he rarely needed to visit.

'My early years were taken up with the crusade against the Lizard-men,' he expounded, as Farred and he rode just behind the head of the column, his soldiers positioned at the front and rear, Hajna and her two companions behind them. 'Vicious creatures, who raid our people and don't think twice about killing women and children. I was often frustrated by a witch who dwelt in the marshland. She protected them, altering the paths through the swamps so that my soldiers got lost, or trapped. I had my suspicions,' he added quietly, glancing behind and then leaning over to whisper to Farred, 'that the Sea Caladri were also involved. No firm proof, but—', he nodded sagely at Farred, as if they both understood that a lack of proof was suspicious in itself. 'Then the bitch died and we got the swamps under control. As soon as that was accomplished, these damn missionaries from the Confederacy began arriving, spreading their dangerous ideas.'

And so to Godfrey's religious persecution. Farred knew it wasn't wise, that he should focus on his mission, but he couldn't help examining the issue.

'What's so dangerous about these priests?' Farred asked. 'If you'll forgive my ignorance on the subject.'

'No need for forgiveness, my son. I am equally ignorant of the issues facing Magnia, I am sure. Or perhaps,' added Godfrey, smiling with satisfaction, 'we should both ask for forgiveness.'

That was the kind of glib comment Farred had got used to hearing from the Archbishop.

'The Empire is a mix of different peoples, and these peoples have many religions: different gods, and different beliefs. Our ability to live together in harmony rests on many pillars, but one of the most important is the Brasingian Church. Here all gods may be worshipped, and all are treated equally. This institution was created by Emperor Ludvig, and is often overlooked or under-appreciated by foreigners, if I may say so. Anyway, to the Confederacy. The religion they are promulgating has it that there is one god only, and all others are false. What does this mean? That those who worship these false gods must be 'stopped' from doing so. Now, I ask you. Do you see how this idea, if allowed to infect the Empire, could cause untold harm? It undermines entirely the principle of our Church, and creates fanatics whose energies are turned to fighting the beliefs of others, instead of respecting them. That is what I am up against here in Gotbeck.'

Farred had been expecting some bigoted defence of Godfrey's persecutions. But he did understand. He saw how the Empire was a different polity to Magnia, and needed more work to keep it united. He saw how protecting religious freedom was crucial to that. He had, he was forced to admit, somewhat misjudged the Archbishop.

'I see,' he said. 'I thank you for the lesson.'

Godfrey nodded solemnly, and they continued their journey.

Godfrey explained that the best place to cross the border into the lands of the Sea Caladri was near. The north-west tip of the Caladri lands, next to Cordence, was some distance from the Cousel and the marshland that surrounded it on its final journey into the sea. Here, the land was dry and mostly wooded. Trails took them through the woods, and they were able to proceed on horseback. As they approached the border they came across a small fort, now a ruin. The woodland had mostly reclaimed it: trees grew from its roof and moss and ivy covered most of the walls.

'There were others built in a line here,' Godfrey explained, pointing to the east, 'maybe a dozen in all. I think they were abandoned soon after they were built. Your cousins are not a warlike people,' he said to Queen Hajna.

'They chose this place to escape war,' she said. 'They have had hundreds of years of peace. In that time, they have become rather good sailors. And that is why we are here.'

She sounded almost jealous to Farred. If her people had been fighting the Shadow Caladri all this time, without help, maybe jealousy was natural.

'I could have some of my men escort you farther,' said Godfrey. 'But in truth, your passage may be more straightforward without us.'

'I believe you are correct,' said Hajna. 'I am most grateful for your help, and I will tell my cousins of the aid you have given me.'

'You are quite welcome, of course,' said Godfrey. He took Hajna's hand and placed a kiss there. He turned to Farred, and they shook hands.

'It may be that the gods decide that our paths will not soon cross again,' said the Archbishop. 'In which case I wish you good luck in your endeavours.'

Farred nodded, then turned to look in the direction they would travel. Apart from the abandoned fort, there was no other sign that the land ahead was claimed by the Caladri. Gentle woodland stretched ahead into the distance and he could see that their trail continued. He wondered whether it was used by Gotbeckers or the Caladri themselves. Some contact, for reasons such as trade, could surely exist here, where it was so easy to cross from one country to another.

He began to follow the trail, nudging his mount carefully ahead, and Hajna followed, with her companions, Marika and Vida, at the rear. They were quiet, almost subservient to Hajna, who always spoke on their behalf. Vida had a sword strapped to his waist, but whether he was a bodyguard, it was hard to tell. Gyrmund had advised Farred that Hajna was a powerful witch, in which case she hardly needed protection.

The four of them followed the trail through the woods. Hajna was content for Farred to take the lead and choose the route. She seemed unconcerned about the direction they took, but while the Queen seemed relaxed about their journey, Farred felt more anxious the farther they went. He didn't know what kind of reaction the Caladri would have to their unannounced arrival.

He wasn't quite sure how it happened, but one moment the path ahead was clear, the next it wasn't. A small group of Caladri riders had appeared ahead of them. Farred touched the hilt of his sword and looked around. Behind them, a few yards down the trail, a second group of Caladri had appeared.

He looked from one group to the next, nervous of them, even though they appeared to have no weapons, either in their hands or at their belts. Hajna took the initiative and approached the group in front of them.

'Well met. I am Queen Hajna of the Blood Caladri.'

'*Queen* Hajna?' responded one of the Caladri. 'Then King Tibor has died?'

'Last summer,' Hajna confirmed. 'In the fighting with the Shadow Ones.'

'I had not heard,' said the Caladri. 'Please accept my condolences. I am Darda. I can take you to see our Council?'

'Yes, thank you. I have with me Farred, a nobleman from South Magnia. He comes with a message from his Prince. I vouch for him.'

'Well met, Farred,' said Darda. 'Since Queen Hajna vouches for you, you are most welcome here. We will be taking you to our capital, Mizky. It is a long ride, we will need to stay one night on the way.'

'Thank you for your hospitality,' Farred replied.

With no further ceremony, Darda turned her horse around and took the trail south. Hajna followed her, and so Farred did likewise, Marika and Vida just behind him. He looked about him as they rode. There was no physical sign that he had crossed into another realm. But nonetheless he felt acutely aware that he was possibly the sole human, in an alien land.

Farred was sitting outside his tent, letting the morning sun warm him after breakfast. He was thinking, and that was never good these days, for his thoughts always turned to Burkhard Castle, and the horrors of the siege he had witnessed there. Bodies piled up at the bottom of the crag, countless Drobax forcing their way up the path, day after day. But he always ended up thinking of Ashere, lying in agony as the poison from an Isharite blade dealt him a lingering death.

'It has to be you, Farred,' Ashere had begged him. 'I can't ask anybody else. Please.'

And what else can you do when someone you love begs you for help? Nothing else, but give them what they want.

His memories were interrupted as two figures approached him—Vida and Marika, the two Blood Caladri.

'We are going to visit the harbour,' Marika said to him. 'Would you like to come?'

'Yes,' said Farred, jumping to his feet. He had come to the conclusion that Marika and Vida were in a relationship, and in normal circumstances he would have avoided getting in their way. But with another empty day ahead of him in Mizky, he was bored.

He wondered what Gyrmund would say, his great explorer of a friend, if he was to learn that Farred was in one of the few places in Dalriya that Gyrmund had never been, and couldn't wait to leave. He smiled to himself. He wouldn't be impressed.

They left the field of tents which was their temporary home, heading downhill to the harbour area of the city, where most of the citizens worked. Vida and Marika walked either side of him, and linked their arms through his. Gyrmund had warned him back in Coldeberg of the over-familiarity of the Caladri, and Farred was glad he had, because it took some getting used to. It was in stark contrast to the Sea Caladri, many of whom openly stared at him as they walked down one of the main streets that led to the sea. They were not hostile, exactly, but he had certainly found them to be unwelcoming, and he was glad to have had the company of Vida and Marika over the last few days.

He had only made one very brief appearance in front of the Caladri Council. Hajna had already met with them beforehand to explain why they had come. Farred's role, therefore, was simply to formally offer the Sea Caladri safe harbour in the ports of South Magnia. From there, their fleet could help to re-open the sea lanes across the Lantinen Sea, which had been closed by the Kharovian navy. Hajna's companion, Szabolcs, had told them that one of the magic weapons they were searching for, the Giant's Spear, was somewhere in Halvia. Re-opening the Lantinen was a necessary first step to finding it.

The Sea Caladri had been polite enough, thanking Edgar for his offer and all the usual pleasantries, but they were clearly not involving Farred in their decision making. So instead, while they deliberated, he was left to his own devices in Mizky.

They reached the sea front. Here, a natural spit of rock that knifed into the sea had been extended by the Caladri to make a large, sheltered harbour, and whenever Farred came down to the sea front, the area was a hive of activity. The three of them sat on a wall to watch what was going on, the sea breeze tugging at their clothes, as passers-by stopped to stare at Farred, the stranger in their midst, before walking on.

A shipyard took up the near side of the harbour. Here many Caladri men and women were working on a large vessel. The carcass was already complete: wooden planks overlapped to create an unusually deep and wide hull. Farred knew enough to identify it as a trading ship, the large hull constructed to carry goods long distances across the ocean. The shipwrights were working on the frame, the internal ribs of the vessel. It was an impressive sight. They worked hard, and each of them seemed to know exactly what their job was, with little direction needed from the master shipwright.

The central part of the harbour was for fishing vessels, which regularly came and went, depositing barrels teaming with fish and crustaceans. The locals bought them freshly caught on the sea-front for their evening meal; the remainder were carted off to the nearby factory to be salted. On the far side of the harbour were Caladri warships, moored onto wooden piers. On his first visit there had been half a dozen; now, there were twice that number. It may have been coincidence, but it suggested that the Caladri Council were gathering a fleet, should a decision be made to sail for the west.

A Caladri man approached them, brawnier than average, with the weather-beaten look of a sailor.

'You're Magnian?' he asked Farred directly, apparently not as shocked by his presence as his compatriots.

'That I am,' Farred replied. 'Why do you ask?'

'I've been told to consult my charts on the routes to Magnia, so it seemed likely that is where you are from. You don't look Magnian, though.'

'My family is Middian in origin,' Farred explained.

'Aah. Not sailors then, I wager?'

Farred chuckled. He had a funny way about him, this Caladri sailor.

'No, I am afraid not. I can't even swim.'

'Well, I know plenty of sailors who can't swim. They're fine so long as they don't fall off the ship. What do you know of this Kharovian fleet then, my lord? Do their ships sail as far south as Magnia now?'

'Not that I know of, not South Magnia certainly. Our fishing boats still go out with no trouble. I doubt that their patrols regularly get farther south than the Guivergnais coast.'

'That's what I would have guessed.'

'Are you the captain of one of those warships?' Farred asked.

'That I am. She's the best of the lot, too. Red Serpent.'

'I don't doubt it. Have you been told to sail to Magnia?'

'Not as such. I've been told I might be asked to sail there. So have a lot of other captains. Since few of us have sailed all that way ourselves, I have been consulting charts, drawn up by earlier sailors.'

'How long does it take?'

'It's not an easy voyage, my lord. You have to sail all the way around the Avakaba Coast, a long way south, where the waters are treacherous, before sailing back up into the Lantinen Sea. The length of the voyage depends on the winds, but it has been done in four days in the past.'

'The Avakaba Coast?'

'You know them as the Lippers.'

'Well, thank you for the information. I am Farred, by the way,' he said offering a hand.

The Caladri took it. 'Captain Sebo,' he said, then gave a twitch of a smile. 'Maybe we will make this voyage together.'

'Maybe so,' said Farred with a smile.

'If so, I recommend my ship,' said Sebo. 'It would be an honour to have you as a guest with us.'

'It would be an honour to sail with you,' replied Farred, now feeling somewhat better about Caladri hospitality.

It would be two more days before the final decision was taken; though as the harbour in Mizky continued to fill with warships, it was plain to see which way it was going. The Sea Caladri would sail a fleet to the Lantinen Sea. Their goals, Hajna explained to him, were somewhat limited: to open up transport across the Lantinen. If that meant conflict with Kharovia they were prepared for it, but they would not be seeking out Kharovian ships, declaring war, or anything of that sort.

Once Hajna had passed on a summary of what was happening, she explained that she would be sailing back to her homeland that very day. She had been away for some time, and she was concerned that her husband, the new king, needed her support.

Farred walked with the Blood Caladri down to the harbour, for Marika and Vida would of course be returning with their mistress. Theirs was a small, sleek ship, which could skim atop the waves and take them swiftly north along the Itainen coast. He said his farewells, receiving a hug from Marika and Vida, then left them to it.

Now you really are alone, he told himself.

On a whim, and with nothing better to do, he walked along the seafront to look at the warships. He wondered whether he could spot Captain Sebo's ship, that he had named Red Serpent. It was busy here, as sailors readied the vessels for the voyage, bringing aboard supplies to keep the big oarsmen fed, weapons should they be needed, and goods for trade. The ships came in different sizes, but the largest were far longer than any he had seen elsewhere. They were also more high-sided than the typical construction in Magnia; altogether, they were an impressive sight. Farred walked along one pier then the next, until he saw a ship painted scarlet red, with the body and head of a great snake on the prow of the vessel.

'So, destination Magnia!' came a voice, and there was Captain Sebo, peering down at him from the deck of the ship.

'She's a beauty!' said Farred. It wasn't the biggest of the ships, but it certainly looked fine, and praising a captain's ship is like praising a mother's child: an obvious compliment, but one that always works nonetheless.

'Come aboard!' the captain shouted, indicating the gangplank that was resting on the wooden pier.

Farred made his way up the plank carefully, wary of slipping. Once he reached the top he saw that it was a significant drop down to the deck.

'There,' said Sebo, indicating a raised platform that had been built along the side of the ship.

Farred stepped from the plank onto the platform, then onto the deck. He looked at the platform.

'For fighting?'

'Yes, it gives us quite a height advantage over most other ships. Fill that platform with archers and you can win most encounters without risking life or limb. Come Farred, let me show you around.'

Sebo showed Farred the deck, which had two masts, with sails that would be unfurled when the captain wanted to catch the wind. There were many other features of the ship he showed Farred, who only half followed what he was being told.

Sebo then showed him below deck. This was where the oarsmen were located, in rows of seats with one oar each, which exited through a hole on either the port or starboard side. The conditions looked cramped even without the seats filled. At the fore of the ship Sebo had a small cabin and at the rear was storage, mainly for food and drink. This was a fighting ship and there was no room to carry large quantities of goods: that required a ship of a different design.

They returned to the deck.

'Will you be travelling with us, then?' Sebo asked.

It was the only offer Farred had, so he was pleased to accept it.

'We are sailing first thing on the morrow, I believe?' said Sebo.

'I'm not sure,' Farred admitted. 'I haven't really been kept informed.'

'Ah well,' said Sebo, looking a little embarrassed. 'You will have to forgive my countrymen. Most of them lead a secluded life here. They don't come into contact with foreigners. Being a sailing man of course means my life is rather different. Anyhow, I will see you first thing tomorrow. We sail for the Avakaba Coast, against the wind, so we will need an early start.'

'I look forward to it,' said Farred, looking about the ship. 'I think I will enjoy the voyage.'

Farred hated it. The roll of the ship as it crested a wave and then dipped down, up and down, up and down, made him violently sick. His body seemed unable to adjust. He couldn't stay on his feet, and any lurch of the ship made him ill. So he stood on the starboard fighting platform, hands gripping the side, head stuck over the edge in case he had anything left to throw up. He watched the south coast of Dalriya, the lands of the Sea Caladri and the Cordentines, gradually slide away as they got farther out to sea, and regretted ever having set foot on the Red Serpent. Once there was no land left to look at, he watched the other Caladri ships, bobbing in the waves alongside the Red Serpent, banks of oars pounding into the sea to keep them moving. Most were warships like Sebo's, but they were also accompanied by the wider shaped trading vessels. Although their design made them less sleek, they sat much lower in the water, and they were able to hold their own with the warships in these conditions.

Captain Sebo approached him, his face a mix of pity and humour.

'Middians make poor sailors, I fear.'

'Why didn't you make that clear before we set sail?'

'I just wanted it confirming.'

'Turn your fucking ship around,' said Farred, 'and take me to the south coast of Magnia. I'll get off there and you can carry on.'

Sebo scrunched up his face. 'Can't do that, I'm afraid. It would take far too long, we'd lose contact with the rest of the fleet. Seriously, Farred, I do have a suggestion. Why don't you try pulling an oar for a while?'

Farred looked at him, wondering if it was a jest. But no, the captain was serious.

'What if I puke up down there? That's not going to make me very popular.'

'I doubt you've got anything left. You might find it better down there. The motion of the ship isn't so severe.'

'Alright. I'll give it a try.'

Sebo led him down, then looked at his oarsmen, giving the matter a little thought, before picking one of them to give up a seat for Farred. Farred clambered clumsily into position, before grabbing hold of the oar in front of him, two handed.

'Just follow the rhythm of the others,' advised Sebo. 'Concentrate on that and you'll get the hang of it soon enough.'

It took him a while. He copied the other oarsmen, whose range of movement was small, their hands always in front of their chests. Several times he got into a rhythm and then his timing went wrong, the blade of his oar dipping too early, or in the wrong position, slapping into the water rather than pulling it. But each time he started again, and began to eradicate the errors, until he found a settled rhythm. Sebo was right. Perhaps it was because the rowing gave him something to focus on, but he felt a lot better below deck. His shoulders and back muscles began to ache, but he wasn't going to show himself up amongst the Caladri, and he was able to push through the pain, his body adjusting to the demands of the motion.

It was hard to tell time below deck. Sometimes it felt like it dragged, each pull of the oar a burden. Then his mind would drift off, thinking of other things, until it was drawn back to the ship and the oar and he wondered how long he had been down there.

Eventually a group of sailors came down to replace some of the oarsmen, including Farred, and he made his way back up to the deck. He stretched out his back, enjoying the sensation after sitting for so long. He looked out to sea. He could see the other Caladri ships; some ahead, some behind. It was comforting to know that they weren't alone in the ocean. But on the other hand, there was no land to be seen in any direction now. He didn't like that feeling, of being surrounded by nothing but waves, not knowing where the nearest shore was.

Sebo was right. He wasn't a sailor.

The captain approached him. 'You did well, I hear?'

'Well, I certainly feel better for it. How are we doing?'

'Well enough. I expect us to make landfall in daylight. We are having to row hard against the wind on the way south. If we have any luck, and the wind stays, our journey will get much easier when we reach the Lantinen Sea.'

Sure enough, it was early evening when they approached a Lipper settlement. Sebo identified it as Chobo. It was perfectly positioned in a wide bay. There was limited docking space, and so the warships waited out at sea while the traders went in first, turning their ships around, then securing their vessels and unloading the goods they had brought to offer to the Lippers. For the rest, there was a long shallow beach which had enough space for all the ships to find a berth.

As they got into the shallows, Sebo ordered his men off, and Farred found himself jumping off the side and landing in the sea, his shoes plunging into the sandy seabed. Ropes were thrown overboard. Farred found a space on one rope, and when all the sailors had a grip, they pulled and heaved, dragging Red Serpent onto the sandy shore. Farred slipped over and fell onto his arse, hands grabbing at him to haul him back up. He wasn't the only one to fall, though obviously the Caladri had experience on their side, not to mention their clawed feet that sank into the sand and found purchase better than his leather shoes.

Once they were out of the shallows and the ship was on firmer ground, it suddenly became much easier, and Farred found himself running backwards, the rope taught, and Red Serpent slid smoothly along the wet sand until it was secure above the high tide mark. Farred found that he had a huge grin on his face despite his wet shoes and trousers, and decided that a life on the seas wasn't quite as hellish as he had found it to be initially, though his favourite part was getting back onto dry land.

The Lippers were already coming out to meet them at the beach, and Farred wandered over, fascinated. They were tall and broad shouldered, with dark skin just like his own. But if they resembled Middians in appearance, they sounded nothing like them. Farred could hear their strange voices talking to the Caladri traders. It was a series of meaningless noises to him—he couldn't make out a single word.

He was surprised that the Caladri traders could talk back in the same language. They laid samples of their goods out on the beach for the Lippers to inspect: worked timber, wool, and iron implements.

Sebo walked over and stood next to him. Farred looked over to the ship and saw the captain's men were busy putting up tents for the night.

'What do the Lippers offer in return?' Farred asked him.

'They have gold, cotton, spices—many things. I am hopeful they will feed us, too. Otherwise it's salted fish for dinner.'

'You have learned their language?'

'Me personally? I know a few words that come in handy. The traders know their language. The people back home do not.'

'What did you say they call themselves?'

'Avakaba. It means The Ones Who Left.'

'Left where?'

Sebo shrugged. 'That I don't know.'

'In Magnia we know nothing of these people. They are our neighbours, but as far as I know we don't trade or communicate with them at all. Looking at this, that seems very foolish.'

'It is very foolish,' Sebo agreed. 'And long may it continue. For the Sea Caladri take goods from the Avakaba, sail north as far as Haskany, even the Jalakh Steppe, and trade with the northerners. It makes us very rich.'

Farred nodded. He could see how.

'You say you sometimes sail as far north as the Steppe?'

'Sometimes.'

'I have a friend who needs to travel there. It is connected with this mission your fleet has been given.'

'Then he would have been far better coming with you and taking a ship there. It is very dangerous to reach the Steppe by any other route.'

'Yes,' agreed Farred. The overland route involved marching through Haskany, under the noses of the Drobax and the Isharites. 'Although if I had to trust anyone to do it, I would trust Gyrmund.'

VIII

MANOEUVRES

THE DROBAX WAS STANDING a good ten feet lower down the slope from the ledge Gyrmund occupied. He adjusted his body line to the angle of the shot, pulled back the string to his ear, held for a second, then released. The arrow struck, and the beast went down.

He turned behind him, and waved Moneva and Soren on.

They didn't have much time.

The Drobax were crawling all over the Dardelles mountain range, sent south by their masters in ominously large numbers. Gyrmund spared a brief thought for whoever this army was being sent against. But he had no time for more, because they had been spotted. If they didn't find a secure place to hide, they were finished.

He jumped down the rocks, risking injury in exchange for speed. When he reached the Drobax corpse he breathed a sigh of relief. He was right, the monster had been standing outside a cave. This was their best chance of escape.

He pulled the arrow from the head of the Drobax, fitted it to his bow and peered into the dark cave. He could feel Moneva's presence behind him and he walked forward carefully. He was wary of marching straight in when his eyes had not adjusted to the darkness, yet fearful of taking too long and being seen entering by the Drobax.

He was right to be careful. As he inched forwards, a figure ran at him out of the darkness. He released his bow on pure instinct and it took down what he could now see was a Drobax. But a second monster followed close behind and Gyrmund had no time to nock a second arrow or draw his sword, instead holding his bow as a staff.

Moneva was a blur that came past him. The Drobax adjusted the swing of its weapon from Gyrmund to Moneva, but it was a clumsy move. Moneva avoided the swinging club and stepped in, burying her sword through its neck, then shoved it to the ground, before finishing it off.

Dropping his bow, Gyrmund drew his sword and stabbed down at the first Drobax, making sure it was dead.

Once done, he turned back to the entrance of the cave.

Soren had entered behind them, and, with Onella's Staff aloft, was concentrating on the cave entrance. The wizard turned to look at Gyrmund.

'I am making the entrance appear like a solid wall of rock. If one of them studies it closely, or leans against it or some such, the illusion will break. That would be unlucky.'

Gyrmund looked around the cave. That would be the end of them. It was a large space, but there was no other exit. They would be trapped inside.

He spied something on one of the walls and walked over to investigate.

'What is it?' asked Moneva, joining him.

There was a slash mark in the wall of the cave.

Gyrmund smiled. 'I'm just wondering. Something very sharp made this mark. And very recently, too. Soren, could you take a look?' he asked, before looking around the floor of the cave as best he could in the dim light.

There had been a large group in here. He approached the far end of the cave. The stink was oppressive, for it had been used as a latrine. He could see what looked like dog hairs on the ground. He turned back, to see Soren looking at the mark.

'Clarin?' asked the wizard.

'That's what I thought,' said Gyrmund. 'It looks just like one I saw him use when we were heading to the Wilderness.'

'Yes, it does,' agreed Soren.

It was only yesterday that Belwynn had contacted Soren to tell them of Clarin's miraculous re-appearance in Heractus. Many of Gyrmund's fellow prisoners had escaped with him, including his friend Cyprian. Herin, however, had not been with them.

'Clarin was here?' Moneva said, incredulous.

'It's a sign that Clarin left for his brother,' Soren said. 'To tell him he was here.'

Moneva looked at Gyrmund.

'It's good,' he said, allowing himself a smile.

Clarin had made it out of Samir Durg. And if the big man thought there was a chance Herin had too, then Gyrmund had to share the same hope.

***

CLARIN FOUND it hard to lift the spirits of his men. It was only natural that each one of them had kept close to themselves a dream, private and intimate, of what they were escaping to.

A reunion with tearful loved ones who had thought them dead? Or at the very least, a bar full of captivated listeners to their heroic stories, while the tankards of frothy beer kept on coming long into the night. But to escape and be immediately impressed into an army in the middle of a civil war? That fell a long way short of the dream.

It wasn't as if he was able to fully explain to them why they should care about this war. The enemy was a complicated, nebulous list of names and groups to them.

The side they were on wasn't convincing, either. Sebastian, Theron and their Knights had captured the king of Kalinth, and the king's son was trying to free him. It was hardly a heroic cause—indeed, half the Knights of Kalinth clearly didn't support Sebastian's seizure of power, taking the side of the prince. They had also bungled their revolution. Theron had apparently sent the enemy army and royal guard home last summer, only for them to reappear as combatants this year.

It was hard for Clarin to fully understand Belwynn's total investment in this conflict. She had stayed in Kalinth for this? While Soren and the others left to continue the quest without her? Something didn't add up.

The army left Heractus for the south-west of the country. The Knights had ridden ahead, on their expensive horses, each of them bringing at least one spare, while the infantry had to walk behind, eating their dust. It was a ragbag infantry force Theron had collected, and to give him some credit, at least he knew it.

Clarin had been put in charge of a division of a hundred soldiers. Apart from his group from Samir Durg, the rest were Madrians, half of them women—followers of Elana whom the priestess had persuaded to fight for the cause. She had gone up in the world, the leader of a powerful Church now. And he had witnessed her using that power. She had insisted to Sebastian that her religion should now be the only recognised creed in the land. That was her price for recruiting so many men and women into the army. And while the priestess had made her demands, Belwynn had smiled peacefully, as if it was the most wonderful outcome in the world.

They camped outside the first night, in a rocky landscape that was the southern end of the Dardelles mountains they had traversed on their way through Haskany. It wasn't a bad spot, with views across the countryside that would afford them early warning of enemy activity.

Theron also went up in his estimation a little that night. By the time his force trudged into camp, the tents had been put up for them and hot food was being cooked. The Knights also took on lookout duty, leaving the infantry to rest after the march. Clarin did a quick round of his troops, trying to take his new officer role seriously, though his heart wasn't in it. Eventually he settled down at a fire with Rudy, Jurgen and the two Dog-men, happy to be left alone with his thoughts.

His thoughts, inevitably, turned to Belwynn. They nagged at him, not letting him relax. Because Clarin was the one who had got his dream. His dream, during the days in the mine, the nights in the pit, was to see Belwynn again. And he had. But it wasn't how he had imagined it. She was pleased to see him, but she hadn't thrown her arms around him and kissed him. He hadn't had a chance to properly speak to her in private, to tell her how much she meant to him. She was always busy, with Elana, or Sebastian, or Theron.

Theron. The man behind this madness. It was Theron who Belwynn spent her time with. It was Theron who she looked at, the way Clarin wanted her to look at him.

He looked across the fire at Rudy and lame Jurgen, forced to walk all day again so soon after their escape, in the opposite direction to their homes. They hadn't got their dreams yet. Clarin had got his, and it had already turned sour. Which of them was the worse off?

***

SEBASTIAN, THERON and Belwynn walked up a gravelled pathway to the home of Diodorus, Count of Korenandi. His house was fortified, much the same as Sebastian's home of Sernea; strong enough to withstand minor attempts at entry rather than whole armies.

Theron lifted a hand to knock on the front door, but before he got the chance, it had swung open, and a servant was gesturing that they should come in.

In the hall of his house stood Diodorus, with what Belwynn presumed were his wife and two sons. It was an oddly formal way to greet them, but she supposed this was the traditional way to welcome guests. Once the introductions and pleasantries were over, the family departed. The Count led them into a side room, where he sat them down in comfortable chairs next to a blazing fire. He offered them a drink called arak, perhaps again what tradition demanded. But they weren't really here for a pleasant fireside chat, and they all declined the offer.

Diodorus poured himself a drink and took a seat.

'Straton is raising an army against you,' he said.

'He has asked you to join him?' said Theron.

'Of course.'

'And?'

'I declined. I am not so popular with the royal family after I surrendered their army to you. There is no reason for me to risk my life to see Straton rise to power.'

'You have also declined our summons,' said Sebastian, sternly.

'I see no reason to risk my life or those of my people for you, either,' countered the Count.

He spoke slowly, with little emotion, but Belwynn detected the undertone of melancholia in his voice and face that she had noticed when they had spoken with him last summer. Then, he had made a wise decision not to fight them. She hoped he would do the same again now.

'These are not easy times,' Sebastian admitted. 'You may think otherwise, but the last thing I wanted to do was stand against my own king. But the future and the honour of Kalinth was at stake. It still is. Standing on the sidelines isn't an option, Diodorus.'

Diodorus took a sip of his drink. 'My father left this county to me and I would leave it to my sons. I would not see it destroyed. If I side with you there will be reprisals from your enemies. It is not what you want to hear, but I intend to stay out of this conflict.'

'You can't,' said Theron. 'We are desperate for infantry. One hundred extra men, well-armed, could make all the difference when we fight Straton. We need you to give us a hundred men. If you refuse we will bring our army onto your lands, take this house, and force you to give us a hundred men. That's the choice you have. A hundred men now or a hundred men later. Staying out of this isn't a choice available to you.'

Diodorus looked at them all in turn, his eyes blinking owlishly. They stopped at Belwynn. There was something about her he didn't like, she could sense it, but couldn't put a finger on it. Something more subtle than hatred or fear. He didn't want her here in his house. She shouldn't have come.

'Is this what the Knights of Kalinth are now?' he asked.

'We have no choice either, man!' said Sebastian, losing his temper. 'You know we fought with the Isharites last summer! They will be back, they want to see Kalinth burned to the ground, our people enslaved. I can't afford division, internal conflict. I can't afford men with the title of count who sit back and do nothing. Give us the men and we'll let you be. We'll return them to you once Straton is defeated. I give you my word.'

'You give me no choice,' retorted Diodorus.

'Now you understand,' said Theron.

Diodorus looked in his drink, as if he would find an answer there.

'I'll give you your men. I'll lead them myself, and when your war is over I'll lead them back home. And if you break your word to me, you will have made another enemy. How many more can you make, before you lose your grip on this country?'

Neither Sebastian nor Theron answered that, though Belwynn was sure they both knew the answer. Their grip on Kalinth was already slipping, and it would take very little for them to lose it completely.

***

THEY LEFT Chobo and shadowed the Lipper coast, using the oars to row farther south. After two days they rounded the southernmost tip of Dalriya, a rocky land where strange animals roamed the shoreline. Great fat creatures that Sebo called suliks lounged on the rocks, then suddenly dived into the sea. Farred saw that underwater they became agile and powerful, and worried that they might attack the ships, before Sebo laughed off his concerns.

Once Red Serpent turned to the north, Sebo unfurled the sails. Until now the crew deck had had little to do, but now their experience was needed to steer the ship and adjust the sails. Sebo was in his element at the centre of things, shouting out orders. At times orders were relayed to the rowers to row hard to get the ship moving again. At others they could rest, as the sails caught the wind and Red Serpent effortlessly cut through the waves.

In the afternoon Sebo gave himself a break, relinquishing the helm to his second in command.

'It's easy to make a mistake when you are tired,' said Sebo, by way of explanation to Farred.

'We seem to be making good time,' Farred observed. Indeed, while he could see ships to the rear of Red Serpent, there appeared to be none ahead of them.

'Aye, the wind is on our side now. There are few hazards, save not to stray out too far to sea.'

'Why is that?'

'My charts tell me to stay clear of the Asrai, who dwell out in the Lantinen.'

'The Asrai?' repeated Farred. This was the name given to a people by the Caladri wise man, Szabolcs, who had said that they took a weapon to the fight with the Isharites. But no-one in that meeting seemed to know who or where they were.

'Before you ask,' said Sebo, 'I've never seen 'em, nor has anyone I know who isn't a drunk or a liar. I just know them from stories and what's on my charts, drawn up by explorers.'

Despite Sebo's words of caution, Farred grew excited at the possibility that he had stumbled onto something.

'Could you show me these charts?' he asked Sebo.

The captain gave him a look.

'This to do with those weapons?' he asked.

'Yes. It could be.'

Sebo reluctantly set off to grab his charts, coming straight back with them. The parchments he brought back looked new.

'I had them copied,' said Sebo, as if reading his mind. 'With the best will in the world, everything gets wet on a sea voyage. I never bring originals with me. Anyhow, I have two maps which reference the area. Here,' he said, passing Farred the first and pointing to the location.

The word Asrai was written in an area of sea out to the west of Dalriya and south of Halvia. Next to the text a hand had been drawn, apparently reaching out from the ocean.

'And here,' he added, passing a second map.

This time the text spelt 'Ashray' rather than Asrai. It was written in a similar location, next to what looked like a collection of small islands.

'And why avoid this area?' Farred asked.

'All Caladri seamen are told to avoid it because it belongs to the Asrai. Various stories say that the Asrai will pull a ship under the water and drown everyone aboard. Or capture the crew and make them work as slaves, never to return home. Or some other variation. With no reason to sail in that direction, no modern mariner that I know of has taken the risk.'

'And what if there is a reason to go?' asked Farred.

'Then still, neither I nor anyone I know would do it.'

With that, Sebo took back his charts.

The Caladri ships harboured on a beach that Sebo said was in the far northwest of the Lipper peninsula. There was no history of trade here and the local inhabitants, if they knew of their presence at all, stayed away.

The crews could fill their skins from a nearby stream, but food was getting scarce and when the sun rose everyone seemed keen to move on. Minor repairs were held off until later, and one by one the crews dragged the ships into the shallows.

The winds continued to be favourable, carrying them on the last leg of their journey to Magnia. It wasn't long before Farred began to recognise landmarks he knew, though they looked different from the new perspective afforded by Red Serpent.

It was still morning when they approached Fripport, located in a sheltered bay near the border with North Magnia. It was the largest harbour in the country and the only place capable of holding such a large fleet. Farred could see Magnian ships moored in one corner—what amounted to Edgar's fleet, but it was insignificant compared to the wave of Caladri warships that were about to join them.

Red Serpent was the first to dock on the wooden piers. Farred almost felt like he would miss her when he found himself walking down the plank and returning to Magnia for the first time in two weeks.

The local officials were already at the dock, waiting to deal with the logistics of mooring the Caladri fleet and accommodating the sailors. Farred spied Aescmar, the leading magnate of the area, directing his men as more and more Caladri ships approached his port.

'You've brought the Caladri with you,' Aescmar said, as Farred approached. 'Edgar will be pleased. I've already sent a rider to tell him the news.'

'You're well organised here,' said Farred, impressed.

'We did get some warning of your approach. Which is just as well, because if we don't see a fleet of this size coming, the whole of South Magnia will be in trouble. Is it right that they have trading ships with them as well?'

'Yes, stocked up with goods from the Sea Caladri and from the Lippers. You would do well to open negotiations with them. I will tell the captain of the ship I travelled on if you like.'

'I am much obliged. Trade has totally dried up since the Kharovians took the Lantinen, and there are many here whose livelihoods have suffered. This could be a boon to them.'

Aescmar was good enough to put Farred and Sebo up in the house he owned in Fripport. The rest of the Caladri were allocated to various patches of land inside and outside the port. Soon a forest of Caladri tents had sprouted up, doubling the population of the town. They were polite guests, however, and there was no trouble. They paid for their food and the traders amongst them wasted no time in bringing their goods to shore, so that an impromptu market appeared. Caladri and Magnians bartered with each other good-naturedly, and in the end there were few locals who failed to turn some profit from the arrival of the fleet.

By the evening of the next day Edgar arrived, and Aescmar was able to accommodate him and his three companions at his house. With him came Elfled, sister of Cerdda of North Magnia. Farred had first gained her acquaintance last year, when he had visited the North Magnians on Edgar's behalf.

In addition, Edgar now had two bodyguards. Brictwin had come, and Farred was pleased that Edgar had followed his recommendation and appointed Morlin as a second bodyguard. The man had served with distinction under Farred in the Empire last summer, and had the ideal temperament for the job. Edgar had been reluctant to replace Leofwin, Brictwin's uncle, who had died while preventing an assassination attempt on the prince. But Morlin was intelligent and easy-going enough to fit in.

They ate a late supper in Aescmar's dining room. Edgar was keen to hear about Farred's adventures since they had left Coldeberg, which he duly recounted, with Captain Sebo adding in details of a nautical nature that he felt Farred had overlooked.

'I must know for sure, though,' said Farred, 'about your own news since leaving Coldeberg. Elfled's presence by your side is a good sign,' he added.

Edgar grinned, and Elfled smiled too, touching the prince's hand.

'I visited with Elfled's family in North Magnia after leaving Coldeberg,' said Edgar. 'Then Elfled and I visited with my mother. Having received our family's approval, Elfled and I can announce our engagement.'

He took Elfled's hand and held it up so that they could see her engagement ring. A deep red garnet was set in rose gold, on a finely worked silver band.

'Congratulations,' said Farred, his words echoed by the others at the table. 'And did you ask Elfled amidst all that approval?' he asked.

'Don't worry about that, Farred,' Elfled said. 'I've already made it quite clear that this is going to be a partnership.'

Edgar rolled his eyes, and Elfled gave him a slap. Aescmar asked them about their wedding plans and Farred watched the two of them talking. It was good to see Edgar so happy. His expedition to the Empire had left him looking exhausted, but Elfled was obviously good for him.

'How have you celebrated your engagement?' Sebo asked the couple.

They looked at each other. 'Coming here, I guess,' replied Edgar. 'We haven't had the time for anything else yet.'

Sebo frowned. 'Not good enough. It would be an honour for my crew and I to take you out on a pleasure ride on my ship, Red Serpent. I promise to make it special enough to suit such a happy occasion.'

Edgar and Elfled looked at one another.

'It would be something we would always remember,' she suggested carefully.

'Why not?' agreed Edgar. 'Can we find the time tomorrow?'

'Tomorrow?' Sebo said. 'Why not now? You two are young enough to stay up a while longer surely?'

'In the dark?' questioned Farred, peering outside.

'There is nothing so special as a moonlight boat ride,' said Sebo, turning to Edgar and Elfled. 'Just don't bring him along. He will just spend his time throwing up Aescmar's delicious food.'

They smiled, agreeing to the idea, and Sebo set off to round up those of his crew who were in a fit enough state to man the ship. The rest of them spoke for a while longer, before leaving Aescmar's house to head down to the harbour.

Aescmar walked ahead with Elfled, while Farred fell in with Edgar. The two bodyguards walked on either side. Farred realised that they now had two people to protect. That fact must have convinced Edgar to take the step of recruiting Morlin.

'This is another great service you have done for me, Farred.'

'You are welcome, Your Highness.'

'I must find a way to properly repay you. I have been thinking about it a little. It is perhaps time you settled down too. Neither of us are getting any younger, after all.'

Farred nodded, trying to be noncommittal. Edgar was straying into awkward territory.

'The easiest way for me to reward you would be to find you a wife who comes with a nice estate. I would like to see you become a bigger landowner here in Magnia. It would help me as well as rewarding you. What do you say?'

What should he say? *Edgar, I like men?* Maybe Edgar wouldn't care if he did. *Edgar, I fell in love with your fiancée's brother and now my heart is broken?*

'It's something I should think about,' he found himself saying.

'Yes, we'll talk more. Oh my.'

They all stopped walking to look.

Sebo had Red Serpent ready. He had placed candles all over the deck and it looked beautiful—ethereal—in the moonlight. Farred wasn't sure that candles and wooden ships were a good combination, but no doubt he was the only one worried about that.

The captain held out a hand to help Elfled up the plank, and Edgar and his bodyguards followed. Farred and Aescmar stood at the shore while Red Serpent slowly, majestically, manoeuvred into the dark expanse of the ocean. As she left the harbour it felt like Farred was watching a heavenly vessel leaving this world and sailing to paradise.

'That is some sight,' murmured Aescmar, seemingly to himself as much as to Farred.

It was, and it prompted in Farred a realisation of sorts. In Magnia his future, as Edgar had laid out, was as landholder, nobleman, husband. But too much of that was a lie.

At that moment Red Serpent, a vessel of light bobbing up and down on a black sea, represented an escape from that future. It was an escape that Farred hadn't even realised he wanted until now.

IX

THE GRASS SEA

C LARIN LOOKED UP AND DOWN the line of knights, queueing up for their turn. They lounged about, bandying insults back and forth as all soldiers do before a battle. But as they neared the end of the line they quietened, grew serious. When it was their turn, they approached Belwynn solemnly, drawing their blades and kneeling in front of her. She put her hands on theirs, said a few words, and they left, a look of serenity on their faces.

Clarin had never seen anything like it. He couldn't tear himself away from the spectacle, all the more curious because it was Belwynn who was carrying out the blessing. Belwynn, a regular girl from Magnia a year ago, now the Lady of the Knights.

'Come on,' said Diodorus, interrupting his thoughts. 'You can get your sword blessed later.'

Clarin followed the count into Sebastian's tent. They had been invited to attend the discussion of tactics before the battle. Theron stood at a table with quill and parchment, as officious as ever. Sebastian and Tycho were also there, along with a knight he had not met yet. Sebastian noticed.

'Clarin, this is Remi, my closest friend. He has been tracking Straton's forces for us.'

Clarin and Remi shook hands. Remi gestured to the parchment, where Theron had drawn a diagram of what they believed to be the enemy disposition.

'Euthymius has largely failed to turn the Knights against us. He leads a small number, probably less than one hundred. The rest of the cavalry are noblemen Straton has recruited. I would expect Count Ampelios to lead this group into battle.'

The knights under Euthymius and the mounted noblemen under Ampelios were positioned on the flanks. Clarin understood that these would be the better fighters, using the power and mobility of their horses to dominate the battlefield.

'The infantry are largely made up men-at-arms raised by the nobility, or members of the temples who have allied with Straton. They have greater numbers than us, but not greater quality.'

Here, Theron had predicted three divisions of infantry positioned in the centre. Behind them Theron had scrawled more words, which Clarin assumed would be the reserve, where Straton himself would command.

'Our problem, then, is matching their infantry,' explained Sebastian. 'I propose we dismount some of our knights, fifty say, and position them in the centre division to strengthen it. Anyone else who can fight will go there, giving the impression of further strength. That includes squires. The knights will have to do without them.'

'Sending squires in to fight?' Clarin said. 'They're little more than children.'

'I'm not happy with it,' said Sebastian. 'But we're desperate. They'll be at the back. Clarin, your unit will be to the left, and Diodorus you will command the right. Watch out for them trying to get around you. I'll let you decide how to organise things, you know what you're doing. I will put myself in the centre with the dismounted knights. I think my presence will reassure them.'

Theron frowned. 'I understand the thinking, uncle, but I'm not sure it should be you.'

There followed a debate between the knights about who should be placed where. There were four of them and four positions to allocate: two on the wings with the cavalry; one with the reserves; one with the infantry. Theron wrote in and scratched out names until they were settled. Sebastian was persuaded to take the reserves. Tycho would fight with the infantry, leaving Theron and Remi to lead each wedge of knights.

Clarin had no problems with the plan. The truth was you could talk for hours before a fight—when it came to it, it was chaos and desperate hacking every time.

Clarin put himself in the centre of the front line. To his left, Tamir led the Barbarians. He was still a tall and formidable figure, though he now fought left handed after losing three fingers in the fighting in Samir Durg. To his right were the two Dog-men, then Zared and the Persaleians. Theron had given them whatever armour and weapons they had requested. Clarin already knew they could fight like monsters, so he had no worries about his front line.

He had told Rudy and Jurgen to lead the Madrians, who stood in four rows behind him. They would have to react once the battle started, supporting Clarin's front line or moving out to prevent any attempts at flanking their position. Clarin could not predict for sure how these men and women would react. For most, it was their first time in combat. They had behaved with discipline to this point, borrowing Elana's icily cool demeanour. But hand-to-hand fighting was something different altogether. He knew that some of them would be able to do it, and some would not.

He could see the enemy infantry ahead. They too had settled into their units and were waiting for the order to go.

The terrain was uneven, with grass and flowering gorse covering the area between the two armies, some of it waist height. He had told his men to tread carefully. There was a slope too, the high point on the right of their position, where Theron's cavalry was located. The dip had more or less flattened out by the time it reached Clarin's position on the left, and gave no particular advantage to either side.

Clarin was relieved to hear the blare of trumpets from behind him. The waiting was over. He picked up his spear and shield.

'March!' he shouted.

They walked steadily, keeping to the same pace as Tycho's central division.

Clarin worried. It wasn't like him to do so. But he felt differently to previous engagements he had been involved in. In those other occasions he was full of emotions. But today he felt empty. It was hard to summon up hatred for the enemy he was about to fight. He didn't know them.

The sound of drums and shouts filled the air. Looking up, he saw the ranks of infantry facing them begin to move. The tension and noise on the battlefield ratcheted up as the two sides moved towards each other. The gap between them started to close more quickly. Clarin could see that the enemy was more numerous. The danger of them outflanking his hundred soldiers was all too real. He could now pick out individual fighters coming to meet him. They presented a wall of shields, with spears, maces and other weapons ready to carve into his own forces.

Then it happened. Clarin felt the danger and the fear. The rage came next, and as the two infantry lines closed, he was ready. Rather than waiting for the Kalinthians to come to his line, he sprang forwards, relying on the Dog-men and the Barbarians to support him.

He shoved his spear forwards. It was turned by a shield. He reached forwards and grabbed at a shield, using his strength to pull the soldier out of the line, where he was quickly skewered by a spear. The Dog-man to his right rushed into the gap, teeth snapping and clawed hands swiping. Clarin risked another lurch forward, slamming his spear over the top of a shield and into the shoulder of a Kalinthian. He released his grip and drew the sword he had named Cutter. The pink crystal blade of the Isharite weapon flashed dangerously.

His front line had supported his move and the Kalinthians who opposed them hadn't coped with it. Defending against his men had left their line of shields ragged, and a gap yawned in front of him. Readying himself, putting his body behind his shield, his face down, his sword arm trailing behind, Clarin grimaced and charged. He buffeted the enemy, using his strength to strike out and barge at those around him with his shield. He had to trust that his soldiers came with him, harrying the rest of the Kalinthian line.

Clarin twisted at the waist and used his hips and thighs to impart power into another barge. He felt the man in front give way, and found himself staggering forwards, walking on top of the man who had gone down. Now he swung his sword over his shoulder. It connected with the man in front, and he found he could push further forwards. Suddenly, he had space around him. He had broken through.

He allowed himself a brief backwards glance. His front line had followed him, carving a hole through the enemy. Now he could take advantage, but he had to be quick. Opening up his body, he slashed his sword at the disorganised enemy around him. He launched himself at one soldier, chopping down so viciously he heard the arm bone crack. He located the next nearest soldier, moving quickly towards him. This one defended Clarin's blow with his shield, and then moved backwards when Clarin slammed his shield at his face. Clarin feinted to strike, and the soldier retreated again. Behind him, Tamir launched a two-handed downward strike, his giant steel blade connecting with the man's shoulder. The blow knocked him to the ground, and it was then easy for Clarin to deal the death blow.

Clarin now led his men against the exposed end of the enemy line. Men who moments before had been ready to come around Clarin's soldiers and envelope them now found themselves fighting for their lives.

Clarin looked up when he heard the thud of cavalry.

Sebastian, quick to understand what was happening, had led his reserves to join in. The remaining enemy infantry, separated from the rest of their forces, ran or died, as Sebastian's cavalry tore into them, lances thrusting down, huge warhorses kicking and buffeting. The Knights knew what they were doing. As Clarin turned his men to face the rest of the enemy infantry, Sebastian was free to take his cavalry in behind them. Straton's infantry was now in a vice, under attack from three directions as Tycho's dismounted knights, Clarin's force and Sebastian's reserves all targeted them.

Victory seemed inevitable, so long as the enemy units were kept isolated. Clarin looked across the rest of the battlefield. He could see Remi's cavalry engaged with the Kalinthian Knights led by Euthymius. Theron's cavalry wasn't in sight. With any luck, that meant they had the upper hand.

Another stretch of fighting ensued, but it must have been clear to Straton's infantry that they were on their own. They began throwing down their weapons, and instead of slaughter, Clarin's force turned to capturing and disarming the enemy infantry. Sebastian left him to it, taking his knights off to join with Remi.

Clarin bumped into Tycho.

'I will put guards on them,' the knight said, gesturing at their prisoners, who had been made to sit on the ground in small groups. 'Can you organise the wounded?'

Clarin nodded. 'You think we've won?'

'Almost certainly. Theron drove Ampelios off the field. I think they will be chasing down those that fled. If I know Theron, he will be trying to capture Straton.'

Clarin ordered his unit to separate from Tycho's, in an effort to bring some order to things. He assessed the damage. One of Zared's Persaleians was dead, bringing the number who had escaped from Samir Durg down to eighteen. They had suffered another half a dozen fatalities from amongst the Madrians, as well as various wounded. As he began trying to work out who needed help, Elana and Belwynn appeared. Belwynn seemed used to such a job and began to organise those that needed to see Elana urgently. Other Madrians began to help, and Clarin decided to leave them to it.

He walked away, keen to know how the Knights had fared. Two knights were riding over in his direction. He walked over to meet them, as did Tycho and Diodorus. It was Sebastian and Remi.

'Well?' asked Tycho.

'Euthymius is dead,' said Remi. 'It was tough fighting—I lost a few, as did they. We have captured the rest.'

'Any news from Theron?'

'Not yet,' said Sebastian. 'We will have to wait a while longer. Well done, everyone. Whatever news Theron returns with, we've scored a major victory and kept the loss of life to a minimum.'

Clarin sat and waited, relief and exhaustion kicking in. The knights saw to their horses first and eventually squires were sent round with food and drink for the soldiers. Elana worked her healing magic on those who needed it. Sebastian gave the order to strip the corpses. Unclaimed bodies would be burned together, he said, since they were all Kalinthians.

Eventually Theron's force returned. They led a large number of prisoners, who walked along in a group, surrounded on all sides by mounted knights. Theron steered his horse over. He was pale with exhaustion but looked satisfied enough.

'Straton tried to escape,' he croaked, climbing off his horse stiffly.

Tycho handed him a cup and he drank deeply before continuing. 'It took a long time to track him down, but we got him. We also captured Ampelios in the first fighting. What news of Euthymius?'

'Dead,' said Remi.

Theron looked about, trying to take in what he saw, but his eyes glazed over. Clarin could see the strain he had been under, not just today but during the campaign as a whole. Defeat would have seen the end of the regime he and Sebastian had established, and a return to the policies of King Jonas. Kalinth would have become subservient to Ishari once again.

On that count, Clarin grudgingly conceded, maybe it had been worth it.

***

THE MOUNTAINS took their toll on Soren's body. Day by day the recovery he had made under Elana disappeared; day by day he found himself reverting to the state he had been found in at Samir Durg. He lacked the stamina he once had, and too much climbing and walking put such a strain on his back that he had to stop and rest before the day was done. Gyrmund, uncomplaining, would have to find food and make camp without his help. He became too exhausted to do the exercises Elana had insisted on, crawling under his blankets as soon as he had eaten supper.

The nights were cold at such a height. Gyrmund and Moneva slept on either side of him. There was a tension between them, and they were avoiding lying next to one another. At first it made him feel awkward to be stuck between them. But after a while he was simply grateful for the warmth.

When he woke on a morning his back had always seized up and he was virtually blind. He would reach out for the staff, panicking if it didn't come to hand immediately, until his fingers grasped the smooth wood. The feel of it as he gripped it in both hands would calm him and his back would loosen. The staff allowed his mind to feed information to his eyes, rebuilding a version of the world around him that he could see and understand.

Then one morning the staff didn't work so well. He could see, but his back and limbs remained stiff. A chill had entered his body, and neither breakfast nor the morning walk removed it. He didn't mention it at first, concentrating all his energy on moving without falling, using the staff to support himself.

The irony was that they were leaving the mountains, descending to the grassy plain of the Jalakh Steppe. They would get the occasional glimpse of it now and then, when they ascended to the top of a peak. The grasslands stretched out seemingly forever, flat like a green ocean. At those moments it seemed deceptively close, and Soren would redouble his efforts, the end in sight. Then hours would pass without a sight of it, just bare rock and stunted trees all around them, and he would come close to despair.

As the sun started to fall on another day Soren got warmer and warmer, trickles of sweat running down his body. He put his hand to his forehead. It was hot and clammy. A fever. He had to tell them. Gyrmund walked them on a bit farther until he found a suitable place to stop. He built a fire and made Soren a hot soup with the herbs and medicines he had to hand. Soren forced himself to drink it before giving in to sleep.

The next morning, he had to be woken up and lifted to his feet. His head pounded so much he felt sick. He leaned on his staff, drawing as much strength from it as he could. He knew they had to get down off the mountains.

That day and the next were lost days of delirium, half-remembered fragments, of Moneva helping him to walk, following a path that led them out of the high ground, of collapsing into the grass of the Jalakh Steppe. Gyrmund and Moneva talking to each other in hushed voices. They needed to find help,

Moneva said. But there was no-one around, not a settlement, not a field or a wall or a single cow or sheep to show that anyone lived here. His fever needs to take its course, Gyrmund said. Soren let himself lean back into the grass. It supported his weight, just like he was floating on water. He let the grass carry him away, his broken body floating along to wherever the wind blew him.

The next memory he had was waking with a canvas roof above him instead of the sky. It felt like he was still floating, but how could he be with a roof above him? Then he realised that the movement was different. It was the slow, bumpy movement of a wheeled wagon. And Belwynn was there. How had she got there so fast?

Soren, can you hear me? She was saying. *Soren, where are you?*

He tried to reply, but all that came out was a croak. It was too difficult to talk, far easier to just close his eyes and let the wagon wheel him along.

He woke up, the memories playing in his head. He tried to clutch at them, tried to make sense of them, but they refused to be caught.

He scrabbled from one side to the next, desperately searching for his staff. There. He gripped it and his sight returned. He pushed himself up to a sitting position. He was alone in a circular felt tent. A round hole in the roof let in sunlight. It was a yurt. A Jalakh yurt. He looked down. His part of the yurt was covered in rugs and blankets and cushions.

He was weak, but it felt like his fever had broken. Gyrmund and Moneva had somehow found help. That was the second time they had saved his life.

Belwynn? He called, remembering hearing her voice, though whether he had dreamt it or not he didn't know.

Soren? She replied immediately, her voice full of concern.

I'm safe, he said. *I fell ill. But I'm alright now. We've made it. We're with the Jalakhs.*

X

IN SHADOW

WHEN BOLORMAA HAD EXPLAINED that all of the Jalakhs were travelling to Tosongat, Gyrmund had assumed that she was exaggerating. It appeared not.

The Oligud tribe who had picked them up and taken the feverish Soren in their wagon had merged with other tribes heading east, becoming a horde on the move. And when they had arrived, Gyrmund could see that other hordes had arrived from every direction on the Steppe. No longer a tribe or a single horde, a nation had decided to come together in this one place.

Surely, this was the most likely location for the Jalakh Bow. But he had to be careful about revealing their intentions.

'Moneva and I would like to look around Tosongat,' he said to Bolormaa.

She looked at him appraisingly. She was wily, still handsome and strong, even though she was now a grandmother. She knew they were up to something, and yet she was the one who had decided to take them with the tribe, a decision that had probably saved Soren's life. Gyrmund couldn't help thinking that she was up to something too.

'Now I see,' she said, 'you are here to witness the Great Contest.'

Gyrmund raised an eyebrow.

'We come here at this time every year that the Jalakhs need a new khan. The Great Contest decides which man will be khan.'

'The greatest fighter becomes khan?' he asked.

Bolormaa pursed her lips. 'That is the idea. The Contest began this morning. You and Moneva should go and watch it. But if you want to watch, you will need to dress appropriately. I will also send Gansukh with you.'

Bolormaa had Gyrmund and Moneva dressed in the traditional deels of her tribe. She advised them that each tribe had a distinctive cut or pattern of deel, so that the other Jalakhs could see which tribe Gyrmund and Moneva belonged with, affording them some protection.

Bolormaa's eldest son, Gansukh, led them through the camps of the various tribes, a maze of yurts that they would have got lost in themselves. Roaming freely about the place, in greater numbers than the Jalakhs themselves, were their horses. A totally different beast to the great warhorses bred by the Kalinthians, the Jalakh horse wasn't much larger than a pony, with shaggy hair. They were allowed to graze wherever they wished, but Gyrmund saw that when their owners whistled they came back, like obedient hounds.

Unlike his mother, Gansukh said little, grunting at them if he wanted their attention. He walked in a young man's swagger, letting all who looked his way know how highly he thought of himself. Gyrmund wondered whether Gansukh considered himself a candidate for the Great Contest.

Gansukh grunted and drew their attention to a large roped off area of short grass, around which many Jalakhs sat or stood.

'This is our Contest,' he said. 'You can watch with me.'

Gansukh led them to a space where they could see. The space inside the ropes was empty, but before long a section of rope was untied. First one rider entered the area, then a second. They were introduced one at a time, their name and tribe called out, after which their supporters, who had gathered to watch, cheered and banged kettle drums. Both men wore scale armour and helmets, and were armed with scimitars, curved swords made for slashing.

Moneva turned to Gansukh. 'It's a fight to the death?' she asked.

He nodded. 'Yes.'

'But that's so wasteful.'

'Only those who truly believe they can win will fight. Otherwise, any man could enter the ropes and the Contest would never end.'

The two adversaries moved to either end of the ropes. There was a shout and the fight began. Both men hurtled forward at incredible speed, their mounts strong and agile. Once they got within distance of each other, their horses sidestepped and they leant in, trying to land a strike while defending themselves and their mounts. The speed of their blade-work was impressive, doubly so when one considered they were using one hand to hold the reins, while constantly nudging their horses back and forth or to the sides, trying to manoeuvre an advantage for themselves, or lead their opponent into making a mistake.

The ring of steel on steel filled the air. Both men landed blows, but they hit the armour of their opponent, skidding off the scales to no apparent harm.

They broke apart briefly then moved back in, their swords a blur of frenetic slashes and blocks. Then one man scored a hit. He slashed at his opponent's hand and lower arm and his blade came back with a spurt of blood, the blow somehow penetrating armour. The fight continued, the injured man not done yet, even though Gyrmund could see a steady trickle of blood coming from his hand. Depending where the wound was exactly, it could begin to make his grip more slippery.

Perhaps it was the injury driving him to take more risks, but the warrior drove in close, aiming a blow at his opponent's head. The second warrior's horse skipped aside at the last second, and he then found the space to land a strike on his opponent's mount. The poor creature collapsed, sending its rider skidding to the ground. Ruthlessly, the mounted warrior wasted no time. He rode in close, leaned over and cut down, twice then three times, until the floored man was dead.

Staying on his mount, he raised his arm in the air, receiving the adulation of his tribe, who made a cacophonous noise. He left the roped area, before the members of the other tribe moved in to recover the body of their fallen champion.

'Both were good fighters,' commented Gansukh. 'But their riding was not so good.'

'What happens next?' Gyrmund asked.

'Next, a champion from another tribe will challenge the winner.'

'Would that be you?' Gyrmund asked with a smile.

'I will enter the ropes,' said Gansukh proudly. 'But Bolormaa will tell me when.'

'When does it end?' asked Moneva.

'It ends when there are no more challengers.'

Gyrmund and Moneva shared a brief look. No doubt this was a tradition that went back many generations, and had its uses, in binding the tribes together. Nonetheless, Gyrmund thought it a flawed system for choosing a leader.

'Is there anything else to see in Tosongat?' Moneva asked Gansukh. 'Except more yurts?'

Gansukh frowned, as if wishing to see anything further was greedy. 'Just our temple.'

'Temple?' asked Gyrmund.

'It is only for priests and royalty to visit.'

'Can we see where it is?'

Gansukh shrugged. 'Follow.'

He took them away from the ropes and away from the yurts. Here, in an area which the tribes had left empty, was the only permanent structure Gyrmund had seen. A large rectangular area was surrounded by wooden walls, only reaching the height of a man. Peering over, Gyrmund could see that inside was mostly open to the elements. On his side of the wall was a ceremonial garden, with developed trees, plants and a pond. He could see walkways had been constructed around the garden. Elsewhere within the walls he could see one story wooden buildings. He could hear rather than see animals: sheep, probably goats, were kept somewhere behind the walls. At the far end, its protruding eaves visible in between the branches of the trees, was a pagoda. It was elaborately designed, with five small towers emerging at the top of the building.

Moneva peered over the wall too.

'It's beautiful,' she said.

'Only priests and royalty are allowed in there,' Gansukh repeated.

Gyrmund and Moneva shared another look. Surely this was where the Jalakhs would choose to keep their Bow.

***

THEY FOUND Soren, awake and alert, sitting up in the yurt belonging to Bolormaa. He listened, leaning back on his cushions and sipping at the drink he called kumis. Moneva remembered giving him the same drink in Samir Durg, when they had rescued him from the Tower of Diis. It had revived him then and it looked to be doing so again—his face less pale, his eyes sharp and inquisitive.

'The question, then,' said the sorcerer, having digested their description of the Tosongat Temple, 'is whether we explain our need for the Bow, and ask the Jalakhs to give it to us. Or try to take it without their knowledge. Both approaches have their dangers.'

'Take it,' said Moneva instinctively. 'They're not going to hand over a precious relic to a group of outsiders. The Temple is barely defended. I can find the bow, take it without them realising it has gone.'

'I'm not so sure,' said Gyrmund. 'I would favour talking to Bolormaa. She may be able to help us.'

'Why would she?' countered Moneva.

They both looked at Soren, who seemed to have the deciding vote.

'If the Jalakhs had a leader, a khan with the authority to grant us the Bow, then I would take that option,' Soren said. 'But they don't. Who would we ask for it? Bolormaa is an impressive woman, but even if she decided to help us, how would she persuade all the other tribes to agree? I think, if we can take it undetected and leave, that is the better option. I could come and help, I'm feeling much better.'

'There's no need,' said Moneva, pleased at his decision. 'I just need Gyrmund to help me over the wall. There's no benefit to more than one of us moving about in there. It just raises the chances of getting caught.'

'Alright,' said Gyrmund, conceding defeat. 'When do we go?'

'Tonight,' said Moneva.

Moneva and Gyrmund crept through the fields of yurts, matching each other in the silence of their movements. The Jalakhs slept on, and if there were any still awake who heard a movement they would put it down to a grazing horse, since each tribe had hundreds if not thousands of the animals moving freely in the area around their camp.

It was the first time they had been completely alone together in a long time. Her mind should have been completely focused on the job at hand, but once they moved out of earshot of the last group of yurts, Moneva stopped.

'Gyrmund,' she whispered.

He stopped immediately, looking about in case she had spotted trouble.

'I need to talk to you. About Samir Durg.' She took in a breath. She had to make herself keep going or she would never get it out. 'I had to sleep with Arioc. I'm sorry.' *Why was she apologising? That wasn't what she meant to say.* 'I mean, it affected me afterwards. When we got back to Heractus. I didn't deal with it very well.'

She paused. She had been thinking about what exactly to say to Gyrmund for a number of days now, and it had all come out a jumbled mess anyway. She looked at him, but it was too dark to read his expression.

'I understand,' he said quietly. 'Moneva, I can never repay you for what you did in Samir Durg. You got all of us out of there, when we all thought we were dead. You're an amazing woman. Truly amazing. I'm sorry if I didn't support you properly.'

She heard his voice catch and a lump came to her throat. Part of her said this conversation was stupid. But another part knew that it was important, and that they should have had it a long time ago.

'No,' she said. 'I didn't want to let anyone in. I wanted to deal with it myself. That's just what I'm used to.'

Gods, how pathetic, she told herself. Since her father had died—no, probably since her mother had died before that, she had been alone. She had learned to deal with things herself. It was better, safer, to be like that. But now, when she heard herself speak, she sounded like a bloody mess.

'I had a lot of time to think in Samir Durg,' Gyrmund said. 'I lost all my family when I was young. An illness—I was the only one who survived. I lived with Farred's family after that. I never spoke about it, no-one ever asked me about it. I got on with things, but I couldn't wait to leave. As soon as I was old enough I went wandering around Dalriya, telling myself how free I was, what an exciting life of adventure I had. But part of that, a big part, was me running away from what happened. Being by myself, not having to care about anyone else, moving on before I put down roots anywhere, before I got close to anyone. In the mines I realised that was wrong. I did want to be with someone, and that someone is you, Moneva. I promised myself I wouldn't give up, wouldn't take the easy option and walk away any more. So I'm always going to be here if you want me.'

Moneva moved into him, put her arms around him and he did the same. She felt a tear rolling down her cheek. A simple hug—it felt so good, made her feel so much better. She needed to allow herself this. Be a bit kinder to herself. If she had done this six months ago she would have felt a lot better a lot sooner.

There, she was doing it again, telling herself off. Gyrmund said she was an amazing woman. Maybe it was about time she believed that and let someone else care about her.

They stood that way for a while before, reluctantly, she pulled away.

'That's enough of that nonsense,' she said. 'We've got a job to do.'

They made their way to the Temple, peering over the outer wall. There wasn't much to see—no lights, no sounds of activity either.

'Alright,' she whispered.

Gyrmund bent at the knees and linked his hands together, forming a step. Moneva put one foot in. He stood up and she pushed up with her foot, placing one hand on his shoulder to steady herself. She touched the top of the wooden wall. It was rough and sharp, so she removed a blanket she had tied around her waist and placed it on top of the wall. She placed her hands on the blanket. Fine. She looked over the top of the wall to the ground directly beneath it. Just grass. Confident, she took all her weight on her arms and vaulted over, landing securely inside the Temple.

If the Bow was stored here, it was almost certainly in the pagoda, on the other side of the complex. She walked through the garden, using the paths and being careful where she placed her feet. It was quiet, the only sound she could detect was animals moving about in the wooden sheds that lined the walls to her left and right. She found herself in the centre of the garden. All the paths seemed to meet here, though they clearly took their own, individual, meandering routes. Here, one huge tree stood, dominating the other vegetation in height. The larger branches that radiated out were themselves the size of trees. Moneva had the sense that it was very old, probably predating the Temple itself, but beyond that she could discern nothing more, not even the species.

Moneva walked through to the end of the garden, approaching the pagoda. Here, it became clear that few, if any, people actually resided in the Temple. Outside the pagoda there were some small cells, nothing more than wooden shacks, so thin and tiny, each with a little individual door, that they could only fit in a bed for one person, with no room to stand. They didn't seem to be permanent living quarters, more like places to sleep while on a vigil of some kind. Jalakhs who were visiting for other reasons, Moneva considered, would almost always bring a yurt with them and have no need for accommodation.

She crept up to some of the cells, listening intently. She could detect breathing in at least two, but the idea that someone was sleeping in one of them next to the Jalakh Bow was a ridiculous one, so she moved on to the last and best option. The pagoda.

It was a pretty little building, full of fanciful curves where each tier of the building met the one above.

Moneva circled around the pagoda, checking for entry points. On the other side to the one she started from was a grand opening. Four pillars supported a roof, and this structure faced a gate in the outer wall, the main entrance into the complex. Moneva walked up a small set of steps and passed between the two middle pillars, moving under the roof. Two double doors faced her, the wood heavily decorated in geometric patterns. She approached the doors and, ever so carefully, pushed at one of them. The door gave, barely making a noise, and she slipped inside.

She hesitated briefly but decided in the end to leave the door open. It was riskier, but allowed some moonlight into the ground floor of the pagoda. Nonetheless, it was still dark, and Moneva allowed her eyes to adjust for a little while. Around the wall were stairs with a railing, circling all the way to the top. A central pillar climbed all the way to the top. She could just make out thin planks of wood radiating out from the pillar above her, with lattice style flooring on top, making a second floor. She walked a full circle around the pillar, returning to where she entered. Four statues had been placed around the pillar. Looking closer, she could see they were identical representations of the same man. Flowers, presumably cut from the garden, had been placed next to each statue. It was hard to understand what she was looking at. She went down on her knees, touching the statue, feeling to the sides. But there were no other offerings but the flowers, and no sign of a bow or a place where a weapon might be kept or displayed.

Deciding not to waste any more time, Moneva took the stairs. She walked up to the next level. Tentatively, she placed a foot on the latticed wooden floor. It held her weight no problem. She moved over to the central pillar. Nothing, and the cobwebs she found told her all she needed to know. No-one ever came up here, except perhaps when the structure needed maintenance work on it.

Knowing she was wasting her time, but just to eliminate the chance, she explored all the way to the top of the pagoda. It was the same story. She had found nothing of any use, and if she stayed any longer she was taking unnecessary risks. She moved quickly now: descending the stairs, then out of the pagoda, closing the door softly behind her. She retraced her steps, back into the garden, and through it to the outer wall she had climbed over. The blanket was still there.

'Gyrmund?' she hissed.

'Still here,' came his voice. 'I've got the blanket.'

Moneva reached up to grab the end of the blanket that hung over her side of the wall. With Gyrmund holding the other end, she used it to pull herself up, feet jammed against the wall until she could reach the top. She clambered over and landed on the other side, pulling the blanket with her.

'Well?' asked Gyrmund.

'Nothing. It's certainly not on display anywhere. There wasn't much to look at to be honest. I'm fairly sure it's not there.'

'Well, we tried.'

'Still,' said Moneva, 'it wasn't a completely wasted trip.'

'How's that?'

Grinning, she pulled Gyrmund in, and they kissed, the passion of it taking her by surprise. At that moment, she didn't care very much about finding a stupid bow.

***

SIAVASH WALKED down the dimly lit corridor until he found the cell with the prisoner he wanted.

'This one,' he said.

The guard stepped forward and unlocked the door.

'Leave.'

'Yes, lord.'

Siavash entered the cell. He allowed himself a bitter smile. This was where he had kept Soren imprisoned, who had dared to challenge him, in the Throne Room of all places. He and Soren had unfinished business. But then, he conceded, without the Magnian's insurrection, Erkindrix would still be the Lord of Ishari and he would merely be a member of his Council. That way of looking at it meant that he owed Soren a favour. He would enjoy deciding what to do with him when he was caught and returned here.

He glanced briefly at the Haskan prisoner. He was unharmed, as Diis had commanded. The man, on his knees in chains, looked terrified. As well he might, Siavash allowed, though what exactly was going to happen here he didn't know. It was time to find out.

He called to Diis. Diis, who had chosen him above Arioc, above all the others. He would prove to his lord that He made the right choice.

Diis emerged, His face inside Siavash's face, His body inside his body. It took all of Siavash's strength to keep Him contained there, for he was a God, who should not be constrained to live inside a mortal's body. He would not need to for much longer. It made Siavash wonder about the hundreds of years during which Erkindrix had been a vessel for Diis, and he found he gained a new respect for his predecessor.

Diis looked about the cell, coal black eyes finding his bearings. The prisoner whimpered and began rehearsing a prayer. But he prayed to some other god and Siavash knew that wouldn't help him.

What news do you have, demanded Diis, speaking inside Siavash's mind, not so very different to when Siavash spoke to Soren in this room.

We have completed the reconquest of Haskany and re-established control over Persala, Siavash informed him. *My reforms to the army are complete and each host is ready to be given their orders.*

He had defeated both Arioc and Pentas to secure complete control over the Isharites, the Drobax, and their dependent states. But he almost felt more pride in his reforms, that gave him greater personal control over the army than Erkindrix had ever had. Betrayals like those of Arioc and Pentas would now be a thing of the past.

But Arioc and Pentas are still at large, Diis bellowed in anger from somewhere inside him.

He whimpered, the prisoner staring at him in horror.

You are right, Siavash admitted. *With all my foolish pride I have hidden those grave failings from myself.*

For each failing you owe me a sacrifice, Siavash. You are stronger than Erkindrix was, and you can endure the punishment.

Yes, Siavash agreed. He would willingly make such a sacrifice.

Erkindrix and the Council made a great mistake. They underestimated the Krykkers and the Kalinthians. This allowed my enemy to use her weapons against me. We cannot afford further mistakes. Soon I will help you to open a portal to my birth world and together we will bring forth a creature that will help us to destroy the Krykkers. When I am in full control of this world I will have the power to bring many such creatures here. But for now, one will suffice.

Siavash couldn't help but exult at the prospect. The destruction of the Krykker race would remove the last great obstacle to a complete conquest of Dalriya.

Now, I will take your first sacrifice.

Without warning, Siavash felt a horrendous, tearing pain engulf him. It was more than a physical pain. He could feel Diis, his claws sharper than diatine crystal, ripping at his very soul. He tried to withstand the pain, tried to maintain consciousness.

Then he saw something out of the corner of his eye. Something that had been hiding, almost fully obscured in the dark prison cell. He saw his shadow move without him, and with a last agonising tear Diis completely severed it. Siavash turned in shocked disbelief, to see his shadow slide around the wall of the room, free of him, moving of its own volition.

Your shadow, said Diis. *It can now do your bidding, allow you to move around Dalriya while your body stays here, safe from harm.*

Siavash was speechless. This was a thing of nightmares, a void of colour moving about the cell. And yet, when he concentrated on it with only a fraction of his powers, he saw that he could indeed move it. Control it.

But a shadow is useless without a body to inhabit.

Siavash understood. He drew his knife, strode over to the prisoner and grabbed him by the hair, yanking his head up.

Not the neck, said Diis.

Siavash did as commanded, plunging the blade with all his force into the middle of the prisoner's chest. The prisoner's scream was cut off when he withdrew the blade and he sagged down, unconscious. Blood started to pour from the injury.

It is better to make the injury somewhere it can be hidden, Diis explained.

Siavash began to appreciate the possibilities. If his shadow was able to control the corpses of his victims, it could pass unnoticed, hidden in plain sight.

He concentrated on his shadow. It approached the prisoner and he forced it to enter, to reattach itself to a body, but this time a different one.

The prisoner's head jerked up.

'Release me from the chains,' hissed his shadow in a Haskan accent.

Siavash stared in shock. It appeared that the Haskan soldier had returned to life in front of him, speaking again with his own voice. But he knew it to be nothing more than a reanimated corpse.

You will go to Kalinth, Diis commanded.

XI

HALVIA

RABIGAR STOOD ON THE WHARF, watching the tall ships of the Sea Caladri out on the shimmering turquoise of the ocean. It was a beautiful sight, one he didn't think he would ever see. But then, he hadn't expected to ever be back home amongst the Krykkers, and here he was.

One of the ships had furled its sails and was now heading in their direction. As it came nearer he could see the oars on both sides rising up and down, propelling it towards them. Red eyes painted onto the sides of the ship glared at them, as if she was a sea serpent come to lay havoc to the coastline.

They waited as the ship was manoeuvred into position. With Rabigar were two chieftains: Maragin of clan Grendal, and Hakonin of clan Swarten. They were going to cross the Lantinen Sea to visit with their cousins, the Krykkers of Halvia. There had been no contact with them for a year, not since the Kharovians had defeated the Vismarian fleet and established an iron grip on the Lantinen. The pirates of Kharovia would not be pleased to see Caladri warships in what they had declared to be their waters.

But they were going to Halvia for a specific purpose, too. Szabolcs, the wise man of the Shadow Caladri, had identified Halvia as the location of the Giants' Spear, one of the missing weapons of Madria. The Giants, everyone seemed to agree, were long gone. The Krykkers of Halvia, therefore, were the first step in tracing the Spear's resting place.

If Maragin and Hakonin were going as representatives of the clans of Dalriya, then Rabigar was going as the holder of another of Madria's weapons, Bolivar's Sword. He touched the hilt of the weapon, scabbarded at his side. His ownership of the sword wasn't a popular choice amongst the Krykkers. No, it was downright unpopular. But he enjoyed a rather unique position amongst the Krykkers now—he was clan-less, exiled from the Grendals for killing Maragin's father, and never formally brought into a new one. Should any other Krykker claim the blade, they would be opposed by all the other clans, demanding to know why it wasn't going to them. No alternative claimant had come forward, and the longer it went on, the more secure Rabigar was.

He had made it perfectly plain that he would not give up Bolivar's Sword. Not to anyone. And it would be a brave Krykker who dared take him on.

The Caladri ship was tied off and the plank came down. Rabigar put one foot onto the wooden board. It flexed worryingly. He hated water and ships, didn't know many Krykkers who didn't. But it wasn't going to stop him. He took a breath and marched purposely up the plank. He grabbed an offered hand when he reached the top and found himself stepping onto the deck.

He was surprised to see a familiar face amongst the crew.

'Farred?'

It was Gyrmund's friend—he had met him in Coldeberg. Quite what a Magnian was doing on a Caladri ship he didn't know.

'Hello Rabigar, good to see you again. This is the captain of the Red Serpent, Sebo.'

Rabigar and Sebo shook hands. He then introduced Maragin and Hakonin, who had made their way on board.

'Welcome aboard all of you. It is an honour to have three Krykker lords sailing on my pride and joy, Red Serpent. Any questions or requests, please don't hesitate to ask. If you'll excuse me for a few minutes, I need to get her going, then I will come and speak with you some more.'

There followed an unpleasant lurching sensation as the ship cast off and the oars began to pull it away from the wharf.

'Well, I wasn't expecting to see you here, Farred,' Rabigar said. He pointed at the Krykker countryside they were leaving. 'Don't know the last time a human was allowed to see this view. Clan Swarten's lands are something of a secret, eh Hakonin?'

'That's right,' said Hakonin. 'It suits us for others to think of all the Krykker lands as impregnable mountains. But my people's lands are the exception. Flat, and good for crops. We're called the breadbasket of the Krykkers. We used to trade with the Halvian Krykkers when the Vismarians controlled the sea. Now you know our secret, I'll have to kill you,' he smiled.

Farred laughed. 'Well, maybe you'll spare me if I exchange a secret?'

'Go on,' said Maragin. 'You have us intrigued now.'

'Well,' said Farred, looking more serious. 'I sailed with Sebo all the way from Mizky. He showed me the charts he used. Two of them have the same people marked at the same place, in the South Lantinen. The Asrai.'

Rabigar looked at Maragin and Hakonin. The two most obscure weapons mentioned by Szabolcs, the Spear and the Cloak. They were closer to finding them both.

Red Serpent joined up with the full Caladri fleet and they made a course for Halvia. The Sea Caladri weren't taking any risks and they were right not to. Captain Sebo pointed out to the starboard side and Rabigar could just make out dark smudges on the horizon, in the direction of the island of Alta.

'They've seen us,' said Sebo calmly. 'They're following, at a safe distance.'

'Will you try to intercept them?' Rabigar asked.

'No. Our orders are clear on that. We have authority to defend ourselves, but we are not to seek out conflict. If they are merely watching, we will let them.'

'And what if the Kharovians are bringing all their ships to destroy you?'

'Then we will be ready for them.'

The Caladri ships cut through the waters of the Lantinen, pulled along by the powerful oars. The oarsmen worked in shifts, allowing small groups to rest and regain their strength. Farred took a turn on the oars, leaving the Krykkers to watch the coastline of Dalriya gradually disappear, before Sebo called their attention to the bow, where the Halvian coast was coming into view.

Hakonin joined Sebo, using the maps in his clan's possession to help find a port for the fleet. The coastline was rocky, as Krykker lands should be. But it meant that it was dangerous for such large ships to get close to shore, which they had to in order to identify the landmarks that would take them in the right direction.

Eventually, and with a minimum of fuss, Red Serpent led the Caladri fleet to an inlet. They sailed down the channel, steep cliffs on either side, before it opened into a wide bay. Here the waters were still, and while there were jagged rocks they needed to avoid, a large section of the bay was salt marsh that was safe enough to beach the fleet.

It took a while for all the ships to execute the manoeuvre, by which time a group of armed Krykkers had arrived, forming up on higher land that overlooked the marsh. What they made of a Caladri war fleet appearing in their bay, no-one could know for sure. Rabigar and his two companions walked off to meet them, keen to explain their appearance before the Halvian Krykkers decided that they were hostile.

As they approached they saw that a good two hundred Krykkers were arrayed in battle formation, fully armed. It was a relief, then, when Hakonin declared that he recognised the leader of the force as a clan chief.

'Crombec!' he shouted. 'I am Hakonin of clan Swarten, come from Dalriya. You knew my father well and you know me.'

One of the Halvians took a step forwards from the front line. He ripped off his helmet, releasing a bush of grey hair, and squinted down at them.

'This is Maragin and Rabigar of clan Grendal,' Hakonin added into the silence.

'That's all very well,' Crombec shouted back at them, before gesturing down to the shoreline. 'But who the fuck are they?'

With a bit of work, Crombec was persuaded to stand down his troops, and instead lead the three Krykkers up into the mountains of his homeland. The Sea Caladri decided that they could not stay in the bay, explaining that it left them too vulnerable to a Kharovian attack, who would be able to seal the inlet and trap them inside. They would sail back to Hakonin's lands in Dalriya and return to Halvia in five days' time.

As they walked with the Halvian Krykkers, Rabigar and Maragin relayed to Crombec the recent events in Dalriya, and the significance of finding the seven weapons of Madria. When he learned that Rabigar was carrying Bolivar's Sword he insisted on handling the weapon, eyes sparkling with joy as he gripped the hilt and squinted at the magnificence of the blade. Rabigar felt a flush of anger, a desperate desire to take the sword back, but he controlled himself, and Crombec reluctantly returned it to his keeping.

Not so very high up they came to Crombec's hall. It was well positioned to get a view of the sea and Rabigar deciphered that coastal defence was the key role of his clan, the Pecinegs.

'I will call a Great Moot of the clans,' he told the three Krykkers. 'That is most likely to unearth any knowledge we may have of the whereabouts of the Giants' Spear. Our legends say that the Giants lived in the far west of Halvia. But that is too vague a starting point for an expedition, if that is your intention. It will also give us the chance to tell you what has been happening in Halvia in the past year. You may not be surprised to learn that we are facing problems of our own.'

Rabigar, Maragin and Hakonin travelled with the Pecinegs to the site of the Halvian Great Moot. Unlike the Great Meeting Chamber of the Dalriyan Krykkers, an underground cavern carved into the mountain Kerejus, Crombec led them to an open-air building. It was circular, surrounded by high stone walls. The walls contained three arched entrances, one for each of the Halvian clans.

Clan Chief Crombec led the Pecinegs through their entrance. Steps led them up to a seating area that belonged to their clan. Crombec sat Rabigar and the others on the front row with him, while the rest of his Krykkers took their places on the tiered rows behind. In front of them was a platform, raised above ground level, where a speaker could address all of the clans at once.

As the Pecinegs took their seats, a second clan began filtering into the building. Crombec identified them as the Vamorins. He explained that they manned the Western Walls, a series of towers that marked the Krykker border with the untamed, western half of Halvia.

They waited until the third and final clan arrived. Finally, the thud of boots on steps could be heard and the Binideqs appeared. Rabigar stared at this third group. There was something wrong.

'Humans!' Maragin hissed.

Mingling with the Binideq clan were human men and women. They took up a good third of the seats, between the Binideqs and the Vamorins.

'They are Vismarians,' Crombec explained. 'Refugees. Some of them have lived in our lands for two years now. We have given them a voice at the Moot.'

Rabigar shared a glance with Maragin and Hakonin. Such a thing would be unthinkable in Dalriya. It was a reminder that they were not in Dalriya anymore, and that the Halvian Krykkers, for all their shared ancestry, had led different lives since they had been separated by the Lantinen Sea.

Once everyone was ready, Crombec took the floor. He explained to the Moot why he had called it, introducing Rabigar and the others. Rabigar went next, explaining in more detail the events in Dalriya so that the Halvian Krykkers could understand why the search for the Giants' Spear was so important. He proudly held aloft Bolivar's Sword, letting the Halvian Krykkers see the weapon they had only heard stories about. He gave way to Wracken, chief of the Binideqs.

'Our guests have brought us news from Dalriya, which we were ignorant of, and for that we give them thanks. Now they must know about events here in Halvia before we can proceed. They should know that the Drobax have become a mighty force on this continent, ferried across the Lantinen in huge numbers by the Kharovians. The Drobax have run amok in the north of Halvia, relentlessly attacking Vismarian settlements. This has been a war of destruction, with the massacring of whole communities. While the Krykkers have fought with our allies, it has not been enough to stop it. The majority of Vismarians now live here in our lands, contributing to our society with their skills. Those that remain beyond the River Drang are those that have found shelter in the most remote and hidden locations. The West of Halvia is a largely wild and unknown land. It is the Vismarians who have explored the western reaches in the past. They are the ones who will know the most about the Giants, if they are willing to share this knowledge with us. I therefore invite Sevald of the Vismarians to speak.'

As Wracken left the stage, this Sevald took his place. He was tall, strong, long-haired like all his people, and if he had any doubts about speaking at a Krykker Moot, they were well hidden.

'I once again take the opportunity to thank all of the Krykker clans for their help to us in our time of need. To the Krykkers of Dalriya my people say this: we understand you arrived here by Caladri ships. Please, the Kharovians outnumbered and overwhelmed our fleet. But we did not give it up. Here, and in other places, our ships are ready. Let us join with the Caladri to defeat the Kharovian menace, that threatens both Dalriya and Halvia.'

He looked at them then. It wasn't desperate, or pleading, but it was a look that demanded a response. Rabigar found himself nodding in agreement, even though he had no control over what the Sea Caladri did.

'As for this question of the Giants. Our stories say the Giants lived far to the west. Where exactly, and how to get there, none of us here know. It is a dangerous land, which none of us have ventured very far into. There are Vismarians, of an adventurous nature, who have journeyed into the west. Nothing good has ever come of such expeditions. In particular...' Sevald paused. He looked reluctant to continue. 'There is a family whose home is in the north west. They—' he paused again, 'they claim to be descended from Giants. They are an eccentric group, even by Vismarian standards,' he said, allowing himself a smile. 'No-one has heard of them in months. They may have been killed by Drobax. The probability is that they have. But I am willing to lead a group back into Vismaria to try to locate them. If anyone can offer you a specific location, or route, it is them.'

The moot continued until everyone who wished to had their say, but no more progress could be made. They had succeeded in getting the support of the Halvian Krykkers, and of their allies, the Vismarians. But the more they had learned, the more the recovery of the Spear sounded like a challenging and problematic task.

It was time to return home. Crombec took them back to the bay where they had arrived, for the rendezvous with the Caladri fleet. The ships were already there. The whole fleet had made the passage, testament to their concerns about a Kharovian attack. Bidding Crombec farewell, they spotted Red Serpent and made for Captain Sebo's ship.

They were welcomed aboard. Farred had made the journey again, though he and Sebo both wore grave faces.

'What is it?' asked Rabigar, sensing they had news to tell.

'The Isharites have invaded the lands of the Grand Caladri,' said Farred. 'The Caladri who had resettled their lands were forced to retreat all the way back into the Krykker mountains.'

'We had expected the Isharites to return, possibly to move against us,' said Maragin grimly. 'We must prepare to defend against them.'

'There's something else,' said Sebo. 'The Caladri who escaped say the Isharites had a monster with them.' He exchanged a worried look with Farred. 'They say they had a dragon.'

***

STRATON AND Ampelios travelled under armed guard in one of the supply wagons as the army made its way back to Heractus. Diodorus and his soldiers left to return to his estates, while the rest of the army began the return journey to Heractus, making a camp in the open a day's march from the capital.

The mood was low. Theron and Sebastian had ensured they remained in control of Kalinth, but it had been an empty victory; an unnecessary loss of life. Theron was drained, physically and emotionally, and went to sleep as soon as he got the chance. So Belwynn decided to seek out Clarin. She had barely had a chance to spend any time with him since he had returned from Samir Durg.

She found him sitting with the rest of the escaped prisoners outside their tents. With no need to worry about enemy scouts any more, the soldiers were building their fires high to keep off the night chill, and drinking up the last of the ale and wine in the army's supplies. Clarin and his friends were no different, but in other ways they stood out. They were an intimidating looking group, scarred men with grim, thin faces. Then there were the two Dog-men, former servants of Ishari who had become Clarin's loyal hounds. With their powerful, protruding jaws, and their clawed hands, they had a monstrous appearance in the flickering light of the flames. These were Clarin's people now. They had all changed since they had left Magnia nearly a year ago, Belwynn knew that. But she felt that Clarin had changed more than most.

He saw her standing a few feet from the fire and hastily got to his feet. He came striding over, his long legs making up the distance in no time.

'Hello Belwynn,' he said. She could smell the alcohol on his breath. 'Would you like a place by the fire?'

'I'm fine. I just wanted to say hello. I feel rude, like I have been ignoring you. But we've all been so busy the last week. I've good news, too. Soren spoke to me from the Jalakh Steppe. He got ill on the journey there, but he says he's recovered now.'

'That's a relief. I'm glad you came, Belwynn. I've been wanting to talk to you. How about we take a walk to keep warm?'

They strolled slowly around the camp, the fires of the soldiers lighting their way in the darkness.

'Sebastian told me that you broke through the enemy line. You've really won his respect, he said they needed men like you. You could have a place here in Kalinth if you want. A valued place.'

Clarin gave a nod. He seemed unimpressed with the compliment and the offer. No doubt he had other things on his mind.

'I know how hard it is for you,' she said. 'With Herin. I had the same thing when Soren was captured. It was the not knowing that was the worst part.'

'Yes,' he said. 'It's not easy. That's not what I wanted to talk to you about, though.' He paused, thinking, as if trying to choose his words carefully. 'When I was a prisoner in Samir Durg I faced the very real possibility that my life would end there. We all did. It makes you think about your life—makes you look at yourself. I asked myself, if I was ever going to get out, what did I want from life? And the answer was you, Belwynn.'

They both stopped walking. Belwynn felt taken by surprise, hadn't seen this coming. She didn't know what to say, just stood there gaping at him.

'I love you,' he continued into the silence. 'I always have, but I was too young and stupid to do anything about it before. But I'm not that man anymore. I want you, Belwynn. I want to make a life with you.'

'Clarin, this is so sudden. I didn't know. It's difficult, I—'

'Theron?' he asked, his mouth forming a sneer when he said the name. 'I've seen how you look at him. But I don't trust him. And he doesn't know you like I do, doesn't love you like I do.'

'Clarin, stop. Stop for a second. I can't think.'

He grabbed her arm in his hand, holding it tight.

'I don't want you to think, Belwynn. Gods, I need you. I need you to say yes.'

He was scaring her now. *How much had he had to drink? How much of this was his emotions from Samir Durg, repressed for so long, now pouring out?*

'Let go of me, Clarin,' she said.

'Sorry,' he said, letting go immediately and looking ashamed.

What do you want from me, she wanted to say, feeling angry. *Why now? When it's too late? If you had said this sooner. If you had arrived in Kalinth even a day earlier, and said all this, I might never have gone to Theron's bedroom. But you didn't, and I did.* But she wouldn't say any of that, because it would only make things worse.

'Clarin, I'm glad that you've told me. But you must understand, I wasn't expecting it. You need to give me some time.'

He nodded, a mournful look on his face. 'Yes. I'm sorry. It didn't come out right.' He sighed. 'I'm a clumsy fool.'

'Come on,' she said. 'Walk me back to my tent.'

When they returned to Heractus, Belwynn and Elana made straight for the Temple of Madria. Elana had to speak to her flock, who needed to be told about the outcome of the battle. The Church of Madria was busy, especially so after Elana's deal with Sebastian that it should be the only recognised Church in Kalinth. They had already taken over all the religious buildings in the capital. Now they had plans to expand into the local settlements and to the larger towns.

Belwynn was keen to spend some time with Lyssa, and escape from the business of war and politics. The girl had been looked after at Elana's Temple while Belwynn was on campaign, her time filled with chores, and she was happy enough. Belwynn had begun to teach her some basic reading and writing skills, for she was completely illiterate. It was a struggle. She didn't really show much interest in it. Belwynn found herself wondering what to do with Lyssa. Other children her age were already learning a trade. Was that best for her? Should Lyssa be treated as Belwynn's own daughter? And what kind of life would that lead to? *Because what am I, exactly?* she asked herself. *Apart from the Lady of the Knights?*

Lyssa was a town girl, and Belwynn resolved to teach her something of country life. They spent a pleasant afternoon on a walk, just the two of them. Lyssa was captivated by everything, from a gurgling stream to a patch of wild flowers, from the birds signing in the trees to frogspawn in a pond. She talked nonstop, and they both felt disappointed when it was time to return to Heractus.

It was remarkable how easily and completely she had withdrawn into this little world, and so it was a jolt to find Clarin pacing about outside the Temple upon their return.

'Do you know what he's doing?' demanded the warrior.

'What? Who?'

'Come see.'

'Alright Clarin, but let me see to Lyssa first.'

She entered the Temple and made sure that Lyssa was suitably supervised before returning outside.

He led her into the city centre. A crowd had gathered and Clarin had to take her closer before she could see why. A man knelt there, hands tied behind him. He shivered, face pale.

'Who is it?' she asked.

'Count Ampelios, the nobleman who surrendered to Theron in the battle. They're killing him anyway.'

Theron approached the crowd.

'No, Theron,' she whispered under her breath. 'Why do you have to carry out every unpopular task?'

'Count Ampelios, you have been convicted by the royal council of treason. Your sentence is death.'

An executioner approached, holding a large two-handed sword. Belwynn didn't recognise him. She was sure he wasn't a knight. If he was an official executioner of some kind, it looked a little better than the Knights doing it themselves.

He didn't waste any time and he did it well. While Ampelios was still kneeling, he launched a massive swing of the blade which cut the head clean off the shoulders. Belwynn turned away at that point, and many in the crowd screamed and cried out.

She looked up. Clarin was looking at her.

'Is that justice?' he hissed.

What did he want from her? It was horrible, did that make it wrong? She wasn't sure what she thought.

'Don't pretend there are easy answers, Clarin,' she said. 'Leniency and gentility allowed Straton and Ampelios to escape and look where that got us. A bloody battle with hundreds of deaths. I don't want that to happen again.'

'Treason?' Clarin said, pursuing the issue. 'He was imprisoned here when the Knights took the capital by force, he escapes and fights for the heir to the throne, and that's called treason? I know treason when I see it, and I'd use that word for someone else.'

Belwynn looked around them. 'Be careful what you say, Clarin, for Madria's sake.'

'Or else I'll have *my* head cut off? I don't understand, Belwynn. What has happened to you that you defend him like this? Why are you here, when Soren and the others are away looking for Madria's weapons?'

'Is that what this is, Clarin?' she retorted, hearing her voice rise with anger and trying to control it. 'Attack Theron so that I will fall in love with you instead? It doesn't work like that.'

He looked at her, a stunned expression on his face.

'I think I'll go,' he muttered, sounding defeated. 'If this doesn't open your eyes, nothing will.'

'I think that's best.'

She watched him go for a while, then walked away herself, keen to get as far away from the scene as possible. Before she realised where she was going, she found herself walking up to the gates of Heractus Castle. The guards let her in and she took the familiar route up the tower steps to Theron's room.

She knocked on the door. There was a rustle and he opened it.

He stared at her, a haunted look in his eyes.

'I saw,' she said simply.

'Oh,' he said quietly. 'I didn't want you to see that.'

He walked over to his bed, wearily taking a seat. 'I'm sorry. You may hate me for it. But if we didn't do that, demonstrate the consequences of rebellion, it would never stop. An endless civil war where we tear ourselves apart, with the Isharites waiting to finish us off.'

Belwynn took a seat next to him.

'I know all about civil wars,' she said.

He looked at her. It was a look of raw gratitude.

'Thank you. For understanding. I never want to do that again.'

He flopped down, putting his head in her lap.

She stroked his hair, looking down at her knight.

You would, though, she said to herself. *If you had to, you would do it again.*

XII

JOINED

HIGH-PRIEST WULFGAR of the Temple of Toric would not have been Edgar's first choice to conduct his wedding. But he was the leading prelate of South Magnia. He wasn't the most spiritual of men either, but there was some benefit to that. He had kept the ceremony mercifully brief and to the point. After exchanging rings, and sharing a kiss, Edgar and Elfled could turn to face the congregation in the Temple as man and wife.

Applause and cheers met them. On one side of the circular central chamber sat the South Magnians. Edgar's best man, Wilchard, grinned over. Leading noblemen such as Otha of Rystham and Aescmar occupied the front rows with their families. Behind them, those less titled such as Oslac, mayor of Halsham, and Ulf the smith had been found room. On the opposite side of the room the front row was occupied by Elfled's family. Her brother Cerdda, Prince of North Magnia, with his wife Irmgard. Their mother, Mette, had also made the trip. Behind them, foreign dignitaries, from as far as the Brasingian Empire, had come to witness the union.

For it was a love match, Edgar was sure of that. But it was also, he knew, political. The rival families of Magnia were uniting. And, should Cerdda's marriage remain childless, any children that Elfled gave him would perhaps one day lay claim to both parts of Magnia.

He shared a look with his new wife, her dark ringlets of hair spilling over her white dress, and he knew he had never been this happy. But he also took a moment to acknowledge those who were not here. His father, Edric, dead these four years, whose statesmanship had paved the way for this marriage. His mother, too frail in body and mind to make the journey. Ealdnoth, his trusted adviser, and Leofwin, his rock of a bodyguard, both killed in Barissia by the bastard Salvinus. The same man who had dared to invade Edgar's realm and desecrate this very temple. No. He would think no more of him today.

Holding hands, Edgar and Elfled led the congregation out into the large temple complex. Toric had blessed the day with bright spring sunshine. They all gathered outside, everyone keen to have a word with Edgar and Elfled before they were called into Wulfgar's hall for the feast.

First was Coen, Duke of Thesse, not the kind of man to wait politely for his turn. With him was Frayne, the Midder chief who had fought with them against the Barissians. Edgar introduced them both to Elfled.

'Ah!' she said. 'The heroes of Lindhafen! I have to thank you for keeping my husband alive last year! I would love to hear all about the campaign. Edgar never talks about it.'

Both men beamed at the prospect of recounting their war stories. Elfled was very good at all this; much better than he was. Edgar detached himself and located Walter, the new Duke of Barissia, who was standing with Russell, a soldier from Morbaine who was here on behalf of Duke Bastien.

'Congratulations,' both men said as he approached, before they each shook his hand.

'Your new wife is stunning.'

'Thank you, Lord Russell.'

'You didn't stand a chance,' Walter added.

Edgar laughed, turning to Russell. 'I wonder when the new Duke of Barissia will be caught? Surely the most eligible man in the Empire?'

Walter made a horrified face.

'Ha, you look just like Farred when I mentioned the idea to him.'

'Where is he?' asked Walter. 'I had been hoping to see him here.'

'He's too much of an adventurer to stay here, I'm sorry to say. He travelled with the Sea Caladri fleet north.'

'I see. I hope he finds success. Freeing the Lantinen would be a welcome development.'

'Couldn't agree more,' said Russell. 'The Kharovians are a menace to all of us.'

'How is Duke Bastien?' Edgar asked Russell.

'Bastien sends his apologies. The duchess is very close to her due date and he wants to be there for her.'

'Of course. Please pass on mine and Elfled's best wishes. And,' he said, turning to Walter, 'I must ask about news from the north.'

'Bad news, I am afraid. We know that Siavash has won control over the Isharites. We had let ourselves hope that a civil war might occupy the enemy for some time. Gustav reports that a great battle took place in Haskany. The

Haskans were defeated, Queen Shira killed. Arioc's army was defeated there too, though he may have escaped. Siavash has restored Haskany and Persala to his empire. It can only be a matter of time before the Drobax are sent south again. They may be sent to Kalinth, or to the Krykkers. But we must prepare for the monsters to return to Brasingia. As we speak, my men are getting Burkhard Castle ready in case we must defend it again.'

Edgar nodded solemnly. He had to ask, though the answer couldn't help but sour his mood. The silence after Walter had spoken hung around him, urging him to offer his aid in the coming conflict. But he wasn't going to do that. Magnians had shed enough blood in the Empire last year. They had helped to defend Burkhard Castle, and they had helped to defeat Emeric. Baldwin now had a united realm with which to withstand the Isharites. This time Walter and Coen could lead the Barissians and Thessians north should the need arise. Surely that would be enough to withstand the new Lord of Ishari?

***

SIAVASH'S SHADOW, occupying the body of the dead Haskan, had climbed into a wagon, been given a guard of elite mounted Isharite soldiers, and driven south-west towards Kalinth.

The journey gave Siavash a chance to get used to the experience. When he slept, his shadow lay unmoving—but not asleep, for shadows didn't know sleep. If a noise or movement alerted it, Siavash would wake, full of confusion until he realised what was happening. When awake, he tried to get used to managing his own affairs, while controlling the shadow's movements at the same time. Gradually, he became able to control both bodies, so long as neither required too much effort. When a job required his full attention, the shadow was left to slump on the floor of the wagon. After experimenting in such a way, he realised that once the shadow was active in Kalinth, he would be forced to stay in his rooms so that he could properly concentrate on its mission. It was a frustration, but would perhaps be worth it once the shadow got to work.

The wagon reached Masada, the fortress that the Kalinthians and Krykkers had taken the previous summer. It had been reinforced and was now fully garrisoned by Haskans. A servant of Diis named Harith was also stationed here. He reported to Siavash alone, and his presence helped to ensure the loyalty of the Haskan soldiers. Siavash was delivered to him, with written instructions. The Isharite broke the seal, looking from the words on the parchment to Siavash and back again, until his eyes widened.

'My Lord,' he stuttered, getting to his knees. 'It will be an honour to serve you.'

'Your service will be remembered,' said Siavash, speaking in a stranger's voice, the voice of the dead man he inhabited. 'Now, waste no time.'

None was wasted. Two horses were saddled immediately. They rode south, crossing the border into Kalinth. They had to be careful now, since this area would be patrolled by Kalinthian Knights. Siavash, his real body all the way in Samir Durg, decided it was best to sleep for the rest of the day and move again at night. His Haskan body was left to lie on the hard ground, eyes open and staring. Before sleep took him, he caught Harith glancing at the living corpse in horror.

That night they moved through the Kalinthian countryside, looking for a victim. Harith argued that the isolated farmsteads were less favourable, since their inhabitants were more alert to danger. The small villages, where many families gathered together, gave them a false sense of security. Siavash accepted this and waited on the outskirts of such a village as Harith approached a house.

Harith climbed onto the roof, where he pulled out an area of thatch, before dropping inside. Time passed and Siavash heard nothing, waiting patiently.

Harith emerged from around the corner of the house, obviously having exited from the door. He was walking backwards, dragging a body behind him. When he reached Siavash he let it drop to the ground. Siavash could see that it was a young man, not yet fully grown into his body. As instructed, the wound was in the chest, and could be easily hidden.

Siavash concentrated, forcing his shadow to leave the body of the Haskan. His shadow resisted. But it had already been detached once before, and this time it left more easily. Willing to find a new home, Siavash was able to insert it into the new body. He stretched, flexed his hands, moved his limbs, before standing up.

Harith was staring at him, jaw wide open in awe.

'You have done well,' said Siavash. 'I will continue alone now. Show me the way.'

Harith nodded, visibly reasserting control over himself. He pointed in the direction to be taken.

Siavash wasted no more time and began walking. It would be wise to leave the vicinity of the village as soon as possible.

He turned at a noise. Harith was riding away, back to Masada, holding the reins of the second horse. Siavash could just make out the dark shadow of the Haskan soldier that had been left on the ground. He turned back, and resumed his journey.

Siavash walked through the night. As the sun began to rise, he found a secluded spot to lie his new body down in so that he could sleep. He awoke at midday and resumed his journey.

He came upon a road, which suggested that he was going in the right direction. Making his shadow follow the road was easy. It needed no food or water or rest. He passed some travellers going the other way. They mostly called out a greeting, to which he responded in kind, never stopping to talk further and arouse suspicions.

In the middle of the afternoon he heard the clip clop sound of a horse and cart from behind. He moved to the side of the road to let it pass. The driver stopped the cart.

'Ayup, young man,' the driver called out. 'Where to?'

'I'm going to Heractus,' Siavash replied. Where else would he be going?

He could see the driver looking him up and down, especially his lower half. What is he looking at? Siavash wondered.

He looked down and saw that his shoes and the bottom half of his trousers were caked in mud. He had to be more careful about his appearance if he wanted to avoid attention.

'I was walking during the night,' he said.

Perhaps that would satisfy the man's curiosity. If not, he would kill him.

The man grinned. 'Hop in the back.'

Siavash looked at him blankly, before turning to look at the cart. It had four big wheels with a wooden box made of rough planks of wood.

'Thank you,' he said to the driver. He placed one foot on a spoke of the rear wheel and then clambered over the side into the box. He moved aside some bags of grain and vegetables to make himself a space and sat down, before banging on the side of the box.

The Kalinthian farmer called out to his horse and the cart began to rumble onwards.

The farmer was waved in through the gates of Heractus. Siavash, ensconced in the back of the cart, wasn't asked a single question. It wasn't just the security that was lax; the walls and defences of the city were ludicrously weak. If the Drobax were sent here, the Kalinthians would be crushed. But Siavash intended to break them without the need to waste an army on the task.

He familiarised himself with the layout of the city first. He knew much about his targets already. He knew that pliable King Jonas had been replaced with a more stiff-spined regime, who had dared to invade Haskany. He knew all about Soren's group, of course: his sister; Madria's priestess; and the others. They had been busy on Madria's behalf, collecting her weapons, engineering the death of Erkindrix, all the while protected by the treacherous Pentas. They were in league with the Kalinthians and Siavash knew they might still be here.

He located the castle, and determined that was where the political leadership governed from. He located Madria's Temple, where her priestess and the rest of her followers worshipped. These, then, were his targets. And in a city where he seemed free to go where he wished, it dawned on him how impossibly easy this was going to be.

When he saw the woman and the girl a thrill ran through his body. He knew her. She had been in the Throne Room of Samir Durg, with Pentas. He followed them as they walked from the castle down into the city centre. He decided to speed up and walk past them, taking a surreptitious look. He reassured himself that she couldn't recognise him, because he wore the face of an unknown Kalinthian man.

There was no doubting the resemblance. This was Soren's sister, an individual he had wrested from the Magnian's mind during his imprisonment in the Tower of Diis. He remembered Rostam striking her to the floor in the Throne Room. It was the one victory that worthless man had ever enjoyed, may Diis take revenge on his pathetic soul.

She had obviously recovered from that episode. If she was here, then it was more than likely Soren was too. Siavash exulted at the possibilities. He could take her body and kill Soren with it. And what of the girl, presumably her daughter? A small body such as hers could make a very useful assassin, perhaps. No-one would suspect her.

He stopped walking and then turned, waiting for her to approach. But she had stopped to talk with a man. He was powerfully built, doubtless a warrior, perhaps a leader here. Siavash edged closer to listen.

'It's a strange logic I admit,' the man was saying. 'But with the Isharites having regained complete control of Persala, Zared believes this is the best time to return to his homeland. Their armies will be moving elsewhere. He thinks if I go with him, I have a good chance of finding it.'

'If you trust him, Clarin.'

'I do.'

'It's just, wouldn't it be better to wait for Soren?'

So, Soren isn't here. Where have you gone, Soren, I wonder?

'Zared thinks that he and the other Persaleians will have contacts there who can help me. The Persaleians might trust me when otherwise they wouldn't. It honestly feels like the best chance to get the Shield now, before it's too late.'

I see, Siavash said to himself as realisation dawned. *They are after the Shield of Persala. A very useful conversation to have stumbled onto. This soldier will find he won't be the only one looking for it.*

'I just wish we were parting on better terms,' said the man she had called Clarin. 'I'm sorry about the way I've acted—'

Suddenly, the man stopped speaking and swung around to look straight at Siavash.

'Can I help you, son?' he said, an angry frown appearing.

'Er, no. Sorry.'

Siavash turned away, flustered. So stupid to have been caught out like that! He walked away towards the centre of town, feeling their eyes on his back as he went.

They know this face now, he berated himself. *I can't let them catch me out a second time. I must get a new one.*

XIII

TO THE ROCK

GYRMUND STOOD OUTSIDE THE WALLS of the Jalakh Temple again, this time waiting for both Moneva and Soren to return. The wizard had insisted on looking inside, in case he could interpret what Moneva had seen differently and find some clues, if not the bow itself. If he didn't, they were stuck for ideas.

He heard a whisper from Moneva and moved over to the blanket that hung over the top of the wall. As he did, he saw Soren's head emerging on the other side of the wall. Soren kept on rising, revealing his shoulders, chest and legs, all the while maintaining a perfectly straight face. He floated right over the wall and then down next to Gyrmund. Gyrmund shook his head, grabbing his side of the blanket and telling Moneva to climb over. He had seen Soren do many things he had not thought possible, and he had never got used to it.

'Well?' he asked when Moneva had made her own way over the wall.

'Nothing, really,' said Soren. 'Moneva is perfectly correct, it's not there. Which means it may well not be in Tosongat at all. It could be kept by a particular tribe...We need to think carefully about our next move before we do anything else.'

Next morning Gyrmund awoke early. He left the yurt he shared with Moneva and Soren. He stretched, wondering what to do with himself.

Some of the Oligud warriors had allowed him to join in with their archery training yesterday, and he was pleased to have demonstrated enough skill that they had invited him back today. The composite bows, the weapon the Jalakhs were famous for, were not much different to his own longbow to use. However, he would never possess the skill of the Jalakhs, who were taught to ride and shoot from a young age. Gyrmund was content with staying on his feet.

He spied Bolormaa, sat around a fire with a group of Oligud women. He edged over. He knew that Soren and Moneva were not keen on involving her in the search for the Jalakh Bow. But maybe, if he was careful, he could find something out.

'Come!' she called over to him.

He sat down next to her. On the fire was a pot of Jalakh tea and without asking him, Bolormaa scooped a cup into it and handed it to Gyrmund. He thanked her, though that was out of politeness. It was very milky, salty rather than sweet, and Gyrmund had not acquired a taste for it. The women were preparing meat, which would be tossed into the tea later on for the midday meal.

'How long until the Great Contest is done?' he asked her, sipping at his drink.

'No-one knows for sure. A champion must last for seven days to become khan. If there is no champion, the Contest finishes at the end of this month. That's in twelve days.'

Gyrmund thought about this. 'So, a champion wins a bout. He is then challenged the next day, and the day after, and so on, for seven days? He will get tired, pick up injuries, while each day he faces a fresh warrior?'

'Just so.'

'Then it is almost impossible to become khan. That is why you have told Gansukh to wait until late on to enter the Contest? That is his best chance.'

'Yes. But many will adopt such a strategy. It is still virtually impossible to last for seven days. Then, as I say, the tribes return to their lands until next year.'

Gyrmund thought some more. 'When was the last time the Jalakhs had a khan?'

'Over sixty years ago.'

Sixty years since the Jalakhs had a ruler? This was a strange people. 'Surely people can't be happy with this system?'

Bolormaa turned towards him. 'I am not very happy, Gyrmund, but some people are. With no khan, the tribal leaders have no authority above themselves. With no khan, there are no wars to fight. Many tribes like things exactly the way they are. And if Gansukh were to win two or three bouts, these tribes will send their best warriors in against him, until one of them cuts him down.'

'Then why is he entering the contest?'

'Because,' she said fiercely, 'Gansukh wishes to be khan!'

Clearly, it wasn't only Gansukh who wished it. His mother did, too. A thought crossed Gyrmund's mind.

'Did Gansukh's father enter the Contest?' he asked.

'He fell on day five.' She said it in a matter-of-fact way, but he could feel the pride and fury that she tried to hide.

Gyrmund sipped on his tea, thinking so hard that he didn't even notice the taste.

'We could help him,' Gyrmund suggested, quietening his voice so that only she could hear.

Bolormaa's eyes locked on to his with an intense look.

'And what,' she asked slowly, 'would you want in return?'

Here it was. Their opportunity to get help, or the moment the Jalakhs turned on them. Gyrmund looked back to the yurt, but Soren and Moneva were still asleep. It was his call.

'We want the Jalakh Bow.'

She cackled then, a sound of surprise and genuine mirth.

'You don't want much, then.'

'Is it here? In Tosongat?'

'Is it here?' she repeated his question, a sly look on her face. 'In a manner of speaking, yes.'

'Could you get it for us?'

Bolormaa's humour faded away, replaced by a deadly serious look. 'If you help Gansukh to become khan, he will give you the Jalakh Bow. This is the only chance you will have of getting it, I should add. So. Do we have a deal?'

Bolormaa offered her hand. Hesitating only briefly, Gyrmund reached out and they shook. She broke out into a big smile. 'Wonderful!' she cried. She grabbed his head in both hands, pulling him in. At first Gyrmund thought she was going to land a kiss, but instead she pulled his head down and sniffed the top of it, before letting him go.

'You haven't asked me why we want the bow,' he noted.

'The Jalakh Steppe is remote, yes,' Bolormaa said. 'But remember, we are neighbours of the Isharites. I am not ignorant of what they are. The Jalakhs need a khan now, more than ever. And those who oppose Diis need weapons to do so.'

Gyrmund nodded. 'I think I may have underestimated you, Bolormaa.'

She flashed him a smile. 'You are very wise, Gyrmund. One thing. You must never speak to Gansukh of our deal. He is a very proud man.'

Gyrmund nodded. No doubt khans didn't like it said that their mothers helped them get the job. He looked over at his yurt again. There were a couple of people he *should* tell about this deal. He just hoped they would understand.

***

SOREN WATCHED Gansukh ride into the roped off arena. He approached the area where Soren was seated, surrounded by the members of the Oligud tribe, and raised his sword. The Oligud screamed and cheered, banging drums so loudly the noise reverberated around his skull. It hardly made his mood any better, and he stared balefully at Gyrmund, who was clearly responsible for all of this, while Gyrmund studiously avoided making eye contact.

Gansukh's opponent was already there, eliciting a similar response from his own supporters, the Yahmet tribe. He had already won two bouts, and was considered to be a tough first opponent for Gansukh.

The shout went out and the two warriors went for each other, blades whirling at incredible speeds, horses agile and clever, seeming to understand what their riders wanted them to do.

Soren felt the nudge of power, buffeting Gansukh's horse, trying to disrupt his sword arm. Soren pressed back, protecting Gansukh from the attacks. The two warriors continued to fight, trying to find an opening in each other's defences, too focused to be aware of this secondary contest. They were evenly matched. It seemed wrong, somehow, to interfere in this fight. But if this was truly the only way to get the bow, he had to do it.

Soren went on the offensive, weakening the strength of the other warrior's blows, reducing their speed. The Yahmet wizard, whoever they were, reacted violently, pushing back with force. But now a third force entered the fray. It began to work with Soren. If Soren defended the Yahmet attack, they went on the offensive. If Soren tried to impair the Yahmet warrior, this third power focused on defending Gansukh.

Then, suddenly, it was all over. Gansukh launched a flurry of strikes and his opponent was too slow to counter them. The first landed, then a second, then a third rattled through one of the slits in the helmet, the blade crunching through bone into brain, killing the Yahmet warrior almost instantly.

Gansukh celebrated his victory and the Oliguds cheered wildly for their hero.

Soren looked about him. Somewhere among this group the Oligud had a magic user of their own.

Bolormaa approached him, a sly kind of smile on her face.

And then it clicked.

'Oh, I see,' he said, as she sat next to him.

'Well done, Soren,' she replied. 'I knew your life was worth saving. Now, all we need to do is keep my son alive for seven days.'

***

IT WAS A strained journey across the Lantinen Sea. They all wanted to get back as quickly as possible, and fears about what was happening in Dalriya made people anxious and short-tempered. Maragin and Hakonin perhaps felt it the most, since they were absent when their clans needed their leadership.

Kharovian ships could be seen to the north, tracking their movements, still not making a move of their own. Their presence added to the tension on board, and Rabigar let out a sigh of relief when he saw the Krykker coast come into view.

When they had docked, they immediately went their separate ways. Farred left for the south, travelling to the lands of men to warn them of the new threat. Hakonin remained, to guard the coast from the Kharovian threat. Maragin and Rabigar took half of Hakonin's Swarten soldiers and headed east, to the border threatened by the Isharites. They would pick up her soldiers from the Grendal clan on the way. They had to hope that when they got there, the border was still intact.

Before they reached the border, they met a defeated army coming the other way. The first few soldiers could be seen emerging from the tree-line ahead of them, and the two forces came together in a rock-strewn mountain clearing. The retreat seemed orderly enough, but Rabigar could see the panic in Krykker eyes and the relief at seeing Maragin with her Grendals.

'I need to speak with the leaders. Gather them here!' she shouted.

The troops under Maragin's command were ordered to help carry the supplies and the wounded. Keeping the Krykkers moving was essential, because it wasn't clear how far behind the enemy were.

It was a sorry looking group that appeared to speak with Maragin. Jodivig, the new chief of the Dramsens, looked fraught and out of his depth. Kelemen, the Grand Caladri governor, was also there, leading the remnants of his people.

'Where's Guremar?' Maragin demanded.

Guremar's clan, the Plengas, controlled this area.

'He stayed behind with a group of our soldiers,' said a Krykker Rabigar didn't recognise. 'He said he would hold them off while we escaped, otherwise it would turn into a massacre. I—I don't think there will be any survivors.'

'Shit,' Rabigar muttered under his breath. There was no love lost between himself and Guremar, but he was one of the strongest clan leaders. If he was gone, that put even more responsibility onto Maragin's shoulders.

'What happened?' asked Maragin.

'A huge Drobax army entered our forest,' explained Kelemen. 'There was no stopping them, we were forced to retreat west into Plengas lands. Guremar raised an army and led it to the border. He prepared well enough, using the high ground. I thought the Drobax would give up, our position seemed impregnable. But then the dragon came—' He stopped, as if unable to continue. But no-one else stepped in. 'It flew above our position. We fired some missiles, but we didn't have many. Nothing stopped it. It flew over and blasted fire, again and again. We had no protection, it killed scores each time it passed. That's when Guremar ordered the retreat.'

Drobax and a dragon. What could the Krykkers do against such monsters? Rabigar looked at Maragin as she looked at him. They both knew the answer.

'I need to see,' he said. 'I need to see them before I leave.'

'I'll come too,' said Maragin.

It went quiet. Clearly, not a popular request.

'I'll take you,' said a voice.

Rabigar turned. Standing behind Jodivig, so that Rabigar hadn't even seen him, was Stenk, the young Dramsen Krykker he had befriended. Stenk, after some persuasion, had arrested Rabigar upon his return to his homeland last year. They had fought side by side against the Isharites in Haskany. Rabigar was happy to see him alive.

'You're the perfect man for the job,' he said to Stenk. 'Now, you just need to take us close enough so that we can see them, then you turn around and come back to join this army, understand?'

'Keep moving,' Maragin said to the rest. 'We'll catch up.'

Rabigar pushed his face through the rock, looking carefully about. There were no Drobax. They were using the path twenty feet away to climb the mountain. It was high up here, high enough to burn the lungs of Krykker folk, never mind creatures such as Drobax, whose bodies weren't used to it. There was no reason for them to come this way anymore.

He pushed through, emerging fully from the rock while glancing at the sky above. By the time Stenk had shown them this location, the dragon was gone. It had perhaps found somewhere to rest. Rabigar didn't know anything about dragons, but he imagined that flying around at this altitude, casting fire, was exhausting.

Maragin pushed through the same section of rock. Wordlessly, they began to look about. The ground was covered in a grey soot. Charred bodies littered the area where Guremar had made his stand. The place still stank of burned meat, and something about that upset Rabigar's insides. He tried not to think about the suffering too much. But soldiers clad in metal armour, exposed to fire of these temperatures, would have died in agony. They had come to bear witness, and to check for survivors, however unlikely. Clearly, there were none here. If Guremar had Rock Walkers with him, they may have been able to escape. But there was nothing else they could do now.

'We'd better head back,' he said to Maragin. 'What will you do?'

'We have no choice,' she said, and he already knew that. 'We must order the tunnels closed and we must evacuate.'

The underground tunnels and caverns were the last line of defence for the Krykkers. They could explode the tunnel entrances, creating an underground lair that was virtually impregnable. Certainly, not a place a dragon could do any harm. But only a few Krykkers could live in those conditions for long. All the rest would have to leave their homeland.

'I will lead the group who stays,' he said to Maragin. 'You will be needed elsewhere.'

She smiled at him. He had thought he would never see that sight again. He stopped talking, so that her smile stayed on her face for as long as possible.

'We both know that's not going to happen. The Rock Walkers will follow me; not you. You are the one who claimed Bolivar's Sword. You must see that through. You need to go back to Halvia to find the Spear.'

'I don't know that,' he argued. 'You can do all that instead of me. Here,' he said, unbuckling the sword. 'Take it.'

The last thing Rabigar wanted was to see Maragin buried alive in the mountain caverns. That wasn't the last image of her he wanted in his head.

She snorted disdainfully. 'Please, no romantic gestures at your age. It's sad. I am the best person to lead the defence here; you must find the Spear; Hakonin must lead our people in Halvia. We both know those will be our roles, so stop wasting your breath.'

Rabigar felt he had never loved, never respected her more than in that moment, when the chances of seeing her again suddenly dropped to virtually nil. Not that he had the right to feel sorry for himself. He had killed his chieftain. He had killed Maragin's father. That act still—would always—stand between them. So Rabigar stopped wasting his breath, and they both returned to the rock.

XIV

CONSUMMATUM EST

LYSSA SKIPPED ALONG THE STREET, pleased to have escaped the Temple.

It wasn't that she hated it there, exactly. The people were sort of kind. But they were always making her do things. She didn't mind it so much when Belwynn made her read, because she liked spending time with her. But she hated it when the women kept making her learn to sew. In Korkis, she was used to doing what she wanted, when she wanted. She didn't want to go back to that life. No way. It was just that, now and then, she needed some time to herself.

Coronos was on guard duty at the castle.

'Welcome back, Your Highness,' he said to her, bowing deeply, before allowing her to pass through.

Lyssa giggled at him. Walking into the castle did kind of make her feel like she was a princess, though.

She went to the Tower where she shared a room with Belwynn, but half way there decided that she wasn't in the mood to sit around. She'd much rather go exploring around the castle.

She walked up and down the corridors. As she walked along she saw Queen Irina leaving the castle library and closing the door behind her. Irina turned to walk in her direction, and it was too late for Lyssa to change course, so she kept on walking towards her. When they passed Irina gave her the look of displeasure she always gave her, while Lyssa kept her eyes on her shoes.

She kept on walking and stopped outside the library. She looked back down the corridor, waiting for Irina to disappear. The Queen was one of the few people who ever used the library, so there was a good chance it was empty now. Nervously, she turned the handle and peeked in.

Yes! It was empty!

Lyssa slipped inside. She liked the smell of the room. There were several shelves of books, and comfy chairs to sit on. She didn't like the room because of the books, though. She liked it because of the secret door she had found.

She went straight there now, pulling at the door that was painted to look like it contained shelves of books.

No-one had exactly told Lyssa she wasn't allowed to go into the secret passage. She knew that Belwynn hadn't lived in the castle very long, and might not even know about the secret door to tell her not to go in. Queen Irina had lived here a long time. She might know about it. Maybe that was why she was here before? Anyway, whoever knew or didn't know about it, to Lyssa it felt like a forbidden part of the castle.

She walked in and pulled the secret door shut. The passage was very narrow and not very high, but they weren't problems for Lyssa. It was almost completely dark, which she didn't like so much, but she crawled along on her hands and knees and that helped her to avoid bumping into the walls.

She stopped when she heard voices. This was where Sebastian's rooms were, and she recognised his voice first. Second, Theron. They were always talking about boring things up here. Nevertheless, she peered into the room.

There were four of them altogether. Tycho was there. He always wanted to arm wrestle with her, even though she always beat him. Remi was there too. He always winked at her when he saw her, but didn't talk much.

She listened in. They were kind of arguing with each other about what to do with Count Ampelios's lands. The Knights seemed to think they were on the good side, but they had just killed Ampelios and now they were taking his family's lands. Theron wanted his friend Tycho to have them, Sebastian said Remi should have them. If they really were good, maybe they should give his lands to people who didn't have any of their own? Maybe they shouldn't have killed him in the first place, then there wouldn't be anything to argue about.

Theron and Tycho left Sebastian's room.

'I'm sure we can find a compromise,' Sebastian said to Remi.

Remi shrugged. 'I don't care. I have more important concerns.'

Sebastian frowned at him. 'Oh? Like what?'

'This.'

Suddenly, Remi drew a dagger, leaned over to where Sebastian was seated, and plunged it into Sebastian's chest.

Lyssa had to grab her mouth to stop herself from crying out. She didn't want to look, but she couldn't make herself stop watching.

Sebastian tried to stop Remi, but the other knight pushed him back with one hand, while pushing the dagger deeper in with the other.

'You thought you could stop us?' Remi hissed. 'You thought you could invade our lands with no consequences? You fool!'

Lyssa turned away. She wished she hadn't opened the secret door now.

Moving slowly to avoid making a sound, she began to crawl back down the passage.

***

BELWYNN HALF-WALKED, half-ran through the garden at the Temple of Madria. She had to stop suddenly to avoid crashing into Elana and Prince Dorian, coming the other way.

'Sorry,' she said breathlessly.

'Is something the matter?' Elana asked.

'Have you seen Lyssa anywhere?' Belwynn asked, slightly embarrassed. 'She seems to have run off without telling anyone.'

Dorian smiled kindly. 'I'm heading back home,' he said. 'If I see her on the way, I'll be sure to bring her back.'

'Thank you.'

'I'll help you look,' said Elana.

'It's alright, I don't want to waste your time.'

'I'll help,' Elana insisted.

They said farewell to Dorian and began to search the grounds of the Temple, where an unruly child might have decided to have an adventure.

'I'm not sure what to do with her anymore,' Belwynn confessed. 'I feel like she needs her time structured properly, learning something useful.'

'Don't fret,' said Elana. 'It's perfectly normal for children to go off exploring. It's good for them. I'm sure she'll turn up.'

'Yes,' said Belwynn absently. Lyssa wasn't in the garden. She had gone into the city, she knew it.

'Belwynn, I haven't told anyone this, not even Dirk.'

This sounded serious. Belwynn gave Elana her full attention.

'Before all this started, back in Magnia, I had a family. A husband and two children. Girls.'

Belwynn's mouth dropped open.

'What happened to them?'

Elana smiled. 'Nothing, I hope. I hope very much that I will be able to go back when this is over.'

'You mean, they're back home now? In your village, what was it, Kirtsea?' Elana nodded.

'How could you do that?' Belwynn blurted out. 'Do they know what you're doing, that you're alive?'

Elana pursed her lips and Belwynn could see tears threatening to spill.

'Sorry, I didn't mean—'

'I didn't choose this, Belwynn, remember? Madria chose *me*. Sometimes I wonder why. But I have to see it through. And what would I tell them, so that they could understand why I left? How could I explain that I still love them, but can't be with them?'

'I'm sorry Elana. Truly. Soren will get the weapons. We'll win, and you will get to go back home.'

Elana smiled wanly. It didn't seem like she believed that. 'Where do you think we should look next?'

'Eh?'

'For Lyssa?'

'I think she went into the city. Hopefully just back to the castle. I'll head there now.'

'I'll come with you.'

They made their way out of the Temple grounds and onto the street outside. They hadn't walked very far when they saw her, walking towards them alongside Dorian. He had one arm around her shoulder protectively, as if shielding her from something.

'Found her heading this way,' he said. 'Couldn't get out of her where she's been. She seems a bit shaken up.'

Belwynn looked at Lyssa, who stared ahead listlessly. She seemed withdrawn, removed from their immediate conversation.

'Are you alright, girl?' Belwynn asked her.

Lyssa turned to her. There was something in her eyes, something like fear, but she didn't say anything.

Belwynn and Elana shared a look. What was up with her? Had something happened?

Before she had time to question her further, Dorian had turned to look back up the street.

'It's Sebastian!' he said.

Sebastian was walking towards them. Belwynn watched him approach. He seemed stiff; older somehow. Perhaps recent events were weighing on him more than she had realised.

'Well met, Grand Master,' said the prince.

Belwynn wondered at Dorian. Sebastian had defeated his older brother in battle but a week ago. Theron had ensured that Straton was now locked up, unable to leave the capital again. What did the younger brother really think about these developments?

Sebastian nodded at them all. 'I have come to talk with Elana.'

He sounded grave.

'We'll go back to the Temple,' said Elana, and she and Sebastian left in that direction.

'Well, I really should be getting home,' said Dorian.

'Thank you for finding her,' said Belwynn, glancing down at Lyssa.

She was startled when she looked at the girl. She looked stricken, staring at the departing Elana and Sebastian in terror.

'What is it?' Belwynn asked her.

'I-I saw Sebastian killed. By Remi.'

Belwynn frowned at her, but getting those words out seemed to open a floodgate in Lyssa. 'I was hiding in the secret passage behind the library, I know I shouldn't have been. Theron and Sebastian were arguing about who should get the lands of Count Ampelios. Theron and Tycho left the room. Then Remi killed Sebastian. Just like that. For no reason. Then—' she stopped, pointing after Sebastian and Elana, who had now gone into the Temple.

'Then you saw Sebastian alive?' Belwynn asked.

Lyssa nodded, looking up at her like a little mouse, expecting Belwynn to solve the problem for her. Belwynn looked at Dorian.

'Maybe you fell asleep, Lyssa?' he suggested. 'Had a nightmare?'

Lyssa looked from Dorian to Belwynn. Belwynn could sense her desperate need to be believed. And maybe, most people would have dismissed her wild story as a dream. But Belwynn had grown up with Soren. She had no reason to doubt the existence of the mysterious—of dark powers. And what she had witnessed in the last year had only confirmed that.

'I think we should check on them, just in case,' she said.

Dorian nodded. 'And, there *is* a secret passage at the back of the library,' he added.

She looked at him. It was no joke he was making. If Lyssa had witnessed Sebastian's murder, who or what exactly had walked off with Elana?

'Come on!' she said, suddenly feeling the need to act quickly. 'Stay here!' she said to Lyssa.

Belwynn and Dorian ran together into the Temple. 'Elana?' Belwynn shouted at the startled followers of the priestess.

One of them pointed down a corridor to Elana's private room, an obvious place to take Sebastian. Private, but dangerous, for there would be no witnesses.

Belwynn ran in that direction, her lungs burning from the effort, Dorian still by her side. He got to the door first, shoving it open.

Despite Lyssa's warning and her own mounting dread, Belwynn still couldn't process the scene before her. Elana lay on the floor, a pool of dark blood visibly growing around her. Sebastian, knife in hand, turned to them, a repulsive snarl on his face. Lyssa had to be right. Sebastian wouldn't have done this.

Dorian charged him, avoided a knife swing, and then tried to wrestle the weapon from Sebastian.

Belwynn barely cared. Her eyes fixed on Elana. The priestess's eyes were open, and she was looking back. She mouthed 'Belwynn'. In a daze, as if she was in her own nightmare now, Belwynn walked to her, kneeling in the blood. She located the wound in Elana's side, putting her hand to it to try to stop any more from leaking out.

'Can't you heal yourself?' she asked desperately.

There was a crash behind her. Dorian had been thrown to one side, the knife clattering across the floor, and Sebastian, with a final look at Belwynn and Elana, ran from the room. Dorian got to his feet. 'I'll get him,' he said and gave chase.

It was deathly quiet in the room.

'Belwynn,' came Elana's voice, weak and breathy. 'There isn't much time. I need you to hold my hands.'

Belwynn grabbed one of Elana's hands and put it to the injured side of the priestess. 'Here. You are on the wound. Heal yourself.'

Elana smiled. It was gentle and full of sadness. 'I can't, Belwynn. Hold my hands. Please.'

Belwynn shook her head. No. This wasn't happening. Elana wasn't going to die.

She took Elana's hand back, sticky with blood. She held Elana's other hand. Elana closed her eyes. A shudder ran through her and she winced in pain.

Belwynn felt something, it felt like a tiny spark in her mind. Some sensation, not quite an itch, or a pain, in the back of her head. A presence.

Then the sensation started to grow and swell, filling her mind, her head, her heart, her body, then her soul. It blazed throughout her like a fire, and it burned like one, blinding her. She cried out in pain, overcome by the force that had entered her. She thought she could hear Soren's voice calling to her, but she couldn't focus on anything, her senses overwhelmed. She knew she was going to lose consciousness. She tried to pull her hands free of Elana, but it was too late.

***

STRATON SLUMPED on his bed, a snot-filled handkerchief by his side, a half-finished meal on the floor. His cold had stolen his appetite and he had no energy for anything, so he sat on his bed, staring about his room, brooding.

Since the defeat he had lurched from impotent rage to a lethargic despair and back again, and this torment, coupled with his confinement, had made him ill. It was a gilded cage he had been given, under guard in his own rooms, treated with the utmost respect, nothing but the very best from the kitchens delivered every day. He would rather have been given a prison cell in the dungeons for everyone to see the truth. But Theron was too clever for that. He had imprisoned the royal family here in their own castle, and yet no doubt the citizens were falling over themselves to praise him for his magnanimity.

The door opened and a knight stepped into the room.

'Excuse me, Your Highness. You have a visitor.'

Straton looked up in a disinterested way.

Dorian. The one member of the family not kept under lock and key, strolling around Heractus without a care in the world.

He looked full of purpose, staring at the knight until the door was shut and they were left alone.

'What do you want?' Straton demanded.

Dorian looked about the room, his eyes coming to rest on the plate of food, the handkerchief, and finally on Straton.

'I've come to get you out of here.'

Straton laughed. There was something absurdly funny about that.

'You've come to rescue me? Where were you when I was fighting for our family against the Knights? When your help might have actually made a difference?'

Dorian showed no remorse. Instead, he walked over to the bed. He grabbed Straton by the front of his shirt.

'Quit whining,' he said, a look of utter contempt on his face.

Straton didn't know how to react.

'You've allowed the Knights to walk all over you, and ruined every opportunity you had to regain control.'

This was so unlike Dorian, so unexpected, that all Straton could do was stare into the seething anger of his brother's twisted features.

'I'm going to make you king, so get out of your pit and do what I tell you.'

XV

BETRAYAL

IT WAS A SOMBRE GATHERING in Maragin's hall, in the high lands of the Grendal clan. Rabigar could take no pleasure from his return to the place where he was raised, despite the flood of memories that assailed him as he once more entered rooms, strode past buildings, looked out on the stark mountain views, that had then been the daily sights of his youth. For, despite their victory in Haskany some eight months ago, the Krykkers had effectively been defeated in a matter of days. The dead littered the mountain slopes of his homeland: butchered by Drobax, burned by dragon fire.

'There is only one location open to us,' Maragin argued. 'The Isharites may fall on Kalinth at any time. The Empire and Guivergne will also fall to a sustained attack, and we cannot be sure that our people will be welcome there for a long spell. We must evacuate to our cousins in Halvia.'

Most reluctantly agreed, having come to the same conclusion. If that decision was easy enough, the logistics of it certainly weren't. It would involve the Krykker people travelling across the Lantinen Sea, with the risk of being targeted by the Kharovian fleet. If it went wrong, it could be catastrophic.

'What of my people?' asked Kelemen.

Rabigar studied him. He had that fierce look that comes when you have gone past exhaustion and you are living off your last reserves. His people had already come close to being wiped out by the Isharites. There were even less of them left now.

'Would they give us sanctuary?' he asked.

'I would say so,' said Rabigar. 'They have given such sanctuary to the Vismarians, and that people could hold the key for us. When we visited, they told us they still had ships. If the warships of the Sea Caladri can keep the Kharovians away, the Vismarians could help to transport our people across the Lantinen.'

'What say you, Captain Sebo?' Kelemen asked the Sea Caladri captain.

'We were given orders to only engage the Kharovians if necessary,' Sebo said. 'But at that time, our Council had no way of knowing that the fate of our cousins, not to mention the Krykker people, would be at stake in such a way. We are ready to do whatever it takes. I suggest a crossing of the Lantinen now. I will need to speak with the Vismarian captains and agree a strategy. What we are suggesting is a very complicated manoeuvre.'

'Are you suggesting your whole fleet sails again?' asked Maragin.

'No. That would be too risky, and may alert the Kharovians to our plans. I will take Red Serpent across on a night-time voyage, to avoid being seen.'

'I'll go with you,' said Rabigar. 'The people there know me now. I'll persuade the Vismarians to help us.'

'So be it,' said Maragin. 'Meanwhile, we continue the evacuation. The Grendals will hold the mountain passes for as long as possible. Our people are to be gathered in the lands of clan Swarten, ready for the crossing. We need those ships, Rabigar, or it will be a massacre.'

***

MONEVA STOOD next to Gyrmund, looking on as the fighters entered the roped area for the Contest.

Gansukh's fourth day, and the opponents were starting to appear thick and fast now, the best of the best arguing over who should be the one to kill him. Bolormaa had warned them of this. If Gansukh lasted seven days, he was khan. Those who did not wish to bend the knee to a superior would risk their lives between the ropes, to end the threat to their independence.

Qadan was the man who had won the right to defeat Gansukh today. He was huge, towering at least six inches taller than his opponent, with broad shoulders and huge limbs. His mount was the largest Jalakh horse Moneva had seen—it had to be to carry that weight and still be able to move fast enough to compete in the Contest.

A roar erupted as he was introduced, and not just from his own tribe. The area was heaving with Jalakhs from all tribes, many keen to see Gansukh defeated, others wondering whether they were witnessing history being made, with the making of a new khan.

Bolormaa and Soren sat next to each other, ready to use their powers to help Gansukh to another victory. They would be opposed by any sorcerers from Qadan's tribe, and, Bolormaa had warned, others who wanted Gansukh to lose.

The shout went out and the two combatants charged forwards to meet in the centre, horses circling, curved swords swirling. Qadan was faster than Moneva thought possible for his size, his blade sizzling forwards to attack and moving across to parry with what looked like relaxed ease. He was not, perhaps, quite as agile as Gansukh. But his blows were stronger, forcing Gansukh to move back or to the side. They allowed Qadan to go on the offensive more often than not, dictating the pattern of the fight.

She looked across to Soren, recognising the signs of strain that showed he was using his powers in an effort to blunt Qadan's attacking prowess. Then, a new expression appeared on his face, one of surprise, or shock.

Moneva nudged at Gyrmund, telling him to look at Soren.

Then, suddenly, the sorcerer shuddered, and shouted out loud.

'Belwynn?' he shouted.

He looked about him desperately, blindly, as if she might be here.

Moneva and Gyrmund rushed over to him, as the members of the Oligud tribe he was sat with stared at him.

'What is it?' Gyrmund asked Soren, kneeling next to him.

'Belwynn!' he shouted out loud again, then slumped over.

Moneva caught him and laid him down on the ground. She placed Onella's Staff back into his hands, hoping that the weapon might revive him, but it seemed to have no effect.

'I don't understand,' she said to Gyrmund. 'Why shout out Belwynn's name?'

He shrugged, no wiser than she was.

Next to Soren, Bolormaa was visibly sweating as she concentrated on her son's fight, lacking the support that Soren had been providing until now.

Moneva turned to the fight. She wasn't surprised to see Qadan gaining the upper hand now, driving Gansukh back, his defence getting more desperate. Then, a brutal blow landed on Gansukh's shoulder, smashing through his scale armour and cutting into flesh. A gasp emerged from the crowd. Gansukh reeled backwards but somehow stayed on his horse, weaving away from Qadan's follow up attacks. Excited talk babbled across the crowd, as they discussed the wound that Qadan had inflicted. Even if Gansukh didn't die right now, his quest to become khan seemed over. Moneva knew it wasn't the gash itself, so much as the damage to Gansukh's movement that was the issue.

If he couldn't move his shoulder and arm properly, he would have no chance of defending against further attacks. The situation was critical.

Gyrmund knelt down to Soren, talking in his ear, even giving him a slap on the face in an effort to wake him.

Moneva could see tears in Bolormaa's eyes, but she maintained her focus. Her face was red with effort.

Qadan and Gansukh clashed again. Gansukh made no attempt to attack, his energies directed at moving, guiding his horse this way and that, unbalancing Qadan so that he failed to land a clear blow. It was an impressive display of horsemanship, but it was surely only a matter of time before Qadan landed a second blow. And that might be it.

Soren stirred, mumbling incoherently.

Desperate, Moneva and Gyrmund lifted him into a sitting position.

'Belwynn?' he asked drowsily.

'Soren,' said Moneva. 'We need you to focus on the fight right now. Gansukh is injured.'

Soren frowned. She saw his knuckles turn white as he squeezed his staff, perhaps drawing on its energy to revive himself. He opened his eyes and stared at the fight ahead of him.

Gansukh parried Qadan's blows, but he was getting weaker. He couldn't lift his arm properly. Qadan was growing frustrated, trying to batter his way through Gansukh's flimsy looking defence, his chest heaving with the exertion, his horse's sides lathered in sweat.

Then, Gansukh turned it around. He went to parry a blow, dodged it instead, then flicked his blade at Qadan's wrist. Qadan managed to hold onto his sword but Gansukh was on to him, lightning fast, sending blows to the left, then the right, at his face, then his sword arm. Qadan never completely recovered, desperately trying to get back to neutral. Gansukh faked a high blow, circling around instead, then plunging his sword into the horse's neck, before withdrawing it in a fountain of blood.

As the horse fell, Qadan somehow managed to land on his feet, charging at Gansukh in a final bid for victory. Gansukh's horse didn't need to be told what to do, skipping out of the way, and as Qadan's blow fell way too short, Gansukh chopped his scimitar down, the razor-sharp edge cutting through bone and detaching his enemy's sword-hand from his arm.

Qadan stood there briefly, gazing at his raised stump, in apparent disbelief that the fight had ended in such a way, before Gansukh finished the job.

The Oliguds cheered, rushing to the ropes to guide their champion back to the embrace of his tribe.

Bolormaa, shaky on her feet, immediately ordered that Gansukh be sat down and his wound inspected. Her son had won, but she wore the face of defeat.

She tutted at the injury as Gansukh was cut out of his armour. He needed rest for it to heal, but if he was to become khan, he had to fight again tomorrow. And his opponent would know exactly where to target.

'It's over,' Bolormaa muttered, but Gansukh raged at her, saying he would never withdraw.

'Her husband died on the fifth day,' Gyrmund said quietly for only Moneva to hear.

They turned away from the scene and went to check on Soren.

He was still sitting on the ground, his staff resting on his knees, a dazed expression on his face.

'You called out Belwynn's name?' Moneva asked him.

'Something's happened to her,' he said dully. 'Something-,' he paused, looking up at them, as if trying to find the right words, and then giving up. 'Something I don't understand. She's not replying to me.'

'Did she say anything?' Moneva asked. She felt a sense of dread. They shouldn't have left Belwynn and Elana alone for this long. It had been a bad mistake. She knew, as much as anyone perhaps, what the Isharites could do. Heractus wasn't safe.

'No. I felt her pain, a sense of loss. And I felt something else. It reminded me of Samir Durg,' he said, his face ashen, 'when Siavash was inside my head.'

A sense of helplessness came over Moneva then, a feeling she had sworn she would never tolerate again. All this time wasted, and they were still no closer to getting their hands on the Jalakh Bow, their one chance fading away in front of their eyes.

She walked over to Bolormaa. The woman looked exhausted, observing her son's wound being cleaned before they would sew it up.

'I need to talk with you,' said Moneva.

Bolormaa looked up at her. She seemed ready to tell Moneva to get lost, before relenting, and the two of them walked away from the crowd gathered about Gansukh.

'We need to try something else,' Moneva said. She didn't have to explain why. Gansukh had barely come through that fight, and no-one expected him to win tomorrow. 'Show me the main challengers to Gansukh; the men who are likely to enter the Contest tomorrow.'

'Why?' asked Bolormaa. 'What will that achieve?'

'I'll make sure they never make it to the ropes.'

Bolormaa stopped walking, instead looking Moneva in the eye. Moneva didn't look away. What was the woman's problem? Had her suggestion gone too far, challenged some sacred rule that Bolormaa wasn't prepared to break?

'Very well,' said Bolormaa at last. 'I will show you.'

***

EIGHTEEN OF them crossed from Kalinth into Persala. Eight Barbarians; five Persaleians; two men of Rotelegen; two Dog-men; and a Magnian. Clarin decided they'd go no farther this day. It seemed a decent place to stop for the night.

A cluster of buildings on the Persaleian side marked the border. Here the authorities used to regulate traffic passing between the two countries, but they were now abandoned. Trade was dead, and the Persaleian government destroyed when the Haskans had invaded and taken the capital, Baserno. They could only speculate about who was in charge now. A Drobax army had been seen crossing from Persala into the lands of the Grand Caladri days ago. That suggested that both Haskany and Persala were now firmly back under the control of the Isharites.

Either the people who lived here hadn't left in a hurry, or someone else had come since and cleaned the place out, because there was nothing much to show for it after they carried out a sweep of the buildings. Still, the inn was cosy, with a good roof. Spring was different this far north compared to Magnia. The days were pleasant enough, but the nights were cold. Cyprian got a fire going in the hearth and they all made their beds in the main hall. Clarin organised two lookouts at a time, in two-hour shifts, and everyone enjoyed a comfortable first night.

When the sun appeared they continued east, using a road that Zared confirmed would take them to Baserno. As they walked along, Clarin quizzed him about his country. Cyprian, Clarin knew, came from the east of Persala, the port city of Lumberco, whereas Zared had told him he had lived in the capital. He would know the area better than anyone else.

'How long will it take us to get to Baserno?'

'At this pace, with no interruptions, three days.'

'What have you heard of the Persaleian Shield?'

'Nothing. This long-ago war against the Isharites you speak of—alliances with Krykkers and Caladri, magic weapons—it's not a story that Persaleians know. Our history begins with Avilius, founder of Persala. We then conquered the north: alone, not with allies; by force of arms, not with magic. Two centuries after Avilius, our armies drove the Drobax away at the Battle of the Tarn. If this war fought with magic weapons did happen, it was before our empire was born.'

Clarin didn't really know his history, not like people such as Soren. Although Belwynn had told him what the Caladri wise man, Szabolcs, had said in Coldeberg, he was more than vague on the when of the story.

'If it did exist,' he persisted, 'forgotten somewhere, where would it have been kept?'

'Baserno. There are two obvious locations: the Imperial Palace, or the Temple of Ludovis. The Temple has a depository where the wealthy can store their money and possessions. It's known to contain many ancient artefacts.'

'Have you been?'

'I've been to the Temple plenty of times. But my family never had anything worth putting into the depository, nor do I know where exactly the items are kept. That's a secret kept by the priests, because the riches held there would be a target for thieves.'

Clarin knew he wasn't the smartest. He'd always been content to leave the thinking to people like Herin and Soren. But he had worked out there was more to Zared than the young man let on. He said his family had modest wealth, that his father was a shopkeeper. But at some point, he had been trained to fight properly. Then, there was the fact that the rest of the Persaleians deferred to him, despite his young age. There was something he wasn't telling Clarin. No doubt he had his reasons. And as long as he helped Clarin to find the Shield, which he'd promised he would, did it really matter?

156

They followed the road to Baserno. This part of Persala was sparsely settled, heath and gorse stretching out in every direction. A good morning's walk saw them approaching a settlement. Zared named it Bineto, a town that straddled the road to Baserno. He described it a focal point for the local area, as well as a market for Kalinthian traders in years past.

Clarin deliberated over their tactics one last time. His instincts told him to skirt around the town, but Zared and the Persaleians argued against this.

'From now on,' Zared said, 'there will be town after town, then cities. There is no countryside we can hide in: this is Persala. Either we pass through these places or we give up.'

Zared's plan was simply to boldly walk into Bineto. Once there, they would get a feel for the situation. If challenged, they would pose as soldiers serving Ishari. Clarin knew they had a chance of getting away with such a ruse. The Isharites had humans in their armies. But the two Dog-men were key. It was known that their kind served Ishari, so their presence made such a claim more convincing. Zared would do the talking if his countrymen began to ask questions. But if it didn't work, they would be in serious trouble, seriously fast.

And it wasn't just that. The farther they got into Persala, the more Zared was gaining control over what they did, and the more Clarin was fading into the background. Had he made a mistake coming here in the first place?

Clarin sighed, shaking himself out of his introspection. They were here now, and Zared's plan was the only one they had. It was pointless to think about it anymore. They walked for Bineto.

Bineto had known better times, that was for sure. The streets were filthy, uncared for. Many of the houses were run down, if not empty, and when they got into the town centre many of the shops were boarded up. The townsfolk had a sullen, fearful look about them. They made for the market area, where a few stalls huddled together in one corner of the square, the rest of it empty.

Zared and Cyprian moved over to the stallholders with purpose, hailing them in loud, confident voices, as if they were meant to be here. The following conversations were quieter, and Clarin, stood with the rest of the group out of earshot, looked about them and tried to think.

There were no soldiers here. That said something. The Isharites had sent an army south—they were set on conquest. They wouldn't want to waste men occupying the towns of Persala if they didn't have to. From what Zared said, there were many settlements bigger than Bineto. It suggested that they would likely be unoccupied, too. The population were cowed, serving their new masters. Should a rebellion stir, troops would be sent in to put it down, from the larger centres such as Baserno. Clarin nodded to himself, feeling like he was gaining a sense of the state of the country. A large population, defeated and leaderless, no doubt many pressed into the Isharite armies. Relatively few occupying troops—just enough to keep them submissive. It was possible, in such a place, for them to pass through unchallenged. To somehow make their way into Baserno. And once there? They had to find a shield that no-one knew existed.

The three Persaleians returned, arms full of loaves of bread and rounds of cheese that they had purchased from their compatriots.

'Well?' asked Clarin.

'Not very talkative—suspicious, as you might expect,' said Zared. 'Siavash is in charge in Samir Durg, his opponents dead or fled. Haskany has no king or queen any more, the country is said to be as reduced as Persala is. The people here pay heavy taxes, mostly in foodstuffs and other items for the armies. Many of the younger men have been recruited to fight, making life harder for those who remain. Other than that, so long as they do what they are told, they are generally left alone.'

'The other towns are likely to be the same?' Clarin asked.

'Yes.'

'Good. Then let's get moving. The sooner we leave, the sooner these people forget we were ever here.'

They continued east, stopping at places much like Bineto. Each town had the same layout, central plazas surrounded by parallel roads. Some were larger, some smaller, but in its essentials their experience was the same at each one. Communities that were suffering, but somehow surviving, under Isharite rule. Zared spoke with the people: sometimes it was traders, at other times mayors or other dignitaries, even passers-by on the street going about their own business. They were cautious, wary of strangers. When pressed, each said the next town along was the same as them. In one town, a place called Pontecchio, they spent the night in a row of empty houses, their occupants either taken away by Isharite soldiers, or had left of their own accord, trying to make a better living elsewhere.

The next morning Zared announced a change of plan.

'There's news of soldiers in the next city,' he explained. 'It would be better for us to detour around it, just in case. It only involves going down some less travelled roads to other settlements, and then cutting back to the main road, bypassing the city. It will add no more than two hours travel time.'

They set off. A small road, better described as a track, took them north of Pontecchio, where they soon found themselves passing the well-tended fields of the Persaleian countryside. It seemed to Clarin that in the rural areas, life carried on not so much different than it had before.

There was something about the outdoors that made Clarin feel better about things. His mind wandered to Belwynn, how he had made a right mess of things in Heractus. He had genuinely thought that he would declare his love, she would return it, and they would settle down on a farm somewhere to live out their days. In hindsight, he had been stupid. She was with Theron now. And maybe, he just had to admit to himself that she was better off that way. That didn't mean it didn't hurt, though. He had already lost Herin. Those were the two people in the world who really meant anything to him.

'We'll head up here,' Zared said from the front, speaking in a voice loud enough to carry to everyone. He was pointing towards a steep slope that led up to a mound. 'We can get a decent view of the area from up there, check we're going the right way.'

Wordlessly, the group followed Zared and the Persaleians up to the top of the mound. It was tough going, Clarin's thigh muscles protesting by the time they got to the top. The group shrugged packs off shoulders and looked around.

There were, indeed, good views of the surrounding countryside. A pile of stones, some very large, had been placed in the middle of the mound. Clarin walked over to inspect it, making his legs stretch out a little after the climb. They had definitely been carried up, he decided. Maybe they were atop a burial chamber of some kind. It reminded him of the vossi mound in the Wilderness, where they had been surrounded by the creatures, close to defeat, before Soren had cast a spell to scare them off. Maybe once, many years ago, vossi had lived here. Or some other group of humans. Or Caladri, or Lippers. Maybe this mound was the most important place in the world to them. Now, no-one even knew what it was.

'Clarin!' came a shout, urgent sounding.

He turned to see Jurgen gesturing at him. He and Rudy were at one end of the mound, looking down the slope.

Clarin ran over, one hand on the hilt of his sword. Men in armour, holding spears, were making their way slowly up the mound, looking up at them. They were spread out, all along the base of the mound.

The Dog-men barked a warning. Turning, Clarin looked at their position a few feet away. He didn't need to go over to confirm that there were men there too. They were surrounded.

At the far end of the mound, where Zared and the Persaleians had positioned themselves, armed men had already made it to the top of the slope. Zared and his men were helping them up.

Clarin took a few paces towards them. Zared gave him an apologetic look.

A spearman stood next to Zared, as big and strong looking as Clarin, with a huge shield. He pointed his spear in Clarin's direction, then at the other members of the group, as more soldiers crested the mound behind him.

'We're going to need you to drop your weapons.'

XVI

EXODUS

THE CALADRI WARSHIPS had already put to sea. Their role was to offer protection to the armada that would transport the Krykker people—plus the Grand Caladri refugees—across the Lantinen. This armada consisted of the Caladri trading vessels, and the Vismarian fleet, which had crossed the Lantinen with Red Serpent. Rabigar had asked for their help, and they had given it. Their leader, Sevald, the same man who had spoken at the Krykker moot, hadn't wasted time debating it, or demanded anything in return; they had gathered their ships and sailors and set off immediately. Rabigar would always be grateful to them for that.

Rabigar stood with Maragin, looking down on the long, patient line of Krykkers, waiting their turn to embark on foreign ships. It was natural to think that they had somehow failed their people. But even now, a wave of Drobax, unstoppable in number, roamed over their lands. And wherever the Grendals had manned mountain passes to fight this plague, the dragon had arrived. Destroying their forces, burning Krykker and Drobax alike until the passes were cleared, only grey ash was left as a sign of its passing.

Maragin had put an end to using her soldiers in such a way. She had blocked all the entrances and tunnels that led underground, except for the one they now stood by. She had conceded all of her clan's territory above ground to the invaders. Halls, houses, fields; all were lost. Whatever could be saved, had been taken underground. Enough food to feed a small army. Underground wells provided an endless supply of water. The Krykker resistance would continue. They would never give up their homeland.

It was time to close the last entrance, before the Drobax reached them. Maragin ordered her soldiers to set fire to the wooden props they had put in place underground. Once they gave way, the walls would collapse, and a tonne of stone come crashing down where they now stood. It was time to clear the area. Maragin had chosen a thousand Krykkers who would stay behind. Many of them were rock walkers, capable of forcing their bodies through Krykker rock. Rabigar allowed himself a grim smile at the thought of them emerging, with night as cover, to slaughter the Drobax above ground, before disappearing again. He wished he could be with them. But as Maragin had said, he had other responsibilities.

He paced backwards, taking a last look at Maragin, before she disappeared into the darkness of the tunnel behind her.

He kept moving back. He felt the ground shake, and saw small stones and debris sift down the wall of rock above the tunnel entrance, as the ground underneath it began to weaken. Then, without further warning, the rock gave way. Huge chunks of it cascaded down towards him, and he skipped backwards faster to avoid the cloud of dust that came behind. He knew that the same thing had happened inside the tunnel.

He waited a while, allowing the dust to settle. The wall and the entrance had disappeared, replaced by an untidy jumble of cracked rock. The Drobax wouldn't even know that an entrance had once stood there, never mind be able to clear a way inside. There was nothing else for Rabigar to see here. Finally, he turned around, and made his way down to the harbour.

Here Hakonin, leader of the Swarten clan, was organising the evacuation of a whole people. The pier was full of Vismarian ships and Caladri traders getting loaded. Once full, they would cast off and sail out to sea, while the next vessel would steer its way in to replace it.

'Get on the next ship,' Rabigar said to Hakonin. 'We need to make sure you get across. You're in charge now.'

'Is it done?' Hakonin asked, looking up at the rocky scree where the tunnel had stood a few moments before.

'It's done. It worked. They won't get in that way.'

Hakonin nodded. He signalled to his household troops, who stood in a group along with family members, and they made their way down to the harbour, identifying a Caladri trader that looked large enough to hold them all.

That was the last of the stragglers. Everyone else was already in the line, waiting their turn for the next ship. They had nearly done it. Only the crossing itself to go, and they would have pulled off a remarkable logistical feat.

Then he heard the noise. Turning, he looked back towards the rocks. He saw nothing, but he knew what he had heard. Drobax.

'They're coming,' he whispered to himself.

Rabigar placed a hand on the hilt of Bolivar's Sword. He would make a stand here if necessary.

162

The noise came again, the shouts of thousands of Drobax, echoing down to the shore from the mountains. Rabigar still couldn't see anything, but with only one eye he knew that didn't mean they weren't visible to others.

The Krykkers in the line for the ships had heard it this time, and panicked voices reached him, urging those ahead to go faster. He turned to look.

'Calm yourselves!' he barked. The last thing they needed after all this was a last-minute stampede for the boats. They were Krykkers. They were better than that.

Some of the Krykkers left the line to stand with him, ready to fight if need be.

'Can you see anything?' he asked one of them, a man half his own age.

'They're on the high ridge, some already past it. They've seen us.'

Rabigar nodded. 'Then they may get here before all the ships have left. We must keep them away.'

'I'll fight with you, Rabigar Din,' the man said.

Rabigar grunted.

They waited, a thin line of Krykkers, Rabigar straining his eye to see, until he saw movement high up. The Drobax were moving fast, keen to get to them before all the ships were cast off. But they were in a disorganised mess, not moving in regiments, but in ones and twos. Rabigar was sure they would be able to hold them off for a while. He looked anxiously into the sky. So long as the dragon didn't make an appearance.

'Look!' someone shouted, pointing.

Rabigar turned to see. Those Drobax who were nearest were under attack. Emerging from the rocks, groups of Krykkers intercepted them. The Drobax behind screamed in anger, their attention diverted to the new threat.

Maragin's rock walkers. Their intervention was already working.

Rabigar smiled.

'We'll be fine. Come on, let's go.'

They returned to their positions in the line. They all cast the odd look behind them now and again. The rock walkers had disappeared, but they had done their job.

The line was diminishing, and soon Rabigar found himself boarding the last ship, a Vismarian vessel. It was big enough to take on the remaining Krykkers, though to Rabigar it didn't have the same feeling of stability he had experienced on Red Serpent. Still, if it got them across the Lantinen he wasn't going to complain.

Taking a place on deck, Rabigar made himself look back towards his homeland. So recently he had gained the right to return, after half a lifetime as an exile. And now he had been forced out again.

There, the first of the Drobax had descended from the rocky scree to the shoreline, looking out at their escaped quarry. Forced out of his home by those creatures. He made himself look, holding on to the image, so that when he needed to, he could recall it and use his anger to do whatever he had to. Because whatever it took, he would return his people to their homeland. That was his vow.

Sunlight reflected off the deep blue of the ocean. The sound of oars hitting water filled Rabigar's ears, as the Vismarian ship followed the rest of the armada west across the Lantinen Sea. Dalriya receded from view and the world of the Krykkers contracted to a few tiny ships bobbing up and down on the waves.

It may be that my people have never been so vulnerable, Rabigar told himself. Krykkers were used to having the safety of rock underneath their feet, if not all around them. Here they were in an alien, dangerous environment, and they wouldn't be safe until they made landfall in Halvia.

Somewhere to the north, not visible from Rabigar's ship, the Sea Caladri warships patrolled, protecting them from a Kharovian attack.

The hours passed, the sun gradually withdrew, making the horizon turn orange and the sea purple. But it was still light enough for the Vismarian sailor to spot the smoke to the north.

He raised the alarm and Rabigar, like many others, rushed to the starboard side to look out. He saw one, then two, then half a dozen: great palls of black smoke could be seen rising into the sky.

'What is that?' asked a young woman.

Everyone else shared a look. They all knew.

'The Sea Caladri are out there,' someone answered her. 'The Kharovians have come.'

There was nothing they could do, except tell the crewmen to row harder. Those on deck looked anxiously to the bow, for signs of the Halvian coast, then back to starboard, for signs of the sleek Kharovian warships. Neither came into view. The smoke continued to darken the sky to the north, until the disappearance of the sun made it invisible. Then, they could see fire where the smoke had been. The two great navies of Dalriya were clashing out there, and it was impossible to know which way the battle was going.

At last, they could see lights on the Halvian shore. It was close. Many of their ships must have already landed, and were lighting the way for those that remained. Rabigar could feel the relief flow through the vessel, after hours of anxiety.

But the relief was premature.

For now a sailor called out a second warning, and this time he pointed into the sky.

Rabigar knew it was the dragon before he saw it. Doubtless the creature was responsible for much of the fire and smoke they had seen to the north. It had now flown south, looking to wreak more destruction.

What Rabigar wasn't prepared for was the fear that seemed to roll off the creature down onto the ship. The people on the deck moaned, no longer able to speak. It wasn't possible to say what, exactly, caused it. The shape of the thing, perhaps—the long tail and neck at each end, the outstretched wings. The size of it, unlike any creature they had seen before. That it was airborne, making it faster as well as more powerful than they were. The fact, of course, that they were stuck on a drifting pile of wood, exposed, with no rocks to hide under.

Rabigar succumbed to the fear, just like everyone else. But his hand brushed against the hilt of Bolivar's Sword and the weapon gave him the courage to react. It was just in time.

Its wings furled back and a great roar erupted from its long throat. The sound of death. The dragon dived through the air towards them, a green devil hurtling through a grey sky.

'Into the sea!' Rabigar shouted. 'Get overboard!' He drew his sword, facing the oncoming beast.

Some were able to react quickly enough, running to the sides of the ship. He heard the shouts and splashes as they hurled themselves into the Lantinen, but he didn't see, for his eyes were now trained on the dragon. It was coming right for him, his defiance provoking its wrath.

The dragon opened its maw and flames erupted down onto him. The sudden heat engulfed him, as if he had fallen into a fire. He held Bolivar's

Sword in front of him. Somehow, the weapon protected him from the flames, deflecting them to the sides. Wherever they went, the ship caught fire, ablaze in a matter of seconds. Even though the flames didn't touch him, the heat became too much for Rabigar and he wilted, collapsing to the deck, only just able to keep his sword aloft.

The dragon passed overhead with a screech of fury.

Rabigar was surrounded by flames and now he panicked, unable to see anything but fire and smoke. It got in his eyes, his nose, his lungs. Desperate, he pulled his cloak over his face and began walking. He resisted the urge to run, knowing he could trip, bang his head, and that would be it. He could feel his skin crackling and burning, but still, he moved carefully. A rope, still taut, blocked his passage and he moved around it, before resuming in the same direction. He was rewarded when he bumped into the side of the ship. Still holding Bolivar's Sword, he swung one leg over the side, before half jumping, half falling out of the burning ship.

He plunged into freezing water. He held his breath, trying not to flail about as held onto his weapon for all he was worth, kicking with his legs, until somehow he emerged into cold air, gasping for breath.

He knew enough that he should tread water at first, letting his body adjust to the freezing temperature of the sea. The flames of the ship blinded him, so that he could see nothing else. Fearful, he scanned the sky for the return of the dragon.

He decided he had to move. Krykkers weren't built for water. His heavy torso, encased in its natural armour, pulled him down, and the blade in his hand prevented him from using the smooth, controlled strokes that would have seen him cut through the water. He turned to face the Halvian shoreline and tried to pull himself in that direction, splashing about and not getting very far. Waves crashed into him, preventing him from gaining any kind of rhythm.

He would not let go of Bolivar's Sword. He would not be the Krykker to lose the greatest treasure of his race, the weapon of their greatest hero. He would rather drown with it than wash up on the shore without it.

He looked about him. Ahead was another Vismarian ship, also set alight. To his right and slightly behind him was the burning remains of the ship he had escaped from. He couldn't see anyone else in the rolling black waves.

Wait, Rabigar thought to himself. *Why is the ship so far to the right?*

The sea. The sea is pushing me in that direction. He looked ahead again. He wasn't getting any closer to the Halvian shore, where the rest of his people had set lights to guide the last of the armada. He was being drawn away by the tide.

Rabigar had to fight down the panic that gripped at his insides, that clamped his throat.

He had to swim hard for the shore now, while he still had enough energy. If he left it any longer he would be dragged further out to sea.

Rabigar put his head down and pumped with his arms, kicked with his legs. He threw his head to the side, gulping a breath of air, before pushing ahead again. He didn't waste energy looking about him, checking how far he had got, he just pushed and kicked, his arms burning with the effort, his lungs ready to burst.

He stopped, looked up. He could see the shoreline, but he was still too far away. He put his feet down. Maybe he was close enough to stand? No.

He started swimming again, but he had given everything he had now. He was too tired, unable to move his limbs properly. He felt dizzy. If he lost consciousness now, he would drown. But if he stopped moving, he was dead anyway.

Drop the sword. Part of his mind was telling him to leave the weapon behind, to save himself. *No. Never.*

He gave it one last push, trying to drag his heavy body to shore. He began to sink under. He held his breath. He could see Bolivar's Sword in his right hand ahead of him, sinking down with him. At least he hadn't let go of the sword, he told himself idly, as the oxygen began to leave his brain. At least they would drown together. That was some comfort.

It was time to give up now. He'd done his best.

Then Rabigar was pulled up, his head breaking through the water, and he took a choking mouthful of air.

Strong hands clamped onto him and picked him up, his whole body leaving the sea.

He looked about, head lolling, feeling impossibly high, as he was carried towards the shore. He heard the slosh of legs walking through shallow water, saw the sandy beach, and suddenly he was flying straight towards it as whoever carried him threw him onto the sand.

Rabigar lay there for a while, unable to move, like a fish out of water.

His hand twitched. He was still holding the sword. He was alive and he still had Bolivar's Sword. It gave him a final spark of energy.

He pushed himself up onto his hands and knees. Half a mile down the beach dancing light caught his eye. When he looked he saw that the shoreline was aflame. The dragon had torched the armada. The Vismarian fleet, saved from the Kharovians, was now destroyed. Just like the ships of the Sea Caladri.

He heard a wheezing sound and turned to look in the other direction.

Rabigar got such a shock he let go of his sword. Stood in the flickering shadows cast by the bonfire behind him, bent over, hands on knees as it got its breath back, was the largest human he had ever seen. At least eight feet tall, it was large in every respect, seawater dripping down from its hair and clothes like a sea monster that had emerged from the depths.

And, for some reason the most shocking of all, it was a woman. This woman had literally picked him up and carried him to the shore. She was still bent double, chest heaving from the exertion. Despite everything that had happened, Rabigar couldn't help but look at her chest heaving up and down, for like everything else about her, it was unfathomably large.

She turned her head, standing up to tower over him, before putting her hands on her hips.

'Well, I've found a right one here, haven't I?' she asked him. 'Bloody dragon come and burned us all to bits, and all you can do is stare at me tits!'

XVII

COMEBACK KINGS

TIME IS A STRANGE ENEMY, Farred mused, as the Kellish countryside slipped by on either side.

Everyone agreed that the fastest way to get to Essenberg from Guivergne was by river barge, but it didn't feel like it when you were sat on the deck, impatiently waiting to reach your destination. Their pace was determined by the flow of the Cousel, and there was little that could be done to alter it. If he had taken the roads, on horseback, at least he would have felt like he was doing something to get there faster.

Farred was satisfied that he had given the Guivergnais good warning of the threat they faced to the north. The Drobax had overwhelmed the lands of the Grand Caladri and had now turned on the Krykkers. They were unlikely to stop there. Moreover, the Isharites had sent a flying monster, that the Grand Caladri had identified as a dragon. They had told Farred in no uncertain terms that the beast was unstoppable.

The Duke of Martras, whose province bordered the Lantinen Sea, was quick to understand the stakes. He had accompanied Farred to the capital, Valennes, to speak with the king, Nicolas. Farred had found Nicolas to be withdrawn and suspicious. He had looked sceptical at Farred's talk of dragons. Well, so be it. Farred had done his part. It was now up to the Guivergnais to defend themselves as best they could.

Eventually, the walls of mighty Essenberg came into view. Baldwin's Bridge towered above them, spanning the Cousel. Two catapults were trained on the river, ready to sink any craft deemed hostile. Emperor Baldwin had built the defences when Guivergne was considered to be Brasingia's greatest threat. To Farred it seemed that such petty rivalries now belonged to an age long gone. But a mere two years ago everyone here would have agreed that the Guivergnais were the national enemy. Time was playing tricks on them all.

The bargemen shouted up to the soldiers, who waved them under the bridge and allowed them to dock inside the city walls. Passengers were allowed off first, and soon Farred was standing on the harbour of the Market Quarter, saying his farewells. He wasted no time in joining the Valennes Road, passing the market stalls, stacked with greens and other vegetables. The food purveyors were roasting lamb with mint and his mouth drooled at the smell of it. He forced himself to walk on, taking the Albert Bridge, the main thoroughfare across the Cousel.

From the north bank he could see the whitewashed, square towers of Essenberg Castle. He made straight for it, walking down streets lined with the opulent town houses of the merchant and noble classes. The central square opened up before him, and his gaze was drawn to the fluttering flag of the Empire atop the castle. A stag, with seven antler tips, each representing a duchy of the Empire. Only four of those duchies had fought for the Empire at Burkhard Castle last summer. But the sickness at the heart of the Empire had been cut out, thanks to the intervention of Farred's prince, Edgar. Emeric was dead and his duchy of Barissia was now in the hands of the Emperor's brother, Walter.

One of the more welcome things that had come from Farred's role in the defence of Burkhard Castle was that he was on close terms with many of the most powerful men in the Empire. So that when he presented himself at the castle, it didn't take long for the chain of command to respond to his arrival.

Rainer, Baldwin's chamberlain, came to meet him personally. He was a reassuring figure: tall, intelligent, with a firm grasp on facts and figures. He wasn't entirely surprised to hear Farred's news.

'We know that Siavash has won control over Ishari. Gustav has warned us of great armies marching south. He is travelling back and forth to the northern realms, so that we have some warning of an invasion. We are expecting it soon. Duke Walter has already based himself at Burkhard, readying its defences.'

Farred remembered watching the Drobax leave Burkhard Castle. He had known then that they would return, but the thought of having to go back there so soon, and face it all over again, made him feel sick.

Rainer read his expression. 'It's not an easy path we have. To my shame, part of me feels glad that the Drobax have hit our allies first, because it buys us a bit more time. The Emperor—he carries the biggest burden of all of us. It is no surprise that he has been suffering with the responsibility. I think it will do him good to hear your news from you, Farred, rather than listening to the same old voices. He has begun to blank us out rather.'

Farred wasn't sure what Rainer meant by that.

'Would you be willing to wait here while I fetch him?' the chamberlain asked.

Farred agreed, somewhat unsettled by the exchange.

Some time passed before Rainer returned, alone.

'The Emperor has asked that you come to his rooms,' said Rainer, looking uneasy.

Farred gave his consent and followed the chamberlain along corridors and up stairs, keeping pace with the lanky official, who no doubt made such journeys several times a day.

Arriving on a quiet corridor, Rainer rapped on a wooden door. A murmur came from behind the door, and the chamberlain opened it, gesturing Farred inside.

'His Imperial Majesty, Emperor Baldwin,' Rainer said, looking red-faced. 'Lord Farred is here.'

As Farred stepped into the room he saw that the emperor was lounging on a bed, wearing shorts and with a bare torso. A fire was going in one wall, making the room unusually hot, and smoky. Sharing the bed was Inge, the young apprentice to Gustav. She wore a silk dress and they each held a wine glass, a bottle and nibbles in front of them on a wooden tray.

He recalled a similar scene last summer in Burkhard Castle, where they had shared a room. Baldwin had been asleep, and Inge had seemed to enjoy intimating to Farred that they were sleeping together. But that had been at Burkhard Castle, during a siege when Baldwin had every reason to believe he had days to live. This was in the royal castle, when presumably his wife and children were in the same building.

'Farred!' exclaimed Inge, 'it's so good to see you again!' Her mocking tone put him on edge, but Baldwin didn't seem to hear it.

'Indeed!' Baldwin agreed. 'I will never forget the debt I owe you, Lord Farred. Rainer barely had to twist my arm at all to persuade me to see you. Even though I understand your news is sure to sour my mood.'

'I am afraid so, Your Majesty,' said Farred, bowing slightly.

Baldwin waved a hand at his chamberlain. 'You are dismissed, Rainer.'

Rainer exited the room, gently closing the door behind him.

Farred proceeded to tell Baldwin of his journey with the fleet of the Sea Caladri, of Rabigar's expedition to Halvia. He finished with the invasion of the Grand Caladri and Krykker lands by the Drobax, and a fire-breathing dragon.

As he did so, Inge crunched on a handful of nuts from the tray, washing them down with her wine, before refilling her own glass and Baldwin's.

'What adventures you have had!' she said when he was done.

Farred would have liked nothing better than to give the girl a slap. But he realised that she was dangerous. He was certainly no match for her.

'It's not all bad news,' said Baldwin thickly.

Toric only knows how much wine he has consumed, thought Farred.

'The Krykkers are no pushovers, and then the Drobax will have to get through Guivergne before they reach our borders. It's about time they got a taste of what we've had, anyway.'

That didn't sound like the Baldwin Farred knew. Inge gave Farred a little shrug. What did that gesture mean?

There was a knock at the door.

'Yes?' said Baldwin in exasperation, as if tired of constant interruptions.

It was Rainer.

'Your Majesty, your queen is asking after you. She is in the hall. I thought it prudent to come and warn you.'

'Shit,' muttered Baldwin.

'Oh, what does that bitch want now?' sighed Inge.

Baldwin looked torn. He looked from Rainer, to Inge, to Farred, as if unsure what to do.

'It would be a great honour to meet the queen,' Farred said into the silence.

'Of course,' said Baldwin. 'What, you've never met Hannelore? Come, come, Farred, let's see what she wants.'

He leaned over to Inge and they kissed, tongues probing each other's mouths, until Baldwin pulled away, got off the bed, and began to get dressed. It was uncomfortable and odd, Farred not wishing to share a look with anyone else in the room.

He was relieved when the three men left the room, Inge remaining sprawled on the bed.

Rainer led them in the direction of the hall.

'Farred, you were in Coldeberg. You saw Hannelore then, no?'

'I saw her, but we were never formally introduced, Your Majesty. It was a busy couple of days.'

'Ah well, we shall correct that.'

'I admired from afar, however. She is a handsome woman.'

'Mmm? Yes. Big chested, if you like that kind of thing.'

The tone Baldwin used made it clear that he didn't. But it was the words themselves that Farred found so odd; so out of character. Had the strain on the Emperor caused some kind of nervous breakdown? If so, how would that affect the Empire's ability to defend itself?

They crossed a courtyard to the hall. When they got inside, it was empty.

'Where is she?' Baldwin demanded.

'Oh, forgive me, Your Majesty. Perhaps she gave up and returned to her rooms, or went looking for you herself. I will track her down, don't worry.'

Rainer gave Farred a look as he left. Had the chamberlain made it all up to get Baldwin out of the room? If so, that was a dangerous game to be playing.

Baldwin sighed. 'A dragon, you said?' he asked Farred.

Farred nodded. 'I heard reports of it. It turned its victims to ash.'

'Farred, think for a second what such a beast could do to Burkhard Castle. I wonder, if you are willing Farred. I'm asking you because I trust you, and you're the best informed. Walter is at Burkhard now, fixing the defences. Could you ride north and tell him? He's a clever man, my brother. Perhaps, given some time, he could find a way to mitigate this threat. Even if there's not much he can do, I think he needs to be told. As soon as possible. Rainer will arrange everything, supplies and expenses, for your time and efforts.'

Suddenly, it was like Baldwin was back—like he had sobered up. And, given what he had witnessed here, Farred didn't think that saying no to the Emperor was an option.

***

CLARIN SAT cross-legged with the rest of his group at one end of the mound. Armed Persaleians had been set to watch over them. Zared and the rest of his men were nowhere to be seen.

So, Zared had played him for a fool. No doubt he had made contact with these allies in one of the many towns they had passed through, arranging to meet at this very spot, so that they could take Clarin and the others captive.

Why he had done it, well—that was less clear. Would he give Clarin and the others up to the Isharites for some advantage? Maybe. After all they had been through together, Clarin hoped not. He couldn't even find much to reproach himself over. He had trusted Zared to get him to Baserno. Had that been the wrong move? Or the best option, that had turned to shit nonetheless? He couldn't decide.

The big man with the spear and shield came over, looking Clarin over. Clarin stared back. He levelled the spear at Clarin.

'Come. We need to talk.'

Slowly, Clarin got to his feet. He shared a glance with Rudy and Jurgen, with the Barbarians, even the two Dog-men. They gave him steady stares. None was panicking yet. They had all survived Samir Durg, after all.

The two of them walked to the edge of the mound and made their way down, taking care since the slope was steep and it would have been easy to slip and twist an ankle. At the bottom two men were sitting on the ground, looking up at them. Zared and another, a man Clarin hadn't seen before.

Clarin and the spearman walked over, the spearman gesturing that Clarin should sit. Once he did so, the man sat down with them, making it a foursome. Clarin looked at the other two. The man next to Zared was significantly older, with a weathered, soldierly face. But there was a similarity in features that must have been more than coincidence, even down to the loss of hair on top.

The older man offered his hand.

'Clarin, welcome,' he said, his voice dry, tired sounding. 'Zared has just told me much about you and I am honoured to make your acquaintance. I am King Mark of Persala.'

Initially Clarin was shocked, even dubious, looking at the three faces in front of him. Then, it all clicked, and he found himself laughing, at his own slowness as much as anything else.

'And this is your son,' he said, indicating Zared.

Both men smiled then, seemingly pleased with Clarin's reaction.

'I'm sorry for the deception, truly,' Zared said. 'I was captured soon after the invasion of Persala, sent to the mines. The Isharites didn't know who I was, but the other Persaleians in the mines did. Not one of them gave me away. They kept my secret, many to their graves. If I had told you the truth, and it had gone wrong, then those men's bravery would have been for nothing. I hope you can understand.'

Clarin shrugged. 'If you did what you thought was right, I'll not judge you. So, what of the rest of us now? Prisoners?'

'Certainly not,' said Mark. 'I needed to see and speak to my son first, to learn exactly what the situation was. How he managed to get back home. He has told me the story, including your mission here. The Shield of Persala, eh?'

'From what I've been told,' said Clarin, 'by people far cleverer than myself, we need it to defeat the Isharites. Have you heard of it?'

'Of course,' Mark said, sounding insulted. 'I was once king in more than name, you know. Privy to all the secrets of the Persaleian Empire. I know it was kept in the Temple of Ludovis, a relic forgotten by most, though not by the priests—they forget nothing.' He looked at Clarin, a reckless smile coming to his face. 'I'm minded to help you get it, too. But know this. I barely escaped the invasion alive. I've been hunted throughout my country ever since. The Isharites would love to display my head on the walls of the capital, to make it clear to my people that they are in charge. That there is no hope. Like my son,' he said, slapping Zared's thigh affectionately, 'I owe my life to others who have risked theirs for me, some paying the ultimate price. In the last year I've hidden up trees; under floorboards; in a hole in the ground no bigger than the size of a coffin. If I'm going to risk my life, and the lives of those who have stuck by me, I need to know that the price is worth paying.'

Clarin nodded. Mark had a fair few soldiers with him. But if this was all that was left of the once great Persaleian army, that had conquered most of Dalriya once upon a time, it wasn't so many.

Mark seemed to be thinking, finalising his plan. Hopefully, committing to the mission.

'Alright. First, we need to ascertain whether the priests of Ludovis still have the Shield. Second, will they hand it over to us? If they do and they won't, we must be prepared to take it.'

'So, what now?' Zared asked his father.

'Now we all pack up and move out. We're going to Baserno.'

***

BELWYNN WASN'T sure she could get through this. Sebastian's funeral yesterday had been bad enough. But Elana...

She was in the Temple of Madria, sitting on a pew, gripping Theron's hand as tightly as she could, as if that would hold back the tears. It didn't.

175

Bemus was at the front, tall and gangly, his glum voice echoing throughout the building as he recounted stories of how Elana had healed and treated the people of Heractus. How he did it without breaking down, when the room was full of people crying, some even wailing, she couldn't comprehend. The stories went on and on, but they were stories people knew, had witnessed, and that made them all the more powerful. They emphasised, too, just what a loss Elana was. Bemus addressed this too in his service, forcefully arguing that her mission should be continued, would live on. But how could it, Belwynn wanted to ask. Lives that had been saved would now be lost.

The image of Elana dying on the floor returned to her mind again, unasked for but irresistible. She had saved so many, and when she needed help there had been no-one. Just Belwynn, kneeling in the blood; useless. She couldn't shake the thought that it was on her. If she had acted more quickly, to stop the thing that had possessed Sebastian, Elana would still be alive. She was Elana's second disciple, and when Elana had really needed her, when she could have made a difference, she had failed her.

As she lay dying, Elana had clutched her hands. Belwynn wasn't sure what she had wanted, but a strange force had overcome her and she had collapsed, unconscious. When she came around, it was too late. Elana was already dead.

She wanted to leave the temple, to run away. But the least she could do, the very least, was to sit and listen.

Outside, Elana's body was carefully lowered into the ground. Belwynn stayed awhile, to speak with the community, before Theron led her away from the Temple and up to the castle. They held hands as they went, both of them instinctively needing each other's company after the losses they had suffered.

It was hard, but they didn't have the time to grieve properly.

Sebastian's body had been found not long after Elana's death. Dorian, who had chased him from Elana's rooms, had left Heractus, with his older brother Straton. Not everyone wanted to believe it. But Belwynn was sure, and she had made Theron understand too. Some creature, some nightmare sent by the Isharites, had killed Remi and taken his body. Despite a thorough search, his body was still missing. As Remi, the monster had killed Sebastian. They only knew this because little Lyssa had been playing in a secret tunnel and witnessed the murder. As Sebastian, it had killed Elana, and almost certainly Dorian. As Dorian, it had killed two more knights, before leaving the city with Straton in tow. The Isharites had taken their revenge for the Kalinthian invasion of Haskany and for the death of Erkindrix. They had killed Madria's priestess. And the creature was still out there.

More was to come.

Belwynn had come close to despair at Elana's death, had assumed that all hope was lost. But she had talked with Soren and he had turned her around. They still had three of Madria's seven weapons. He believed he was close to getting a fourth. Clarin had gone to Persala to find the fifth. They had to continue.

Belwynn and Theron took the familiar route through the gates of the castle and up to his rooms. Tycho was already there waiting, no doubt with a list of tasks for Theron to tackle.

The Order of the Knights of Kalinth had lost their Grand Master. It wasn't official yet, but everyone knew that Theron would replace his uncle. His first task would be to hunt down and kill the creature that had torn their world apart. Belwynn hadn't even dared to voice her fears on the subject. What if it couldn't be killed?

Only the weapons can kill it.

A voice in her head. But not like Soren's. Not words, even. More like thoughts, or ideas. Belwynn clasped the sides of her head, sinking to her knees.

Theron and Tycho both stood at once, turning to her with concern.

'What is it Belwynn?' Theron asked.

'A voice! I don't know-'

Since Elana's death she felt different. Something had changed. Was she going mad?

You know who I am, Belwynn.

***

THEY TRAVELLED mostly in silence, Dorian hunched over the reins, staring ahead as if in a trance, the two horses clip-clopping their way along the road south from Heractus. Straton had tried to make conversation, but his younger brother wasn't interested, seemed to be locked away in his own private world. The back of the cart was empty, save for an item, the same size and shape as a body, wrapped up in canvas.

'Just ignore it,' Dorian had told him when he had spotted Straton looking at it.

So Straton didn't look at the item in the back of the cart, ignored the smell of rancid meat, didn't interact with his brother. He sat there, and thought. He'd never been much of one for thinking—he'd never pretended otherwise. He was a doer, and that was how he liked it. But in the last few months he'd been forced, with no company but his own, to think. A lot of the time he thought about Theron, of the various punishments he could inflict on him when he was defeated. But instead, he knew he had to think more clearly about *how* to defeat him. He had thought he had done it, escaping with Ampelios, raising an army together, allying with Euthymius. But Theron had beaten them. That had hurt.

Defeating Theron was his greatest desire. But Euthymius and Ampelios were dead. How was he going to raise an army again, with no support but from his brother, who seemed to be suffering from some kind of brain-sickness?

The cart stopped and Straton's eyes flew open. He'd drifted off to sleep, lulled by the movement of the cart and the lack of conversation.

'We're here,' Dorian said.

Where was here? Straton looked about, still befuddled from sleep. Then he saw the elegant spires of the High Tower, seat of the Knights of the Kalinth. What was Dorian doing, leaving Heractus just to go to the headquarters of their enemies?

'Get down,' Dorian added.

Nervous of his brother, Straton got down and followed him round to the back of the cart. Oh no. He had hoped he would be able to forget about the contents of the canvas sacking, but Dorian reached over and grabbed an edge, sliding it along the cart towards them.

'Help me with this.'

Straton took the weight on one end, holding what was unmistakably the legs of some victim his mad brother had slaughtered.

They carried the body about a hundred feet into the woods by the side of the road. Straton stood panting with the exertion. His brother seemed unaffected. In fact—

'Go back to the cart and wait for me. I won't be long.'

This was now getting too odd to just go along with.

'Dorian, let's get out of here. We'll raise an army together, fight the Knights.'

'Yes,' his brother replied. 'We'll do all that. I just have one thing to do here first. Wait in the cart for me.'

This was ridiculous. He had a good mind to drive off and leave Dorian here. If it was anyone else but his own flesh and blood, he would already have done so by now. As it was, he would give him one last part of the hour to get back, then that was that, brother or no.

A rustling sound from the trees made him turn. At last, Dorian had returned, and he had brought someone.

Straton recognised Galenos, Grand Master of the Knights, or at least that had been his title before he was replaced by Sebastian and imprisoned in the High Tower. Dorian guided the man over to their cart. Straton had met him enough times over the years to know it was Galenos, but he looked different. Thinner and frailer than the man who had enjoyed his position as the second most powerful individual in Kalinth. Well, no doubt Straton had looked better before his captivity.

Dorian indicated that Galenos should get into the back of the cart. The old Grand Master looked anxiously from Dorian to Straton. Straton thrust a thumb towards the back of the cart.

'Get in,' he said. If Galenos thought he was going to give up his seat in the front he was sorely mistaken. Straton was just pleased that Dorian had left the dead body in the woods.

They climbed into the cart.

'Galenos has agreed to help you to become king,' said Dorian.

Straton turned to Galenos who gave an anxious nod.

'Many thanks, Grand Master. In return I shall ensure that you are fully returned to your rightful position, and that the traitors, Counts Sebastian and Theron, are hunted down and executed.'

He smiled magnanimously, frowning when Galenos didn't respond.

'Thank you, Your Majesty,' the old man managed at last.

Straton held back a shake of the dead. It seemed like the old man had lost it. Still, not such a bad thing for him to have an enfeebled Grand Master when he took the throne.

'This will help us to bring many knights to our cause,' said Dorian. 'But we will need more soldiers.'

'Yes, well I've been thinking about that,' said Straton proudly. 'With Ampelios dead, the biggest landholder in Kalinth is Count Diodorus. He fought against me last time, but maybe he can be persuaded to switch sides.'

'I'm sure he can be.'

XVIII

THE JALAKH BOW

ZARED WAS GIVEN THE LEADERSHIP of those who would enter Baserno. With him went Clarin and the rest of their group, plus ten of Mark's soldiers, led by the big spearman, Duilio. It was a big enough number for a fight if it came to that. Mark would wait for them outside Baserno with the rest of his force. If their attempt to get the Shield led to disaster, he would still be around to continue the resistance to the Isharites.

Thick, curved walls greeted them as they approached the capital, interrupted by squat round towers. It looked impregnable, and yet the rumour was that Arioc and Shira of Haskany had taken the city in a day. Clarin would have liked to witness such a feat.

They passed through the West Gate, lodged between two of the round towers, in one large group. Zared claimed that they were a unit of the Isharite army ordered to the capital. They were waved through with little fuss. Clarin didn't know whether the guards at the gate believed them, or were somehow in on the deception. Recent events had made it clear that he didn't have much control over what happened in Persala. He had to go with it, hoping that they somehow got their hands on the Shield.

A wide road took them in a straight line from the gate towards Baserno's Central Square. Clarin gawped at the great city. They passed statues of Persaleian gods and heroes at regular intervals along the route. The buildings they passed were constructed of white marble, with gloriously tall pillars everywhere. Carved creatures appeared on the pillars and walls, leering down at them as they passed. And huge windows, everywhere. Clarin had never seen so many all in one place—indeed, was convinced that nowhere else in Dalriya could rival it.

It was odd. There was no obvious sign that it was a city under occupation. The buildings and statues had not been despoiled. No foreign soldiers patrolled the streets. There was no symbol of Isharite power that Clarin could see. He thought of the walls of Samir Durg, sparkling with diatine crystals, and of the huge towers they had fought through on the walls of the Isharite fortress. The Isharites had made no effort to turn Baserno into an Isharite city. It seemed that once the Persaleians had capitulated, the Isharites had largely ignored them.

Then he realised what the difference was. Baserno was quiet, the streets half empty. He compared it to Essenberg, the great city of the Empire. In Essenberg, there was constant noise, movement, bustle, at any time of day and long into the night. Baserno was sedate; polite. Where had its people gone? Some into the army, some sent to the mines in Samir Durg, others Toric only knew where. Nowhere nice. Visually, Baserno had been left virtually untouched, but the people who actually made it a city had been scattered. They were walking through a diminished version of Baserno—a museum—not the real city at all.

When they arrived at the Central Square, Clarin's jaw dropped a second time. He could see Rudy and Jurgen, and the Barbarians, sharing awed expressions. For some reason he had been expecting to see the Imperial Palace, the Temple of Ludovis, and that would be it. Instead, he found himself looking at a huge square filled with buildings that would each be the centre of attention in virtually any other city. There were a dozen temples altogether. Then there were monuments, obelisks, giant statues, theatres, fountains, bathhouses and a large circus with a race track. It made Clarin wonder why one city would need all this for itself. And it made him realise that all the other cities of Persala he had seen were attempts to copy Baserno. Inferior versions of this city had been spawned for miles in every direction, aping the design and layout, unable to come close to matching the grandiosity.

The population of Baserno was reduced, that much was plain, but nonetheless thousands of citizens were still crammed into the Square. This was where people met to socialise and do business. Vendors hawked their wares, many selling from within the temple precincts which were hubs of noisy activity. Their group of twenty-eight was not so many that it made a difference to the atmosphere. Those that did pay attention to their arrival were the street peddlers who approached them with their goods or shouted out their offers as they walked past.

They stopped when they reached the huge, rectangular site that was the Temple of Ludovis. Tall pillars stretched to the sky, holding up a substantial peaked roof. Through the gaps between the pillars, Clarin could see a walled building.

'Some of us need to go in,' Zared said quietly to those around him, 'ascertain the situation. The rest be ready to move in if they don't hear anything. No more than an hour afterwards.'

'I'll lead the second group,' offered Duilio, one hand clutching his huge spear. 'Me and my men are more the fighting type than the talking type.'

Clarin thought he may have found a kindred spirit, but nonetheless he offered to go in with Zared. He wanted to play a full part in finding the Shield.

So it was that Zared, Clarin and Cyprian took the steps up to the Temple, while Duilio and the rest waited for them outside.

Up the steps and past the pillars was an area set aside for stallholders, positioned either side of the route into the main building. It was busy, and they found themselves squeezing through a throng of shoppers before they got to the open doors of the main temple building. Zared didn't pause, marching straight inside and accosting one of the priests.

Clarin looked around the interior of the building. Smaller pillars ran up the length of the building, with decorative arches between them. They supported a gallery above, from where people looked down over the main space. The floor was made from coloured mosaics, natural scenes with animals and plants decorated the edges of the floor, while in the centre were scenes featuring Persaleian men and women, or perhaps their gods. An altar to Ludovis stood in an open space at the far end of the building. Statues lined the walls, each one given its own alcove with a pair of pillars and a peaked roof. The altar and the statues drew worshippers, but all about the space Baserno citizens mixed with the orange robed priests of Ludovis.

Zared caught Clarin's eye and gestured that he should follow. The priest led them towards the far corner of the temple. They approached a second priest, talking quietly with two visitors. He was short, broad-shouldered, with hair turning grey. He glanced their way, continuing his conversation. They waited patiently before he extricated himself from his conversation. The first priest whispered in his ear before leaving them to it.

'Prince Zared,' he said, tilting his head in a small bow.

'Flamen Aulus,' Zared replied. 'Thank you for seeing us.'

'Of course. Any news of your father?'

'He is well. I am representing him today.'

'I see. I am pleased to hear of your father's health. These are truly difficult times. I understand that you have come looking for the Persaleian Shield?'

'Correct. These are my friends, Cyprian and Clarin. We escaped from Samir Durg last year.'

Aulus raised his eyebrows at the news.

'We have made contact with other groups outside Persala. There is an alliance to defeat Ishari. To do so, we need the Shield.'

'The Persaleian Shield has been in the hands of Ludovis since time immemorial. During that time some have sought to claim it, but it has never been given up.'

'Now is the time to do so,' Clarin found himself saying.

'So you say,' Aulus responded frostily. 'Only a select few even know of its existence. What has prompted the interest?'

'Other weapons have already been collected,' Clarin said. 'The Dagger of the Lippers, the Sword of the Krykkers, the Staff of the Caladri. It is time for the humans to make their contribution.'

Aulus looked at them, his expression giving nothing away.

'I will give you a chance to claim it,' he said at last. 'If what you say is true, and it is the will of Ludovis, it will be yours to wield. Come,' he said, starting off.

'Where to?' asked Zared.

'The treasures of the Temple are not kept *in* the Temple. That would be very foolish. We are not fools, Prince Zared.'

When they exited the Temple, Aulus was quick to spot the rest of their force lounging about outside.

'I hope there are no plans to take our treasure by force,' he said sternly. 'That would not work. The Shield is in a secret location. I don't know where it is. You could pull all the nails from my hands and feet, pull out all of my teeth, and I wouldn't tell you, because I don't know.'

'Please, Flamen Aulus,' said Zared, visibly taken aback by his words. 'We are not here to take it by force, I assure you. Those men are here for our protection. This is dangerous work we are about.'

'Very well. Then you will ensure that we are not followed.'

'Of course.'

Zared's eyes shifted in his head at the predicament. 'Cyprian, stay with the others. Impress on them the need to stay exactly where they are.'

Cyprian nodded and headed over to begin speaking with Duilio and the others.

Oh shit, Clarin said to himself. *We're on our own.*

Aulus led them north out of the Central Square, up what must be the Great Road. The road stretched from Haskany in the north to Cordence in the south, one of the great legacies of the Empire the Persaleians had created. It made Clarin wonder who else had passed this way, which great emperors and armies had set off from Baserno to conquer the other peoples of Dalriya.

Soon, though, Aulus took them off the Great Road, right then left, then right again. The streets of Baserno all ran parallel to one another, so while Clarin didn't feel completely lost, it became hard to spot recognisable features, as one street looked much like the next. They were walking through a residential area. The houses were still built from the same beautiful marble as the rest of the city, but it was eerily quiet, as if most of them were empty.

Finally, Aulus led them to an unexceptional looking house half way down the street. Clarin had to admit, it was a better place for the priests to hide a treasure than in the temple itself.

Aulus approached the wooden door and knocked, slowly, five times. They waited. Clarin wanted to ask who lived here, but that would be revealed soon enough. Patience was needed.

Eventually they heard the noise of several locks sliding open and the door was opened. An old man appeared before them. He had unkempt hair and a long, straggly beard. His clothes looked like they hadn't had a wash since last spring.

'Aulus,' he said in a croaky voice, as if not used to speaking.

'I bring visitors who would speak with you, Ennius. This is Prince Zared, son of King Mark.'

Ennius stared suspiciously at Zared, then gave a harrumph. 'Mark was a usurper, traitor to the imperial line. He brought this catastrophe on us!'

Zared stared wide-eyed at the old man, before recovering somewhat. 'I am not here to discuss politics,' he said.

'And who is this lump?' Ennius asked.

'I am Clarin.'

'Clarin who? Clarin from where?'

'I am from Magnia.'

'A Magnian, by Ludovis!' Ennius declared, bushy grey eyebrows rising up and down. 'The only people in all of Dalriya to resist the Persaleian Empire! If they were all as big as you, I can begin to understand why. Come in, then,' he said, turning around and disappearing inside his house.

They followed Ennius into his front room. A small fire in the grate gave out smoke and not much heat. There were enough chairs for all to take a seat. Ennius didn't offer food or drink, instead he sat waiting for someone to start.

'Zared and Clarin have requested the Shield of Persala,' Aulus explained.

'Very well,' said Ennius, apparently unimpressed by the news. 'That's simple enough. Just give me a name. Tell me who wants it and it's yours.'

Clarin thought about it. Was it some kind of riddle? Who wanted it? Well, *he* did. He had come all this way for the Shield. And what was more, he fancied wielding it, too. Soren had the staff, Moneva the dagger. Why shouldn't he have the shield?

'Clarin,' he said.

Ennius turned to Aulus. 'He comes all the way from Magnia, dares to ask for our Shield, and then gives me his own name? Why have you brought these fools here?'

Oh, Clarin said to himself. *That's clearly not what he was looking for.*

'King Mark,' said Zared.

Ennius gave another harrumph and turned away from them all, staring into the fire.

Zared looked to Clarin in mute desperation.

Think, Clarin, he told himself. *Who wanted the Shield? Who wanted the weapons?*

'Madria,' he said.

'You'll have to do better than that,' Ennius said, still staring furiously into the fire.

Have to do better than that, Clarin reflected. But he hadn't sounded quite so cross. Was he getting closer? If not Madria, then who?

'Elana?' he offered.

Ennius stopped staring at the fire and turned to look at Clarin. Deep brown eyes stared at him, suddenly magnetic in their intensity.

'Not quite correct, unfortunately,' Ennius murmured, his voice quite different now—hushed, expectant.

Clarin felt angry with frustration. What kind of test was this? If Madria was close, and Elana closer, then who?

186

Elana was the priestess of Madria. Belwynn was her disciple. But why would Belwynn be correct if Elana wasn't? He almost said her name, then stopped. *Don't be stupid, Clarin,* he told himself. His infatuation with her was muddling his thinking.

'Go on,' said Ennius, in the same voice.

I don't have a name, old man! He wanted to shout. *Oh, sod it.*

'Belwynn.'

'Yes,' Ennius said simply.

'What?' blurted out Aulus and Zared in unison.

'That is the correct answer,' Ennius said simply. 'The Shield must be passed into this man's keeping.'

'How do you know Belwynn?' Clarin demanded.

'I don't, you great Magnian muttonhead! Aulus, will you fetch it?'

'I don't know where the Shield is kept, remember Ennius?'

'Oh yes. I forget myself. It's just next door.'

'What?' asked Zared.

'It's kept in the house next door,' Ennius repeated. 'It's easier that way.'

The Persaleian Shield was circular, covered in leather that had been painted red, black and yellow. In the middle the head of a bearded man had been painted, with two horns emerging from his forehead.

'Ludovis,' Ennius explained when he saw Clarin looking at it.

The sight of the shield had a profound impact on Clarin, while the touch of it caused a shiver to run through the tips of his fingers to the rest of his body. It was clear to him that this was much more than an ordinary shield, yet if he had been asked to explain why, he couldn't have put the feeling into words.

They all knew there wasn't time to waste. Reluctantly, Clarin wrapped the shield in sackcloth and strapped it to his back.

'Farewell Ennius,' he said, still without understanding what had happened in the old man's house.

'Use it well.'

Aulus led them back to the Temple, where the group was still waiting for them.

Zared nodded curtly to Duilio and the rest of his men. Their eyes widened, but they controlled their reactions. They all knew that their mission was only half complete until they had safely left the city with the weapon.

'Thank you, Aulus,' said Zared, shaking the flamen's hand.

'I pray that what we did today takes you a step closer to liberating our country,' Aulus said. 'Good luck.'

With that they left the Temple of Ludovis behind. Clarin gave the Central Square of Baserno one last look. The Shield of Persala had been resting here long enough. It was time to use it.

***

ELANA'S DEATH had wounded them all. It had never been spoken out loud, but Gyrmund was sure they had all shared a sense that they were doing this for her, collecting the weapons for Madria's champion. Now she was dead, struck down by some hellish creature that had taken Sebastian's form. Gyrmund found it hard to take. He had seen a touch of innocence to Elana. A gentle goodness that had been unique to her.

But if Gyrmund was struggling with his grief, the reaction of the other two was more severe. At least Soren knew that Belwynn was alive and safe. But this didn't seem to soften him. He wore a hard face now. It reminded Gyrmund of the Soren who had appeared in Edeleny, grabbing the Grand Caladri elder Agoston, taking his magic in order to restore his own powers, before discarding his husk of a body. And Moneva, who had only just come out of her shell, only just begun to start smiling again, was even worse. She barely spoke to anyone, a look of murderous intent fixed on her face.

The morning after Gansukh's fourth fight three Jalakh warriors were found dead. Their throats had been slit in the night. Angry recriminations followed, the Oligud tribe accused.

But Gyrmund knew it was Moneva.

A challenger still appeared on the fifth day to fight Gansukh. It had been a close contest for a while, Gansukh having to fight with an injured arm. But after five minutes one of the Jalakhs in the crowd started screaming, before a sudden haemorrhage left him sprawled on the ground, blood shooting out from his nose and mouth as if his head had exploded. Soren, face grim, had bent the rules, targeting a Jalakh wizard rather than the fighter in the ropes.

The chaos completely distracted the other tribes, while Soren and Bolormaa turned all their power on the fight. Gansukh's opponent could barely move, held in a web of magic, before Gansukh slew him with a strike to the head.

The Oligud warrior was livid, railing at his mother and Soren, demanding that she send the three foreigners away. But that was the last thing Bolormaa was going to do.

The sixth day began with two more murdered warriors. Gansukh entered the ropes, but there were no challengers.

On the seventh and last day, the Day of Destiny, Gansukh again entered the ropes unchallenged. A sea of Jalakh people, sullen faced, cowed, all bended the knee.

They had a new khan.

'They can't come in,' said Gansukh, gesturing angrily at Gyrmund, Moneva and Soren.

The new khan was already asserting his authority. But his mother wasn't so easily put off.

'They got you here,' she whispered to him fiercely. 'When they've gone you can forget that, take all the credit for yourself. All the Jalakhs will forget it. But while they're here, no-one will forget. So I suggest you give them what they want soon, then let them go.'

Gansukh's face curled into a snarl. He looked at Gyrmund and the others, but what he saw was Soren, the implacable wizard who had given him his victories in the ropes, and Moneva, a killer who worked in the shadows, and he seemed to think better of resisting them. He screwed his face up, thinking.

'Just him,' he said, pointing at Gyrmund.

Gyrmund looked at Moneva and Soren, raising his eyebrows.

They shrugged their acceptance and Gyrmund stepped forwards.

Gansukh, content that he had been obeyed, turned around and walked through the gate in the outer wall of the Temple.

A small group followed behind. As well as Bolormaa and Gyrmund there were a few other notables of the Oligud tribe, and a few of Gansukh's friends, men who would now perhaps become his generals.

A trio of priests met Gansukh as he entered the Temple grounds. He bowed his head, and they each placed a wreath of flowers around his neck, before leading him on.

Ahead was the entrance to the pagoda, which Moneva had described to Gyrmund, though this was the first time he saw it for himself. A small set of steps led up to the entrance, while four pillars supported a roof that extended out towards them.

Bolormaa saw him looking at the pagoda and fell in with him.

'Gansukh will spend the night in there,' she explained, as the three priests led them past the entrance. 'Our rituals say he will enter as an Oligud and awake tomorrow as a member of all the tribes—as a khan.'

She spoke with pride and reverence.

'Your husband would be proud,' said Gyrmund.

'He is.'

The group left the pagoda behind and joined a path that wound its way into the sacred garden. The priests stopped when they faced a giant tree that stood in the centre of the garden. They all stood facing the tree in a semi-circle, before one of the priests produced a saw and handed it to Gansukh. He approached the tree, studying it for a while.

'This one?' he said, pointing at a huge branch that grew out in the direction of the Jalakh tents. Gyrmund smiled as he saw that it pointed directly at the location where Moneva had climbed over the outside wall, in a failed attempt to find the bow.

'A wise choice, great khan,' said the priest.

Gansukh set to work, making a notch cut first, then cutting into the branch slightly further along, pushing back and forth with his saw. It was as thick as some trees, and it took him a while to cut through, as the rest of them just stood and watched. He grew red-faced and sweaty, and had to stop to rest more than once. But he cut through the last section cleanly, the branch dropping to the ground.

The three priests gathered around the fallen branch.

'See!' one proclaimed. 'The Tree of Destiny has provided us with the Jalakh Bow!'

'What?' said Gyrmund, turning to Bolormaa in shock.

'The priests will now use this branch to make the Jalakh Bow. Gansukh will hunt antelope, and the horn and sinew of the beast he kills will be used in the construction.'

Gyrmund found this difficult to process. 'So, wait? The Jalakh Bow doesn't exist? You said it was here, in Tosongat,' he said accusingly.

'I said it was here in a manner of speaking. The Jalakh Bow is made by order of the khan. Legends say that the Tree of Destiny grew when the original bow was planted into the ground. Or maybe the original bow was also made from this very tree. Come, Gyrmund,' she tutted, that sly smile of hers reappearing. 'You didn't think the *original* Jalakh bow, made from wood hundreds and hundreds of years ago, would still be in existence?'

Gyrmund didn't know what to say.

'But don't think we are giving you an ordinary bow. The Jalakh Bow is made from the Tree of Destiny, using methods preserved by our shamen. It will be the finest weapon in all of Dalriya.'

'How long does it take them to make it?' he asked.

'Not long. But it must be allowed to properly dry. You will be able to use it in days.'

Gansukh approached him, along with his councillors and friends from the Oligud tribe.

'You will take care of our bow?' he asked Gyrmund.

'Of course, Your Majesty. It is an honour to receive it.'

Gansukh nodded. 'My first act as khan is to give away our most precious weapon. But my mother insists that we share the same enemies, so it will still be used for the Jalakh people.'

'I will use it wisely and I promise to return it to you when it is no longer needed.'

'So be it,' said Gansukh, waving a hand in the air as if to be rid of the whole business.

Gansukh, his mother and the rest of the Oliguds left the way they had come.

It took all three priests to carry the branch away. They were presumably going to start work on it immediately.

Gyrmund was left alone in the garden. He looked up at the tree, at the cut where the giant branch had been. He approached, placing one hand onto the trunk.

'Thank you,' he said.

XIX

BEYOND THE DRANG

IT HAD TAKEN TIME TO GATHER THEIR WITS after the dragon attack. Rabigar had been relieved to learn that the Krykker losses had been a few hundred. He had feared they were much worse.

The dragon had fired the Vismarian fleet, and the Caladri trading vessels, but most people had already made it onto shore. They had run into the swamps and hills of the Pecineg clan. The dragon had not pursued them, flying away over the ocean.

The Sea Caladri had not been so fortunate. Only four Caladri warships limped back to the shore of the Halvian Krykkers. They spoke of a sea battle where they had gained the upper hand over the Kharovians, until the dragon had turned the outcome of the battle, destroying ship after ship, until the Caladri that remained broke away in an effort to escape. They confirmed what Rabigar had already suspected. Captain Sebo's Red Serpent had been in the thick of the fighting and had gone down. They held out little hope that many more than a few other ships had escaped the destruction. The Sea Caladri fleet, the greatest in Dalriya, was no more.

They hadn't dallied. Rabigar couldn't blame them. Picking up those of their race who had crossed the Lantinen, they departed south, to deliver their devastating news to their countrymen. The Krykkers were now stranded, the ships of the Sea Caladri and the Vismarians all lost in one day. More than one Krykker could be heard lamenting over their chances of ever returning home. But Rabigar had other priorities. He was here to find the Giants' Spear, and that was his only concern right now.

His hopes, it seemed, lay in the form of Gunnhild, the Vismarian woman who had saved his life. She had lifted his sinking body from the seabed and deposited it onto the sand.

The Vismarian leader, Sevald, explained that he had led a small party north in the hopes of finding a family who had knowledge of the paths into the wild lands of western Halvia. He had returned with Gunnhild. She had agreed to take Rabigar into the west. But there was a catch. The area they needed to reach was swarming with Drobax.

So it was that Rabigar left the land of the Pecinegs with an army. It contained about two thousand souls altogether. Chief Wracken of the Binideqs led his soldiers, who would guide them through their clan-lands to the River Drang, that marked the northern border of the Krykkers. Jodivig, chief of the Dramsens, had recruited a force of Dalriyan Krykkers that matched the numbers under Wracken. Sevald came with his Vismarians, men and women who knew the lands north of the Drang. Finally, Ignac of the Grand Caladri led a small group of his exiles. Some of them, like him, were mediums. Their magic might prove useful once they entered the dangerous lands to the north.

As they followed Wracken's force north, Rabigar fell in with Sevald and Gunnhild. The woman's stride was huge, meaning she had to walk in an odd sort of dawdle to travel at the same pace as Rabigar.

'Where did your family live?' he asked her.

'We hunted in the far north, where the cold turns your snot to ice and freezes your eyes shut in the night. Our size allowed us to survive up there, where tiny men like this would shiver and cry,' she said, giving Sevald an almighty slap on the back. He smiled good naturedly at the ribbing.

'We would hunt all manner of beasts, living off elk and bringing back bear and wolf pelts to trade with the lowlanders. What a life it was.'

'What happened?'

'The Drobax came. So we started hunting those bastards instead. But we must have upset someone, because they came for us. And I don't mean like Drobax usually do, running around aimlessly like squirrels looking for their acorns. This was an ambush—well planned. I saw my father go down. My brothers escaped to the north, but I got cut off from them. I pray they got away, that they're hiding in the icy wastes, somewhere too cold for the Drobax to follow. Anyway, I was chased miles to the south. That's where Sevald found me, talking some nonsense about giants and spears.'

'What do you know about the giants?' Rabigar asked.

'Oh, plenty of stories about the giants in my family. Stories that we're descended from a giant. The truth is they left for the west. A long, long time ago.'

'How do we find them? Or find where they went?'

'Farther west of where the Vismarians and Krykkers live there are miles and miles of ice fields. Not much lives out there. If you tried walking that way you would fall through the ice, sooner or later. Even if you're a lucky bastard, and all the odds are in your favour, it will still only take a few days before the ice gets you. The only way to travel west is down the Nasvarl. The source of the Nasvarl is in the northern wastes. But they say it flows west, all the way to the edge of the world. If we head northwest from here we will reach a good spot in the river that thaws early. From there we can head downriver.'

Rabigar heard the Drang before he saw it. Chief Wracken had chosen to reach the river at sundown, when their activity was less likely to be noticed by any Drobax in the area. Rabigar looked out from the southern bank and saw the Drang was wide and full, bringing huge quantities of meltwater from the highlands of Halvia to the Lantinen Sea. A strange looking apparatus had been built in the river.

Chief Wracken sent twenty or so of his soldiers towards it and then, noticing Rabigar's interest, approached him to explain.

'We've destroyed all the other bridges across the river. So far, it's kept the Drobax from crossing in significant numbers. This is now the only way for us to go beyond the Drang.'

As Rabigar watched, the Krykkers on the bank began to lower a drawbridge-like contraption onto a small, artificial looking island that lay about a quarter of the way into the river. Once lowered, they crossed the drawbridge onto the island, where a second drawbridge was lowered onto a larger, natural island that lay in the middle of the river. It was big enough for a few wooden buildings to have been erected on it. Rabigar could see that two further drawbridges would complete the route and allow them to reach the north side.

'Ingenious,' he said, enthused. 'It allows you to cross but denies passage to the Drobax.'

'Yes. I will leave a few men on the south bank and on the middle island for when we return, just in case we need to make a quick crossing.'

Wracken ordered his soldiers to cross first, securing a bridgehead, before the rest of the army followed behind.

Despite the late hour, they had attracted the attention of a small number of Drobax. By the time Rabigar got across, the brief encounter was over, a pile of Drobax bodies casually dumped next to where the latrines had been marked out. But it didn't bode well.

They were quick to make a camp. Each of them carried a sharpened wooden stake that were used to build a defensive perimeter around the camp. Wracken insisted that the Binideqs would handle the night watch, and so Rabigar settled down to eat his rations with the Dalriyan Krykkers. He was surprised to see a familiar figure come over to join him.

'Stenk? I had no idea you were here!'

'Jodivig asked me to come,' Stenk said proudly.

The truth was, Rabigar was surprised to see the young Dramsen Krykker. Stenk had fought in his very first battle with Rabigar last summer, against the Isharite army in Haskany. But, Rabigar supposed, that now made him a veteran. When you factored in the many losses suffered by the Krykkers, and accounted for the fact that Maragin had kept many of the best warriors with her in the underground tunnels of the Krykker mountains, that made Stenk one of the more experienced fighters they had left to call on.

'We're going to find a spear?' Stenk asked, his brow creasing in confusion.

How many of these soldiers really understood what they were doing, Rabigar wondered. Events had moved too fast to fully explain things.

He drew Bolivar's Sword. 'When Bolivar defeated the dread lord of Ishari at the Battle of Alta, he had six other champions with him.'

He turned to see that other Krykkers were looking at him, listening intently to what he said.

'There was a Lipper, with a dagger. A Caladri medium, with a staff. A human, with a shield. A Jalakh archer. And there was a giant, who wielded a great spear. We need to find this spear here in Halvia, far to the west. When these weapons are assembled, we can use them to defeat the Isharites.'

'How?' pressed Stenk. 'How will these weapons rid the Drobax from these lands? From our lands back in Dalriya?'

Rabigar felt all too aware of the eyes on him. They were hungry for answers—certainties—when there were none.

'Remember,' Rabigar answered, making sure his voice carried. 'My friends stole into the very heart of Ishari, the fortress of Samir Durg. Who did they kill there?'

'Erkindrix,' someone offered.

'Yes, the dread lord himself. And who knows what weapons they had with them? Not our sword, for no Krykker went with them.'

'The dagger and the staff,' said Stenk.

'Correct. With just two of these weapons they entered the dread lord's own lair and killed him. And at that very time the forces of the Emperor of Brasingia were defending Burkhard Castle, that great fortress that our ancestors built. When Erkindrix was slain, the horde of Drobax, the Haskans and the Isharites, all turned around and fled. So, imagine what will happen when we have all seven weapons together.'

Rabigar's people nodded, satisfied. None of them was so foolish as to believe that they were saved. But they believed they had a fighting chance, and that was all a Krykker should ever ask for.

Wracken woke them while it was still dark. He wanted them to move out without being seen.

Bedrolls were packed, stakes collected, and breakfast taken on the march. But they weren't free of the Drobax. When sunrise came they could be spotted: small, grey figures, coming in and out of sight. Rabigar saw one looking at them from the top of a hill. Later, someone pointed out a small group, walking through the trees to their right, before the woodland hid them from view again. The Drobax were following them, on each flank, but keeping their distance.

Sevald and the Vismarians now led the army, choosing which route to take through their lands. They avoided the deeply forested areas, in case the Drobax were waiting for them there. But Vismar was wild terrain: heavily wooded, no roads, and full of rocky outcrops, streams and other obstacles. Each time they had to slow down to cross a stream, or their vision was obscured by knoll and hummock, or they descended into a valley, there was a threat of ambush. Scouts had to be sent out, and the constant state of vigilance began to drain energy and fray tempers.

It happened when they were climbing out of a valley. Screams behind them signalled that the Drobax were finally attacking. Wracken's Krykkers at the rear turned to face them. Meanwhile, streaming down the valley slopes on either side of their position, more Krykkers came.

'Up!' Sevald shouted. 'We need to take the high ground.'

The Vismarians moved forward at pace, aiming to climb out of the depression. Jodivig, leading the Dalriyan Krykkers, followed the Vismarians.

Rabigar went with them, slipping and sliding on the muddy path as he tried to get purchase. They rounded a corner where they stopped, running into each other. Ahead, the Vismarians had come up against a force of Drobax who had been waiting for them. Logs had been placed along the path to block their progress. Drobax hurled stones and rocks down on the Vismarians, who backed away from the trap.

They were surrounded on all sides. But what sent a chill down Rabigar's spine were the voices. He saw them. These Drobax were taller and broader than any he had seen before. They were shouting out instructions to the rest of their kind.

'Hold!' some of them shouted, keeping the Drobax behind the logs where they held an advantage.

There was something so unnatural about seeing Drobax opening their mouths and speaking that Rabigar stood rooted to the spot, unable to react.

Meanwhile, the Vismarians turned and retreated, Sevald leading his warriors back down the path. Rabigar could see Gunnhild at the back, her giant frame a target for Drobax rocks, battering them away with her shield.

Jodivig ordered the Dalriyan Krykkers to move back down again, to make room for the descending Vismarians.

The Drobax on the flanks now reached them. Rabigar grabbed his shield from his back, drew Bolivar's Sword and met them. He slashed at one, too quick for it defend with its club, his blade crunching into its shoulder and sending it sprawling to the ground. A second he smashed into with his shield, shoving it backwards, then thrusting his sword forward so that it slid into the chest cavity of the creature. Yanking it out, he saw that a group of Krykkers had come with him.

'Pull back!' came a voice above them.

Rabigar looked up to see one of the larger, new breed of Drobax some distance up the slope, shouting out commands. It looked straight at him, and its sharp face made a vicious grin. It knew the Drobax had the advantage so long as they kept Rabigar's force surrounded. All it had to do was contain and wait for reinforcements.

Rabigar turned to see that Sevald had arrived and was talking with Jodivig. The Krykker chieftain's eyes were wide, close to panic. Rabigar joined them.

'Rabigar,' said Sevald. 'They're too entrenched up there. We need to break out the way we came in.'

Rabigar looked down to where the Binideqs were engaged with the Drobax who had come at them from behind. More Drobax were descending the sides of the valley.

'Alright,' Rabigar said.

It seemed the only option, but it would cost lives. And once they moved, the Drobax at the head of the valley would leave their enclosure and come at them from behind, squeezing the door shut in their trap.

'Rabigar!' came a shout.

It was Ignac. Together with a group of his Caladri he was trying to get to Rabigar, but the path was too congested.

'We can protect your backs while you break out!'

'Agreed!' Rabigar shouted back.

He held Bolivar's Sword aloft, trying to get the attention of those around him, before pointing it back down the valley, to his target. Without waiting any longer, he moved, Krykkers and Vismarians following him down the path.

Rabigar led his force off the path and up the side of the valley on his left. Here, they could present their shields, held in the left hand, to the Drobax descending to meet them. The first Drobax swung down at him using all its strength. He braced himself, taking the blow that rattled up and down his arm, before swinging out with his sword, chopping away the legs of the creature. It came to earth with a crash and as it sprawled there Rabigar was free to pick his spot, pushing the tip of his blade under the chin and into its head.

He kept moving, circling around the rows of Binideq Krykkers who stood on the path, before coming at the Drobax on their flank. Two of them moved out of position to meet him and he charged them, flinging all his weight behind his shield at the first, knocking it to the ground and barely staying on his feet. He whirled around, sword and shield in front of him in the hopes they would take the expected attack from the second Drobax. The strike came, a short spear glancing off his shield and striking him on the chest, leaving nothing more than a scratch on his tough, armour-like skin.

Jodivig, following in his wake, smashed a battle axe into the back of the creature's neck, completely severing the head which sailed into the air, eyes still staring out in a look of surprise.

More Krykkers came behind them, short weapons for close work at the ready, and Rabigar led them into the Drobax. The battle mist came over him then, the unthinking part of his brain taking over, reacting to threats by raising his shield arm, lusting for blood with his sword arm. Bolivar's Sword hummed like a death machine, dripping red with Drobax blood.

The stink of battle rose as the body count grew, the ground treacherous with piss and shit and gore. The Drobax had brought the numbers, but the Krykkers were better armed and better trained. Finally, the Drobax gave ground under the onslaught.

The Krykkers punched through, retracing their steps down into the valley, aiming to come back out the other side. But although the Drobax had fallen back, they had not retreated. Their leaders, the large ones who spoke, ordered them to harry, as they marched along the path that led through the valley.

Rabigar stayed at the front, leading the army forwards. He began to ascend back up to the other side. The battle fury was beginning to leave him now and he felt aches and pains. His legs felt heavy, his lungs burned. Behind him his comrades were struggling with exhaustion, some walking wounded, others supporting those too injured to walk by themselves. He looked back across to the other side of the valley and saw half a dozen small figures—the Caladri mediums—holding back a force of Drobax ready to descend the valley towards them.

Up they marched, desperate to escape the trap that the Drobax had laid for them. Rabigar allowed his mind to briefly consider this. Until now the Drobax had been a mindless enemy, reliant on orders and firm control from their Ishari masters. But this new breed of Drobax seemed to change that. They could communicate, give orders, prepare an ambush and ensure that it was carried out. All of which made the threat from the Drobax even more grave.

The creatures continued to hound their movement, while staying clear of Krykker steel. But eventually Rabigar crested the top of the valley. The front ranks dragged themselves onto the flat terrain above, just as the Drobax at the other end of the valley were released and threw themselves down, howling for blood.

Rabigar looked about him, wondering where the most defensible location in these parts would be. He found Jodivig and Wracken. The Binideq leader had taken a blow to the side of his head, his hair matted with blood. Sevald joined them too. Below, Rabigar could see Gunnhild bringing up the rear of their forces as the Drobax closed in on three sides, her shield deflecting blows, her giant hammer forcing the creatures to keep their distance or else risk being flattened.

'Can we get to a fort or defensive structure?' Rabigar asked Sevald.

Sevald raised an eyebrow. 'There's too many of them,' he said simply. 'We could struggle to a hill or some such, but all that would do is prolong the slaughter.'

'We need to fight our way back to the Drang,' Wracken added. 'That's our only hope of survival.' He spat a mix of saliva and blood onto the ground. 'And that's a faint hope.'

Rabigar shook his head. 'I need to get the Spear.'

'Are you mad?' Wracken demanded angrily. 'Look where that nonsense has got us!'

Rabigar pointed down at the horde of Drobax coming towards them. 'Look what will happen if we don't. You think the Drang is going to keep them out forever? This is a taste of what awaits.'

Ignac appeared. 'We can transport a small number away a short distance. I don't know the area, but perhaps past the valley,' he said, pointing vaguely to the north-west, beyond the Drobax enclosure.

Sevald shrugged. 'It may work, if there are no Drobax waiting for you there. The terrain is gentle enough.'

'Then that's what we do,' said Rabigar. 'Myself and Gunnhild are the two who need to go. If Ignac can send more, whoever else that wants to and could be of use.'

'I'll die with my men,' stated Wracken flatly.

Sevald and Jodivig echoed his sentiments.

'Could you come with us?' Rabigar asked Ignac. 'A medium may be useful to us.'

Ignac nodded. 'Coming with you would make the teleportation easier. That leaves three of our enchanters left who can stay with the army.'

Rabigar saw Stenk waiting a few feet away. He wanted his young friend to live. But were his odds better with the army, retreating to the Drang, or heading west through the treacherous lands of Halvia with him? It was impossible to know.

'Do I have permission to take Stenk if he will come?' Rabigar asked Jodivig.

'Of course. Good luck.'

They all shook hands there and then, for there was no more time to waste. As soon as Gunnhild arrived, she was guided over to the waiting group. Without argument, she took Rabigar's hand in one massive palm and Stenk's in the other. The Caladri mediums made their magic and Rabigar felt himself moving, just like he had done before when Ignac had found Rabigar and his friends wandering lost in the forests of the Grand Caladri. Most of his senses were taken from him, leaving the sensation of movement. It stopped almost as soon as it had begun, leaving a sick feeling in his stomach.

He opened his eye and focused on his surroundings.

They stood in a meadow, a few feet from a stream in one direction and a wood of birch in the other. It would have been possible to believe that they were miles away from the bloody confrontation they had just been a part of, if it wasn't for the sound of howling Drobax carried to them on the air.

Rabigar looked at his companions: young Stenk, giant Gunnhild and the Caladri magic user, Ignac. This was all that was left of the army that had intended to march to the Nasvarl. They had fatally underestimated the strength of the Drobax.

'It was as if they were waiting for us right from the beginning,' he said.

'It was the same with my family,' said Gunnhild. 'They have leaders now.'

'Will the others manage to get back home?' Stenk asked.

'No problem,' said Rabigar quickly.

Maybe Stenk believed him. He could see from the expressions of the other two that they didn't.

'Thanks for bringing me,' Stenk said quietly.

'Glad you're here,' said Gunnhild. 'You can keep an eye on that one,' she said, pointing at Rabigar. 'I swear, all he does is stare at me tits!'

Stenk's eyes bulged as his gaze was drawn, irresistibly, to the chest area of the giant Vismarian.

Gunnhild slapped her thigh and gave a rambunctious, uninhibited laugh, loud enough to alert every Drobax in the region to their precise location.

XX

THE GIFT

FARRED LEFT ESSENBERG BEHIND, taking the Great Road to the north.

It wasn't long before he began to pass groups of people coming the other way. These weren't merchants laden with supplies for the capital. These were family groups, taking with them all the possessions they could carry.

When he asked why, he got the same answer. An army of Drobax was heading for the Empire.

The people were mainly from Rotelegen; some from Grienna. They had learned from what had happened last year. Rotelegen wasn't safe. The imperial army wouldn't defend it. The best option was to abandon the duchy, find refuge in Essenberg, and hope that the Drobax would leave again. Hope that Burkhard Castle could hold against the enemy a second time.

Farred rode on, apprehensive about what he would find when he reached the fortress.

He never made it.

Riders appeared on the road ahead. Scouts of the imperial army.

One of them recognised Farred and stopped to speak with him. Walter, Marshall of the Empire and Duke of Barissia, was returning to Essenberg with urgent news.

Farred waited. Soon, Walter's small force of riders appeared. Walter was at the front and next to him was Gustav, Archmage of the Empire. The duke hailed Farred with a smile and asked him to ride with them. He didn't have time to stop.

'I wasn't expecting to find you on this road, Farred,' Walter said. 'Last I heard, from Prince Edgar, you were sailing north with the Caladri fleet.'

Farred briefly explained to the duke, and to the archmage who listened in, that the invasion of the Krykker lands had led him to warn the human realms of the threat. Walter and Gustav shared a dark look at the mention of the dragon.

'How are we supposed to defend against that?' demanded Walter wearily.

Gustav shook his head, seemingly bereft of answers. He looked at Farred. They had developed a close relationship of sorts in Burkhard Castle. Walter had persuaded Farred to support Gustav when he made his transformations into a hawk. It had been an experience Farred had never really got used to, and didn't talk about.

'The Isharite sorcerers have been more active recently. Defending their borders, preventing me from crossing into Persala. The appearance of their army wasn't a total surprise, therefore—though I only saw it once it had crossed into Trevenza. In most respects it is the same as the force that came at us last year. Thousands upon thousands of Drobax. Isharites, Haskans and other forces in support.'

'Jeremias and Adalheid are evacuating Rotelegen,' Walter added. 'We defend Burkhard, just like last time.' He gave Farred a grave look. 'You and I knew they would return.'

Farred nodded. This was all well and good, but he had a concern he couldn't shake off. He resolved to tell them both.

'You may have a problem,' he began. 'Baldwin and Inge. It began last summer, at Burkhard. Maybe I should have told you then. But when I was in Essenberg, they were in bed together. Baldwin didn't seem himself—'

He stopped, not knowing what else to say.

Walter and Gustav shared another look.

'We know,' said Walter quietly, clearly finding the topic awkward. 'My brother has a lot of pressure. Everyone, inside and outside the Empire, looks to him to deal with the Isharite threat. But we all learned something last year. He *can't* deal with it. *We* can't. That's a difficult position to be in. Deep down, he knew this day would come again. So, this affair, it has been a diversion for him. A distraction for his mind until the time comes to fight again. And, after all, emperors and kings with mistresses isn't exactly uncommon.'

'I understand that,' said Farred, unconvinced. 'But Inge isn't a simple mistress,' he said, glancing briefly at Gustav. 'She has powers. I fear she has some control over him.'

Gustav twitched his mouth. It was now his turn to look uncomfortable. 'Inge has power, yes. Is she using her magic on Baldwin? Perhaps,' he admitted. 'But women have ever sought to beguile men, whether they are magic users or not. And men—' the archmage paused, struggling for the right words.

'Sometimes they want to be beguiled. That is what I believe is happening between Baldwin and Inge.'

'If your concerns remain,' said Walter, studying Farred's reaction, 'know two things. I have already sent messengers out to all the dukes of Brasingia, warning them that they will soon receive imperial orders to raise an army and take it to Burkhard Castle. And now, Gustav and I ride straight for Essenberg, where we intend to persuade Baldwin to send out such an order. Have faith in my brother. He has always done what is right.'

***

BELWYNN AND Lyssa left their room for the other side of the castle, where the chapel was located.

You have it? she asked Soren, desperate for some good news.

Sort of, he replied. *The Jalakh priests have made it. They need to finish it before we're allowed to take it.*

Alright. Come as quick as you can. We need you here.

We will.

Right. Now it was time for her news.

Soren, there's something else.

Yes?

I can sort of speak like this to someone else now. Since Elana died. I can speak with Madria.

Silence. Soren probably thought she had lost her mind. Had she?

You're speaking telepathically to Madria?

Yes. It's more feelings, and ideas, than words. Maybe this was what Elana experienced, why she thought she knew what to do but was vague on the details.

Are you sure? What I mean to say is, are you sure it is her and not someone else in your mind? Remember, in Samir Durg, Siavash was able to enter my mind and talk to me.

Yes, it's her. I'm positive. Well—I'm pretty sure it's her.

Belwynn, just be careful. Don't do anything hasty. I'm going to come back as fast as I can.

Alright Soren. Bye.

See you soon Belwynn.

Don't be hasty. That was easier said than done. A monster was on the loose in Kalinth. It had already killed the two most important people in Heractus.

Now Prince Straton and Galenos, the former Grand Master of the Knights, were busy raising an army for it. Doing nothing just wasn't an option.

They walked into the chapel, usually reserved for the royal family. Today it was needed by the Knights, for a ceremony that would normally have been conducted at the High Tower. It was meant to be a celebration, though Belwynn had mixed feelings about it.

Pages guided them to their seats near the stage. Belwynn found herself next to Philon, the young sandy haired knight who had first approached her for a blessing last summer. He had been rising up the ranks quickly since that day.

'My lady,' he said politely. The nervous knight from last summer had been replaced by a man of quiet confidence, Belwynn noticed. It had been less than a year, but they had all changed since then.

Belwynn peered to the front where a group of six young men—children, some of them—were kneeling on the floor.

'There he is, Lyssa,' she said, pointing out Evander, his broad back and neck length dark hair allowing her to identify him.

Lyssa stood up and looked over. She sucked in a breath.

'We don't call out to him, remember,' Belwynn said quickly, causing the girl to sit back down with a grumpy expression.

'Theron says these squires owe much to your efforts on the training ground,' Belwynn said to Philon.

'Some,' he agreed modestly, 'though it varies. Certainly, young Evander has been well trained by Grand Master Theron himself. I could add very little to what Evander already knew.'

Grand Master Theron was a title Belwynn struggled to get used to, for many reasons. It was a title she thought she would always associate with Sebastian, and it sounded strange attached to anyone else—even Theron, who surely deserved it. Then, of course, it represented the end of their brief affair. The Grand Master devoted himself to the Order. Like all knights, he could have no wife. Belwynn's little dream, that Theron would leave the Order for her, was over.

As she was thinking of him, Theron appeared on the stage, with King Jonas. The king looked older than when she had first met him—face puffy, muscled torso now partly turned to fat. She wondered what Jonas thought of recent events. His two sons escaped from the capital, raising an army against his captors. Had he heard the rumours that his youngest, Dorian, was no longer Dorian at all? That he was a monster? She felt a pang of grief for Dorian, almost forgotten amidst her deeper pain at the loss of Elana. He had seemed a gentle, benign soul. He hadn't deserved such a fate.

The chapel quietened, and Theron spoke a few words of introduction to the knighting ceremony. The congregation hung on his every word. There had been no dissent whatsoever to Theron's elevation to the head of the Order from the men who had worked and fought with him over the last few months. He was the obvious choice—in truth, he had been the driving force behind their achievements, albeit too willing to take on the unpopular tasks to spare his uncle from them. But out in the country, opinion was more divided. He wasn't as universally respected as Sebastian had been. And he had a formidable rival in the former Grand Master, Galenos. That made the choice of who to give loyalty to more difficult. It made the option of avoiding making a choice at all, the easiest course to follow.

This ceremony was all about addressing that problem. With the loyalty of some in the Order in doubt, Theron was making new knights. Belwynn didn't like it. Evander was far too young and inexperienced to be knighted, to go into battle with Theron and Tycho. But she knew that Theron was desperate, that he needed all the manpower he could get.

And so, Evander and five other youths well short of the usual age, were called up one at a time to the stage, where they knelt in front of their grand master and their king. First, Theron delivered the blow, a cuff on the side of the head, landing from ear to neck. Then, Jonas lifted his sword and tapped the flat of the blade once on each shoulder. The Order had lost six squires and gained six knights.

After the ceremony, Belwynn and Lyssa joined a circle of people congratulating Evander and the other boys. Theron and Tycho were there, beaming with pride; Tycho punching each boy on the arm several times in pleasure.

Bemus approached her, his long face as serious as ever.

'We are ready when you are,' he said, as if passing down a death sentence.

Theron grabbed her elbow. 'Good luck.'

'Evander says he will look after me,' said Lyssa, in a blatant attempt to avoid being taken down to the temple, where she would doubtless be made to do chores.

Belwynn was about to tell her no, when she caught Theron's stern gaze. She stopped herself. Evander was a knight now: it would be disrespectful to imply that he wasn't capable of protecting Lyssa.

'Of course,' she said. She made her excuses and followed Bemus out of the room.

Belwynn steeled herself to enter the main chamber of the temple, which just two days before had held the funeral service for Elana.

I'm not sure I can do this, she said to Madria, the new voice in her head.

You have a unique gift, Belwynn, Madria replied, the thought appearing in Belwynn's mind rather than the words themselves. *It is time you used it to its full potential.*

The heads of Elana's congregation turned to look at her as she followed Bemus up the central aisle. Some smiled supportively; some didn't. She was known to most as Elana's second disciple, the organiser who used to decide which patient had priority. To others she was the Lady of the Knights, the woman who lived up at the castle. These people had idolised Elana, followed her every word. Belwynn wasn't sure what they thought of her. Or how they would react when she tried to claim leadership of the movement.

Bemus said a few words, his voice a comforting drone. The man already thought of himself as the new leader, she knew. Not that he saw her as an enemy—just less equipped to lead than he was.

Bemus retired to a seat on the front pew. All eyes turned to Belwynn.

She thought of her gift, then, as she prepared herself to use it once more. Her telepathy. She had been able to speak with Soren like that since they were very young—neither could recall exactly how or when it had started. Belwynn had always assumed it was because Soren could do magic. That it was because of *him*. Then she thought of her singing, how she could use it to connect with and touch an audience, sending them into a collective stupor. What if the telepathy and the singing were, in fact, the same thing? What if her ability to speak to Soren's mind was down to *her*, not him?

She looked out at Elana's flock and a feeling of serenity descended on her.

'I bring a message from Madria,' she said, projecting her voice to the very back of the chamber.

She was met with a range of expressions. Surprise. Doubt. Scorn.

She concentrated.

It's just the same as singing, Belwynn, she told herself.

I bring a message from Madria, she said.

Gasps of fear and shock filled the chamber. People looked at one another, desperate to know whether they had shared the same experience.

Belwynn's voice in their head.

Bemus slipped from his pew to his knees, his long body crumpling.

'Tell us her message!' he pleaded.

XXI

REVENGE

*T*HERON SAYS WE NEED TO FIGHT THEM NOW, Belwynn said to Soren.

Despite trying to explain to him how much the situation in Kalinth had changed, Soren didn't seem to fully understand. He counselled her against hasty decisions, asking her to stay where she was.

We have the bow now, he said again. *We'll be there in a matter of days.*

Get here as soon as you can, she asked him. *We're leaving today. We can't afford to wait and let them grow any stronger.*

Alright, said Soren, sounding disappointed that he hadn't dissuaded her, anxious about her claims that she was in communication with Madria. *We'll get there as soon as we can. Look after yourself.*

Barely a soul remained in Heractus, as the army assembled in the fields outside the city walls. Belwynn had emptied the city, recruiting its people to her cause using her gift of telepathy, magnified by Madria's power. Already believers, thanks to Elana's work, they now submitted themselves to Belwynn's instructions, who told them that this was a battle that simply had to be won.

The Temple of Madria had been left in the hands of those too aged or too young to join the army. Much to the girl's disappointment, Lyssa was amongst them. She had tried to persuade Belwynn how useful she would be to the army, but Belwynn had put her foot down. She couldn't afford to worry about the girl's whereabouts on top of everything else. Men, women, and those not old enough to be called either, were now ready to fight and die for this cause. Madria told Belwynn that it was necessary, that there was no guilt; no sin involved. Belwynn wanted to believe that.

Theron was grateful, for she had solved his ever-present problem, the lack of an infantry force. He led the cavalry part of the army, the Order of the Knights of Kalinth, or at least those knights who had chosen him over Galenos.

More soldiers had come in from the countryside to swell their force. Theron's estates in Erisina had been stripped of men of fighting age; likewise Sebastian's estate of Melion, which Theron had now inherited from his uncle. Theron's friend Tycho, the new owner of the estate of the traitor, Count Ampelios, had arrived back only yesterday, after raising a force from his new lands. Finally, Leontios, the young knight who had been tasked with defending the eastern border out of Korkis, had been recalled with his forces.

It was desperate times, the country left completely undefended. If the Kharovians or Drobax should descend from the north, they would find no-one to halt their passage to Heractus. Belwynn had asked Theron whether it would have been better to wait behind the walls of Heractus and see whether Straton's army materialised, but Theron had ruled that out. His knights needed to fight out in the open. He had described a scenario where they were stuck in the city, the rest of Kalinth taken by their enemies, starving and forced to eat their horses for food. The image had done its job of persuading her that they needed a battle.

So they marched for the south-west of the country. Philon returned to the army to pass on the information that his scouts had collected. Reports said the enemy army was led by the princes, Straton and Dorian. They could only assume that Dorian was the creature that had killed Elana and Sebastian. Many noblemen had flocked to the banner of the two young men, responding to their claims to leadership of Kalinth, their accusations against Theron, and the opportunity for advancement if they were successful. Galenos, formerly a prisoner at the High Tower, had allied with them, and many knights had chosen to fight with him. Diodorus, the Count of Korenandi, had added his soldiers as well, despite having fought with Theron only three weeks past. The enemy were growing in size, and this only reinforced Theron's view that they needed to deal with them immediately. Hanging over their heads was the fear that they may soon face an even greater threat. The Isharites could turn their attention to Kalinth. If they were to stand any chance, they had to avoid further civil war.

They marched hard all day, not stopping until they had crossed the Pineos. This part of the country was controlled by their enemies, and Belwynn could sense tensions rising as Theron gave orders to make camp, ensuring that sufficient knights were put on watch to give them warning of an attack.

Without realising what she was doing, Belwynn found herself walking off the path, until she came to a flat piece of rock by the river. She placed a palm on its surface as tears came to her eyes.

She had come upon this rock once before, when another army of knights had marched from the High Tower to Heractus. She had sat here in the sunshine with Elana and Dirk, as the priestess had healed her first disciple. A group of young knights, led by Philon and Leontios, had approached and asked her to bless their swords. Elana and Dirk were both gone now. She would have to sit here alone.

When she sat down she saw a figure making its way from the camp to her location.

'I thought I might find you here.'

Theron took a seat next to her and they sat together in silence for a while.

'What are you thinking?' she said at last.

'Lots of things. Maybe I've made a terrible mistake. Would Kalinth be better off if I hadn't started all this?'

'No. We freed Soren. Moneva killed Erkindrix. They've got the Jalakh Bow. The Isharites will be defeated. Thanks to you.'

Theron smiled. 'Thank you. I needed to hear that.' He tapped his scabbard. 'I seem to remember the Lady of the Knights giving out blessings here. Maybe she could bless this poor knight's sword? I think I will need to use it tomorrow.'

'Of course. But you think we will fight them tomorrow?'

'Yes. Neither of us will give ground. There's an inevitability to it now.'

'You need to tell me what you want Madria's soldiers to do. And there's something else.'

Theron looked at her, one eyebrow rising inquisitively.

Belwynn stared into his eyes.

Can you hear me? She asked him.

Theron's eyes widened. He frowned, concentrating.

Yes, he replied.

Belwynn smiled with pleasure. Although she could now communicate telepathically with Madria's servants, none of them could talk back to her. But somehow, she had known that Theron would be able to.

'Good,' she said out loud. 'When the battle starts tomorrow, you can tell me what to do.'

Soren! Belwynn tried one last time.

Where the hell was he? Surely he wasn't still asleep at this hour! Had something happened to him?

She couldn't know, and she had to put it out of her mind. Because the enemy had been sighted, and it was time to fight.

From her location behind the army, Belwynn ordered Madria's followers to their position. They marched, the flags showing the Winged Horse of Kalinth rippling in the breeze. They were to be the centre of the army, and they must not break. She communicated with them, reassuring them that whatever happened today, they had Madria's grace.

On either side came the rest of those who would fight on foot, men drawn from the estates owned by Theron and Tycho. Some were trained—some were even former knights. But most had never fought before.

The elite fighters were the knights, who were all on horseback. Theron led the right flank, Tycho the left. Leontios had been given another rapid promotion, leading the small force of reserves. Evander, one of the newest knights, would fight at Theron's side.

Move them forward fifty paces, Theron said to Belwynn from his position on the battlefield.

Their ability to communicate gave Theron an advantage in managing all these disparate forces.

Forwards, Belwynn relayed to her followers, and the Madrians walked in a disciplined line, gripping their spears, matching each other's stride, until Belwynn called a halt. The leaders of the other infantry units had orders to follow the Madrians, and they now marched, stopping once they had drawn level.

Those with the best eyes pointed ahead. They could see the enemy army. Belwynn peered ahead, just about making out shapes moving on the horizon—the enemy units getting into formation.

How many? She asked Theron.

Less than we have.

It was what they had hoped. The Madrians gave them an advantage in numbers. And in the end, more knights had sided with Theron than with Galenos.

Theron ordered them to advance another fifty paces, then he declared himself satisfied, waiting to see what the enemy would do. What they did came as a surprise. A small group on horseback detached themselves from the army, carrying the white flag of parley.

What is there to talk about? Theron asked her suspiciously.

The group stopped at the midway point between the two armies and waited.

Well? Belwynn asked Theron.

Well I suppose I will speak to them.

Me too, she demanded.

Alright, he said, in a resigned way.

Belwynn asked Leontios for a horse, while she told the Madrians to rest and meditate.

She climbed into the saddle and rode ahead, passing between the units of infantry.

Theron and Evander appeared from the right flank of the army, Tycho from the left. They trotted their horses towards the middle of the field.

Waiting for them were five figures. The soldier holding the flag she didn't recognise, but she knew the others. Diodorus, puffy-eyed and sad looking, sat his horse a few yards away from the others, as if he didn't want to be there. And so he should, thought Belwynn. Galenos and Belwynn had never exactly met, but they had once shared a look in the Great Hall of the Knights, at the High Tower, as she roused his order against him. He grinned at them now, seemingly confident about the revenge he would get for what they did to him that day. Finally, the two brothers, Straton and Dorian. Except they weren't brothers, for surely Dorian was dead, his body inhabited by the same monster that had killed Elana.

'You've got a bigger army than you did last time,' Straton said to Theron conversationally when they drew up. 'Where are they all from? There can't be many soldiers there.'

'They're loyal Kalinthians,' said Theron, 'prepared to fight our enemies even if you have chosen to fight alongside them.'

Diodorus had the grace to look to the ground at that comment, but the others didn't. Straton gave a light smile, looking away, somewhere into the distance.

'Loyalty?' retorted Galenos, his voice high-pitched and hysterical sounding. 'You have the gall to sit there and lecture us on loyalty? Oh, I will enjoy your humiliation today. Very much.'

'Have you asked us here to trade worthless insults?' Tycho said angrily. 'What does your leader say?' he added, gesturing at Dorian. 'The monster that inhabits the bodies of its victims! What kind of creature do you take your orders from?'

'It is time I introduced myself to you,' said Dorian. At least, it spoke with Dorian's voice, but it was clear to Belwynn that it wasn't really him. 'I am Siavash, Lord of the Ishari. I have come at the bidding of Diis, my master. When I visited in Heractus, I killed the leader of the Knights and I killed Madria's champion. My armies have conquered the Krykkers of Dalriya. The fleet of the Sea Caladri is destroyed. As I speak, our armies descend on the Brasingian Empire, on our remaining enemies in Halvia. The war is over. I have brought you here to make it clear to you that your continued resistance is pointless. If your people lay down their arms, they are free to return to their homes. Kalinth will be incorporated into the Isharite Empire. Straton will rule as king. I will not seek vengeance or pursue vendettas. If you choose to fight, all you will achieve is the slaughter of Kalinthians.'

Siavash? The man who had replaced Erkindrix? Belwynn wondered at it. She wondered why he would risk coming to Kalinth alone, albeit he had succeeded so far.

Tycho was one step ahead of her. He urged his mount forwards, drawing his sword as he did, before shoving the sharp end of the blade into Dorian's chest.

Siavash cackled. He grabbed the blade, pulling it out. No blood came with it.

'You cannot kill what is already dead,' he explained simply.

'You strike under a white flag?' Galenos demanded, looking outraged.

'I strike a demon!' Tycho retorted.

'Enough,' said Theron. 'We did not come here to surrender. Your revelations change nothing, except to make us more determined to defeat you today,' he said, pulling at his horse's reins, turning away from them.

'I will let you live,' said Straton quietly. 'I will rule justly. Theron, we have no real choice in this. Don't kill our people without reason.'

Theron ignored him, moving off. Belwynn glanced surreptitiously at Siavash, before following him. The Lord of Ishari had killed Elana, Madria's champion. Did he suspect that Madria had chosen a new one? It didn't seem so.

They rode back to their lines.

'It changes nothing,' Theron insisted.

None of them disagreed. But now they knew that it was Siavash who somehow resided in Dorian's body. And that he couldn't be killed.

Soren! Belwynn called with desperation.

But Soren didn't answer.

I'm not waiting any longer, Theron declared.

Trumpets blared across the battlefield. The Knights on each side of the army began to move forwards. They were the best fighters, the ones who could win the battle for them. Straton's army, inferior, held their position on higher ground, waiting for them to come.

Belwynn knew enough about battles, mainly from listening to Clarin's stories, to know that Straton's army would have dug in, prepared unpleasant traps and other surprises for the horses. They would defend, and somewhere the knights under Galenos would be waiting, ready to counter-attack.

The Knights picked up speed, streaming away from their lines. There was a nervous energy amongst those left behind, who had to wait for their turn to fight.

Like so many others, Belwynn peered ahead, fruitlessly trying to make out what was happening, to see whether the two sides had engaged yet. Theron had told her, in no uncertain terms, that she must stay with the reserves, and give out her orders from there. A small, basic tower had been constructed here, giving Belwynn and Leontios something of a view over the battlefield. It was enough for Belwynn to oversee her unit of Madrians. For Leontios, it would help him to decide when and where his small force should intervene.

We've engaged, Theron finally told her. *They've dug in. It's hard to get to them.*

Belwynn passed the message on to Leontios. The young man nodded coolly enough, but Belwynn had some idea how difficult it was for him to wait it out while his brothers were fighting.

Belwynn! It came as a shout, Belwynn shocked by Theron's voice echoing around her head. *We're in retreat! Tell Leontios! You need to move the infantry forwards to cover us!*

'Leontios, they're retreating back here, I think he wants you to help, I—' Belwynn paused, as Theron passed on more information. She went cold, her mouth opening and closing in mute shock.

'What is it?' Leontios demanded, his face full of concern at her reaction.

'Theron says it's the Drobax. The Drobax are here.'

March! Belwynn ordered the Madrians. *There are Drobax coming! Be prepared!*

What kind of affect her words had on them, she could only guess. But they did as she ordered, moving forwards in close formation. The other infantry units began to follow. Belwynn couldn't warn them. She tried to reach out with her mind to them, but there was no connection that she could use. They were unknowingly walking into a Drobax horde coming for them, and she doubted whether they would hold out for long.

Leontios took his mounted reserves to the left, swinging around the infantry units, whereupon he would lead them into the Drobax coming their way, trying to give the rest of the Knights time to retreat and regroup. He had insisted on leaving someone behind with Belwynn, and so Philon stayed with her on the tower, watching his friend ride away into battle.

The meeting before the battle made more sense to Belwynn now. Siavash's offer of an end to the conflict. The confident grin of Galenos. Straton's diffidence. Diodorus's shame. They had all known about the Drobax. Known that if it came to a fight, they were going to win.

Then she could see and hear the Knights. They made a noise like thunder, Theron's and Tycho's forces both returning to their original positions on either side of the infantry.

Halt! she ordered her soldiers, keeping them in place while the Knights arranged themselves. They seemed to be spreading out much more thinly than before, leaving larger gaps between each other. She could hear shouts but couldn't make out the words. She could hear the neighs of horses as their riders frantically turned them around, trying to get them into position. Somewhere out there, too far away for Belwynn to see, Leontios would be harassing the enemy, buying them precious time.

Belwynn! Every message Theron sent now came as a shout. *Get them ready. When the Drobax come they need to advance to meet them.*

Belwynn relayed the instructions to her soldiers, and it was just in time, because the Drobax now came into view. They howled when they saw the Kalinthians, picking up the pace from a fast march to a jog. There was little real order to their march, each creature travelling at its own pace. Belwynn could see their weapons, mostly crude wooden things, in their hands. Few wore armour. But it felt like none of that mattered, because more and more kept coming. The horizon darkened with Drobax, and yet there seemed to be no end to the numbers.

Belwynn told the Madrians to ready themselves: lock their shields in place, point their spears ahead. The Madrians let out a roar of their own as they did so, finding strength in the shields of the men and women who stood to either side of them.

Now! said Belwynn. The Madrians moved as one, shoving shields forwards to stop the Drobax, striking out with their spears at unprotected flesh. They had a few seconds of freedom, targeting the exposed Drobax who had arrived without the safety of a shield wall. But that was all they got, because then the Drobax coming behind hurtled towards them. The Madrians locked shields together, presenting a wall of death. The Drobax crashed into it, pushed forwards by the weight of numbers behind them.

From Belwynn's position it resembled a wave crashing against rocks, her Madrians arriving first, then behind them the rest of the Kalinthian infantry, following their advance. Finally, the Knights on each side moved ahead, using their height and long lances to skewer the Drobax before they got too close.

It was a strange sensation, then, as Belwynn ignored all else and focused on her Madrians. They punched ahead with their left arms all at the same time, smashing teeth and noses with their shields, then lunged forward with their right arm, a forest of steel coming at the Drobax all at once, impossible to escape. It was like Belwynn was the queen bee, and the Madrians her workers, following her orders without thinking for themselves. No fear; no sense of self-preservation. When one of them fell, they were replaced. This sense of unity, of harmony, was enough to withstand the greater numbers of Drobax.

Belwynn couldn't say how long this lasted, before she was pulled out of her reverie by Philon.

'My lady,' he warned her, pointing ahead.

Belwynn's Madrians had withstood the Drobax attack, but the infantry forces to their left and right could hold no longer. Men were turning and running from the monsters, and once a few of them left, more and more followed, in an effort to save their lives. Staying to fight suddenly became futile, and the units collapsed, turning to flee and outrun the Drobax while they still had a chance.

They ran in the direction of Belwynn and Philon, some dropping weapons in their haste to escape. The Drobax gave chase, though surely it was only a matter of time before some of the monsters moved around Belwynn's Madrians and surrounded them.

Philon gestured behind them. 'They're running to their deaths,' he said, bitterness filling his words. 'They'll never cross the river.'

Belwynn turned around to look. The fast flowing Pineos waited for those who made it that far. Some might gain the bridge in time, but most would face the choice of turning to face their pursuers or taking their chances in the water.

'I need to get you out of here,' he added.

The fleeing Kalinthians were drawing the Drobax towards their position, but where could they escape to?

Belwynn pointed towards the Madrians ahead of them.

'Take me there,' she said.

Philon looked around, his expression full of indecision. There was the bridge across the Pineos, perhaps still the safest option. He looked across the battlefield to where Theron fought. He could get her on a horse and ridden to safety from there, but they would have to get through the rampaging Drobax to reach Theron's knights. The Madrians ahead of them were closer, but how long would they hold out?

'I need to be with the Madrians,' Belwynn insisted.

'Alright,' Philon reluctantly agreed. 'Come, we must be swift.'

Descending the tower steps, Belwynn found herself running after Philon towards the battle, while not much more than a hundred feet away, Kalinthians were running past them in the opposite direction. They began to attract the attention of the Drobax following the Kalinthians, some of whom broke away in their direction. However, the thought of running hard back the way they had come seemed to dissuade them, and they reverted to their original quarry.

As they got closer, Belwynn could see her fears becoming realised. The rear of the Madrian unit was being attacked by the Drobax, who had all but encircled them.

'Come,' said Philon, urging her on, though her breath was getting ragged now.

Three Drobax came to meet them. Philon, sword already drawn, approached them, but he couldn't stop one of them moving for Belwynn. She drew her short sword.

'It's alright, Philon,' she assured him, sensing his anxiousness. 'I can hold it off.'

She focused now on the creature, holding a wicked looking club. She had been taught enough of sword fighting not to panic. It came for her, but she used her footwork, moving to the side as it approached. It made a vicious swing in her direction anyway, but the club sailed harmlessly past. Belwynn knew that a proper soldier like Clarin would have attacked at that point, but she simply backed away, not willing to risk getting into trouble. The creature grinned at her, but she wasn't intimidated by that. She feinted at it with her sword, making it think twice about charging at her. It moved towards her, twirling the club, perhaps ready to be a bit more patient this time.

But it didn't have time. Philon appeared behind it, chopping down with his sword on its skull. It dropped to the ground, where he made sure it was dead. He had already dispatched the other two Drobax.

However, the fight had drawn more Drobax in their direction. It didn't look like they would be able to get past them.

Help me, Belwynn ordered the Madrians, not really thinking, just acting.

They came at once, swiftly moving from defence to attack. The Drobax were forced to turn and meet the threat.

Philon ran at the Drobax, using his sword to punish them for turning their back on him. Between the advancing Madrians and the knight, the Drobax were either killed or forced to retreat.

Belwynn slipped in amongst the Madrians, safe for now.

Hold! Fight for Madria! she ordered them.

But they were being pressed from all sides, and Belwynn could tell that they wouldn't be able to hold for much longer. When their defences were breached, there would be no chance of an escape to the river. They would be surrounded and slaughtered.

XXII

REAPPEARANCE

THEY LEFT BASERNO BEHIND THEM, Clarin carrying the Persaleian Shield on his back. He enjoyed the weight of it; enjoyed being close to it.

Would Zared and his father allow him to keep it? Allow their people's shield to leave Persala? He couldn't be sure. If they didn't intend to let him have it, why take him to Baserno with them in the first place? Unless they had somehow known that he was the one who could claim it from the old flamen, Ennius. Ennius had only given up the shield when Clarin had said Belwynn's name. The strangeness of that stayed with him. Why Belwynn?

Zared and his father's champion, Duilio, were focused on leading their group to the rendezvous location with King Mark. Maybe then Clarin would get some answers.

They soon left the Persaleian roads to cut across country, heading for one of the old places of Persala, away from the towns and prying eyes. By a track that continued on to a collection of farm buildings stood a giant old oak tree, that had perhaps served as a meeting point when the Persaleian Empire was at its height. Here they threw off packs and sat down for a bite to eat.

Zared paced up and down, waiting for Mark and his force to arrive.

Clarin sat with Rudy and Jurgen, watching the Rotelegen massage his leg. Jurgen had taken a spear to the calf muscle in Samir Durg and had been lame ever since.

'You two must be tempted to head south from here, to your homeland,' Clarin commented.

The two cousins looked at each other. 'We've discussed it,' Rudy admitted. 'Don't know what we'll find there if we do, with Isharite armies heading every which way. And from what you say, finding yon shield could do more good for our people than anything else. But home does call to me. We have family who would be surprised to see us alive, that's for sure,' he said, grinning at the thought.

'I appreciate your help and loyalty,' said Clarin, 'and I'd be honoured if you stayed. But I'd understand if you didn't.'

Jurgen nodded. 'I can't go on walking like this for much longer. My body needs rest. But like Rudy says, two of us marching south, into only the gods know what kind of mess? You've kept us alive this far, Clarin. Against the odds. I'm not keen on doing something hasty and throwing our lives away after what we've lived through.'

Shouts disturbed their talk. Clarin jumped to his feet, Rudy pulled Jurgen up to his.

'Soldiers!' came the warnings. Presumably they weren't Mark's.

Duilio's men pointed to the east, from the direction of Baserno. Tamir and the Barbarians pointed to the fields that stretched to the north. Disciplined ranks of spearmen marched towards them from both directions, supported by cavalry. They numbered in the hundreds, too much of a match for their group of twenty-eight.

Cyprian ran back to their camp from the direction of the farm.

'Soldiers coming!' he declared, then looked at their faces. 'What?'

'There's soldiers coming from every direction,' Zared said, a sad smile on his face.

They stood together, weapons drawn. No-one asked Clarin what they should do. They knew there was no answer.

Clarin pulled the sackcloth off the Shield of Persala, inspecting its decorated leather surface, before putting the strap around his shoulder. If it came to a fight, at least he would get to use the shield once—get to see exactly what it could do.

The three forces closed in on them, in a perfectly executed trap.

'They must have known we were coming here,' murmured Tamir, the tall Barbarian chief hefting a long spear.

The Barbarians were ready to go down. So too were Rudy and Jurgen; the Dog-men; and Zared's Persaleians. Men who had suffered and weren't scared of death if it was coming. Duilio's ten men looked more nervous, but held their weapons at the ready nonetheless.

The first two divisions stopped some fifty yards away, but the third, from the farm, kept coming closer, until they too came to a halt.

Four figures detached themselves from the front line and strode farther towards them. They were strange companions, but all Clarin could really focus on was one of the men in the middle of the group.

Because it was his brother. It was Herin.

Shock slammed into Clarin at the sight of his brother. Herin caught his eye, smiling sardonically at him. But Clarin pushed the shock away. Maybe it was because he was holding his sword, Cutter, and his new shield, ready for battle, that he was able to do so. Some of the others: Rudy, and Cyprian, called out to Herin in greeting. But Clarin knew better. He knew Herin too well to mistake the look on his face, to mistake what this was.

'Hello brother,' Herin said.

'I looked for you. For weeks. We all did,' Clarin said, waving his sword at his friends.

'I knew you would,' said Herin. 'I'm sorry. But I knew you would leave me in the end. And you did.'

'Why did you do it?'

'Because while I was stuck in the mines with all of you, I realised a truth. The Isharites are going to win this war. And, so the old saying goes, if you can't beat them, join them. I knew none of you would be willing to follow where I had to go. You would have tried to stop me, Clarin. You would have come with me, and tried to change my mind. It was better this way.'

Clarin shrugged his shoulders. 'Maybe I would have. I'm glad you're alive, by the way. But you're wrong. Very wrong. We've already killed Erkindrix. We're going to destroy the Isharites. And that means we'll destroy you, too.'

'With that shield?' Herin asked, a smug look on his face.

He turned to the creature next to him and nodded. The creature was Drobax-like, but larger. It reached into a bag it was carrying and dragged out a bloody mass, holding it by the hair. It took Clarin a moment to process what he was looking at, before the creature presented it to them, holding it out for them all to see. It was a decapitated head—Mark's head.

Zared let out a bellow of rage, but his men acted quickly, grabbing him, pulling him to the ground before he could run at Herin.

'Someone's upset,' said the creature.

Gasps of horror met this statement. Clarin couldn't help but stare in revulsion, bile rising to his throat. A Drobax that could speak?

'What kind of abomination is that?' Duilio demanded.

'That's not very nice,' said the creature, casually dropping the head onto the ground.

'This is Kull,' said Herin. 'Did you ever wonder why there were just men in the mines in Samir Durg? Well, now you know why. Your womenfolk were busy breeding with the Drobax to produce a superior stock. Something Ardashir had been working on apparently—Diis protect his soul. Drobax with the strength of humans, who can talk, and think. The new officer class of the Drobax army.'

Now it was the turn of the Barbarians to curse and rage, moving forward threateningly. It must have been their tribes who had been used by Ardashir in such a hideous way.

Herin held a hand up. 'Please. Gods, I'm not saying I approve. No offence to you, Kull, but the whole thing disgusts me.'

Kull put on a hurt face, his expression and mannerisms oddly human.

'But it takes me back to my original point,' Herin continued. 'The Isharites are going to win. It doesn't matter what I think about it. They've already destroyed the Krykkers, destroyed the fleet of the Sea Caladri. Kalinth is about to fall. There's really no-one left to stop them. I'm not going to die trying. Neither should you.'

'They should all die,' said another voice.

Clarin turned his attention to the other two men standing with Herin. Next to him was a flame haired human. At the end of the line was an Isharite, who stared at them with hatred under the hood of his black cloak. He was the one who had spoken. Neither man wore mail. Both, Clarin suspected, could be wizards. Herin had not just brought an army with him, but magic users too.

'What do you want?' Clarin asked reluctantly.

'Mark and his men are dead. No-one is coming to help you. All I want is the shield. You can all walk free. Now, I know you're not going to agree to that. I can see it in your eyes, all of you. This is what will happen. I will send my Haskan soldiers and Drobax against you, Rimmon and Peroz here will use some pretty terrifying magic, too. You'll fight well. Clarin, we'll all get to see what that shield does. No doubt it will turn you into an even mightier killing machine than you already are. But you'll die in the end. And between you, you'll kill, let's be generous, a hundred of my soldiers. But I don't care about them. I don't even know their names. They won't be missed. I'll be more upset about your deaths, to be honest.'

Clarin glanced at his men, back to Herin and his lieutenants. Nothing Herin had said was untrue. Where was he going with this?

'So, here's my offer. I swear on our father's life that it is a faithful one. No-one dies here but you or I. We fight one another for the shield. You don't get to use it in the fight, of course,' Herin said with a smile. 'That would be unfair. The winner gets the shield. The losing army walks away. If I lose, my forces leave and let all of you go free, to fight another day. If I win, I let your men leave Persala in peace.'

'Ridiculous,' said Peroz, spitting with fury. 'I order you to kill them all now. You will be punished severely for this.'

'See,' said Herin, turning to the Isharite, 'I don't think so. If I win, I'm giving Siavash the Shield of Persala and the head of King Mark. I don't think he's going to care about my methods. If I lose, all he'll have to punish is a corpse.'

'Don't do it, Clarin!' Zared, surrounded by his men, was crouching on the ground, his face raw with anger and grief. He'd only been reunited with his father three days ago. Herin had taken Mark from him. 'We're ready to die.'

'How did you know we were here?' Clarin asked his brother.

'Siavash knew as soon as you left Heractus.'

All this time? Clarin said to himself. They'd let them get the shield from Baserno, just waiting to take it from them.

'Like I said, Kalinth is about to fall, if it hasn't already.'

Clarin looked at Herin, fear and anger boiling inside him. 'Belwynn is in Heractus,' he hissed.

At least Herin had the grace to look apologetic. 'I'm sorry about that. Then you may still have a chance to save her. Throwing away your life now gets you nothing, save a sense of false heroism.'

'Alright, brother,' Clarin said, unable to avoid putting heavy sarcasm into the second word. 'I'll fight you.'

'No!' said Zared, storming over, pushing away those who tried to stop him. 'You think we can trust these bastards!?'

'We've agreed to it,' said the red-haired Haskan, speaking up for the first time. 'we've sworn to respect the outcome of the fight.'

Clarin held up a hand as Zared reached him. 'Listen,' he said quietly, just for the young man to hear. 'If you're right, if it's all a trick, then we all die anyway, the outcome's exactly the same. If it isn't, you and your men escape this. Persala gets a new king-in-exile. Your father's fight carries on. You have to take that chance, Zared.'

Zared looked at him, pain visible in his features. He didn't say anything, but he turned and walked away, rejoining his men.

Clarin pulled the strap over his head and laid the Shield on the ground. Herin drew his own sword, built from dark blue coloured diatine crystal, and walked over to meet him. He saw Clarin looking at his weapon, before smiling.

'So, we both fight with these things now,' he said.

'I'm stronger than you, brother,' Clarin warned him. 'You know I'll beat you.'

Herin's smile disappeared. 'We'll see, Clarin.'

They backed away from each other, preparing to begin. When Clarin looked over at Herin, he couldn't help but step back in time. As a child he had idolised Herin, desperate to learn sword-craft from his father just like him. When he grew big enough, he had had two teachers, his father and his older brother, and he had loved every minute of it. Loved travelling around Dalriya and working with Herin, content to let his brother make all the decisions for them because he was so happy they were together.

Well, times had changed. He had to forget the past. Herin had made a decision that he could never follow, and now he had to kill him.

They closed in on each other, both holding their swords two-handed. Herin was more aggressive than Clarin had expected, trying to land a blow from the outset, and Clarin had to defend and keep moving, before he was able to counter-attack, using his strength to push Herin away.

Men from both sides shouted encouragement, advice and insults, but the noise soon faded into the background. It became just Herin and Clarin. They had sparred together countless times, knew each other's strengths and weaknesses intimately. Clarin could never have guessed that he would ever have to use that knowledge to kill his brother.

Herin came at him fast again, feinting high and then spinning his blade low. Clarin's attempted block didn't go low enough and Herin's blade landed, rasping his ankles. Herin had left himself open, though, and Clarin was able to give him an elbow in the face before he leapt away. Now Herin let Clarin come on to him, moving left to right, forward to back. This was more Herin's way, using his speed and agility to entice Clarin into making a mistake, or if none came, slowly tiring out his bigger opponent. Clarin gave him nothing. He stuck to his form, not doing anything rash, not wasting energy. But his blows were that bit heavier, that bit more dangerous than Herin's, and he only needed one to get through.

Herin advanced again, plunging his sword with incredible accuracy into the gap above Clarin's right greave. A sharp, burning pain erupted where the crystal blade struck. But again, Herin's aggression gave Clarin the chance to land a blow of his own. Herin pulled his sword up to block his head and the top of his body, but Clarin put all of his weight into a mighty blow that crunched onto Herin's thigh, twisting the armour. Herin pulled away, but Clarin was satisfied to see that he was now limping. His brother's movement was compromised, and Clarin had the advantage.

Maybe that realisation was what prompted Herin to launch another, reckless attack. He moved inside Clarin's swing, thrusting his blade up, piercing through chain mail and into Clarin's armpit. Clarin lurched to the side, delivering a massive two-handed swing that connected square on with Herin's bicep. Herin pulled away. He still held his sword, but it dangled limply. He could no longer move his arm.

This was it. His brother could no longer move properly, or swing his sword. Herin transferred the weapon into his left hand, not looking like he was ready to give in. But he couldn't win from here.

Clarin was sweating profusely from the fight. He felt his face burning up. He edged towards Herin, who backed off now, wary of getting involved in another exchange after coming off worse each time. Clarin darted forwards in an effort to close the gap, but Herin anticipated it, scurrying away.

Clarin felt dizzy now. He had to stop to get his breath back.

Herin waited, watching him closely, not making a move of his own.

Clarin hefted his sword up, readying himself for a final effort. He tried to wipe away the sweat that was dripping into his eyes. His sword suddenly weighed a ton. Then, it slowly dawned on him, his mind so foggy that his thoughts travelled at a snail's pace. This wasn't normal. Herin had only scratched him three times.

Poison.

His brother must have put poison on his blade. That was why he had attacked so much, why he had been prepared to take Clarin's blows. Because each cut Herin had made had put more poison into Clarin's bloodstream.

Clarin turned to face his friends. They won't have realised. He had to warn them. But his throat had constricted and he couldn't get any words out.

Now Herin came for him, slowly, stalking like a cat with a baby bird. Clarin could barely focus on Herin's approach, his eyes watery, his gaze hazy.

Herin skipped towards him. Clarin tried to swing out, but his legs were jelly and he tottered forwards, dropping to his hands and knees, his sword sliding from his grasp.

This was unfair. If he was going to be killed by his own brother, at least let it be from a fair fight. Not this way.

Not like this.

He looked up, trying to make his eyes focus.

A blurry black shape came towards him.

The last thing Clarin saw was the sole of Herin's boot.

XXIII

RESCUE

*B*ELWYNN! WHERE ARE YOU? came a shout. It took her a moment to process it. Part of her mind told her it must be Theron, but it didn't sound like him.

Soren!?

We're here, he added. *Where are you?* he repeated.

I'm with the Madrians. The— she panicked, desperate to get her words out, struggling to describe her situation so that he would understand. *The infantry on the battlefield. The ones who are still fighting.*

Right. We're coming.

Hold on! she directed her soldiers. *Reinforcements are coming.*

Theron? she shouted. *Soren is here!*

Seconds passed without a reply, and she feared he was dead, but then she heard his voice.

Good, he said, no doubt struggling to talk to her while fighting. *Stay alive, Belwynn.*

Belwynn was now forced to fight as the Madrians were surrounded and one by one, pulled down and killed. Philon fought by her side, more than once stopping a blow that would likely have killed her. She tried to keep the rhythmic work of the Madrians going—left arm shield, right arm spear—but they were tiring now, and the truth was few of them were soldiers.

It was hardly noticeable at first, but the pressure on them slowly started to ease. Then, it became clear that the Drobax on the left had started to reduce in number. They began to disappear altogether. Belwynn looked over in that direction and saw three figures walking towards them. Three figures she knew very well.

Soren held aloft Onella's Staff, and around him was a large, invisible shield of magic, which the Drobax couldn't penetrate. It was just the same as the spell he had used in the Wilderness to defend against the vossi, rebuffing all attempts by the Drobax to penetrate it.

Next to him was Gyrmund, the two men leaning on each other for support as they slowly approached. Gyrmund held a bow, and was loosing arrow after arrow at the Drobax. Each time he released the string, a thrum echoed across the battlefield. It was a sound that Belwynn realised she had been hearing in the background for some time now. Each arrow sped from the bow at a frightening velocity, and each seemed to find its mark, puncturing through flesh and armour alike, embedding in Drobax chests and skulls.

Ahead of them Moneva led the way, her two short swords drawn. Whenever a Drobax got too close and was repulsed by Soren's magic, she was there to strike it down, moving the corpses out of the way so that they didn't trip the other two.

They continued to advance, clearing a path through to Belwynn and the Madrians. The ground was littered with Drobax pierced by arrows from Gyrmund's bow, and yet he still had more to fire.

'The Jalakh Bow,' Belwynn whispered to herself as she watched them approach.

The Drobax had had enough. No longer willing to stand and wait for their turn to be killed, they turned and ran away. It turned into a wider rout. On both sides of the battlefield, Belwynn could see the Drobax detaching from the knights and running back the way they had come.

She walked over to her brother, each collapsing with exhaustion into each other, no need for words. Pulling herself away, she embraced first Moneva, then Gyrmund.

'You got the bow then?' she asked.

Gyrmund smiled ruefully. 'Not a moment too soon.'

'Your fingers!' said Belwynn, staring where the skin had been rubbed off and was red raw.

'Hmm, don't think I've ever fired that many arrows at once,' he said, keeping his smile.

'I'm sorry about Elana, Belwynn,' said Moneva. 'The creature is here?'

Belwynn nodded, pointing to the other side of the battlefield, where the enemy was located, still not defeated. 'The creature is Siavash,' she told them.

Soren's face twisted up, full of hatred.

'Then let's waste no more time.'

'It isn't Siavash himself,' Belwynn tried to explain. 'He has somehow occupied the body of Prince Dorian. Tycho struck him with a sword before the battle. It didn't do anything. I think, because the body is already dead.'

She watched their faces register this: repulsed, fearful, hate-fuelled. They all knew they had to kill the creature.

'How did you get here?' she asked them.

They turned around, looking towards the left flank of the army. Two figures were heading in their direction. One was Tycho, hobbling as he walked and grimacing in pain as he leaned on the second man.

Pentas.

'How-,' began Belwynn, astonished to see the wizard here.

Soren shrugged, allowing himself a grim smile. 'The Isharites failed to kill him. He found us on the Jalakh Steppe. Got us here.'

Pentas gently lowered Tycho to the ground.

'Philon!' the big knight called over, his lungs apparently unharmed, even if he carried a bad leg injury.

Philon came over, and they clasped hands.

'I'm done,' Tycho admitted. 'Can't walk or ride. Will you take my place? We've taken a battering but some of them can still fight. We need to take the bastards out while we still have the chance.'

Theron joined them, tired looking but uninjured. He assured Belwynn that Evander still lived. Leontios arrived soon after, his small band of knights somehow escaping their encounter with the Drobax horde relatively unharmed.

With screams coming from the direction of the River Pineos, the Knights were forced to agree that they had to deal with the Drobax to the north first. They couldn't just allow a slaughter of Kalinthians to take place, nor leave an enemy force at their back.

Theron, Leontios and Philon led those Knights free of injuries to the river. The injured knights and the Madrians remained, casting anxious looks to the south where Siavash, Straton and the other leaders were presumably dealing with the repercussions of the Drobax retreat.

It was difficult for Belwynn to bear. Injured men and women looked at her, mute pleas for help on their faces. Elana would have been busy healing them by now. But Belwynn didn't have such powers. She could talk to them, instruct them to fight and kill, but couldn't save their lives when they were dying. She was a poor replacement for Elana, and she wished the priestess was here.

Instead, she walked amongst them, praising their efforts, reassuring them that Madria was still with them. A small group were fussing over a body, and Belwynn saw that it was Bemus. Elana's disciple had fallen amongst her flock, his body mutilated from half a dozen wounds.

'On your feet, those who can,' came the rich voice of Pentas the wizard, full of authority. 'They are coming for us.'

He pointed ahead. Rows of infantry were coming into view, a slow, methodical approach compared to the Drobax. In between these units, and on the flanks, were mounted soldiers, the Knights of Kalinth loyal to Galenos.

Theron, Belwynn said, *they are coming for us. Come back as soon as you can.*

Will do, Belwynn, he replied. *Try to hold them off.*

Belwynn ordered the Madrians to form ranks. They did so without complaint, but they were heavily outnumbered, by fresh troops.

If Siavash attacked now it would be over in minutes. But his infantry moved slowly, and his cavalry went at the same pace.

Belwynn glanced behind her. She imagined she would see Theron and his Knights riding to the rescue, but they weren't in sight.

'Soren!' Pentas shouted.

It looked like Galenos's knights were done with sticking to the pace of the infantry. Perhaps the Grand Master only now realised just how vulnerable his enemies were, with the knights off the field. For a charge had been ordered. They left the infantry units behind, riding for Belwynn's Madrians. Each carried a lance under an arm, which they would soon level and aim at the front rank. The flag of the Kalinthian Knights, detailing Stephen defeating the Dragon, came with them. Belwynn suspected that Galenos himself rode there, keen to take his revenge on his enemies.

The Madrians had to hold against them. If they turned and ran, it would be a massacre.

Pentas and Soren walked towards the approaching cavalry, past Belwynn and the Madrians, then stood waiting. Some of the knights looked confused, unsure whether they should target the two wizards or ignore them.

Then, both acting at the same time, they unleashed. Fiery bolts leapt from Pentas's outstretched hands and from Onella's Staff.

Bright flames burned across the intervening space and struck mounts and riders alike. Horses crashed to the ground, turned and sped away in fear, ignoring their rider's commands. Soldiers fell from their mounts, pulled on reins in a panic, crashing into one another as they did so.

Pentas and Soren began to walk forwards now, sending more fiery arcs at individual riders foolish enough to stay too close.

Gyrmund then joined in, releasing the string of the Jalakh Bow, the thrumming sound echoing around. His arrows could travel farther than the wizard's flames, targeting those knights who thought they had gained a safe distance. The Knights wore full armour, but the arrows more often than not found a way through anyway—puncturing chest mail, finding unprotected faces. If in doubt, he targeted the horses. Although armoured, there were bigger gaps in the beast's defences, and Gyrmund's accuracy with the bow allowed him to find them.

The charge was over almost before it had begun. The flag lay smouldering on the ground: maybe Galenos with it. Pentas and Soren had devastated the enemy with their power. And for the first time since the Drobax had appeared, Belwynn believed they would win the battle, because they now had two wizards with them, and the enemy had none.

With the outcome of the battle poised on a knife edge, the enemy continued their march. Shouts rang out, as they tried to speed up the march of the infantry. Belwynn understood that Straton's best chance was to drive her Madrians from the field before Theron returned. Pentas and Soren still stood against them, but how much more did they have to expend after seeing off the knights?

The infantry came faster, save for the unit on the right, which began to fall behind.

Hold firm, Belwynn instructed the Madrians. *The Knights will return soon.*

The enemy drew closer and now Belwynn could see the front rank. Leading the soldiers was Siavash, still in the body of poor Prince Dorian. His men marched with him, fooled into thinking they fought to return their royal family to the throne.

I can see you, came Theron's voice. *We will be there soon.*

Relief flooded Belwynn.

The enemy now came faster. Soren and Pentas unleashed their magic yet again. The soldiers either side of Siavash were caught in the flames. Clothes

232

were set alight, as warriors desperately covered faces with arms, or rolled on the ground to put out the flames.

The fire didn't stop Siavash, however. His clothes burned away, his skin melted, but the body of Prince Dorian kept on coming. An arrow whistled into his chest, but he still came on, pulling his spear back. It plunged into Pentas. The wizard grabbed the shaft, trying to stop Siavash from pushing it further into his body.

Soren raised Onella's Staff, but Siavash reacted quickly. Pulling the spear from Pentas's grasp, he cracked the blunt end of the weapon into Soren, once then twice, the second blow knocking him over.

Belwynn ran towards them, leaving the Madrians behind, desperate to stop Siavash. She watched as he turned back to Pentas, raising his spear to finish the wizard off.

Pentas shot an arm out, sending a blast of magic that sent Siavash flying into the air, landing in a heap several feet away.

Pentas dropped to the ground.

Soren slowly pushed himself up with his staff.

Siavash got to his feet, Dorian's body smouldering from the flames. But it seemed that nothing could kill him.

The Kalinthian soldiers had stopped. They now looked at their prince, clothes and skin burned away, but still standing nonetheless. Only now would they begin to ask themselves what manner of creature they served.

Belwynn still ran. To her left, she saw that Gyrmund and Moneva came too.

Gyrmund stopped, fitting another arrow to his bow. He fired true, a second missile slamming into Siavash. The creature took a couple of steps backwards from the impact, but otherwise the weapon didn't harm it. If neither Soren or Gyrmund could kill the thing, what could do they do?

You must destroy it, Madria told Belwynn.

But how?

Belwynn and Moneva arrived together, Siavash studying them, a grin on his face.

He made a feint towards them before moving at astonishing speed towards Soren, whipping his spear in a long arc. It connected with Onella's Staff, knocking it from Soren's hands and sending it spinning away.

Belwynn knew what that meant for Soren—the loss of sight and movement. Did Siavash know, she wondered.

He cackled. 'I knew we would meet again, Soren,' said Siavash, though he sounded like Dorian. 'We have unfinished business, you and I. So killing you would be a disappointment. Pentas, on the other hand,' he continued, gesturing at the prone wizard, 'took much longer to destroy than I would have liked.'

Moneva came for him then, swinging with her short swords, but she was unable to get close. Siavash sent a straight jab with the spear at her chest, before swinging low and taking away her legs. He looked at Belwynn, then, but dismissed her as a threat, before turning back to Moneva with a smile.

'Another chance for revenge,' he cooed at Moneva, 'on the one who dared to kill Erkindrix. Diis will be pleased with today's work.'

'Moneva!' Belwynn shouted at her. 'Give me the dagger!'

Lightning fast, without hesitation, Moneva grabbed Toric's Dagger from her belt and threw it to Belwynn.

Without time to doubt herself, Belwynn caught the weapon, grabbing the hilt in her right hand, and advanced on Siavash.

'Now Belwynn!' shouted Pentas.

He had risen to a sitting position and now tugged at Siavash's spear with his magic. Siavash pulled back, loathe to lose his weapon.

Belwynn launched herself at him, raising her right hand high and bringing the blade down on top of his skull.

'Die!' she screamed, and as the words left her lips she felt a channelling sensation. The forces that had entered her upon Elana's death now awoke, streaming from her body, down the length of the weapon, and into the head. Her arm jolted, and a bang, like an explosion, could be heard.

Then Dorian's body suddenly went limp. It fell to the ground, and Toric's Dagger came free as it did.

Siavash was gone.

Theron and his Knights arrived soon afterwards. They stopped short of engaging with the enemy. Those who had attacked with Siavash remained on the battlefield, apparently leaderless. Some had witnessed Dorian's death; some had seen enough to question whether it had been Dorian at all—but many still saw Theron as the enemy, and the situation remained delicate. Over on the right flank, the second unit still kept its distance.

Belwynn, Soren, Gyrmund and Moneva gathered around Pentas. He was deathly pale but still conscious.

'A shadow,' he said, trying to explain what Siavash had done. 'Diis must have separated Siavash's shadow from his body, allowing him to occupy the bodies of those he killed. That's how he did this.'

'And he's now dead?' Moneva asked.

'The shadow is destroyed. Siavash is unharmed. He and Diis must still be defeated.'

He coughed, desperately trying to find his breath. Soren gripped his hand. After a while Pentas managed to calm his breathing enough to talk again.

'I am sorry about Elana. Mostly, of course, because if she were here I might be saved.' He smiled wanly at this, though Belwynn struggled to see the humour in it. 'Siavash succeeded in killing Madria's two servants. He thought he had won.' He turned to look at Belwynn, grimacing in pain. 'Now he knows otherwise. He must know that you are Madria's new champion, Belwynn.'

The others looked at her after that statement, questions in their eyes.

'He will come to kill you,' Pentas continued. 'But you can kill him. You can kill Diis,' he wheezed, struggling to speak. 'As ever, it's the weapons. You must find the remaining weapons before it's too late.'

Belwynn nodded. 'We will,' she said. A promise to a dying man she had no idea how to make happen.

Nonetheless, Pentas seemed satisfied that she understood.

Events on the battlefield grabbed their attention. The second unit of enemy infantry, seemingly reluctant to move until now, had begun to march towards them. Above the front line they held a white flag.

'Go,' said Soren to the others, still gripping Pentas's hand. 'I will stay with him.'

Theron was dismounting, as Belwynn, Gyrmund and Moneva made their way over to join him. The four of them walked the short distance to a location between the two armies. The second unit halted, and two men left the front rank, one of them the flag bearer.

'Diodorus,' Theron said in disgust, recognising the count who walked besides the flag. 'The traitor has come to wriggle out of this mess.'

Diodorus signalled to the soldiers who had fought with Siavash, until two men detached themselves from their ranks and came to join the parley.

The two groups of four eyed each other warily, one of the soldiers staring fearfully at the Jalakh Bow that Gyrmund carried.

'Dorian is dead?' Diodorus asked.

'Yes,' Belwynn said. 'Though it wasn't Dorian.'

Diodorus nodded in his sad way. 'I realised that much,' he said.

'I recognise you,' Theron said to one of the other soldiers. 'You are Proteus, a Knight of Kalinth. You fought for Galenos?'

'Yes,' the man said defiantly.

'Does he live?'

'He died, engulfed in the flames sent by your warlocks,' Proteus replied bitterly.

Theron nodded, unmoved by the man's hostility. 'Well?' he said, turning to Diodorus.

'I am here to submit to you as victor. We will lay down our arms if you spare the men's lives.'

'We will do no such thing!' objected Proteus. 'We have the numbers still!'

Diodorus swivelled his large head to look at the knight. 'If you try to fight on I will order my men into battle against you. It's over.'

'Treacherous swine!' Proteus declared.

'Just state your decision, Proteus,' Theron interjected, face implacable.

Proteus looked from one to the other before giving up. 'I have no choice, do I? I will order a surrender.'

Theron nodded. 'I accept. Though don't think you can escape this with your life, Diodorus,' he warned the count. 'The punishment for treachery must always be death.'

Diodorus nodded. 'I know that,' he said. 'Though I would ask a favour. Dorian—or whoever he was-'

'Siavash of Ishari,' said Moneva.

Diodorus raised an eyebrow at that, and Proteus frowned, unable to comprehend the statement.

'He took my two sons from me. Kept them as hostages to ensure I fought with them. They are back at the camp. He told Straton to—to kill them should I waver.'

His eyes went down to the ground, wrestling with his emotions, before he looked up again. 'I would appreciate your help in finding them. I would like to know whether they live or not. They are young boys, innocent in all this.'

'Very well,' said Theron. 'I will accompany you.'

They walked back to their soldiers.

It is over, Belwynn said to the Madrians. *Rest now.*

They returned to Soren.

'He is gone,' he said to them as they approached.

Pentas's eyes were closed now. Without those red eyes he looked like a normal, unremarkable man. Of course, that couldn't have been further from the truth.

'Where would we be now without him?' Belwynn asked out loud.

'Do you remember when we first met him, waiting for us on the road to Coldeberg?' Gyrmund asked. 'That was the first time he saved our lives.'

'He got us out of Samir Durg,' Moneva said quietly.

'He had been holding back the Isharites for a long time before that,' added Soren. 'I don't know how we will manage without him.'

No-one had an answer to that. Pentas had said that she must do it, but why had the burden suddenly fallen on her?

'I'm going with Theron,' she said, keen to escape the question.

Belwynn and Theron rode with Count Diodorus to the enemy camp. Wagons full of supplies, soldiers' tents, and the other accoutrements of war lay all around, though few soldiers remained.

'Where did the Drobax go?' Belwynn asked.

'Back where they came from,' Diodorus replied.

Belwynn remembered Siavash boasting that he had conquered the Krykker lands. She spared a thought for Rabigar, hoping he had somehow survived.

'It was hastily done,' Diodorus added. 'The Drobax had marched all the way here. They were tired, leaderless. But there are many of them. I fear they will be back.'

Theron shrugged. 'If the Krykkers truly are defeated, the Drobax will not only be sent here, but all over Dalriya. Nowhere is safe. That's why we must stand against the Isharites.'

Belwynn put a hand on his arm. He sounded tired; empty. He had been arguing for the Kalinthians to stand up to Ishari for years. And he had ended up fighting his own people instead. She understood his despondency.

'There,' said Diodorus, pointing at a covered wagon. 'My boys were kept inside.'

They trotted their mounts over, dismounting just before it. Belwynn felt an unpleasant ache in the pit of her stomach. She didn't want to find two dead boys here.

They walked to the back of the wagon. A man leaned against it. It was Prince Straton.

'When the Drobax ran past,' said the prince, with no preamble, 'I thought then we might lose after all.' He shook his head wryly. 'Seems like I'll always lose to you, Theron.'

The prince looked at Diodorus's expression.

'Oh! Your sons!' he said. 'You know I would never have done anything to them, don't you?'

Straton turned around, pulling aside the canvas. 'Come out, boys!' he said. 'Your father's come for you, just like I said.'

Two boys, neither as old as ten, came to the back of the wagon. Diodorus walked over, lifted them both out, one in each arm, and deposited them onto the ground. He knelt there, hugging them and saying nothing. Belwynn, Theron and Straton walked away a few paces, giving them some room.

Straton looked over at the family.

'I'm not a monster, you know,' he said defensively.

'You've been serving one,' said Theron accusingly.

'Dorian?'

'You know it wasn't Dorian,' said Belwynn, her anger at the prince bursting out.

Straton nodded. 'He said he'd make me king,' he said simply, as if that explained it all.

Theron shook his head.

'It would have been better. Now the Isharites will come and destroy Kalinth,' he said to Theron.

Theron looked at him, teeth gritted.

'There's no longer any need for you to worry about that,' Theron declared, before launching himself at Straton. He knocked the prince to the ground, diving on to him and drawing a knife from his belt.

'Theron!' Belwynn shouted.

But he didn't stop, pushing the knife into Straton's neck, holding it there until the prince stopped struggling.

Belwynn didn't try to stop him.

Theron rose to his feet. Straton's blood covered his face, neck and chest. Turning to Diodorus, his fingers gripped the hilt of his sword.

'Theron,' said Belwynn, 'don't you think we've shed too much blood now?'

He turned to face her. 'Too much? Maybe my mistake has been in not shedding enough.'

'What, then? You'll kill him in front of his children? He could still be an ally.'

Theron drew his sword and approached. Diodorus looked up at him, saw Straton's body sprawled on the ground, then gently moved his children to one side.

'You are pardoned, Diodorus, if you swear to serve me faithfully from now on. Not to serve the kingdom, or some other oath you can wriggle out of. Me.'

Diodorus got to his knees. 'I swear it, on the lives of my boys. I am yours to command.'

***

CLOUDS SCUDDED across the sky and a breeze kept them cool, as soldiers, servants and other hangers-on took the Great Road north.

Farred didn't fully understand how his decisions were leading him to return to Burkhard Castle. He had certainly never wanted to go back there, let alone go through the misery of another siege. Edgar had offered him a wife and lands just three weeks past. He had turned the offer down. Some men might call themselves stupid for doing so. But Farred was beginning to believe that it was fate that was bringing them all back to Burkhard. And fate cannot be denied.

If his thoughts on their destination were bleak, Farred was at least relieved at the manner of their departure. Archmage Gustav had spoken privately with Inge, and Duke Walter had done the same with Baldwin. Whatever had been said worked, for the Emperor wasted no time in sending out his orders and preparing to lead his army to the fortress in person. Baldwin had given all the signs of being back to his old self, and that was surely what the Brasingians needed.

It had been an affecting scene when he departed, Queen Hannelore visibly upset as she bid her husband goodbye. The two daughters wept for their father too, though the young boy didn't seem to understand. There was only a small chance that they would see him again.

Farred saw a figure on the road up ahead and called out a warning. The horses were stopped and men checked their weapons, just in case.

'It's Gustav,' said Inge, her eyes the sharpest, or else she knew by some other means.

Baldwin and Walter nudged their horses forwards. Farred, intrigued, joined them.

Gustav stood on the road, no mount in sight. Farred knew full well how he had got there, though that was never explicitly discussed in front of the emperor. He still had that healthy appearance about him that Farred didn't associate with his kind, but he was tired looking. There was something else too, a troubled look in his face.

'You have news?' Baldwin asked his wizard.

'Yes, Your Majesty. The Isharite army approaches the border of the Empire. The Rotelegen are making good progress with the evacuation, and Duke Jeremias should arrive at Burkhard not long after you do.'

'I sense there is something else, too,' said Walter.

'Indeed, you are perceptive as ever, Your Grace.' Gustav seemed to consider his words for a moment. 'There is no other way to say it,' he decided. 'The Isharite army has a dragon with it.'

Four weapons claimed, three still to go.

The Weapon Takers will return one last time in Book Four, *The Giants' Spear*.

Many thanks to everyone who has supported me.

Special thanks to Marcus Nilsson & Phyllis Simpson for beta reading.

CONNECT WITH THE AUTHOR

Website:

jamieedmundson.com

Twitter:

@jamie_edmundson

Newsletter:

http://subscribe.jamieedmundson.com

'The best way to thank an author is to write a review.'

Please consider writing a review for this book.

Turn over for a sneak preview of the sequel to
The Jalakh Bow...

THE GIANTS' SPEAR

Prologue

Siavash sat on the throne where Erkindrix had once sat. His arms rested on the carved red crystal. It was his now, and he had got more than used to that idea. Golden light shone down from the dome high up in the vaulted ceiling, bathing him in warm colours. He would have felt like a god, if he didn't already have one living inside him.

Diis was with him: an oppressive presence, impatient for the victory over Madria that still eluded them.

His mind repeated the moment when that bitch, Soren's sister, had struck the corpse of Prince Dorian with the dagger. There had been a blinding flash, a bang, and Siavash's shadow was shattered, evaporating away into nothingness. It was lost to him forever—and lost cheaply, because he had not even succeeded in defeating the Kalinthians.

The doors opened and the Magnian, Herin, strode in, walking towards the throne in a self-assured way. Siavash could feel Diis focus his malevolence on the human, and Siavash could see the human's spirit quail, though he maintained an admirable show of bravado.

'I am honoured to present you with these gifts, Lord Siavash,' he said, bending down on one knee in front of him. From a sack he pulled a decapitated head.

'King Mark evaded us long enough, but he has met his end now,' Herin said, holding the face towards Siavash so that he could see the former King of Persala's features. Siavash had never met the man, but his informants had already confirmed that this was indeed the head of the king-in-exile.

'My force also successfully recovered the Shield of Persala, as you ordered,' said Herin.

Dropping the head unceremoniously to the floor, he now held up the shield, the leather exterior decorated in the gaudy colours of the Persaleians.

Siavash felt Diis stir, a mix of hatred for the object brought before him, and elation—that at last one of the weapons of Madria was in their hands.

'You have served us well,' Siavash admitted, 'and will be rewarded. I need generals with the ability to carry out orders. You will be given your own host to command.'

Herin lowered his head, acknowledging the scale of the reward. 'I am honoured,' he said, raising his eyes to look at Siavash once more. 'What orders will this host have?'

'The same as three others. All four hosts will leave for Kalinth immediately.'

'Four?' Herin asked. 'All for Kalinth?'

'The Kalinthians must be crushed!' Siavash shouted at him, letting loose the anger and loathing he had carried since his defeat. 'Everywhere in Dalriya, and even in distant Halvia, our enemies are subdued or on the verge of defeat. And yet that pathetic kingdom still holds out. Almighty Diis demands its destruction!'

A shadow passed over Herin's face, but he bent his head in obeisance yet again.

'Leave your gifts here and go,' said Siavash, tired of the man's presence.

He waited for the Magnian to exit the doors at the end of the throne room before calling out to the shadows behind him, where he had his private rooms.

'Well?' he shouted irritably. 'Come, then.'

Out came Peroz, servant of Diis. Siavash had reformed the Isharite military, so that every unit had at least one servant attached to it, reporting back directly to him. It imposed discipline and loyalty, reducing the chances of another such as Pentas from betraying them.

Siavash allowed himself a smile at the thought of the red-eyed wizard. He recalled the sensation as the spear, wielded by his shadow in the body of Dorian, penetrated deeply into his enemy. It hadn't quite all been for nothing in Kalinth, he reminded himself.

'What of him?' Siavash asked Peroz.

'He can't be trusted, my lord.'

'I don't trust him. That's why you have this task. But he's able.'

'He fought and killed his brother for the shield. But then he let the rest of our enemies leave, no doubt to return to Kalinth.'

'There's something I've learned of humans,' Siavash explained to his servant. 'Despite all the evidence of what Diis will do to this world, they still think they will be saved. If they show loyalty, or are useful in some way, they think we will spare them, their family, their friends. It is the way their minds work. This Herin will do as he is ordered because he thinks it will save him.'

Siavash studied Peroz, looking to see whether the lesson had been taken.

'And if he doesn't,' Siavash added, 'you know what to do.'

THE GIANTS' SPEAR

Continue the quest in Book Four of
The Weapon Takers Saga.

Printed in Great Britain
by Amazon